Witch!

Chane rolled his bare torso across Aurelia onto the bed. "Winsome, robbing witch! You want more than my life, do you?"

Ria tried to buck him off. "Imbecile!" she cried. "Unhand me! I took nothing of yours."

"No?" he growled. "I think you lie. I think you have something of mine here."

His long fingers slipped inside her bodice, grasped the soft fabric and rent the garment to her waist.

Chane blinked as he beheld an image on her fair skin, a coin-sized, black-rayed sun rimmed with red tattooed on one smooth shoulder. Disbelieving, he touched the mark, running a finger over the inked lines, expecting them to rub away. Instead the contact worked magic on him, changing his dark mood as the dawn changes night to day.

Ria whimpered. A shiver of excitement ran through her shaking flesh and bone and sanity; reason left her as Chane bent his raven head to the tattoo on her shoulder.

"You are a witch, Aurelia Kingsley, a flagrant, heartless witch," Chane swore as his dark hand pressed her milky skin....

Dear Reader,

August brings us another batch of great titles!

In *The Seduction of Deanna* by Maura Seger, the next book in the BELLE HAVEN series, Deanna Marlowe is a woman torn between family loyalty and her passion for Edward Nash.

Sir Alexander Sommerville is determined to restore his family's good name, yet the daughter of his worst enemy, Lady Jesselynn, becomes an obstacle to his plans in *Knight's Honor* by Suzanne Barclay, the story of the third Sommerville brother.

Deborah Simmons gives us *Silent Heart,* the story of Dominique Morineau, a woman forced to leave her home in the midst of the French revolution, only to have a silent stranger once more draw her into the fray.

And rounding out this month is *Aurelia* by Andrea Parnell, a swashbuckling adventure of a young woman who enlists the aid of a hardened sea captain to help find her grandfather's pirate treasure.

A month of four rough-and-tumble Westerns is on tap for September. We'll be featuring some of today's hottest authors, including Pat Tracy and Mary McBride, so don't miss a single title. Watch for them wherever Harlequin Historicals are sold.

Sincerely,

Tracy Farrell
Senior Editor

Aurelia

ANDREA
PARNELL

Harlequin Books

TORONTO • NEW YORK • LONDON
AMSTERDAM • PARIS • SYDNEY • HAMBURG
STOCKHOLM • ATHENS • TOKYO • MILAN
MADRID • WARSAW • BUDAPEST • AUCKLAND

Harlequin Historicals first edition August 1993

ISBN 0-373-28786-0

AURELIA

ANDREA PARNELL

loves to travel and is strongly addicted to American history; she enjoys creating characters whose lives show the strength and forbearance that gave us our heritage. A native of Georgia who lives near Atlanta, Andrea is a former home economist and author of both contemporary and historical romance novels, and the mother of fantasy author Dan McGirt.

With love to my not-so-distant relatives,
Hugh and Linda Hudson, Leslie, Albert, Will,
and Ethan

Chapter One

Savannah, Georgia
1783

"He frightens me."

"Don't be a mouse, Clair," Aurelia Kingsley said tersely to her sister as she led her toward a small ramshackle cottage on one of the poorest streets of Savannah.

The redcoats had quartered horses and men in this ward near the river. Signs of abuse were plentiful in broken windows, shutters ripped off and splintered for use as firewood and dusty, pitted streets that turned to muck following every downpour. The place had deteriorated since the redcoats evacuated the town a year before; the rabble who now filled the sorry houses had not the means to improve them.

From within one of the houses came an angry shout and the jarring sounds of a scuffle. Clair leaped the space of three steps then ran until she had gained a place beside Aurelia. At the moment she wished she were a mouse, scrambling through these dreaded streets with nothing more to fear than a hungry, prowling cat. As it was, everything terrified her, and most particularly the man they were going to see.

"I can't help being scared," Clair complained, shuddering when the sun disappeared behind a bank of clouds. "He is like a scaly dragon in a lair." Her apprehension mounting by the moment, she tightened her grip on the string bag of parcels she carried and livened her steps to avoid falling even a pace behind the bolder Aurelia.

A dragon indeed, thought Aurelia. Would that he were. For where there were dragons there were knights. And if she could have a wish granted, she would ask for a champion. A searching look at her surroundings quickly emphasized the futility of her daydream. Knights and champions belonged to a distant wondrous past, as did all things worthwhile, it seemed. To end her troubles and Clair's she had to trust her wits and hope that they did not fail her.

All was quiet again, but from darkened rooms behind dirt-speckled windowpanes Clair felt the sharp stare of curious eyes. From the gloomy alleys she heard the secretive scrapes of the feet of those hidden in the blackness. Her voice trembled as a pair of those feet seemed to take up the cadence of her own footsteps. "This street unnerves me, too," she whimpered, not daring to look back and fearing to look ahead to what she knew was her destination. "Must we go today, Ria?" Clair queried pleadingly. "Everytime I enter that house I expect to see the floor littered with bones, or him spewing fire."

"Do hush, Clair. He is a harmless old man and your grandfather at that." Ria suppressed her own unease—none of which arose from the prospect of seeing her Grandfather Dagian. She believed they were being followed, but dared not relay her suspicion to Clair. She was well aware two girls burdened with what were obviously bundles of food were tempting targets for the ne'er-do-wells who haunted this district since the war ended.

She was glad to pull Clair within the ebbing shadow of her grandfather's house. As expected, the footsteps that had quickened to a run stopped with unmistakable suddenness. When Ria looked around, the person following them had slunk away into the nearest alley and the street was clear of all but a stray black dog and an old woman with a bundle balanced atop her head.

With Clair clinging to her elbow Ria started up the steps. The weathered planks were sound, though the iron railings that led to the scarred red door were broken and hung loose from their mountings. The knocker was a bit of brass on a chain. Ria thumped it vigorously against the top panel of the door, dislodging flakes of peeling paint from the aged wood. After no more than a moment or two, the heavy, creaking door swung open. Within the dim wake of light cast inside, a short but powerfully built man stood and motioned to the girls.

"Inside with ye." He wore a seaman's garb and with it a broad belt and a scabbard holding a blade that looked to Clair as large as a cutlass. His face was wide and his skin like tanned leather, his hair long and ragged and in need of a good soaping. A scar ran across one cheek, a jagged line of red from a cut that had healed badly. Where the scar ended a glint of gold shone from a ring affixed to his earlobe. "Ol' Dag's awaitin'," he said:

"Your message said he was ill." Ria dropped her bundle on a bench in the hall. Clair deposited the one she carried beside it.

"That 'e is. An' short o' patience." With a curt nod of his head he ushered the girls into a room illuminated only by a crack of light from beneath a dust-laden window curtain. Ria held her breath against the odor of rum, stale bread and sickness that was as heavy as the darkness.

Certain Clair would swoon from the stench if she did not act, Ria hastened to the window and quickly flung back the curtains flooding the musty room with brightness. Clair, clutching her hands together, hung back in the doorway, her skirt wavering over shaking knees.

"Curse you, Dom!" a voice roared from a shadowy far corner of the room as thin arms crossed over eyes too quickly introduced to the light. "I'd pitch you to the sharks were I—" Through the bend of his arms he saw the red-haired girl framed by the window she was trying to open. "Ahh. 'Tis you, is it, Ria."

"It's Ria, yes, Grandfather Dag. And Clair." Turning, Ria beckoned to her sister to join her as she crossed a worn scrap of a carpet to where her grandfather sat propped, with the aid of three or four badly soiled pillows, in a tattered damask-covered chair.

With what was close to a smile on a face made only slightly less fierce by age, the old man glanced at the doorway, knowing he would find Clair hanging back. He accepted a rather weak curtsy from her and made no complaint when she stiffly settled into a ladder-back chair near where she stood. Her reluctance to greet him did not pain the old man. She was a gentle sort and no less for it. She knew as did he that it was Ria, his Aurelia, who held his heart. Of his two granddaughters, Ria carried the Dagian fire in her blood; he'd known it since she was a wee thing.

Ria bent and kissed her grandfather's wizened cheek. But neither age nor infirmity had taken the harsh look out of a pair of sea green eyes. Only a brief glimpse into them made it plain why many a man had cowered beneath a gaze from those cold eyes, why many a man had carried the searing memory of them to the grave.

For Ria, the coldness in those eyes warmed as much as was possible. "Leave us, Dom," the old man ordered his faithful manservant in a surprisingly strong voice.

"Aye, cap'n." Dom nodded and padded away.

Ria knew her grandfather no longer left this room, once the tiny parlor of the tumbledown cottage. With a leg gone and the stump of it ever festering, he had only the strength to drink his rum and chase his memories. She had reason to be glad this was one of the rare days he was lucid. Most times when she visited he was out of his head with fever or drink. But even then, out of kindness and love, Ria sat and listened to his ramblings, never flinching at the rawness of his tales, never knowing how much of the colorful past her grandfather recounted was real and how much was imaginary.

"Bring me that parchment, girl, and pen and ink."

Ria looked around in surprise and saw a small table laid out with the materials her grandfather called for. Dutifully she fetched what he required. On another table she found a stained and streaked writing board he could balance on a pillow in his lap. When he had what he needed, she pulled a three-legged stool alongside his chair and sat and watched as he spread the parchment.

As he worked, dipping the pen, drawing, writing, he became completely absorbed in his task, seeming to forget Ria and Clair were at hand. An hour passed, and close to another with Clair fidgeting and nibbling her lower lip. For Ria the hours stood still. She watched in fascination as with his left hand—the right missing three fingers hacked off in a fight—Grandfather Dag dexterously executed and coded a beautifully detailed sea chart.

From over his shoulder Ria studied the intricate rendering. Only when his head lifted from the work and he laid the pen aside did she speak. "You are still quite the artist, Grandfather."

"Ha!" The green eyes glowed and a dreadful smile turned up his thin lips. "An artist! I drank the blood of one once, I believe." He laughed, a grating rasp of a sound, as he saw the skittish Clair wince and shrink in her chair. Ria thought he was about to lapse into a spell of preposterous tale-telling, but instead he quieted and dipped the pen another time, then with a dash added a finishing flourish to his work. Giving it a final scrutinizing look, he raised the completed map before his face and blew on the ink to dry the last of the lines.

"Grandfather, you really should not say those incredible things to Clair," Ria, more accustomed to his brusque ways, chastised good-naturedly.

"Break my bones!" he shouted. "That the day should come when the word of Dagian should be questioned." He swore and brought another rush of high color to Clair's face. "Never mind it." His harsh voice lightened a bit. "It's enough you don't flutter like that pretty bit of lace." The blazing eyes shifted momentarily from his precious Ria to the nervous Clair. "Nor have too many of your father's high qualms. Nay. There's more to you than spit and polish." Unexpectedly he grabbed Ria's hand and clutched it hard. The strength remaining in his grip amazed Ria. "You're all Dagian, girl. Through and through, thick blooded, Dagian blood."

"I am a Kingsley, Grandfather," Ria reminded him, sure now her grandfather was slipping into one of his reveries. Once before he'd called her a Dagian, which was peculiar, as it was his given name.

Her mind began to wander. She'd been eleven, twelve perhaps, and it had been her birthday. What a day that had been. Grandfather Dagian's gift to her had been a remarkable one: a tattoo exactly like the one he wore, a black sunrise outlined in fiery red. He himself had inked the design on her right shoulder as he told her in the boldest of language that he was known on the seas as the pirate Black Dawn.

A smile and a wistful look crossed her face. She remembered so well how her excitement at having the pretty little picture had dulled the pain of the tattoo needles. Even more vividly she recalled her father's anger when she'd recounted the story and shown him the mark. He'd flown out of the house, raging. Alarmed at having upset her father, she had scrubbed until her skin was raw, trying to wash away the mark. Afterward Grandfather Dagian had sailed away and not come back until Dom had brought him to Savannah a good four years later, ill and with his mind failing.

Perhaps it was true, as she'd once overheard, that in his youth her father had taken his mother's family name. He'd never spoken of Dagian, never let his daughters know they had a living grandfather, not until the old man had begun to visit Savannah with regularity some few years before the incident of the tattoo. Certainly there had always been a pointed difference between father and son; even as a child she had been aware of it.

Marcus Kingsley had been an educated and genteel man. Grandfather Dagian was neither. His had been a rougher and meaner beginning, a pirate's life of danger and death. If even half of his stories were true, Grandfather Dagian had been a man who made his living at the expense of others. Yet he was a man who had given his son a better start in life, sent him to the best schools, underwritten his endeavors in the colony.

The old man had not let go of Ria's hand and now the pressure from his firm grip shook her out of her recollections. She saw that those green eyes, so like her own, had a strange glaring light she had never before witnessed in them.

"Hear me, Ria," he said, trying to whisper and sounding as if he spoke in a low growl. "Your father, rest his soul, made me swear I would never taint your life or Clair's with the legacy of my deeds, but the time has come I must break my word." He drew in a long, labored breath. "You be a Dagian and worthy of that heritage, bloody though it be. Take this." He thrust the map into her hand. "I give you your birthright." With a shuddering sigh, Dagian fell back against the dingy pillows. Unmistakable fatigue marked his face but it had not yet found its way into his voice, which came stronger than ever. "You bear the mark. Take the prize."

"The map, grandfather," Ria said softly. "I thank you for it."

"Nay, girl." His head with its thatch of grizzled hair shook emphatically. "Not the map. What it will lead you to. Follow it. All else you need you have. You bear the mark."

"Grandfather—"

He would not wait to hear her out. "I know your plight. Dom told me of it," he said. "You have need of Dagian's trove."

He was out of his head again, no doubt, either from the pain in his leg or from the encroaching ailment that cursed the minds of the old. Grandfather Dag, by all standards, was ancient. The old man groaned. Ria looked around anxiously for Dom, but he had not come down the stairs.

"You could have it set in a frame and hung in your room." Clair, trying her best to say something pleasant and to overcome her aversion to her Grandfather Dag, rose uneasily from her chair for a look at the map Ria held.

"Set in a frame!" Dagian roared. Clair stumbled back to her chair, certain he had singed the lashes from her eyelids. "By the fires of hell! The *Aurelia* is seaworthy! Go, girl. Sail!"

Sail. Ria would have liked nothing better had she known how. Would that she had the funds even to hire a crew. The future that awaited her in Savannah made her shudder. But Grandfather Dagian's eyes were too full of fervor to note the threadbare hems on the dresses his granddaughters wore, or to see that their gloves had been mended many times over. Likely as not within a month she and Clair would be looking for the means to earn their keep with honest work. The money their father had left was gone. Grandfather Dag was even worse off, his house a shambles and his clothes in a sadder state than theirs.

As he quieted she rolled the map and fitted it into her patched silk reticule. Her grandfather was tiring more, his eyes rolling back, the light gone out of them. Wishing she could do more than bring him fresh bread and vegetables from the garden, she touched his hand and softly told him goodbye. Let him dream if he would. Let his dreams take him out of his shoddy room, let them give him back his leg, his youth, his ship. He was happy in his dreams and she wished him that.

Dom came upon them so suddenly and silently that he startled both girls.

"He has exhausted himself," Ria explained. "And he has been imagining things...."

"Not this day, miss." Dom's crusty voice was like a cold wind off the sea. "This day 'e's as sound o' mind as ye and me."

"You did not hear him," Ria returned. Clair, shaken by the exchange, eased from her chair and clutched her sister's arm. The dark-skinned Dom with his burnt coal eyes frightened Clair almost as much as her grandfather. "He drew this map for me and said—"

"I knows what 'e said, miss."

"But you were upstairs," she protested as she felt Dom's dark eyes impale her with an unrelenting stare.

Her grandfather's companion had never warmed to either granddaughter. Ria supposed he had a seaman's suspicion that women were bad luck and could not rid himself of it even on land. In earlier days when her grandfather had been well and she had visited him on board his ship, Dom had always given her a wide berth. That was not possible in the small house, though he did his best to avoid her. Indeed, she could not recall a score of words spoken between them before this day.

"I always know what the cap'n's thinkin'." There was a chill in his voice. "Difference is I know 'e's never said a word as wasn't truth." He paused for so long that Ria made to walk past him but stopped when he produced from his pocket a small pouch of worn black leather. "'E 'ad me ready this for ye."

The bag dangled enticingly in front of her but Ria reached for it hesitantly. When it dropped into her hand she heard the jangle of coins.

"I can't take Grandfather Dag's money," she said in alarm. "He needs it more than we do. Clair and I are fit enough to work before we go hungry." She tried to return the pouch, but Dom crossed his thick arms over his sturdy chest and refused to take it back.

"'E's enough left to last as long as 'e will." The fierce look on Dom's face made Ria feel, momentarily, as timid as Clair. "Do as 'e's bid ye. Make the Black Dawn proud agin afore 'e dies."

It was Clair who led the way from Grandfather Dagian's house, her small feet moving so briskly Ria scarcely had time to conceal the black pouch in her reticule before she was down the steps and hastening to keep pace with her sister on the street.

"He is mad," said Clair. "And I will not go back. Ever. I don't care how ill he is."

"Why is it you've always the courage to carp at me and never an ounce for anyone else?" Ria asked irritably. She herself was saturated with guilt. How could she have taken her grandfather's money? What weakness had seized her so that she had walked out of his house without leaving the bag behind as her conscience had hinted she should. Had she lost her senses? Her pride? Or had she kept what was given to her because a small part of her wanted to believe that a map drawn by a senile old man truly led to a pirate's bounty? Or that the bag of coins she hadn't had time to count equaled enough to pay for an expedition? It was impossible. Wasn't it?

From trembling lips that indicated hurt feelings, Clair raised a weak protest when Ria changed direction. "Where are you going, Ria? Not to the docks. You know the place scares me nigh as much as Grandfather Dag."

"It is necessary, Clair," Ria said gently. "I want to take a look at the *Aurelia*." Her father's ship, hers since his death, sat at its moorings on the Savannah River. Hyatt Landis, her father's solicitor, had taken charge of it. The ship was prey for vandals, and Hyatt, who had newer ships of his own now, had lately been demanding she sell the *Aurelia*.

Ria sighed wistfully. She'd refused until the choice was close to being made for her. The charges for keeping the *Aurelia* moored were mounting, besides which, she owed Hyatt for the repairs he had commissioned. She did not expect him to wait much longer for payment of her bill. The scoundrel! How she would like to show Hyatt for the blackguard he was. Convulsively, her hand squeezed around the lump Grandfather Dag's coins made in her reticule.

Hope rose and fell inside her. A bag of pennies likely. Copper dreams.

"Look! There's Hyatt," Clair announced none too happily. She didn't care for Hyatt. He reminded her of a bird, an image made apt by the beaklike crook of his nose.

Ria saw him near the *Aurelia*'s longboat, flanked by two other men. One was tall, lean and black-haired, and by his stance and expression the dominant one of the unknown pair. He also stood in stark contrast to Landis, a head taller than the solicitor, lean and long where the other was thick-bodied and short of limb. His companion was fair-haired, not a man to turn a lady's head, but attractive in an unobtrusive way.

But it was the black-haired man who held her eye, his leanness giving way to a look of sleek power, his glistening hair blue-black beneath the sun, the strong line of his jaw a backdrop for a softly curved and sensuous mouth. His shoulders were broad enough to carry a gilded suit of armor, Ria mused.

The wind caught the black-haired man's words and carried them along the wharf before any of the party was aware the girls approached.

"She's a fine vessel, sound and fast by the look of her hull," he said. "A runner."

"And the only ship in the harbor for sale," Hyatt Landis pointed out, getting a snort from the gap-toothed William Pollack aboard the longboat. Pollack was Landis's man and lived aboard the *Aurelia* to keep her safe.

"That, too," said the black-haired man, smiling. "She will do if the price is agreeable."

"Count yourself touched by luck. You can have her at a bargain," Hyatt hastened to say. "No local buyer will have the *Aurelia*." He noted the reaction to his words and hastened to explain himself. "Not that she isn't as seaworthy as you've noted. It has nothing to do with the ship. The former owner—"

"The present owner is here," Ria said sternly. "And if the *Aurelia* is sold it will be at a fair price for her worth."

The solicitor had the shifty, uncomfortable look of a man up to no good. Ria felt her anger rise as she closed the distance between them. What right did Hyatt have to tell of her family's disgrace, as she was sure he had been about to? And after all her father had done for the man. The nerve of him! If Marcus Kingsley did not garner the solicitor's respect, he at least deserved his silence.

"Why, Ria! And Clair. I did not expect . . ." Hyatt, flustered, red-faced, pulled a linen square from his coat pocket and mopped his damp brow. But he recovered quickly, easily slipping into the role of proper gentleman. "What a pleasure to see you," he said smoothly. "I was just telling Captain Bellamy about the *Aurelia* and how anxious you are to sell."

Chane Bellamy had spun on his heels and met the furious glare of eyes the color of a storm-churned north sea. If not for those striking eyes, the girl's face might have been almost plain; her lips were drawn tight and there was a high color in her cheeks. And her hair was red, a mass of unbridled flame about her head. She wore a pigeon gray gown with an ecru lace collar that must have been handed down through several generations. The somber look of her costume was entirely wrong, too puritan for the stunning hair and eyes. Should he wonder at her station in life, the gown told him plenty: it had a tired, overworn look, the satin piping on the sleeves and the hem of it frayed beyond mending.

The same was true of the other girl's faded saffron gown. His eyes lingered on her, longer than was courteous. No misuse of color or ill choice of style could dull her beauty or hide the bounty of her curves. Her hair was an exquisite mass of red blond curls that framed a perfect china-doll oval face, which was shyly downcast. Her eyes, the brief second he'd seen them beneath the golden lashes, were a soft glowing brown, like big amber gems catching the sunlight. Her skin, fairer than her irate companion's, was the palest alabaster and looked as if it would be softer than a whisper to the touch.

Any other time he would have been raring to practice his seductive skills on either of the two. But not now. Trouble over a woman had helped put him in his present difficult spot. At the moment, he did not feel kindly disposed toward any one of the fair sex.

From nearby, Chane Bellamy heard his friend, Axel Gresham, gulp a breath and knew that he, too, had been struck by the quiet girl's extraordinary beauty.

"You did not tell me anyone was interested in the *Aurelia*," Ria addressed Hyatt curtly. "As you should have."

"He came to my office only this afternoon."

"And I am very anxious to buy, Mademoiselle . . ."

Hyatt rudely overlooked the introductions. "Of course, I planned to notify you immediately after Captain Bellamy had a look at the *Aurelia*," the solicitor responded with a smile, though he clearly did not like the implication that he had acted beyond his authority. "As it's turned out you've saved me a trip to Palmira."

Ria doubted he was glad of it, since he visited as often as he could find an excuse. Soon he wouldn't need one. He'd asked her stepmother, Opal, to wed him and as Palmira belonged to Opal, Hyatt would shortly be living in the house with the three of them.

"So I have," Ria responded. The thought propelled her into a high temper, which took her beyond careful consideration of what she said next. "But perhaps you have wasted the captain's time," she said, resting her hands on her hips, thereby sending her silk reticule swinging like a pendulum from one wrist. "I have decided the *Aurelia* is not for sale."

"Ria!" Hyatt sputtered, his eyes going first to her face and then suspiciously to the scrolled paper protruding from the reticule she'd hastily concealed in the fullness of her skirts. "What alternative is there but to haul her out to sea and let her rot?" he demanded. "Or would you rather leave her to the mercy of your father's enemies?" Mottled color spread on the skin above his collar. "My generosity is at an end, I warn you. I will not carry the expense of a useless ship and take on two grown women who are too stubborn for their own good."

Chane Bellamy listened carefully to the exchange and watched intently the emotions that flared in the girl's green eyes. There was more afoot here than a disagreement over the sale of a ship. Whatever that difference was did not concern him; the *Aurelia* did. His vessel, the *Trinity,* had caught fire and burned a week past. He'd lost none of his crew and the cargo had been offloaded the day before. But without the *Trinity* he had no way to complete the mission he had set for himself. He needed a replacement vessel, and fast. The *Aurelia* was it and he meant to have her.

"Mr. Landis," Chane said, his voice glazed with the accent of his native French tongue. "If you would allow me to talk to the *Aurelia*'s owner alone, it is possible we could come to an agreement."

He had a quiet arrogance about him. Ria heard it in the deep resonance of his voice, saw it hidden in the intense blue eyes, shadowed again in the tilt of the strong square chin. He was accustomed to having his way. And he was assessing her, giving her a critical look now that he had torn his eyes from Clair. She felt him searching out her weaknesses as one might look for cracks in the foundation of a building . . . to find a place where one might begin to tear it down. She tried to picture herself as he saw her, a silly, penniless girl defying her elders. Pitiable.

Bellamy. *Captain* Bellamy. So, this was the man she'd heard so much about. On the church grounds following Sunday service, Elizabeth Carter had been telling her friends how many dances she'd shared with a handsome sea captain at a ball held a month before. "Sky blue eyes, hair black as a raven's wing, light on his feet as a gypsy dancer," Elizabeth had described him. Ria remembered, too, the quick disdainful turn of a shoulder and raised chin when Elizabeth had seen her approaching; the snooty girl and her friends had then walked off without so much as a word to Ria.

Hidden in the folds of her skirts, her hands were clenched into tight, aching fists. This Captain Bellamy who was so light on his feet was looking at her as if he could control her as easily as he could ask her to dance.

Her anger flared again, and Ria vowed silently, as she felt his eyes upon her, that this time Captain Bellamy would not get his way.

Chapter Two

"She will change her mind."

"What makes you certain of that?" Axel Gresham asked as he strode with his friend toward the welcoming doors of a tavern near the docks.

"Because I intend to persuade her." Chane Bellamy shrugged. He wasn't as sure as he sounded that the girl would relent; she seemed to have taken an instant dislike to him.

His experience with females ran to dealing with those who were overly fond of him. This Ria was different. But he did not intend to leave the matter to fate. Tomorrow he would pay her a visit at Palmira, the plantation Landis had mentioned. He knew the place, he'd seen the house, a mile outside the city and one of the better designed mansions in the vicinity. He had admired its wide verandas and beautiful gardens that were so like those his mother cultivated at Eglantine, his father's estate on the island of Martinique.

The girl was obviously trying to hang on to a memory. Landis had said the ship belonged to her father and that the girls had fallen on hard times since his death. She was sentimental, he supposed.

"And why should she be different from any other woman once Chane Bellamy has cast his eye on her?" Axel asked, interrupting Chane's reverie.

"Why indeed? But it is the other one I would rather be dallying with. Convincing her to change a stand would be more the pleasure." He gave his friend a knowing look. "A true beauty."

"That she is," Axel agreed, remembering the lovely blond girl and searching his memory for a time he'd ever seen a prettier or sweeter face. "Almost enough to make you give in to your father's demands, I'll warrant."

"Close but not quite," Chane said stiffly, unpleasantly reminded of the hot exchange he'd had with his father before his departure for America. He supposed his father's wishes were not unreasonable. A man wanted heirs and that was the way of things. But be damned if he would stand for being ordered to take a bride and sire a son within a year. Certainly not by that fragile French mademoiselle Renaud Bellamy had too conveniently invited to spend the winter at Eglantine.

Chane shrugged, uncomfortable with the recollection. He'd insulted the girl, perhaps ruining his father's business opportunities with her family. But the Bellamy fortune would not fall on the loss. As for taking a wife, he had no need of one, not with willing women as plentiful as fish in the sea. If the time came that he desired a son, as his father had sworn he would, it could be done without saddling himself with a wife. Wives were too inclined to roam—he had bedded his share of dissatisfied ones looking for adventure—whereas a mistress was more inclined to devote herself to pleasing her lover.

His opinion, however, did not get him out of the spot his runaway temper had put him in. Frowning, eyes glowering as he remembered that last heated quarrel with his father, which had stopped just short of blows, Chane fell silent beside Axel. He should never have let Renaud Bellamy goad him into agreeing to that idiotic wager. Because now, with luck running against him, he would likely find himself just under a year from now saddled with a wife, after all—one of his father's choosing, one with all the attributes of a spotted toad. He knew his father's vindictive streak.

Axel pushed open a stout plank door that opened to the bawdy sounds of laughter and song from White's Tavern. Chane followed him in. The crowd was heavy with sailors either assigned to or seeking assignment to the numerous merchant ships in the harbor. The air was clouded with smoke and heavy with the reeking odors of salt-soaked clothing and sweat.

A plank table in the quietest corner was unoccupied. Axel made for it and was not in his seat a full minute before a barmaid came to take his order. Axel smiled, knowing it was not his plain face that had brought her so quickly. His companion was the one who drew her, as he had the eye of each and every loose skirt in the room.

Fortunately, Axel Gresham was not a man troubled by envy for his handsome friend. He got his share of womanly company from being near Chane, and it was his belief that in the long run of it, he fared better than he would have on his own.

"Yer a handsome one," the girl said to Chane, standing so close to him that he could not speak without getting a mouthful of some part of her. "What will it be for ye?"

Wrapping his hands around her thick waist he set her back a step, but there was a twinkle in his eye that kept her from being offended. "Ale and a bit of room," he said. "My friend and I have to talk."

"Pity," she called with a backward glance as she strutted off. She'd noticed the cut of his clothes, the fine fabric, the

silver of the buttons on his coat and the wide buckles of his
shoes, no petty sailor that one. She made a point to tell him
when she brought his ale that she would not mind saving a
place in her bed for him whenever he was in port.

"Bust my britches! Lorelle Telfour!" Axel boomed, eyes
widened in disbelief.

Chane, whose back was to the door, twisted his chair, legs
and all, to see if his friend spoke the truth. "Hell take me,"
he mumbled. If there was anything he did not welcome on
top of the fight with his father and the loss of his ship, it was
a confrontation with the Telfours. And that included Lorelle, as well as her cousins, Yves and Gustave, who could
not be far behind.

Looking neither left nor right, the raven-haired Lorelle
paraded through the closely set tables and headed directly
for the one occupied by Chane and Axel. Her perfume, a
heavy blend of orchid and spices that conjured up images of
the tropics, preceded her, causing all heads to turn her way.

"So I must come this far to find you, Chane Bellamy,"
she said, her voice not quite striking the note of sweet re-
finement she sought. "But what good fortune I am having
today that you are the first person I see in Savannah."

"Lorelle, this is not a place for ladies." Chane stood, angry enough to give Lorelle Telfour the swat she deserved but
principled enough to escort her out of the tavern before the
lustful attention she was drawing from the rough, sea-weary
patrons got out of hand.

He was a moment too late. A sailor at the nearest table,
too far into his ale, had breathed in the potency of Lorelle's
perfume. Grinning, the man pushed himself from his chair
and with a big paw of a hand grabbed the silken hood of her
cloak.

"'At's a fancy lady-flower ye got, Captain." He snatched the covering from her head and without letting go of the garment, jerked Lorelle into his arms. "An' I wouldn't mind 'aving a bite o' the cabbage meself."

Lorelle shrieked at being fondled by the grimy sailor, but he was too drunk to care about the trouble he'd started.

"Set her loose." Chane made a stab at politeness.

The sailor laughed and jabbed a hand into Lorelle's skirt. "Be generous, Captain. There's plenty 'ere to share."

The man's caress ended with a sharp pinch on her buttock. Lorelle shrieked louder, giving Chane no choice but to pull her forcibly from the sailor's arms. The sailor, however, would not be denied. Staggering, he grabbed blindly for Lorelle again.

Breathing out a weary sigh, Chane caught the drunken man by the collar and flung him across the room. Like a spinning top the sailor twisted and spun, laughing as he tried to regain his balance but succeeding instead in bumping half a dozen patrons and toppling two tables. When he landed in a heap against the bar, Chane reached into his pocket and extracted a coin that he flipped to the tavern keeper.

"For the trouble," he said, though he had half a mind to let the sailor pay for the spilled ale.

Lorelle had her arms wrapped around Chane's neck. "Chane, darling, take me out of here," she whispered as she hung on to him.

Chane held his tongue as he half carried, half walked Lorelle toward the door. The words he wished to say to her were no better than those of the sailor he'd sent flying. More trouble would come from this, he knew, and he could see by the furrow of Axel's brow that his companion was thinking the same.

Lorelle clung to him, her arms and legs so tightly pressed against him that he might as well have been wrapped in the

web of a spider. A spider was precisely what Lorelle brought
to mind. She was a stunning girl, and with her dark hair and
eyes and full curves, as luscious as they came. He granted
her that. He'd been attracted to her when she first arrived
on Martinique, until he'd learned that her exuberance ran
to brazenness. There was a bit of tomfoolery he would undo
if he could, meeting her on the beach those few times, slipping into her bedroom many others. But he'd not taken her
innocence; that had been gone long before he met her, if
she'd even been born with it.

Lorelle's feminine wiles knew no limits, and no amount
of tutoring had made her into the true lady her uncle, Rossy
Telfour, wanted her to be. She was trouble in a pretty pack-
age. And she had decided it was Chane Bellamy she wanted,
not her fiancé, her cousin Gustave, as the Telfour family had
planned.

Axel, who would have much preferred to finish his ale in
peace, held the tavern door open for Chane and Lorelle to
pass to the street. "You can let her down now," he said
when they were outside.

"I am trying." Chane cleared his throat and swallowed
the curses on the tip of his tongue. "Let go, Lorelle."
Frowning, he pulled one of her arms from around his neck,
but no sooner had he divested himself of it when the other
arm wrapped even more tightly where the first had been.

"Hold me," she whispered, nuzzling her face into his
neck. "I cannot stop shaking."

Chane, sighing heavily, caught both her wrists at once and
thrust her away. "You are afraid of nothing, Lorelle. Now
get on with you before Gus comes along."

"Speak of the devil," warned Axel, a troubled look
clouding his eyes.

Chane, too, saw the tall fair-haired Gustave Telfour hus-
tling down the street at a near run. Beside him was his nearly

identical younger brother, Yves. A few paces back, her clenched hands at her breast, Lorelle's distraught maid followed. Gus was swinging a cane, a heavy gnarled length of wood with a gold handle shaped like a ram's head. He carried the instrument because he thought it lent him a dapper sophistication and because it had proved a ready weapon at times.

"Take your hands from Lorelle!" The cane held high like a lance, he shouted for all to hear.

Chane groaned as Lorelle, who also saw her cousin approaching, entwined herself around him once more. "Pull her off, will you, Axel."

"And get my skull cracked? Not bloody likely," Axel replied, though he took a stance that made him ready to dispense whatever assistance Chane might need once the Telfours reached them.

Gus was scarlet faced with anger and breathing like a wounded bull. "I said unhand her, you lecher."

As if he meant to run him through, Gus jabbed the sharpened tip of his cane into Chane's shoulder, using the moment Chane staggered back to pull Lorelle into his arms.

Lorelle's pretty face contorted. "Leave me be, Gus!" she demanded.

Having Lorelle in his arms was a treat Gus rarely experienced. The scent of her perfume, the warmness of her, made him momentarily forget what he was about.

Lorelle, on the other hand, knew whom and what she wanted. Not pleased when Gus continued to hold her against her wishes, she raised a foot and stamped down hard on his instep.

"Owww! Hold her!" Gus's face registered pain as he handed his squirming fiancé into his brother's safekeeping.

Gus had not lowered his cane. Embarrassed at being publicly scorned by the woman he loved, again he jabbed the cane's tip, hard, into Chane's shoulder.

The tight muscles in Chane's jaw twitched. "Mind your manners, Gus." He pushed the cane away.

Enraged, Gus poked harder, trying to shove Chane off his feet as, from the corner of his eye, he saw Lorelle eyeing his rival with undeniable desire. "I'll teach you manners, you whoreson!" With another thrust he drove the metal tip soundly into Chane's shoulder and held it there. "You, who dragged Lorelle into a place fit only for sea scum and light-skirts."

Chane, breathing deeply to control his temper, raised a hand and slowly shoved the cane away. "If you care so much for her honor you shouldn't leave her on these streets unchaperoned," he told Gus.

Gus's face contorted like that of a scalded pig. With an angry shout he thrust the cane again, but this time Chane's hands were swifter, grabbing the shaft in midswing, wrenching the golden handle from the other man's grasp.

"Damn you!" Infuriated at being disarmed so easily, Gus growled and made a reckless dive at Chane.

A quick dodge and a swing of the cane landed a blow to the side of Gus's head and knocked the elder Telfour to his knees.

"Hit him harder, Chane!" Lorelle cried, her dark eyes dancing with black lights of excitement as she jammed an elbow into Yves's ribs and broke free of his hold.

"He's got trouble enough," Chane mumbled, experiencing a taste of sympathy for Gus.

Lorelle bounded toward Chane, but his hostile expression halted her long enough for the maid to catch hold of her arm. Blast the little vixen, he thought. This was not the first time he and Gus had come to blows because of Lorelle. She was a hellion in silk skirts, and Gus need not expect a peaceful life should he succeed in making her his bride.

"Want a hand?" Yves, more even-tempered by far than his brother, offered his help. Gus had not yet recovered enough to rise but waved his brother away.

"Rot you!" Gus shouted at Yves. "Now you would come to my aid, but not before."

While Gus swore and Yves protested, Chane broke over his knee the gnarled shaft of the cane Gus had been too quick to wield. The splintered halves he tossed at Gus's feet. Even so, Chane felt no sense of satisfaction as he and Axel left the Telfours outside the tavern. Lorelle was calling to him that she would see him again as soon as she could manage. There was no mistaking, from the foul look Gus gave beneath the egg-sized lump on his brow, that one Telfour was already thinking of a way to even the score.

"I'm telling you the girl humiliated me before two gentlemen prepared to pay a good price for the *Aurelia*." Hyatt Landis paced the brick-tiled floor of the cool downstairs parlor of Palmira. "And Pollack was there to witness her disrespect," he added. "I do not like being shamed in front of a hired man!"

Opal Kingsley was standing near one of the big French doors that opened onto the veranda. "She has little left but her pride, Hyatt. I'm sure she didn't mean to show you in a bad light."

"She meant nothing else," Hyatt complained, stopping only long enough to take a large swallow of the mint tea Opal had prepared for him. "What business do those two have on the docks alone, anyway? As if there isn't enough talk about them!"

"They had been to see Grandfather Dag." Opal, having moved from the window to Hyatt's side, took the drained teacup from his hand, afraid that in his present state of mind his tight grip might break it. "He is ill."

"Ill in the head," Hyatt supplied. "Not to be trusted. He ought to be locked away."

Opal smiled sweetly. "I believe that is the case of it. He has not left that house in more than a year."

"I meant he should be locked away somewhere that would end his influence on those girls. The fool thinks he's some grand old pirate king."

Opal laughed and touched Hyatt's arm. "I would not put it past him to be all he claims. Why, when he used to come here years ago, when he was in his prime, he was the most formidable mortal I ever looked on."

Hyatt clasped Opal's small warm hand as his gaze drifted across the delicate features of her face, the spun-silk hair the color of ripened corn, eyes sparkling with the brilliant lights of the stone after which she was named. Could it be true she was more beautiful than the first day he'd seen her and wished she weren't Marcus Kingsley's wife?

She spoke his name, her voice soft as a lullaby, her touch soothing as a breeze. She calmed him, cleared his head. It was one of the reasons he loved her, wanted her as his wife. The other was Palmira. He'd coveted the house from the day Marcus Kingsley had laid it out. He'd been a poor young solicitor in a place where there was little need of his services. Marcus had seen his plight and given him enough work that he did not go wanting. Marcus had pitied him, asked him to dine frequently with the Kingsley family. The hint of a bitter smile crossed Hyatt's hawkish face, like the shadow of a cloud drifting past. A man's pity was no better than a knife in the gut.

Many things had changed over the years. The Kingsley fortune was gone while his was growing; the Kingsley name, once the proudest in the colony had been disgraced, tainted with shame; that of Landis was one to respect. Marcus Kingsley, once lordly, handsome, rich, lay moldering in the grave while Hyatt Landis courted his widow and made plans to possess his house.

Hyatt smiled fully, calm now as a gull floating on a current of air over the ocean. His life was close to perfect. Very close. Only two flies rested in the ointment: Kingsley's daughters, Ria and Clair. He had hoped that with the money from the sale of the *Aurelia* the sisters could be persuaded to leave Savannah. Too much animosity for Marcus Kingsley remained for his daughters to be accepted in society again. Hyatt did not want his marriage to Opal spoiled by the whispers that followed the girls. Of course, presently, he was much praised for his willingness to assume responsibility for the obstinate Kingsley sisters. But praise had a way of turning to contempt, and that he would not abide.

"Ria will have to change her mind," he said smoothly. "Pride or not, the *Aurelia* must be sold."

"Let me speak to her," Opal said.

Hyatt considered that. "Yes, that might be best." He wasn't one to back away from anything, but he was glad Opal had volunteered to tell Ria what had to be done. The girl had a way of looking at him as if she could read his mind. Marcus had been the same way, though his perception had not always served him so well.

Hyatt drew a long, labored breath. "Be sure she understands there is no choice in the matter. Either she sells willingly or I will claim title to the vessel and sell her at auction for what is owed me. Then I will have those two wed to the first unfortunate men who will take them."

Opal patted his hand. "It won't come to that," she said. "Ria will listen to me."

"She had better," he warned. Then, smiling, he kissed Opal's smooth forehead.

"I will make her understand, Hyatt," she said.

"And I—" Hyatt crossed the room slowly to reclaim his hat "—will send word to Captain Bellamy before he decides to look elsewhere for a ship."

From the veranda Ria stepped quietly into the library and eased the doors shut. "Damn him!" she said. "Damn all of them!"

Clair, aghast at her sister's use of profanity, clasped her hands over her ears. "Oh Ria, please don't swear. It isn't..."

"Ladylike?" Ria paced behind the big mahogany desk that had been her father's. "What difference does it make if we comport ourselves like ladies or not? We are pariahs, anyway. Snubbed on the street, not invited to the houses of people who once were our friends. I won't be surprised if we're asked to refrain from attending Sunday worship." Her eyes narrowed. "And all that is preferable to being at the mercy of Hyatt Landis."

Clair cautiously removed her small hands from her ears. Ria was talking so loud she was afraid Opal would hear. "Shh," she said, glancing at the hall door. "Hyatt says people would be nicer to us if you didn't insist on telling everyone that Papa was innocent."

Ria stopped abruptly in her tracks and set her fists on her hips. "He was."

"I know he was. But people don't want to hear about it."

Ria's eyes blazed. "People ought to hear the truth."

"Maybe they ought to, but sometimes it hurts too much and they would rather hear what they want to believe."

Though she was angry enough to bite a nail in two, Ria gave her sister a tender look. She understood what Clair was saying. Life would be easier for Marcus Kingsley's daughters if they condemned their father's actions. At least then they might elicit sympathy. Poor Clair. Being shunned by almost everyone she had once believed a true friend was devastating to her. She missed the life they'd had before the war.

Ria knew it was mostly her fault that they were virtual outcasts in Savannah. But she did not believe and would never stand for anyone saying that her father was a traitor who had led his men into a trap and deserted them to be slaughtered. No man had been more forceful in his support of independence for the colonies. No man had been more willing to risk his life to ensure it. Marcus Kingsley had been maligned. Before he had been given a chance to prove his innocence, he had been shot down.

How anyone could blame Major Marcus Kingsley for that disaster in the marshes was beyond understanding. The traitor who had shown the British a secret passage through the eastern swamps had not been her father's man. That he had named her father as the one who ordered him to do so could have easily been challenged and disproved. But it had not been a time of reason, not when hundreds of men had lost their lives, many sons and fathers from the finest families around.

General Howe himself had been court-martialed for allowing the British to surprise his garrison. The general had been acquitted. He'd lost his reputation but not his life. The unnamed man who'd shot Ria's father still walked the streets of Savannah. The traitor who had maligned her father had disappeared into the marshes he knew so well— where Marcus Kingsley's body had been left.

Life was hard for any who bore the Kingsley name. And though Ria and Clair were less despised than their father, they were definitely unwelcome in the recovering social life of Savannah. Where was the rhyme or reason of it? Their father was a man who would have given his own life before he betrayed the cause he had embraced. And Ria would prove his innocence one day to all who denounced him.

"Ria, what are you thinking about?" Clair's voice sounded small in the big room, with its nearly empty shelves. Most of the volumes her father had spent years collecting had been sold, as had half the furnishings in Palmira.

"I was thinking of money," Ria answered.

Clair laughed. "I wish for it, too. But what's the use? We have none."

"In fact, we do." Ria reached inside the waistband of her skirt and produced the bag Grandfather Dag had given her.

"You said that was likely only pennies," Clair responded, puzzled.

Ria loosened the leather drawstring of the bag and emptied its contents onto the red felt blotter in the center of the desk. "I was wrong."

Clair jumped to her feet and hurried to the desk to fill her hands with the dozens of gold coins in the bag. "Oh, Ria! So much! Who would have thought . . . ?"

Ria, who had been surprised to discover the coins when she'd opened the bag in her room, gave Clair a moment to revel in the experience. "It is enough to pay Hyatt the money I owe him and to provision and outfit the *Aurelia.*"

Clair's glittering eyes lost their happy glow and took on a fervid look. "You aren't thinking of doing—of going—Oh, no!" Hands trembling, she grasped the edge of the desk for support. "Ria, we can't."

"Why not?" Ria asked, secreting the bag once again inside the waist of her skirt. "What do you think Hyatt has in mind for us once he's wed Opal?"

Clair's expression made it clear she knew what her sister was thinking. "He wants to send us away," she whispered. "That is why he insists you sell the *Aurelia*. He wants us to have enough money to go away."

Ria swallowed. Her throat felt dry. "He has also threatened to marry us off to the first two men *he* finds suitable." She shook as she imagined the choice Landis would make. "I won't have Hyatt Landis telling me what to do," she said coolly. "I've made my own plans. I'll outfit the *Aurelia*. And if Grandfather Dag was telling us the truth..." Her eyes had grown nearly as luminous and wide as Clair's. "Well, these coins had to come from somewhere."

Clair shivered. The idea that her grandfather might actually have been a pirate, a murderer and thief, as he claimed, was horrible to her.

"What if none of it is true? What if he found those things long ago or if Dom stole them from someone? Have you never wondered how Grandfather Dag keeps that house, poor though it is?"

"These coins are Spanish," Ria countered, "and old. Doubloons, I think. Dom didn't get them by knocking some sailor on the head. At least not here or in recent times."

"Ria, you can't. I can't. I would die of fright among pirates."

"Don't you understand, Clair? Pirates are mostly gone nowadays. What Grandfather Dag has told us happened—" she paused and searched what she remembered from her lessons "—happened half a century ago. Why, Grandfather Dag is fourscore and better himself. The map he's given me is for the location of treasure he's hidden."

Clair's lower lip and chin trembled. "Still, I can't..."

"Clair." Ria put an arm around her sister's shaking shoulders. "The worst that can happen is that we will have an enjoyable sea journey. If the map proves false I shall still have the *Aurelia* to sell, if need be."

"I can think of a hundred things that could happen in between," Clair said. "And the worst of it is being at sea with men we cannot be sure we trust. You've seen the sea dogs who come ashore here. Some of them look as if they slit throats for pleasure." A deeper note of desperation crept into her voice. "Ria, how could we ever be sure . . . ? Think of the things they could do to us."

Ria's back was ramrod straight. "Clair, you aren't afraid of doing this, are you?"

"Yes. I'm terrified."

"Don't be." She bent and touched her head to Clair's, reassuring, though she was not half as confident as she sounded. "I have it all worked out. We need not concern ourselves with choosing a crew. As I see it, there is only one man we have to be certain we can trust."

"One? Who?"

Ria had a man in mind, a man whose image burned in her mind as if it had been printed by a brand. A man whom she had seen only once and in the poorest of circumstances. A man who, however misguided her reaction, had immediately made her aware why it was that men and women sought each other out; a man who needed the *Aurelia* as much as she needed a captain; a man whose very stature conveyed courage and strength.

"The captain," she told Clair, not daring to say his name. "If we can trust him he will see to the others."

Chapter Three

On the grounds of Palmira, the midmorning sun struggled to spread its golden light through a leafy canopy of ancient moss-strung oaks. Racing through the mingled pattern of shadow and light was a chaise pulled by a fleet chestnut mare. From beneath her clicking hooves came a spray of mud from the roadbed until, with a grinding of wheels, the conveyance stopped before the sprawling, tabby-walled main house.

"Where have you been?" Clair hastened down the low steps leading from Palmira's front veranda. She hurried across the shell-strewn drive to where Ria had brought the chaise to a halt. A slave boy, one of the handful remaining as more and more of Palmira's fields were left uncultivated, hurried to lead the horse away.

"To Grandfather Dag's," Ria answered, keeping her voice low. She had seen Hyatt Landis's saddle horse tied in front of the stable, and two others with it.

"Why?" Clair took no pains to hold the hem of her faded blue plaid dress out of the dampness left from a night of rain. "Is he worse? Why did you not waken me?"

Ria removed her bonnet. She smoothed back the hair that had blown free of its pins when she'd urged the horse to a trot in her hurry to get back to Palmira. Not that haste had done her a good turn. Hyatt Landis had already arrived, though she had hoped to get back before he came. Ria wanted to tell Clair what her meeting with Dom had yielded. But there would not be time. Already she could hear footsteps behind the front doors.

The footsteps ended. A moment later one of the wide doors was thrown open by Sada, Opal's most trusted slave, a big-boned ebony-skinned woman who had been given to Opal from her father's household in Virginia at the time of her marriage to Marcus Kingsley.

"Mr. Landis want you in the parlor," she said.

"In a minute," Ria called to her, hoping the woman would go away so she could at least give Clair a warning of what was to come.

But Sada stayed at the door and held it open, her ears, Ria knew, open as well. It would not do to spill secrets before Sada. She was loyal to her mistress. And fond of Hyatt. No one could fault her for that, but like so many in Savannah, she held Ria and Clair in part responsible for Opal's misfortune at being the widow of a man branded a traitor. Unlike Marcus's daughters, Opal had acknowledged publicly her belief of her husband's guilt, and that she had been unaware of his allegiance to the British.

Opal no longer tried to convince the sisters that they, too, had misjudged their father. Consequently, a division existed between stepmother and stepdaughters.

Ria understood Opal's need to marry Hyatt Landis. Palmira was going to ruin. Opal had neither the experience nor the resources to run a large plantation. Palmira needed a man's hand, and one that could reach into deep, coin-lined pockets to carry the plantation until crops once again yielded a profit.

"He be waitin'," Sada prompted as she waved her big apron to keep the flies and mosquitoes from swarming in the open door. "Best you hurry on."

Clair, fearful of causing another disturbance, caught her sister's hand and tugged her toward the house. Ria looked a fright, but there was no help for it with Hyatt tromping up and down the parlor and Sada grumbling beneath her breath. "He's hopping mad," Clair whispered.

"He will be worse," Ria told her in the same low voice. And let him be, she thought. She didn't like Hyatt, hadn't from the first time he'd come to Palmira. The way he patronized her and Clair had always irked her. For some reason her father had seen promise in the young Landis, promise that had proved out. Hyatt had done well for himself, too well. Unfortunately, Ria had no way to prove her suspicions that his prosperity during wartime was of dubious origins.

Then there was the surprising way in which he had produced the documents allotting Opal sole ownership of Palmira. On the day Marcus wed Opal he had reassured his daughters that half of Palmira would always belong to them, even if other children were born to him of his new wife. And Marcus Kingsley had always been a man of his word.

"You chose a fine time to take a drive," Hyatt berated Ria as as she marched into the parlor.

"Yours is not the only business of importance to me, Hyatt," she said resolutely. "I had another, more urgent matter to attend to.

The mottling of color that inevitably displayed his mood crept from Hyatt's neck to his ears. "Look here, Ria. Your impertinence is—"

"Captain Bellamy." With a quick turn of her head Ria cut Hyatt off and addressed the man who had followed her in.

"Mr. Landis has forgotten there has been no proper introduction."

His laugh was an affront to the man who had brought him to Palmira, but he could not hold it back. Any other woman he knew would have fled from greeting a guest with her hair streaming free of its coiffure and her skirt flecked with mud. This one seemed oblivious of her appearance. Nor did Landis's reproofs set her back as they might a thinner-skinned woman, like the sister who stood wringing her tiny hands and looking for all the world like a pretty rabbit ready to take flight. They were not much alike, those two. The one called Ria reminded him of a frisky filly taking a nip out of another horse and daring it to repay with a kick.

A couple of long strides carried him to where Ria stood. "Chane Bellamy at your service, mademoiselle."

"I am Aurelia Kingsley." She held out a hand to him. His eyes were the bluest she had ever gazed into, a feature she had overlooked in her anger the day before. They flashed at the sound of her name.

"So the vessel bears your name, mademoiselle."

As he clasped her hand he made a slight bow. In spite of herself Ria found his greeting a welcome change from the rude one Hyatt had given. The tension in her eased a little. She had grown so accustomed to rudeness, it seemed, that she hardly knew how to respond to politeness.

"Yes," she said, smiling and awakening enough of the dormant cordiality inside her to speak softly. She could almost feel, physically, in the center of her, an unwinding of locked-away emotions. Hurriedly she pulled them back, turned the key, regretting her momentary lapse, for it had allowed her to feel more in the touch of his hand than the contact merited. Besides the strength in a grip that was firm but gentle, and the pleasurable warmth of his wind-roughened skin, she felt an unbidden sensation leap into her flesh. She had a quick, wild vision of herself twirling across a glistening ballroom floor in Captain Bellamy's arms. It was an unfortunate thought, one that made her immediately stiffen and pull her hand from his. "And—and this is my sister, Clair," she said, gathering her composure.

Clair reluctantly allowed Captain Bellamy to take her hand, which he seemed to do with much more pleasure than when he'd greeted Ria. For Clair he smiled as if no one else were in the room. Clair blushed profusely when he extended the intimacy of the gesture to a touch of his lips on the smooth back of her hand. "Mademoiselle, you are a treasure for the eyes."

Ria's cheeks warmed as well. She shared Clair's discomfort, though she would have sworn all the way to heaven that it was his forwardness with her sister and not a sense of being slighted that bothered her. All the way from Grandfather Dag's house she had wrestled with what she had to do and all the reasons for it. That she must back down from her firm stance of yesterday did not sit well with her. But she wanted no more obstacles to execution of the incredible plan that had formed in her mind during a sleepless night.

She would bargain with Chane Bellamy to captain the *Aurelia*. He was in need of a ship, she of a navigator—and time was of the essence. If Hyatt learned of the money Grandfather Dag had given her he might demand all of it in immediate payment of her debts. Without the money she could not trade for the assistance she needed. So Bellamy it must be, and the deal fixed today. Theirs was to be a business agreement, nothing more.

Of course she would have no difficulty keeping to the conduct she had in mind. She had completely expelled those foolish romantic thoughts of the day before. For all his manners and good looks she would have preferred another man had she had the leisure to search one out. But Dom knew of Bellamy and swore the captain would be trustworthy.

Ria's brow creased as she looked at her pretty, flustered sister. That he had noticed Clair, found her beauty alluring, as all men did, would be a complication. Clair was vulnerable and the captain had the worldly look of a man whose experience with women was vast. Could she expect him to be trustworthy in that regard as well?

"Captain Bellamy wishes to buy the ship, Ria. He and I have agreed on a price." Hyatt had cast to the wind all semblance of courtesy where Ria was involved. He wanted her out of Palmira, out of his life with Opal, the sooner the better. He'd had enough of Ria and her insolence. Besides, no one would miss her if he hastened her departure from Savannah.

"I will have a say in what is agreed on." Ria cut Hyatt a look that disguised none of her contempt for him.

Hyatt, reddening, took a threatening step toward her. "The papers are drawn. You will sign—"

A warning look from Chane clipped him short. Hyatt had judged the captain a man of soft disposition, one who was easily persuaded; it seemed he might have underestimated him.

"If it pleases you, we can discuss the terms you have in mind," Chane said to Ria.

The devil take Landis. The man's antagonism toward the girl was about to cost him the vessel he wanted. Obviously the attorney knew nothing about the workings of a woman's mind. Aurelia Kingsley needed a bit of gentle handling to bring her around. She was as skittish as the wild little filly she reminded him of, but she had warmed to him. He'd felt the subtle change in her during the brief moment he'd held her hand. A bit of coaxing, a few carefully chosen words, and she would agree to what he and Landis wanted. Then let the pair of them hash out their differences.

"It pleases me," Ria returned. Straightening her spine she turned her back on Hyatt but spoke purposely loud for his benefit. "We will talk alone."

Hyatt was seething with barely controlled anger. He silently cursed Marcus for not having stored the papers concerning the ship with the grants for Palmira. Had the man been more consistent, with Hyatt Landis's help Opal would have gained ownership of the *Aurelia* along with Palmira.

Leaving Hyatt and Clair in the parlor, Ria led Chane Bellamy to the library. She felt stronger, more committed to her purpose in the room where the memory of her father's presence was strongest. Indicating a chair for Chane, she eased behind the shiny mahogany desk and seated herself in the leather-covered chair Marcus Kingsley had used when he read or worked at the figures in his ledgers.

Chane had in the pocket of his coat a packet of papers. He removed it, took one from the fold and spread it on the desk before Ria. "The figure is what I am willing to pay for the *Aurelia*," he said. "A good sum more than your solicitor suggested."

"He is not my solicitor," she said sharply. Her eyes dropped to the paper. The amount was adequate. Dom had told her the vessel's worth. He had also told her what it would take to provision the ship for the length of time she planned to be at sea. The total was close to the amount Grandfather Dag had given her, minus what was due Hyatt. Hyatt, in any event, would have to be satisfied with the amount she gave him. She did not think he would quibble over the point. He would be rid of her and of Clair.

Chane watched the girl, proud and willful in her shabby dress. But what did she hope to gain by this quarrel with Landis? She had already given way on her intention to keep the vessel; otherwise she would not be negotiating with him. Landis was full of himself and deserved the girl's wrath. But Chane could not help believing she was only biting off more trouble by openly defying the man.

"I am prepared to pay you in gold and I would prefer that the transaction be completed today." He had allowed enough time for her to ponder his offer, and he was not about to let her run roughshod over him as she had Landis. Either she accepted or he would start to Charleston with tomorrow's sun. There he was likely to find a vessel to fill his needs.

Ria lifted her head. The man's impatience was only lightly veiled. She must gather her nerve and put her proposition to him. "You may have the *Aurelia* at your price," she said. "But not today."

His temper boiled up inside him. He was in no frame of mind for female ploys after yesterday's incident with Lorelle. Still, it was with an even tone of voice that he said, "It seems you have wasted my time again, mademoiselle."

He rose and would have stridden out the door but her beseeching voice called him back. "Captain, you may have use of the ship as soon as you please."

Yes, then no, then yes again. Puzzled, he looked at the girl. Her eyes had a strange look, like that of the sea in the dead calm before a storm. Was she daft? Had he mistaken dementia for spirit? Or was she simply playing for a higher price? He thought the latter.

"You have before you my only offer, mademoiselle," he said, stepping near the desk and taking an imperious stand before her, his legs spread wide and his hands locked behind his back.

"If you will hear me out, Captain." She gripped the arms of the chair. She wished he had kept his seat. In his intimidating posture he towered over the desk, casting a large shadow that caught her squarely within its outline. For a moment she faltered. Suppose he should refuse, or worse, laugh at her? No. She would not think that. She would think only of success. "My sister and I would like to leave Palmira," she said, raising her head so that she could meet his eyes and gauge his reaction. "Mr. Landis has plans for us that we do not wish to follow."

So it was a favor she sought, a way to escape Landis. To oblige was no trouble to him. "I can help you find passage wherever you wish to go," he said.

"We wish you to take us."

He shook his head. "I am bound for Martinique," he said. "I have a cargo I must deliver posthaste."

"Martinique would not be out of our way," she replied.

"You have relatives in the West Indies?"

"No," she answered. "Our only relative is here. Our grandfather. It is his wish that we leave. There is a place he wishes us to go." She reached into the folds of her skirt and produced a reticule from which she extracted a piece of parchment. Carefully she unrolled it, folded back a portion then spread it over the paper that listed his offer. "He has given me a map."

A map? The girl was muddled. And she had wasted his time. He was behind schedule for his return to Martinique as it was. He'd have turned and left except that the chart she unrolled caught his eye, first a peculiar emblem in the corner, then the chart itself. A sea map of the waters he'd recently sailed, with the coastlines and currents marked as only the best seaman could do.

"Who drew this?" he asked, spreading his palms upon the desk and leaning over the parchment for a better look.

"My grandfather. Grandfather Dag."

"Your grandfather is a fine mapmaker, a man who has spent many years of his life at sea," he observed. The detail of the map astounded him. He'd have liked a look at the half she kept hidden. He wanted to compare the rendering of the waters so familiar to him to his own knowledge of them. It occurred to him at the same moment that there was a reason she was showing only the upper portion. "What is this place you wish to go?" he asked.

"I will first need your agreement that you will take us."

Their eyes met, his questioning, hers beseeching. "Who is this Dag?" he asked. "Why does he send you to a place you cannot speak of?"

"He is Dagian," Ria answered. "He uses but the one name.

"Dagian," Chane mumbled, thinking. The mark in the upper corner drew his eye, a sunburst inked in black and outlined in red. "Dagian. Dawn," he said. "The pirate Black Dawn."

"You know him?" Ria asked in a whisper.

"By repute." Chane's look challenged her. "Who in the West Indies does not know of the Black Dawn? Or even now shudder when they hear his name? He was a scourge to all who hoisted a sail and took more in plunder than a hundred men could make use of in a lifetime. The rumors are many that he hid the best part of his loot and never went back to claim the prize." He stepped back, crossed his arms. His eyes turned a wintry blue. "But Dagian was hanged. He is dead. Long dead."

"No." She could not get her voice above a whisper. So, the tales of bloody deeds, the legacy of plunder, all true. She had only half believed before now, she realized. Only half trusted that the map would lead to more than disappointment. Suddenly she knew it was fact. Grandfather Dag was the man Chane Bellamy spoke of, wicked, cruel. And the map beneath her hand on the desk led to his lost trove. "He lives, if his existence could be called life." She sighed nervously. "I am his granddaughter."

"And it is to Dagian's trove you would have me take you." Now he understood her strange words regarding the ship. She wanted assurance he would abide by the agreement to take her where the map led. To guarantee his compliance that he would, she would reserve ownership of the vessel until the journey was complete.

"Yes," she said, her calm facade belying a furiously pounding heart.

Chane looked about the room for a bottle. He had need of a drink. But the hollow shelves and empty tables yielded nothing. He turned back to the girl. Her story was fantastic, and yet he found himself swayed to believe it.

Ria saw his doubt. She had taken a chance telling him as much as she had. But she had not judged him a man to accept less than complete candor. They had not discussed terms but she was prepared to be generous. If Dom had not exaggerated the treasure's worth, generous recompense to the captain who took her to Dagian's trove would not be a problem.

How much was his compliance worth to her? Chane wondered. "I will see the whole of the map before I raise anchor," he said at length. "And the ship is mine once the search is done."

A tremor shook Ria, then a feeling that a great burden had been lifted from her shoulders. "You will do it?"

He had not laughed. He believed. He was a better man than she had thought. He'd even staved off Hyatt's verbal assault of her, a truly chivalrous act after the way she'd treated him the day before. For the first time in years Aurelia Kingsley felt her life just might be put right again. With the treasure she could take care of Clair. She could find a way to avenge her father, to prove he was not a traitor, to make his murderers pay for their cowardly deed. This was all going so much better than she had hoped. She wasn't quite ready to trust Chane Bellamy fully, but perhaps that time would come.

Still she did not dare to smile, to tempt fate by acknowledging his assent until she heard him say the words. Then—

"Yes, Aurelia Kingsley. I will take you to Dagian's trove."

She could not contain her happiness then. It bubbled from her like fresh cool water from a spring. She smiled, her eyes lit like lanterns.

Chane smiled too, devilishly. What had he to lose by helping her? He'd sworn he would not return to his father's house. He would found his own. He had boasted to Renaud Bellamy that in the space of a single year he would purchase a plantation to equal Eglantine. His face darkened as he remembered what he must do if he did not meet his wager. A rash agreement to be sure, though he would be hanged before he told his father so.

His smile deepened as his mind leaped ahead. If the Black Dawn's trove was as rich as rumored, the girl, Ria, might have given him the way to make good on his boast. If not, he was out only a few months of his time.

Those months could not be overly hard to bear with two tantalizing women on board. One sugar, one spice.

Chapter Four

"Add your terms to the contract," he said, "and my own as follows. The ship is mine should our venture succeed or fail. I am captain of the *Aurelia* from this moment on—there is to be no dispute of that once we are under way. We will make port in Martinique and I will conclude my business there before the expedition to recover the treasure begins. Should the map prove false, I will pay you your due for the *Aurelia,* return your sister and yourself to the nearest safe port and secure passage to the destination of your choice, thereby ending any and all obligation to you."

"So be it," she said.

Chane Bellamy paced as he walked with the rolling, smooth gait of a proud seaman. Ria's heart fairly leaped along behind him. She was so anxious she could scarcely form letters with her trembling hand. Now and again she was forced to stop taking dictation to take deep breaths as her mind raced to imagine all she might do with the riches awaiting her.

She would be free. Free of Hyatt Landis. Free of the taint of traitor. Free—

"I would have your pledge in gold," he intruded. "Half the amount will suffice at this time. I will use it for payment of stores we take on board here. There is room for no more as my cargo will fill the ship. The other half needed for the expedition we can secure in Martinique.''

Ria completed what he had required of her and looked up to find he had returned to a crossed-arm, wide-legged stance before her desk, as if he were about to address his crew on the eve of a voyage. He was straight and tall as a mainmast, and by the look of him—that determined set of his jaw, that stalwart cast in his eye—a crew would think twice before they balked at an order from Chane Bellamy.

''You will have it before you leave tonight,'' Ria promised. She paused to blot the new contract then turned it lengthwise on the desk for him to read. ''You may sign,'' she directed.

Chane took the document and read. The girl had a fine hand and she had written his words precisely as he had spoken them. Her tidy penmanship bore a marked contrast to her appearance—the flyaway hair, the shabby dress. She was a paradox, this one, a bundle of contradictions, calculating and temperamental, independent and vulnerable. Already he had acknowledged a grudging respect for Aurelia Kingsley.

He returned the paper to the desk and pushed it unsigned toward her. The bargain suited but for one thing. ''There is the matter of the treasure,'' he said.

A sudden lurch came to Ria's fast-beating heart. She had expected this and purposely waited for him to broach the topic. ''I am prepared to give you a tenth,'' she responded.

A burst of laughter erupted from him. ''Indeed.'' One black slash of a brow rose sharply. The fine white teeth flashed with a brief sardonic smile. ''A half is what I require.''

Ria's own dark brows rose in a haughty line as, hidden in her lap, her nails dug into her damp palms. ''Half is quite out of the question.''

"Half it is," he insisted with all the bluster of a wind-filled sail. "You do not consider that I must provide a share to every man of my crew else they are likely to leave us both paupers in a watery den."

Ria swallowed hard. A mutinous crew was not something she had considered, but she quickly grasped the possibility of such a danger. The treasure they sought, if indeed as vast as Dom had indicated, might sway the principles of even moral men. Notwithstanding a real peril, she was certain Chane Bellamy, for his own gain, exaggerated to some degree.

"A quarter then," she relented, refusing to be manipulated like some witless person.

"A third," he countered, admiring the way she had quickly seen through his ploy to gain a greater share of the loot, but not quite ready to end the haggling. "A third or it is no bargain. And," he emphasized, "should I find my life and that of my men in grave danger then 'tis half or I turn back the expedition."

Ria set her mouth to disagree but saw in the steely glint of his eye that he was set firm. A third was no more than she'd expected to yield. Increasing his share if there was danger could be debated should a threat arise.

"Done," she said and added a final line to the contract, promising one-third of the treasure to Chane Bellamy.

She had dipped the pen and was about to add her signature to the paper when Chane stopped her, his hand lightly holding hers as he caught and stilled her pen in midair.

"If the contract is to be binding we are in need of witnesses," he advised, his fingers moving lazily along the silver shaft of her pen, stroking that instrument and Ria's soft fingertips. "One of my men rode to Palmira with me and waits in your stable. Or there is Landis as well—"

His hand was warm, his touch immobilizing, until Ria realized she was purposely allowing the contact to last. She withdrew her hand with a suddenness that left the pen to tumble and roll and spill blotches of black ink upon the wide desktop.

"No!" she said abruptly. "Landis is to know nothing of this. Let the terms be known to you and me alone." She half stood, searching her pocket for a handkerchief to mop up the spilled ink. She found none but Chane tossed her his, one of fine soft linen. Ria used it without compunction rather than have her father's desk blemished by the ink.

"It is of no account," he said, referring to the ruined handkerchief. "Let us get on with our business."

"Clair will serve as witness for my part," she offered.

"Agreed." Chane sent for his man. He, too, had no desire to reveal to Landis the strange bargain he had made with Aurelia Kingsley. The fewer who knew of it the better. He had not greatly exaggerated the difficulties of a crew who believed they were being cheated. Even the best chosen of men might turn rogue for a chance at great wealth. Chane needed no convincing that secrecy was the best protection for all.

He noted the look of consternation on Landis's face as the seaman entered Palmira. The solicitor did not like it that he'd lost control over the situation. But Chane cared little if he wounded the man's pride. Chane as good as had his ship, and more.

The signing was done in a moment, with Clair shaking as if she'd taken a winter chill and Chane Bellamy's man acquiescing without question to his captain's request. Ria suspected Hyatt Landis lurked beyond the study door, his ear to the keyhole. Let him listen. He would learn nothing, and tomorrow when she paid him his due, he would have no further hold on Aurelia or Clair Kingsley.

"A moment, please," Ria said to Chane when Clair and the other witness had left the study. She felt a shiver as she spoke, nearly as strong a tremor as she had observed in the anxious Clair. What she was about to ask required an admission of unequivocal trust in her Captain Bellamy. "You intended to pay me for the *Aurelia*," she began. "Gold, you said."

What now? he wondered, scowling. Had she secured his agreement and now his signature only to tell him no money for provisions would be forthcoming, that he must stake the venture until the treasure was found? He was primed to vent his rage should that be the case.

Ria saw his doubt and hurried to assuage it. "A request only," she said softly. "I would not have Landis suspect the reason that Clair and I will be sailing with you on the *Aurelia*. If he saw the coins I have—they are old, doubloons, I think—he would know.... Here," she said, delving unabashedly into her bodice for the secreted pouch of coins. She weighed the bag in her hands then loosened the leather strings and withdrew a handful of gold pieces. These she gave to Chane.

Chane looked closely at the coins. The gold, warm from the heat of her body, weighed heavily on his palm. He thought of the warmth that must reside in her flesh, how it might feel to warm his hands upon her silken skin. His eyes burned hotly as he glanced up at her. "Spanish, indeed," he remarked, handling a few of the thick rounds of gold, turning them in his fingers so that the candlelight fell stronger upon them. "Doubloons. Yes, old. From Dagian?"

"A gift," she said, her heart swelling with pride as she thought of her grandfather's peculiar but touching expression of love. "The price of the expedition."

He closed his hands tight around the coins, joining his heat with that of Ria's. "You wish me to exchange them?"

"Landis would wonder at their origin should he see them. I do not trust him, nor do I wish to further rouse his curiosity.

Chane slid the coins into the sheepskin pouch he carried in a pocket of his coat. "Leave Landis to me," he said. "He'll not trouble you before we sail."

"And when will that be?" The thought of sailing away from Savannah made her breathless, but she tried to appear nonchalant.

"Ready yourself," he said, eyes spearing her. "The *Aurelia* sails at dawn in two days' time. You and your sister may come aboard tomorrow."

At that she could no longer hide her excitement. Her smile was broad and bright as the moon. "Aye," she said.

The stars shone dully through the hazy sky of the humid night when Hyatt Landis arrived at the docks. He swung down from his lathered horse and paid a lad to watch the animal until his return. Pollack, who should have been there to meet him, was nowhere in sight. Landis glanced around impatiently, finally locating the man asleep in a longboat tied up at the wharf. Griping at the inconvenience, he climbed down to the gently rocking craft and shook Pollack awake.

"Ehh—what—" Pollack grumbled, moving leadenly, rubbing his eyes and stretching his long arms until his mind cleared and he remembered that he'd been waiting to row Landis out to the *Aurelia*.

"Look alive, man!" Hyatt said to him. "We may yet have a long night ahead of us."

"What's 'at?" Sluggishly, Pollack crawled upon a seat of the longboat and dropped the oars into the rowlocks.

"Something is afoot," Landis said. "Clair Kingsley is locked in her room sobbing and Ria is so smug her face might break." Impatiently, he directed the seaman to shove off. He had personal articles aboard the *Aurelia* that he wanted to remove before Bellamy took possession of the vessel. "Something is afoot," he repeated, "and Bellamy is at the heart of it. He has formed an alliance with those girls, I know it." Head bent to the wind he sat in the prow of the longboat. "Though what they could offer a man like Bellamy is beyond me." Landis pulled his cocked hat lower on his forehead.

Pollack, his round head encased in a knitted cap with blue stripes, rumbled out a laugh as he pictured the luscious Clair Kingsley in his mind. "I'd take anything that quiet bit o'muslin offered me, I would," he said with a lustful gleam in his eye.

"Ha! What do you know of ladies?" Landis queried. "Or of gentlemen? A man like Bellamy has no use for a mouse like Clair. As for Ria, dallying with her would be like taking a dip in vinegar."

"'Tis 'is loss on either count." Pollack tightened his grip on the briskly swinging oar before he missed a stroke.

"There is something else," Landis mused as the longboat bumped the barnacled hull of the *Aurelia* and Pollack tied up the craft. "Have you heard anything amiss in the taverns? Anything of Bellamy?"

"Nay." Pollack swung to the rope-ladder bound to the ship's side and, with lumbering skill, hoisted himself to the deck. While Landis followed, laboriously pulling his weight from one webbed rung to the next, Pollack recalled one scrap of talk he had overheard. "But Dagian's man, Dom, 'as asked about o' yer Captain Bellamy."

Pondering the bit of news, Landis trimmed the lantern Pollack had left on deck, and cautiously made his way to the main cabin of the *Aurelia,* spitting out a curse when he stumbled over a coiled length of rigging.

"She had something she did not want me to see that day she came upon me talking with Bellamy," Landis said when he and Pollack entered the shadowed confines of the cabin. He began piling articles in a box: a half bottle of good brandy, books, a change of clothes he had left in a cupboard, spare linens, a captain's glass—let Bellamy supply his own. He did not take the sextant, knowing Bellamy would question the lack of one. He left the ship's log; it told no tales that would condemn him.

Box stacked high, he took a last possessive look about. He would be glad to see the *Aurelia* gone. Marcus Kingsley had honeymooned with his second bride aboard the ship, a voyage Landis also had made in his capacity as solicitor. Only a thin wall had separated him from the newlywed Kingsleys, and Landis had listened to the muffled sounds of lovemaking and grown to hate his benefactor. That had been the beginning of it, an oath made to himself that he would possess Opal, would hear her moan and beg for him as she had for Marcus.

Two years had passed as he endeared himself to the new Mrs. Kingsley. Marcus himself had come to think of Landis as a son by the time the colonists took up arms against the British.

"Who?" Pollack asked for a second time. "Who 'id what?"

Drawing a scowl from Landis, Pollack uncorked the brandy bottle and chugged from it.

"Ria," he answered. "Some papers, as I recall, and most assuredly from that mad grandfather of hers." He rubbed the back of his hand across his furrowed brow. "But what could the old fool have given her that she would bother to conceal it?"

Pollack shrugged and turned up the brandy bottle Landis had relinquished, draining it. He hiccuped. "Yer question begs an answer. I could 'ave a look."

"Yes," Landis agreed, having already come to the conclusion that he should try to discover what the girl was hiding. He had a plan that was sure to net him what he sought. "Tonight," he said. "While she sleeps. Anything of value she is likely to keep on her person when she is awake."

Pollack grinned, stuck his tongue through the wide gap in his teeth and licked his fat lower lip. "Aye," he said.

Each bedroom at Palmira opened to a hall and also had outer doors to the wide stone-floored veranda that surrounded the house. The Kingsley sisters' rooms were at the back of the east wing, Opal Kingsley's suite at the corresponding corner of the west wing. A courtyard garden filled with winding arbors of sweet purple wisteria separated the wings. Native live oaks ringed the house, enormous trees with gnarled tentacled branches curling from the umbrella tops to the fertile ground. A man up to no good could hide beneath the oaks and bide the time to make his mischief.

William Pollack waited only a quarter hour to be certain no one stirred within the house. He made his move then from beneath the tent of a tree, gliding across the smooth swept grounds in his stocking feet, padding softly across the stone veranda. He smiled to himself as he went about his misdeed. Landis could not have given him an order he would have taken to more eagerly than he did to this one.

A last look about the dark grounds satisfied him he was not likely to be discovered. His hands went to his pockets as he approached one of the rooms. Smiling, he withdrew the tools he required. A hook of wire and the thin blade of a folding knife successfully released the latch that held shut the louvered doors leading to Clair Kingsley's bedroom.

With the shred of moonlight the crack in the door allowed
through the narrow opening, Pollack eased inside, tensed
and held his breath. Behind a drape of netting, Clair lay
upon the snowy sheets, angelic face reposed in deep sleep.
Her gown was white as the linens, her pale skin nearly of the
same hue. Pollack's first gulp of air came heavily, like lead
in his chest, at the sight of her. Another part of his body
grew heavy as well.

Do not touch the girl. Landis's warning nagged his memory. *Give her a scare, that is all.* Pollack sneered at his absent master, but obeyed. He was not a man to wonder on
which side his bread was buttered. Landis kept his purse
full. He would not cross the man, no matter how much he
itched to climb atop the sleeping girl. But Landis, Pollack
recalled, had said nothing about looking. And look he
would.

Moving silently, he crossed the room and eased the netting curtain aside. With awkward slowness he lifted the
coverlet draping Clair's body, nearly choking on a groan
when he uncovered the pale, bare, shapely ankles and
calves. Her gown was of sheer lawn, a wispy fabric that
draped her lush curves like translucent silk. Pollack spent a
long time staring at her, searching in the dim light for the
dusky spots of color where her nipples capped full round
breasts, for the shadowy patch of curls where her thighs
met.

The blade of his folding knife was still outstretched, an
instrument of temptation to Pollack, who, unable to re-
strain himself, hooked the steel blade of it into the ruffled
hem of Clair's gown. Taking his time about it, he lifted the
soft fabric above her knees, over her creamy thighs, beyond the wisp of reddish color that seemed to invite his
hand.

Clair stirred when a draft of cool air swept over her, disturbed by the rustling of her gown, a tickling as it moved on her legs. She had been sleeping soundly until the change in temperature stirred her subconscious thoughts, catching her in a dream full of dangers she could not escape, fears that lapped at her feet like treacherous waves in a troubled sea. Moaning, yearning for escape from her nightmare, she turned on her pillow and hastily opened her eyes to the darkness.

Had she kicked the covers away, bared her legs to the cool wind that fluttered past the bed curtains? Clair lifted her head from the pillow, saw that the hem of her nightgown lay bunched and twisted about her waist. Aghast, she quickly cast it over her naked legs and sat up, then froze. Her spine tingled, the silky hairs at her nape lifted and curled. Among the dusky shadows a shape moved, a specter that loomed larger and larger the longer she stared.

"Riaaa!" When she screamed the specter became a blur of black then disappeared behind a click of the veranda door. She was sure.

In her own room, Ria leaped to her feet, flinging bedclothes aside. Clair's nightmares, so frequent following their father's death, had been on the wane for months. Still, the terror in her cry was unmistakable. Ria knew what would follow, the bout of hysteria, the uncontrollable crying. She also knew she must bear the blame for this outburst, for the renewal of the night terrors. Clair was horrified at the thought of going to sea.

A shared dressing room adjoined their rooms. Clad only in her nightgown, Ria rushed past the trunk she had started packing, through the dressing room and was at her sister's side in moments, her arms about Clair's tremulous shoulders. Deep sobs shook her sister from head to foot.

"Hush, hush," she whispered as Clair grabbed her and held on so tightly she could hardly get her breath. "Dreams cannot hurt you, Clair."

"I saw a man," Clair mumbled, wiping dampened hair and tears from her face. "He was there." She pointed toward a tall oval cheval glass set so that it gloomily reflected the sisters as they sat side by side on the bed.

Ria observed the murky animated reflections. "Only that," she said, relieved. "You saw yourself."

"No. No, I did not," Clair insisted. "I couldn't have. He was walking. He had been here at my bed. The curtains were open—" she touched the silk netting "—the door, too." Overcome by a new bout of shivering when Ria released her and turned to examine the door, Clair drew her knees snug against her chest and hugged them tightly with her arms. "He . . . touched me."

Knowing Clair would not be satisfied until she had proved only the two of them were in the bedroom, Ria lit a candle and walked about the room, illuminating each of the four corners, finding nothing to account for her sister's fear. The door leading to the veranda was shut and latched, as was the one opening into the hallway and as had been the one to the dressing room. She had, however, heard a sound long before Clair screamed, a clink of metal, a scrape, then nothing. Not so unusual in a house the size of Palmira, a house with a hundred shutters and dozens of doors, a house surrounded by a thick swamp and a dense woodland filled with hungry prowling creatures.

Nightmares were commonplace for Clair. Ria returned to her sister's bed, placed the burning candle on the nightstand. "You are all right now, Clair," she said softly.

Clair nodded and clutched Ria's hand. "Stay with me, Ria," she pleaded. "Please."

"I will," Ria promised, smiling softly at Clair. "I prefer my own pillow, though," she said, rising quietly and walking toward the dressing room. "And getting it will take but a moment."

William Pollack snuffed out the flaming candle stub he held above the paper he had found only seconds before inside the pillow slip on Ria's bed. He had not seen much, but a man of the sea needed only a glance to know that what he held before him was a treasure map. Pity was that he did not know his letters better. He might have been able to distinguish a destination, even a course to set. Now the girl was coming and he did not have time to study or copy what he had before him. Hurriedly, as Ria's footsteps drew near, Pollack rolled the map and shoved it into the pillow slip.

He had been ordered to look for and identify some papers, not steal anything. Landis did not want the Mistress Kingsley alarmed by knowing her house had been broken into. Except for that, he might have been allowed to have his way with the girls instead of contenting himself with a quick look at pretty Clair. Still, that was a sight he was not likely to forget soon, what pretty Clair hid beneath her skirts. He had seen, he'd warrant, what no other man's eyes had beheld.

A step ahead of Ria's return Pollack slid through the veranda door, grinning his wide toothless grin. Landis's plan had worked almost perfectly. Just as the man had said she would, Ria Kingsley had rushed to her sister when she screamed. But the bolder Kingsley girl had not given him quite enough time at the map. What would Landis say to that? he wondered.

The smell of melted wax, the lingering essence of smoke, brought Ria up short. Already suspicious, despite her assurances to Clair, Ria entered her room cautiously, scanning it as she had Clair's. Among her own possessions the oddest feeling took hold of her, as if she had been given eyes that saw a trail made in the air, the invisible path of an intruder. But that was impossible. Her room was quiet and still and empty, the doors closed and locked.

Trying to shake off her suspicion, she hurried to her bed. Had she tossed her pillow aside as she left her rest? Perhaps. And perhaps not. She picked up the down-filled sack, searched the covering linen slip and, comfortingly, found her map safe as she had left it. Still, it was with some anxiety that she knelt to the floor beside the bed. She whispered a word of relief when she found that the pouch containing those coins she had not given Bellamy was still safely tucked under the carpet beneath her bed. And yet—

"Ria!" Clair's voice held desperation. Pillow and pouch in hand, Ria hurried to her sister, unable to shake the dread that perhaps Clair was right after all.

"Well, man. Out with it. What did you find?" In his study Landis, attired in a scarlet silk lounging robe, lay back upon a plump velvet settee.

Pollack, his undertaking having revived his thirst, eyed the cabinet he knew held an assortment of spirits. "A map," he said. "A map bearin' the mark o' the pirate Black Dawn. A map to a treasure."

Landis sprang to his feet. "You have it? You brought it?"

Pollack snorted and gave him a curious look. "Nay," he replied. "Ye said take nothin'. I did as ordered."

"Dolt! I did not anticipate a treasure map."

"And I did not 'ticipate ye changin' yer mind over what ye wanted done." Pollack audaciously opened the polished doors of the cabinet that had drawn him ever closer, selected a bottle and popped out the cork. His single concession to civility was to make use of a glass. He selected a tall one and poured it full to the gold-rimmed brim.

"I suppose it is too much to hope that you could reproduce it?"

"Copy it? Nay," Pollack said. "Readin' an' writin' ain't what ol' Pollack does best." He laughed. "'Sides, even if I knowed letters, the light was poor an' the time short." He looked up from the rim of his glass. "The girl came back."

"She did not see you?"

"Nay," he said. "No one at Palmira is wiser fer William Pollack's visit."

Including Pollack, Landis thought, and then his mind was ablaze with possibilities. Following Pollack's example, he selected a bottle from the cabinet, choosing a fine Madeira and a slim-stemmed crystal glass that he filled with the golden liquid. He'd never believed the tales about old Dagian, but suppose he was wrong? "What store do you put in these tales of the Black Dawn?" he asked the seaman.

"'Ey do not do 'im justice by 'alf," Pollack proclaimed. "The Black Dawn was the dyin' curse o' many a sorry bloke. Even now no man o' the sea will draw near 'is bloody 'ouse."

Having paced the full length of his study, Landis whirled about. He would like a look at that map. But the chance was poor that Pollack could get his hands on it a second time without being seen. Everyone, including Opal, knew Pollack was Hyatt Landis's man. Was it worth the risk? The map could be insignificant, merely marking a spot Dagian had returned to and emptied of treasure long ago. Or it could lead to the site of his last untouched hoard. Landis blurted out a curse. Why had Pollack not used his head and brought the document to him? Angrily, he glared at the man. "Could this map be genuine?"

"Only ol' Dagian could tell us 'at," Pollack wisely remarked.

"Go to him! Make him tell you!"

"Nay!" Pollack shook his head until the ragged tassel on his knit cap waved like a banner. "Not fer you. Not fer gold. 'Is man'd gut me an' boil me 'eart. 'E's swore 'is life to that ol' devil."

The flinty look in Pollack's eyes warned Landis that further insistence was futile. He would have to find another way to uncover the truth about the treasure map. "I will have to make Ria tell me," he said.

"She was packin'."

"Ria?"

"Aye. She 'ad a travelin' trunk open an' near full."

Landis, in his consternation, snapped the stem of his glass but moved neither left nor right as the shattered remnants fell at his feet. He was seized by the certainty that the map Aurelia had from her grandfather was the key to a hidden fortune. That Marcus Kingsley's offspring might rise from the mire to which he'd brought them galled Landis no end. Greed, too, played upon his mind.

"She is going with Bellamy," he ground out, recalling the long session between the captain and Ria in Palmira's study. "The bloody bastard has bargained with her for a share of the loot. Damn her! She's as much a poisonous thorn in my hide as her father was." His eyes narrowed and his lips thinned. "But I can best her as I did her bloody father."

"'Ow's that?"

With a new vigor in his body, Landis took the empty glass from Pollack's hand, refilled it and handed it to the stunned man. "Drink up, my friend," he said. "You and I have come to a parting of the ways."

"Eh?" Head twisted to one side, Pollack looked threateningly at Landis. He had done many a foul deed for the solicitor and he was not about to brushed aside with a mere glass of whiskey.

"As it appears, man. Only as it appears." He patted Pollack on the back. "You have no further use for me nor I for you. Tell Bellamy you would like a spot aboard the *Aurelia*."

A light shone anew inside Pollack's small dark eyes. A grand plan. He might have thought of it himself. Let Bellamy find the treasure if there was one, then he'd take it from him. "An' bring ye the Black Dawn's loot," Pollack ground out.

"Half for you and half for me," Landis stated jovially, then dropped his voice ominously low. "And see the Kingsley sisters cannot darken my door again." Eyes hooded, he offered his hand to Pollack, a rogue's covenant.

Pollack linked his filthy, callused hand with Landis's smooth, manicured one and sealed the black bargain.

"Generous ye are, sir," he said, grinning. *An' a bloody great fool to think ye will see William Pollack again.*

Chapter Five

A deepening shadow slipped past the noon mark on Palmira's wide front door. Far back in her wing of the house Ria guessed at the time and concluded that the hours before she and Clair left for the *Aurelia* were growing short.

Pausing at her work, Ria wiped a straggling lock of red hair from her sweat-dampened face. So much to be done. She had to pack for Clair and herself. All morning her sister had been completely helpless to do anything in a hurry and too close to hysteria to be scolded for not doing her part. By now Opal, would be wondering why the girls had failed to appear for their usual morning ride, but Ria had a ready answer for her stepmother. She would cite Clair's sleepless night and claim fatigue from sitting up with her sister.

"Aren't we telling anyone of our plans?" Clair fidgeted with the few toiletries on her dressing table, selected a bottle or two, then changed her mind and put them back to ponder her choices a little longer.

"Only when it's time to leave," Ria reminded her, impatiently scooping all Clair's jars and bottles into a tapestry bag and binding it tight. "Opal would feel honor bound to tell Hyatt of our planned departure. I, for one, have said my last word to him." Until our return, she added silently.

Clair flitted from her dressing table to sit on the edge of a dainty chair, wringing her hands as Ria went through her wardrobe callously discarding some garments while she tossed others into the trunk.

"I do want that one," Clair said of her favorite quilted white velvet ball gown, it was old and out of style, but it had been her first and Papa had picked it.

Ria dismissed her protest and tossed the gown aside. "Too heavy for where we are going," she said, choosing instead a honey-colored traveling dress of cotton twill. "Wear this when we leave," she instructed. She had a dress of identical cut, only hers was the color of ripe plums and had never looked right with her brilliant red hair. She had worn it often as a riding costume and it was worse for the wear, but who was to care if she looked shabby for one more day? Only Clair.

The discarding of her favorite gown was enough to send Clair into a greater twitter. "Oh, Ria! Are you sure about this journey? Are you sure the map means anything? What if Captain Bellamy steals it from us? Have you seen the way he looks at me? What if he—"

Ria's cheeks burned as she bent over Clair's trunk, tucking in the bag of toiletries and tossing in the cake of rose-scented soap she had brought from her room. "Yes, I have seen the way Captain Bellamy looks at you, Clair."

She answered but one of her sister's questions. "He is like all men, foolish over a pretty face. And yours, my sister, is prettier than most."

"I wish it wasn't," Clair said emphatically as she spun about to view herself in the mirror. "I wish my face was plain as an old cow's and that no man would notice me at all."

"You would like that even less," Ria assured her.

"Oh, no—"

A rap at the door hushed the girls. Ria scrambled to her feet. That nosy Sada had been snooping around and would spread the news in a heartbeat if she discovered Ria and Clair were preparing for a journey. Stumbling over the sorted piles of clothing and shoes, Ria hurried to answer the door. She was a second late reaching it. Clair had forgotten to secure the lock and Opal, with a look of concern on her face, swung the door open.

"Sada said you had been to the attic and brought down your traveling trunk and Clair's." She looked around the clothes-strewn room, saw the open trunk, Clair's frantic face. "What is this, Ria? Can you be leaving Palmira without a word to me?"

"I p-planned to tell you, of course," Ria stammered. "But I knew you would be upset and I wanted to leave and say goodbye at the same time."

Opal stepped inside. "Palmira is your home, Ria. And yours, Clair."

Clair gulped but Ria would not be dissuaded. "Palmira is *your* home," she said. "Clair and I do not belong here any longer. Next month you will wed Hyatt and—"

Opal's voice was anguished. "I had hoped you could learn to like Hyatt, that we could be a family here."

Ria shook her head vigorously. "Captain Bellamy has promised to take us . . . elsewhere," she said, looking away.

Opal turned her pinched face to Clair. "Is this what you want?"

Clair's chin trembled, her soft brown eyes misted with tears. She was afraid to go, but afraid to stay as well. She liked Hyatt little better than Ria did. "Yes," she answered weakly. "Yes, it is."

Opal hurried to the girls and embraced them, surprised and ashamed she felt relief at learning that Ria and Clair were leaving. Yet she had done her best for them, she believed, and if it was impossible for them to be happy at Palmira again then perhaps it was best for them to go. She looked forward, she admitted, to beginning life anew with Hyatt. This parting of the ways, unfortunate as it was, would be easier for all. "I will miss you," she said softly.

In the *Aurelia*'s main cabin Chane Bellamy's young cabin boy unpacked his captain's newly purchased belongings and arranged them neatly in the cupboards of the spacious compartment. At a small square table secured to the polished floorboards by iron bolts, Chane sat with his first officer, Axel Gresham, drinking steaming coffee as they looked over the cargo manifest and a list of crew members from the *Trinity*. Many names on the crew list were marked through. For a week or more his men had been idle, and faced with the uncertainty of Captain Bellamy's securing another vessel quickly, some had signed on with other captains. By latest count Chane would need to replace some half a score.

"That will do for now, Tad," he told the bright-faced, towheaded youngster. "Make ready Mr. Gresham's cabin as I instructed you."

The lad nodded and hurried away.

"I suppose I owe you a round of ale," Axel remarked to his friend. "You said the girl would come around and you were right. You have your ship." He smiled. "I salute you."

Chane's expression, serious as he checked the manifest, was suddenly lighter. "Speaking of the girl—girls," Chane corrected, "you like them, do you not?"

"As I like all women. They are not hard to look on."

"You have no objection to their joining us on board."

"As guests?"

"As passengers."

"Not in the least," Axel said, though he could not imagine why the girls had a sudden need to travel to Martinique. "But for what purpose?"

"I have agreed to help Aurelia Kingsley find a pirate's treasure."

Axel said nothing for a minute. Chane enjoyed a good joke as much as the next man—but rarely a joke at his own expense. "You have agreed to what?" he ventured at last.

Chane's expression was serious. "You have heard of the pirate Black Dawn?"

"As has every man of our occupation." Skepticism deepened Axel's voice. "What has a dead man to do with this?"

"A dead man does not. Dagian is alive. I spoke to the man who cares for him." He noted Axel's look of mounting disbelief. "Dagian is grandfather to the Kingsley sisters," he explained. "He has given them a map and I have promised to take them where it leads."

Eyes narrowed, Axel tipped his chair back on two legs. "I am not so gullible as to believe that."

"Believe it. I shall need your help in this. Do I have it?"

Axel wondered if there was a word of truth in what his friend said and was swayed to the likelihood there was not. Quietly he drank coffee and waited for the punch of the jest to come, until as the silence lengthened, he could not stand it. "What is it you want me to do?" he burst out.

"Voluntarily offer your cabin to the Kingsley sisters."

"Voluntarily," Axel said, deciding he would play along with whatever Chane was up to. "My cabin, my life. I am at the service of the Kingsley sisters."

"Thank you, sir," Ria said softly.

The feminine voice coming over his shoulder brought Axel to his feet. He stared at Chane a moment, his face contorted by confusion and surprise. So this was not a joke at his expense. He wished it had been merely that. He was overcome with foreboding when he turned to see Aurelia Kingsley and her sister, Clair, waiting with Tad in the doorway. Nevertheless, he greeted the sisters warmly and promptly made his name known to them. "I am Axel Gresham," he said. "Welcome aboard." To Chane, low and anxiously he whispered, "I hope you know what you are about."

Not far away in a warehouse office, Gus Telfour concluded the business that had brought him to Savannah. He had sold his load of rum and molasses, though at not so good a price for the rum as he'd hoped to find. Chane Bellamy had been a step ahead of him again, arriving first and selling Eglantine's rum at premium prices. The merchant he had dealt with first had vowed Eglantine's rum was superior and rated the higher price. Gus, stung, had tried selling to every other merchant in the city, but the answer and the price had been the same everywhere.

He'd had to settle for second yet again. Bellamy had the luck of the saints and the charm of the devil. Lorelle, who reluctantly accompanied him on his rounds, had pouted since the day of the irksome exchange he'd had with his rival. Gus would have preferred attributing Lorelle's ill mood to distress that he had been slightly injured attempting to save her honor; he had received a nasty scrape on one hand. But he suspected the cause of her melancholy was that she had not seen Bellamy again.

Rage, a deep quiet rage, fermented within Gustave Telfour. He looked upon his sulky fiancée as he might the rarest, most beautiful, lush fruit from his Caribbean homeland. But never, ever, could he look at her without wondering if Chane Bellamy had tasted her ripeness, partaken of her sweet flesh while he, destined to be her husband, must beg for a favoring look and grovel for the slightest touch.

"Have I told you that you are especially beautiful today?" Gus whispered into Lorelle's ear as they left the warehouse and walked to the inn where they were to join Yves.

Lorelle patted her ruby lips to yawn as she eased away from Gus. "Twice," she said.

" 'Tis still true," Gus told her.

She did not reward him with a look. Her eyes were far too busy searching the bustling street for Chane Bellamy. Lorelle was disappointed, so it was no wonder that when she sat down to dinner with Gus and Yves and the dutiful servant Louise, her ears pricked up at the sound of the name *Bellamy*.

"What's that? Bellamy's done what?" Gus, too, was immediately interested in what his brother had to say.

"He has purchased the runner *Aurelia* and is nigh done filling the hold," Yves said. "I hear he is engaging his crew."

Had Lorelle not been present Gus would have expressed his true feelings about Chane Bellamy so expeditiously finding a vessel to replace the one that had burned. How he had rejoiced at the prospect of Bellamy being delayed for months while he sought a new ship. Gus and his party would be departing for home within days, and he had eagerly looked forward to Bellamy remaining far, far away from the island. The look of pleasure Yves's news brought to Lorelle's dancing eyes further stoked the fires of jealousy in Gus.

"Did you hear the day he sails for Martinique?" Lorelle shamelessly inquired.

"Soon, but that is a guess," Yves told her, and then out of sympathy for his brother added another tidbit. He had

chanced to see a red-haired girl on the *Aurelia*'s deck and
had learned from one of the vessel's new crewmen that there
was another woman below. "He has taken aboard a pair of
passengers, sisters, comely both of them, though I am told
one far outshines the other."

For once it was Lorelle who glowed with jealousy. She
could think of only two reasons for Chane to take female
passengers to Martinique. One reason was for the sake of
pure and simple pleasure. More than any man she had
known, Chane relished the pleasures a woman could give.
The other reason infuriated her even more. Several months
back, the island had hummed with gossip about the Bellamy household. Renaud Bellamy wanted his son to take a
bride. Lorelle wanted to be that bride. She was quite willing to do anything to achieve what she wanted. The mere
thought that Chane might have chosen some cool-blooded
colonial bitch for the honor tore at Lorelle's insides.
Frowning, brooding, she pleaded a headache and had
Louise accompany her to her room.

Gus's own experience with jealousy made the signs of it
in Lorelle evident to him. Vexed at every juncture by Chane
Bellamy, he wondered if it might be to his advantage to
somehow ensure that the *Aurelia*'s sailing was delayed. If
Chane were out of Lorelle's sight for long enough, perhaps
she could get him out of her mind forever. Perhaps then she
would agree to the nuptials he was so anxious to finalize.

"Have we a crewman we can trust?" he asked his brother.
"One not known to Bellamy?"

"Spruill," Yves answered. "He's loyal and he has no love
for Bellamy. Renaud, you recall, is responsible for his
brother's hanging."

Gus recalled the incident. Spruill's half brother had
abused then murdered a servant girl from the Bellamy estate. Renaud Bellamy himself had hunted down the guilty

man and seen to his conviction and hanging. Spruill was the man Gus needed, but only if Chane would not recognize his face. "He's not known to Bellamy?"

"Nay," Yves assured him. "He was at sea when his brother's neck got stretched. Bellamy will not know the fellow, and as the brother went by the name Griggs, he has no way to connect the two."

"This Spruill, would he object to causing a piece of trouble aboard the *Aurelia*?" While Gus had had no hand in the misfortune that befell the *Trinity,* he was not above a bit of calculated bad luck for Chane Bellamy's new vessel.

"Spruill would welcome the chance to do Bellamy a bad turn if that is what you are asking."

"Have him join the *Aurelia*'s crew," Gus directed his brother. "And have him see me before he goes aboard."

An hour after the Kingsley sisters boarded the ship, Clair, aided by a relaxing brew of herbal tea, napped in the double berth of Axel Gresham's cabin. The compartment had a tiny stateroom that Ria had ordered made up for herself later in the day. She did not want to disturb Clair and chance having to spend the remainder of the afternoon calming her sister again, so while Clair slept, she went for a stroll on the familiar deck of the *Aurelia,* determined the unpacking could wait.

She was close to bursting with pent-up excitement when she sprang upon the deck and saw William Pollack busy at checking the rigging. The sight of the man had the effect of a dark cloud snuffing out the warmth of the sun. He reminded her of Hyatt and all she had suffered beneath the solicitor's pressing thumb. Furthermore, she could think of no good reason for Pollack's remaining on board long after Hyatt had been paid what he claimed was his due.

"Evenin', Miss Kingsley," came in a mumble from between the gapped teeth. Grinning, the man made a mock tip of a hat as she came upon him. "Fair weather we be 'avin'."

"Pollack, you are overstaying your welcome," she snapped. "Hyatt no longer has a say in what goes on aboard the *Aurelia*."

"Aye." Pollack nodded. "But Captain Bellamy does, an' 'tis 'e what signed me on."

She saw Bellamy on the quarterdeck assessing the ship and crew with the clear searching eye of a hawk, that he might know every inch of her mast and rigging, every fold and corner of her sail before she put to sea. He was much too occupied with giving orders to his men to notice Ria's approach.

"Captain!" she called.

He turned but he had no smile for the girl. His men were busy and a woman on deck on the eve of departure could only be a distraction. Still, there was veiled politeness in his greeting. "Mademoiselle Kingsley," he said, overlooking the deepening frown on her lips. "You and your sister are comfortably settled, I trust?"

"Settled, yes," she snapped back. "Comfortable, no. And I will not be until that man is off this ship." She pointed at Pollack. "I demand you dismiss him!"

Chane groaned as she raced up the steps to reach his side. He had suspected he would regret making the bargain with Aurelia Kingsley. He had not expected to do so this soon. Temper rising, he braced for her assault. The first line of it came unexpectedly, from the scent of sweet fresh flowers rising from her heated skin. Damn the wench! The woman herself looked nothing like the promise of that alluring scent. She was red-faced and angry when she gained the quarterdeck, her unruly red hair flying like a cat-o'-nine-tails.

Eyes narrowed, arms crossed, he met her broadside, waiting until she was within two paces to speak. "Has he harmed you?" he asked, looking aside at Pollack and noting that every man of his crew within earshot had paused to listen to the coming exchange.

"No. But—"

"Has he threatened you?"

"No. But—"

Chane gritted his teeth. "Then I suggest, Mademoiselle Kingsley, that if you find the sight of my men distasteful you remain below." With that he turned his back and continued with his work.

Ria sputtered out a gasp. But she would not be denied. Hands on her hips, skirt tail fluttering, she stalked around to face him down. "I will not remain below!" Her eyes, brilliant green shards, flashed furiously. "For the time being the *Aurelia* still belongs— Oh!"

The grasp of his strong fingers around her arm was as painful as the pinch of a grappling hook as he dragged her from the deck, her feet barely grazing the boards as he swept her along. She was too stunned, too humiliated to cry out, not until they were well below.

"How dare you!" she shouted. But by then he had propelled her into his cabin and had kicked the door shut and let her loose.

Ria rubbed her upper arm and scowled, certain her flesh must already be lined with bruises. She would have paid him in kind with her teeth and nails had not a good look at his face stopped her. A muscle in his taut jaw jumped fiercely and his teeth were set hard together.

He stood so close she could feel his hot furious breath on her face. She gasped with relief when he moved away, but quickly learned that was only to give himself room to wave a finger before her eyes. "Feel fortunate, mademoiselle, that I did not toss you over the rail and rid the ship of that quick temper of yours."

Involuntarily, Ria shook. He had grown a foot taller, or so it seemed. His eyes glared like burning coals. His voice roared like a bellowing gale. Stunned, she backed away a step but she did not back down. She raised her hand as he had done. "Don't you bully me!" she warned.

"Bully you?" he said hotly. "Nay. But there is a part of you I would like to blister, and I promise, Mademoiselle Aurelia Kingsley, lady or not, if you again attempt to undermine my authority with my men, your hide will suffer."

"I did no such thing! Pollack cannot be trusted. If you insist on keeping him you will regret it. We all will."

Chane breathed a heavy sigh. "Then regret it we will. The man stays."

Ria's effort to remain resolute was not aided by having lost all her hairpins while racing across the deck. Her heavy red hair fell around her shoulders as if she had just climbed out of bed.

"I think, Captain Bellamy," she said crisply, "that you are an incredibly stubborn man."

"Yes." His eyes had cooled a little but not his voice. "That I am, and you will do well not to forget it."

Chane left her with a warning to stay below until she was invited on deck, hardly believing she was ever likely to do as ordered, and wondering what there was about the unkempt girl that was attractive. She had a shrewish nature, and complete disregard for her appearance. Perhaps it was her fiery spirit he found enticing. Just how deep did that fire go?

Ria declined a supper invitation from Captain Bellamy and Mr. Gresham. Clair was not ready for that. Ria could not, however, decline an after-dinner glass of sherry in the captain's quarters. She had promised to allow him a look at the map before they sailed, and it was time to make good her promise.

The cabin seemed different by lamplight, more the way she remembered it from when her father had occupied it. The rich rosewood paneling glowed softly, the brass fixtures sparkled, the teal blue velvet curtains and bed fittings visible through the open doors of the sleeping compartment seemed to absorb the warm golden light. The ship itself was quiet, most of the crew having gone ashore for a last night of revelry before they sailed. Mr. Gresham was on the bridge, and Clair, finally reconciled to the journey, had chosen to remain in the cabin and read.

Chane Bellamy was different by lamplight as well. Ria could hardly believe the quiet voice and gentle expression belonged to the same man who had coerced her cooperation earlier in the day. He had bathed and changed his clothes, he was clean-shaved, his black hair damp and glistening. The snowy linen shirt, the crisp nankeen trousers and spotlessly fresh thread hose he wore made her acutely aware of the state of her much abused traveling dress. At least she had put her hair right and washed her face with the dwindling rose soap so she did not feel herself a total catastrophe when she accepted the glass he promptly offered.

"I thank you," she said. The sherry was good, calming.

"I shall send a glass to your sister if you think she would like it."

"How very kind of you," Ria said. "I believe she would." Smiling, she lounged back in the comfort of a cushioned bench built into the compartment's outer wall. "Sherry helps her to sleep soundly."

Chane quickly dispatched Tad with a small silver tray and Clair's glass of sherry.

When the lad was gone he made certain the door was fastened, then turned to Ria, completely ignoring her conciliatory attempt at conversation. "You have the map," he stated bluntly, his glass set aside. "I would like a look at the whole of it while there is still time to put you ashore if I do not like what I see."

"Of course I have it," Ria snapped back, her body suddenly tense as she stood and retrieved the hidden reticule from within the waistband of her skirt. She briskly crossed the floor to the table Chane had cleared, and spread it before him. "Are you certain you are capable of understanding it?"

"Let us hope so," he countered. "So that we do not both find ourselves upon a fool's errand."

The table was situated to make best use of the daylight that streamed in the stern's bank of windows when the sun was high. At night a globed lamp mounted on the wall lit the table's surface. To better catch the light, Chane lifted the map and held it at a slant before him. As he bent his head to the parchment he detected a soft fragrance emanating from it, as spicy sweet as a floral garden, a scent of roses he had come to associate with Aurelia Kingsley. A strange choice, it seemed, for the peppery mademoiselle. Could it possibly be that the essence, so much hers, hinted at a secret nature, one that was gentle, sweet and feminine, one she never showed?

After a moment, he glanced at the girl. She had returned to the soft bench beneath the windows. In her present quiet state, in the lamplight, she was attractive enough. Her shapeliness made up for what her face lacked in traditional prettiness. If he wanted to do more than rankle her on this journey, which, from what he had learned looking at Dagian's map, would be a long one, he must mend his ways. Her complete cooperation was essential to the success of the mission.

No wonder she had challenged his ability to understand the map. It gave no straight shot to the hidden loot. Using a series of numbers, Dagian had made a puzzle of the co-ordinates to be used once they made land. But if Chane did not miss his guess, a key hidden somewhere in the rendering of the map would make it possible to decipher the first set of numbers; these would take the bearer of the map to a point where another clue might be found. There he must hope he could recognize the key to the second set of figures.

A man who misread what he found might run in circles until he went mad. He believed Aurelia Kingsley knew how to avoid a point-to-point search. If he could get her to reveal what she knew it would save them both time and trouble.

"Mademoiselle Aurelia," he said, his voice so much gentler that she was immediately suspicious.

"I prefer Ria," she answered. "And that we at least attempt to be friends while we engage in this enterprise."

"As you wish, Mademoiselle Ria. Your grandfather has shrewdly concealed the coordinates we need to follow his map."

"Oh?"

"A pirate's trick," he explained innocently, "in the event his map falls into the wrong hands. This one," he swept his hand across the map, "a man with a good mind and an excess of time could decipher. But if I had the key to the code your grandfather has used, it would be far easier to begin. Have a look," he said, inviting her to the table that he might more closely observe her reaction to what he said, though he did not truly expect her to admit any collusion. She would be wary of giving away that information so early in the journey, and might, he feared, refuse to give it until they actually went ashore to begin a search.

Ria came as he requested and looked at the map. Alone she had studied it a hundred times, but the nautical notations had proved beyond her understanding. At least now she knew why. Leaning over the table top, she placed her forefinger on a group of figures below the tiny diagram of a ship set offshore of the Guiana coast on the continent of South America. "The coordinates are hidden in these figures?"

Chane smiled. She had reaffirmed his belief by showing she knew the ones that held the secrets. The man Dom had told him as much, he'd said Dagian had given the information needed most to his granddaughter, but to her alone.

"Aye," he said, leaning so close that his black curls brushed her forehead.

Ria jerked away from the unexpected touch. "And the k-key," she stammered. "Can you find it?"

Chane smiled. She was as sly as her grandfather, pretending she knew so little when in fact she knew all that was needed to follow the map. "I know where to look," he boasted.

His air of confidence alleviated all Ria's concern that her grandfather might have given her a map to the gates of paradise and forgotten to leave the key.

"Then you have no doubt we can find the treasure?"

"I have none at all," he assured her as he slipped a glass stopper from the sherry bottle and poured a second round for the two of them. Let her keep her secrets now if she must. He'd get them from her when the time for that came. "In three months' time the Black Dawn's trove will be aboard this ship." He gave her a glass and lifted his high proposing a toast. "To red hair and riches," he said.

Ria added her toast to the daring one Chane had made. "To adventure and success and kind sea captains," she whispered.

Chane set his empty glass aside and rolled the map. "You may leave it with me. I would like to study it more at my leisure."

The eyes which had been starry flashed. Ria was having none of that. "You may see it as you wish," she told him. "But until we are well at sea off Martinique, it stays within my sight."

Chane laughed. It had just occurred to him that the fire in Aurelia Kingsley came to her honestly from her pirate's legacy. With a small bow he caught her hand and laid the rolled map in her palm, continuing to hold her hand as he said, "You do trust me just a little, do you not, Mademoiselle Ria?"

"A little," she said shakily. Ria could scarcely stand still with the man holding her hand. She felt as if he had enveloped all of her in a quick scorching wash of heat. A blush lingered long after he let her trembling hand fall free. Nonplussed, Ria drank down her sherry far too quickly.

Neither she nor Chane heard the catlike ascension of the seaman Spruill as he made his way up a line he had strung from the railing of the quarterdeck above the window of the captain's quarters.

Ria fell asleep long after Clair in her larger berth had begun making up for sleepless nights. Ria kept thinking of Chane's bold toast. Clair would have been horrified at such a personal pronouncement. Ria liked it, thrilled to it. And then there was the way he had held her hand, as if it were the most delicate object he'd ever touched. She had never felt so alive, so full of hope and wonder at what life might hold.

Counting those possibilities one by one, as another might count sheep she drifted off only moments before the door of her cabin eased open a crack. The slight sound disturbed her rest but did not fully awaken Ria. With a soft silky moan she rolled over in the cozy bunk.

She was perfectly safe, her mind dreamily assured her. She had purposely closed the door fast, her experience during the last night at Palmira making her doubly cautious. Beneath her pillow she had placed her father's old but serviceable flintlock. If not the best of shots, she could at least hit anything as big as a man.

Slipping into a blissful slumber, Ria welcomed a dream of ocean swells and sun-kissed shores and treasures hidden beneath a stretch of silvery sand. She gazed upon rows and rows of weathered chests pulled from beneath the glittering sand, chests filled with shimmering gold and a twinkling rainbow of jewels.

Even in sleep the expectation of great wealth gave rise to endless thought and speculation. She pictured reams of silk and bundles of satin destined to be the most beautiful of gowns, soft leather shoes, elegant, sweeping fur-lined mantles, delicate ivory fans, a majestic white saddle horse, perhaps two, and a man so handsome she needed his strong arm to steady her giddy feet as she walked beside him.

The floor creaked under stealthy feet, but Ria slept on, absorbing the intrusive sound into her dreams, imagining the aged lid of still another sea chest creaked open.

Crouched on all fours where he was least likely to be seen, the lithe, darkly clad Spruill scampered like a hungry wharf rat across the bare floor of Ria's stateroom. There were not so many places to hide a thing of value in the small niche of a compartment. If the girl slept soundly he should have time to search everywhere. He began with her trunk, thanking the stars that the bowed lid of it lay open as he plunged his dirty hands into its depths.

Depending upon touch as he could see nothing within the trunk, Spruill churned Ria's meager garments ripping most of them as he searched the linings and looked for hidden pockets where she might have concealed the map.

Finding no parchment among the clothes, Spruill gritted his teeth and moved to examine the single cupboard in the compartment, inch by inch silently easing the wooden doors open. While the sneak commended the silence of his probe he unknowingly exposed his presence another way. Ria, lulled into ever deeper and more placid sleep by the peaceful roll of the ship and the pat of the waves upon the bow, found her slumber at last disturbed by the acrid odor of an unwashed body.

Kerchoo!

Spruill, surprised, fumbled the lady's kidskin boot he held. The thump of the boot's stacked wooden heel striking the hard floor assailed Ria's ears. As she gasped, she saw, in the faint light, her belongings cast helter-skelter upon the floor and beyond them a low scurrying shadow. Heart skipping, Ria bounded up in the bunk and scratched beneath her pillow for the pistol hidden there. Where she aimed she couldn't have said, but, determinedly, she swung the weapon before her and attempted a challenging shout. Her voice faltered and squeaked out a feeble whisper. "Who is in here?"

Spruill quaked and flattened into a corner as if he'd been crushed by an unseen weight. He had been willing to risk all for the map, but now, as he saw the long barrel of the pistol, it seemed hardly worth the cost of his life. He looked toward the door and the dim band of light he would have to rush through if he tried to escape. As he gauged his chance of success he recalled that the captain's cabin was but a dozen steps away. Even if the girl missed her shot Spruill could well imagine Bellamy bursting upon him before he could gain the deck. The bastard would break him in two, and that would be the best of what he got for his treachery.

By the contradictory way that luck sometimes favors the wicked, Spruill was spared. In the passageway beyond Ria's compartment Chane Bellamy was, at the moment, returning from the bridge to his empty quarters. He could not help noticing that the door of the foremost compartment the girls occupied stood ajar. Curiosity piqued, Chane heard a throaty, if somewhat unintelligible, whisper from the cabin's darkened interior. "Come here," came the message.

Or so he chose to believe. Virgins, if they were innocents, did not frighten him as they did many men. Every woman, he eased his conscience, must surrender her maidenhead at one time or another; if she did so willingly he did not see that he was obligated to wed the lass.

He heard the invitation again, this time a low pleading cry. Framed in a pale backwash of light from the passageway's flickering lamp, Chane stepped within her doorway. "Ria?" he whispered.

Crouched upon her bed, blinded with panic and fear, Ria mistook Chane's entry for the departure of whatever fiend scampered about in her room. Involuntarily, her eyes clamped shut as her fingers squeezed off a shot from the flintlock. Simultaneously, she screamed, loud enough to bring even the nethermost crew member at a run if the shot she had fired had not served that purpose already.

Chapter Six

"**D**amn!" The grazing shot burned Chane's flesh before thudding into the paneling behind him. The pain and force of impact knocked him to his knees. Uncertain who had shot him and what harm the knave might have done the Kingsley sisters, Chane stifled an agonized moan as he gripped the doorframe and attempted to pull his leaden limbs upright. Before he regained his balance Spruill lunged past, head tucked, arms shielding his face.

White with fear, his desire to survive foremost, the wily seaman ducked into the darkness beneath the stair treads that led to the deck, biding his time until all who had come running at the sound of a shot had descended the stair and stood crammed in the narrow passageway.

Ria, smoking flintlock clenched in her hand and still with no clue whom her rifle ball had struck, saw the blurred shapes of two men mesh, then separate before her. Then one of them disappeared from sight. Fearing the worst, Ria sprang from the bunk and raced to the downed captain, but neither she nor any of those men who moments later came to his aid saw the crouching Spruill slither from beneath the steps and slip away.

"Bellamy!" she cried when he raised his head and the light fell on his face as he braced against the bloodstained door casing. "My God!" Aghast at what she had done, Ria attempted to aid Chane but hurriedly dropped her arm to her side when a beastly growl dared her to touch him.

Chane, cheeks white while his eyes glowered a burning red, struggled to his feet. He let loose a string of vile oaths and another vicious snarl as Ria stumbled back, afraid that in his rage he would do her more harm than she had done him.

"You conniving wench!" He swore through gritted teeth. "What are you about?"

"I didn't know it was you," she rasped.

Like a madman bent on destruction he wrenched the pistol from her quivering hand and cast it to the floor. Ria he snatched hard against him, knocking the breath from her trembling breast and snapping her neck so hard she thought it would fracture. Crushed against him, Ria felt sweat pop out in fresh beads on his chest and saw it stream from his forehead, mingling with the blood that flowed from his wound. The moisture quickly soaked his shirt and saturated her soft cambric nightgown until the dampened flimsy garment was pasted to her skin as his shirt was to his. That discomfort was nothing compared to his black vengeful look, which burned her like a blast of scalding steam.

She gasped as an arm about her waist squeezed. "What purpose is there to killing me?" he demanded.

"I—I only meant to protect myself," she stammered. "How was I to know it was you?"

He swore and pressed her against the unyielding panels of the cabin wall crushing her so hard with his tensed body that she was as devoid of breath and lost to the light as if she had slipped into a sable sea and been swept under the hull of a great ship.

"I suggest, mademoiselle," he ground out derisively, "that before you fire a pistol, you know your target."

Ria gasped for air and struggled to get clear of him, pushing desperately at his massive straining chest, but his hard thighs pinned her firmly. Where they lay against her she battled the rugged strength of every throbbing muscle. It was a losing battle, her body a small and fragile flower against the power of a storm. She bent beneath him, her slender frame rapidly absorbing the penetrating, maddening heat of him, her flesh trembling in response to the unmistakable turgid maleness pressing threateningly into her belly.

Even as he held her, fear of his wrath took over. She shrieked and gave him another forceful push. "I would fire at anyone who enters my room uninvited and sneaks about up to no good."

"With your door open you invite everyone. For any purpose." His voice was sharp, his shadowed face mocking. "And perhaps that is exactly what you did."

She was too filled with fury to answer and too nearly suffocated by his closeness to bear much more. "Let me go!" she demanded.

Axel brought a truce between the two. He lit the lamp in Ria's cabin, showing clearly the ripped and scattered clothes and ransacked cupboard. Chane was mildly appeased but not ready to forgive. His wound ached and his pride had suffered. To think he had imagined this red-haired, tart-tongued witch invited him or any man into her cabin for a night of pleasure. And to think he had considered, for even a moment, that he would find anything more than torment and trouble in her witch's arms.

Chane ordered a search of the ship, though he suspected it would be futile after so much time had elapsed. The culprit would be long gone if he'd stowed aboard, quietly at his post if he was one of the crew. If that were the case, the men had ways of ferreting him out. In time, the devil would get his reward. A stranger, however, they had little hope of finding roaming the streets of town. Though it galled him to know the one who should carry the pistol ball he had taken would escape punishment for his deed, Chane would not consider a delay for what would inevitably be a lengthy and useless search of the city. What was more important was to learn if the map was safe. With Axel and himself well inside the sisters' cabin he slammed shut the door and again lambasted Ria with a look that made her shudder.

"Well, did the man get what he came for?"

Stunned by his turnabout and a surprising concern for her person, Ria blushed and grabbed for a sheet to cover her soiled and clinging nightdress. Once covered she assured the men she was untouched.

Chane snorted as if he had heard a fine jest. "Do not overrate your charms, mademoiselle. Where is the map?"

The meaning of his words sank in like a sprinkle of salt upon a wound. Ria's blush darkened to the red of rage. In her deepening ire she forgot her modesty and spun around, dropping the cloaking sheet as she sank upon the tousled bed, completely unaware that her thin gown against the lamp's bold light made a liar of Chane Bellamy. Mumbling a prying question of his parentage, she turned her backside and tore into her pillow, unhappily revealing her hiding place but finding the map, like her honor, untouched.

"You will release that to my safekeeping," he ordered.

"No—" Ria started, but relented when she saw the scathing look from Chane had not diminished. "Take it!" she said, supposing she now had no choice but to trust him while he had every right to cast her ashore for having wounded him.

As Chane seized the roll of parchment, a red blond head peeked nervously from behind the door of the sleeping compartment. Clair's pretty teeth rattled so that even Chane took pity and nodded a reassurance to her. "All is well, mademoiselle," he said softly. "Ease your worries." Clair flickered a smile but did not venture from behind the shield of her door. For Ria, Chane retained a biting tone. "Share your sister's bed," he ordered. "Axel will sleep in your bunk this night."

Ria's budding apology died on her lips. "That is unnecessary," she insisted tartly. "The thief is unlikely to come back tonight. Clair and I should be entirely safe without a guard."

Chane's sharp brows lifted diabolically. "Here Axel stays, mademoiselle. If I am to close my eyes I must be sure my men and I are safe from you." With a snort of disgust he turned on his heel, but not without a backward glance and a last word. "And now," he said, "before I am bled dry from this wound I must find a man to put a stitch in it."

He had meant to stoke her guilt, and he had. Her eyes dropped with shame as she saw that a trickle of blood still oozed from the injury. He would surely like to take a whip to her and flail until her skin likewise bled. And she deserved it. Another inch or two to the left and she might have as easily taken his life. Venting a repentant sigh, Ria recalled that she had tended many an injured man during the siege of Savannah and sewed stitches in many a ragged wound. "I could be of help to you, Captain Bellamy," she offered. "I have a needle and good silk thread—"

Chane turned fully toward her again, his blue eyes glowering with such a lethal look that poor Clair, though he meant her no harm, shut her door against him. Ria, who knew quite well that for her there was more seething anger in the man than even that menacing look told, turned anxiously to Axel Gresham. Chane, however, was quickly on his way, not even looking back as he spit out his reply. "I'd sooner have the devil's hands on me," he said.

Clair, trembling anew, peeked out a second time when she heard Chane leave. Assured he was gone for good she rushed into the room and threw her slim arms around Ria. "I wish Grandfather Dag had never given you the map," she declared as rivulets of hot tears began to stream from her eyes. "We have been in danger ever since."

Ria sighed, her raw nerves and the wild excitement having drained the energy from her. "And before, Clair," she reminded. "Only with no chance of better things. Anyway, you have no reason to worry now. Mr. Gresham is a gentleman. He will protect us."

"Rest assured." Gresham nodded and confirmed her trust. "No one will pass that door to do you more harm."

Ria half wished the kindly Axel Gresham with his ruddy cheeks and fair hair were the new captain of the *Aurelia*. He displayed none of Chane Bellamy's vile temper and churlish manners. Though solidly made he had an inspiring air of calm about him and, at a good head shorter than Bellamy, he was comfortably closer to the size Marcus Kingsley had been.

Most redeeming was the effect he had on Clair. He was the only man they had met of late who did not make her sister cringe and hide. He even had the decency to blush when circumstances dictated. Ria gasped as she realized, now that they were alone, the reason for his vibrant flaming cheeks. Hastily she sought a robe among her scattered clothing and flung it about her shoulders.

Spruill wasted no time fleeing the *Aurelia* while confusion reigned below decks. If any man saw him leave, he did not take notice with the sky black as ink and skiffs loaded with drunken seamen coming and going until close to dawn. Only when the sun crested and it was time to hoist the sails did the truth come out as Spruill's name boomed unanswered when the *Aurelia*'s roster was called.

Chane Bellamy, beside Axel at the wheel and hampered by a left arm too sore to be of much use, cursed the missing sailor. But he had too much else on his mind to worry over the truant man. Should their paths cross again he would learn for certain if Spruill's duplicity had cost him a night of sleep and nigh a pint of blood. A troubling alternative did not occur to Chane until sometime later, but when it came to him it was a vexing one. If, in fact, Spruill had missed the sailing because he had drowned in his cups or had lain too long in the arms of a tavern trollop, then a culprit hid yet among his crew.

"Tell me more of the map," Gus demanded of his hired man. Spruill's story had earned him a hero's welcome aboard the schooner *Conquest,* Gus Telfour's ship.

The sailor's small dark eyes darted about Gus Telfour's cabin, lingering longest on Lorelle Telfour, who with her fussy maid listened to the man's report. "Were only by skill I slipped past 'em to start. Come close to gettin' me bloomin' 'ead blowed off or I'd 've got me 'ands on that map."

"Tell me more of the map," Gus demanded.

"Tell me more of the ladies," Lorelle put in.

"Fetchin' pretty the both of 'em." With a tip of his capless head to Lorelle Telfour, Spruill replied, enjoying his brief moment of her ardent attention.

"Forget them!" Gus barked and cast a grievous look at his ladylove. "Tell me of the map!"

"A bloomin' treasure map like I said." Spruill swore. "But for 'angin' by me 'eels so long I might 've seen it better. But a bloomin' bloody treasure map it was." He nodded again to Lorelle. "Beggin' yer pardon, miss."

"Damn you, Spruill!" Gus swore at the man, ending his moment of glory. "Could you not have used more care, man, and brought me the map?"

Spruill squirmed. "I did me best, cap'n. Askin' a man to come to blows with Bellamy is askin' a lot. 'Ad I not been blindin' quick to put me fist to 'is block o' a jaw an' knocked 'im between me an' a flintlock I'd not be 'ere now tellin' you yea or nay or nothin'."

Lorelle, who sat with her mouth hooked in a frown of irritation, eased her sore spirit by laughing haughtily. "Monsieur Spruill is a better man than you, Gus, if he landed a blow to Chane."

Spruill seized another chance to shine. "Aye, 'at I did, miss. 'E'll not forget the cuffin' I give 'im any sooner than 'e forgets the pistol ball 'at tore 'is arm 'alf off."

"He was hit?" Lorelle, face pinched and white, overturned her chair in her haste to get to her feet. A hand to her heart, she rushed at Spruill, nearly drowning him in her potent perfume. "Chane was shot? How badly?"

"'At I cannot say, miss, but I can assure you I left 'im lying on 'is back wishin' 'e'd never crossed a Spruill."

Spruill's boast fell on deaf ears. Lorelle had heard all she cared to from the swag-tongued sailor. Her eyes, fiery darts of hatred, aimed at Gus. She cocked an accusing finger at him. "This is your doing, Gus. You go to any length to keep me from Chane but now—this bloodshed—you have gone too far. If he is badly hurt, I warn you, the day will come when you regret it."

With a proud twist of her black-maned head, Lorelle stormed from Gus's cabin, an apologetic Louise in her wake, promising she would calm her angry mistress and do all in her power to make things right.

"Lorelle—" Gus started after his beloved but stopped, embarrassed at being humiliated to the point of servility in front of an underling and knowing, in her present mood, he was likely to get his eyes scratched out and handed back to him.

"She has a tender heart," he lied. "Your ill-timed talk of wounds has upset her."

"Sorry, cap'n," Ducking his head, Spruill apologized, though he had quickly grasped the way of things. Tender-hearted as a shark that one was, and anxious for a taste of Captain Telfour's blood.

Behind his chair, Gus clicked his heels together. "There is a thing that puzzles me, Spruill," he said.

"Aye, cap'n."

"If you did not shoot Bellamy, who did fire on him?"

Spruill guffawed. "'Ere's the biggest rub of all, cap'n." A grin split the swarthy darkness of his face. "The lady done it. 'At one with the fiery 'air."

Relishing that news as much as any he'd ever heard, Gus poured a shot of rum for Spruill and waited with mounting impatience as the thirsty man gulped it down.

Wiping a drip from his chin, Spruill eyed the tempting bottle but quickly saw he'd enjoyed all the hospitality he was likely to get from Gus Telfour. The man had swung his chair about and straddled the seat of it, resting his folded arms on the spindly back. "Tell me again," he said. "All you heard Bellamy and the girl say. Leave out nothing," he warned. "Not even the smallest detail."

"It were the map o' the Black Dawn, she said. 'Er grandfather, and I believe 'er in that. She be like 'im, I swear, hair like a blazin' dawn. A she-devil she were, brandishin' 'at flintlock. She lacks Dagian's aim, I judge. Thank the kind saints for 'at."

"She must have said more," Gus goaded. "Or he did. Where is the treasure buried? Did you hear that, man?"

"Aye. That I did." Spruill had calculatingly held back a tidbit or two of what he had learned, waiting until he was sure of the best way to gain a reward for his efforts. "An' the tellin' of it ought to be worth a weighty share for old Spruill should you decide to go after it for yourself," he ventured. "Seein' it was me that risked me life learnin' a thing you never would 'ave knowed about."

"So you did, man," Gus agreed. "And a double share is yours should we venture after the loot."

"Triple," Gus insisted. "It's a rich trove, I heard 'im say. You would not miss it."

Gus's mouth watered, though not so much over the hidden treasure as over the chance to get the better of Chane Bellamy. To take Dagian's trove from beneath Bellamy's nose would show Lorelle once and for all who was the better man. "Triple," he said. "A triple share to you, Spruill, if what you know is worth it."

Spruill nearly choked on his good luck at getting such an easy agreement from tightfisted Gus Telfour. Spruill, a poor sailor all his life as his father and grandfather had been before him, saw his best and only chance in a lifetime to rise above the lamentable squalor that was his heritage. "The Guiana coast," he said hoarsely. "Dagian's trove lies buried on the Guiana coast."

Gus laughed bitterly and looked at Spruill as if he were crazed. "The Guiana coast is no cemetery plot, man. It stretches for hundreds of miles, sand and swamp and savages known to have a taste for human flesh." His laugh rang out like the bleak toll of a cracked bell. "You have earned yourself a share of nothing, Spruill."

Spruill shrewdly waited a moment and then he spoke. "Aye, cap'n. An' so it seemed to me when I first thought on it. Without the map, the Black Dawn's treasure might well be lost in the middle o' the sea. But then it come to me like a shinin' beacon on a rocky shoal.''

"What?'' Gus growled.

"We need not know the very spot the treasure's 'id. We need not 'ave the map.''

"Nay...'' The perverse wisdom of what the sailor hinted took shape in Gus's mind. He punched a fist to his palm. "Nay,'' he said. "Bellamy will do that for us. Let him search and brave the savages. We need only stand by while our work is done for us.''

"An' take 'im unawares when 'e's found the trove,'' Spruill supplied. The narrow shoulders squared and the dark face lit. "Worth a triple share or not, cap'n?''

Gus had risen and poured a drink of rum and bitters for himself. He swigged a long draft of it, then slapped Spruill on his bent back. "Well worth it, Spruill,'' he swore. "The *Conquest* will shadow the *Aurelia* wherever she sails, and when the lady has bedecked herself in gold and jewels and finery we will take our pleasure of her as we might any fancy piece who hikes a skirt.''

"Aye, cap'n. An' leave 'er spread naked to the wind.''

"Stripped and shamed,'' Gus said for his ears rather than Spruill's. Taking more and more solidly to the plan, he cast a hard warning look at the sailor. Men of Spruill's station were not noted for reliability nor closed mouths. "You tell no one of what you heard or saw aboard the *Aurelia*.''

"Nary a word,'' Spruill swore, making a cross upon his breast.

"And tell no one the plan we have made,'' Gus said. "Or I swear I will cut out your tongue and hang you by your thumbs on the mainmast where you will stay till your dried carcass whips like a sail above my ship.''

"No one'll serve you better than Spruill," the man swore, meaning all that he said. He would be Gus Telfour's man, do or die—or until a better chance at riches came along.

A similar thought crossed the mind of William Pollack as he cocked an ear to the shipboard gossip that a dullard named Spruill had taken a drunken notion to bed down with one of the lady passengers aboard the *Aurelia*. And her with a flintlock under her pillow. Pollack laughed to himself. He did not need to guess which of the Kingsley sisters would shoot a man without a thought. Though he did wonder how it happened that the captain had come up wounded in the fray. Curse Aurelia Kingsley for that. For her folly, they were all feeling the lash and sting of Bellamy's foul temper.

"On your post, you scurvy knave," Chane growled to a brutish sailor called Norbie, who lagged at his work while the snowy sails billowed, seized the wind and sent the *Aurelia* skimming over the choppy waters offshore. "Make haste," he warned, his red-rimmed eyes narrow against the brisk chill breeze. "Or I'll heave you over the side and let you swim to where I found you."

"Aye, Captain!" the man returned, making his ox's legs step lively as he put his shoulder and his weight to his job.

"Women," the stocky Norbie grumbled to the sailor nearest him, a man as new to the crew as Norbie was. "Shot by a woman, our cap'n." He shook his big head. "Always trouble when 'ere's women on board."

William Pollack's eyes caught a fiendish gleam. "Ye breathe the truth, mate. Trouble an' ill luck they are. An' these two— Do you know them, mate?"

"Nay," the man said. "They are only a pesky pair of gentlewomen." He laughed. "If there be such."

"If there be such they are not these two." Pollack's voice fell low as he glanced cautiously about. "Born o' bad blood they are."

"Misbegotten, eh?" The seaman's interest was piqued. If the two were coarse women and not ladies as they seemed, there might be a bit of fun to be had for a crewman as well as the captain.

"Nay, not that," Pollack said. "Blood o' the Black Dawn they are."

Norbie shuddered. "In truth, mate?"

"True as I stand 'ere," Pollack swore. "Watch your back, mate, when those two be about."

"'E's a fool to let those two keep a pistol," Norbie said. "A bloody fool, our captain."

"Aye, you may be right, mate," Pollack agreed. His back was to Norbie as he grinned broadly. He had done a good day's work already and the sun was not yet high. One tiny crack might sink a ship, and he had put the first breach in the *Aurelia* by setting a doubt between one man and the captain. By the time the party found Dagian's trove, Pollack was certain he would have the entire crew ready to rise up against Chane Bellamy.

The gap-toothed grin lasted long after Norbie was gone. There was not a man aboard better fit to pilot a ship or who knew the *Aurelia* better than William Pollack.

Chapter Seven

Late in the day, the fifth at sea, Ria sat below with Clair, industriously engaged in a game of cards, a game that failed to occupy her mind or satisfy a growing restlessness within. She would be driven to distraction, she believed, if Chane Bellamy did not allow her on deck soon. Was the man never to forgive the accident that had left him wounded? Did he expect her to stay out of sight the entire voyage? She could not.

Ria sighed, closed the fan of cards she held and listlessly dropped them upon the tiny table.

"Ria," Clair protested. "The hand isn't done."

"No more," Ria said, loosening the top buttons of her perspiration-dampened bodice so that what little air there was might reach her flushed skin. "This cabin is stifling. I'm going to stroll into the captain's quarters or I swear I will either faint of heat prostration or be stooped like an old woman from sitting so long."

Clair fanned nervously with the hand of cards she still held. "Ria, you can't. Tad has not been down to tell how long the captain will be on deck. *He* might come back while you're there."

Ria was at the door. "If he does, he can hardly fault me for stretching my legs in the only place large enough to walk more than three steps. Besides, he is always above after his noon meal and until the evening one. Will you join me?"

"No," Clair said. "I'll have a nap while you're gone."

Only a little apprehensive that she might be discovered, Ria left her sister. In the days since they had sailed she and Clair had been confined below deck, she assumed, as punishment for the damage she had done the captain. Both women had come to know Chane's cabin boy quite well. The lad had pitied their plight as he brought their meals and news of the weather. On the second day out, seeing how they fidgeted in the tight little compartment with but one small window, he had cautiously offered them a secret hour or so of respite in the captain's spacious great cabin, first making certain Bellamy would not return to find them.

Ria had welcomed the opportunity to stretch her cramped limbs. There, while Clair nervously reclined on a cushioned bench Ria could throw open a window and bathe in the golden light of the sun as she breathed deeply of fresh salt air. Most of the time she walked the cabin, strolling the bare polished boards until she knew them all to the pegs that held them fast. Oftentimes she would make a game of circumventing the tacked-down, thick and plush Persian carpet Chane had added to the compartment's decor.

To repay Tad for his risk, Ria assumed many of his chores in the cabin, dusting, straightening, clearing the table of the captain's lunch and setting the plate for the evening meal. Never, though, had she ventured into the compartment before Tad slipped below and arranged a signal should the captain leave his post. But on this day, with the weather grown hotter and the air so still it could almost be seen, she could not wait. Besides, the captain had proved to be a man of habit, one who kept rigidly to a predictable schedule.

The cabin was dim as she eased inside, the sky beyond the windows banked with swells of thick dark clouds that marked a distant storm, a storm they would surely sail into the midst of by evening. She knew at once it was the pending change of weather that accentuated her restlessness, though she did not fear a storm. She loved watching the great roiling black clouds sweep across the open sky. She loved sitting quietly and listening to the imposing symphony of rolling thunder and flashing lightning as it jibbed and crackled in the air.

Tonight would be such a night and she welcomed it. She welcomed anything to break the gloom of monotony that threatened to snap her mind, including the work which beckoned in Chane Bellamy's cabin. Without lighting a lamp she went straight to it. Tad had left plenty to occupy her, the bed unmade in the sleeping room, the covers in a wild tumble behind the sheltering curtains, a plate of half-eaten food upon the table. Chane had left his boots beneath his chair, those dashing knee-high ones of tanned leather with the wide flared bands topping the snug shaft. Ria stored them in a cupboard with his other footgear, and set to work scrubbing a stain from the shirt he had heedlessly tossed to the floor.

The stain, she saw as she dipped it into a basin of water, was blood. She burned with guilt as she rubbed a cake of soap over the blotch on the dampened cloth. If the wound she had given him still bled after so much time, it was not healing as it should. In this hot clime, that could mean infection had set in. If it had, there was the likelihood of fever, even the chance of death. All her fault.

Her stomach knotted as she turned to hang the scrubbed shirt over the runged back of a chair. All the fault of her blind, stupid fear that she might lose the map. Close to shedding tears Ria crossed the cabin. The least she could do was straighten out that tangle of a bed so that the captain might comfortably rest upon it when he came down for the night.

The curtains were drawn, a single layer of crimson silk that rippled and shimmered like a pool of water when she opened one of the windows. A fold of silk had spilled across the sturdy oak commode that flanked the headboard of the bed. As Ria reached to straighten it she saw that the puddled cloth also covered a heavy banded chest of brass and wood, the captain's strongbox. A handful of gold coins glittered temptingly from within the open box. Ria could not dissuade herself from looking to see what else lay inside or from wondering what utter foolishness had prompted the captain to leave the box open and unguarded.

The *Aurelia*'s logbook lay flat on the bottom and with it several lumpy leather pouches evidently full of coins and notes. Nestled among them sat an elegant velvet-covered box of the sort used to store jewels, and the map.

The map! "Oh!" Ria gasped. There in a corner of the box, nearly lost in a shadow, lay the rolled parchment, tied tightly with a length of blue satin ribbon she had once worn in her hair. Alarmed to see it so vulnerably displayed, Ria reached into the strongbox for the map as might anyone who had come into the compartment. How could he be so careless? After he had demanded she release the document to his safekeeping, how could he be so completely lax in the care of it?

In an instant all her guilt-laden concern for Chane Bellamy sped away like the fading sun before a threatening storm. If the safety of the map mattered no more to Chane than this, let him wonder what had happened to it. Ria, feeling quite justified in what she did, retrieved the map and slid it inside her bodice. Perhaps with just the slightest niggling of conscience, she closed the lid of the box and bolted the lock in place. She supposed Chane had a key, if he had not also carelessly lain it aside somewhere.

With a loud huff of disdain for the absent captain, Ria turned to leave the compartment, but she made only a step before a hand snaked from behind the swaying bed curtains and snared her slender wrist. A yelp of protest did not stop her being forcibly dragged within the curtains.

"Witch!" Chane, who had been lying in the unmade bed all along, his body like a burning fire, rolled his bare torso across her. Clad only in his breeches and a strip of bandage that crisscrossed his left shoulder, he stared wildly down at her. His lean sweaty face had a rasp of black beard and the haggard, wild-eyed look of madness. "Winsome robbing witch! You want more than my life, do you?"

His glassy-eyed look paralyzed her for a moment, a moment he used to sweep her flailing arms above her head and rivet them to the mattress. Caught like a helpless lamb at a shearing, Ria bowed her back and tried to buck off his weight, but accomplished as much as she might have trying to lift a stone with a feather. "Imbecile!" she cried. "Unhand me! I took nothing of yours."

"No?" he growled as he maneuvered both her wrists into the iron grasp of one of his large, rough hands. "I think you lie, witch. I think you have something of mine here."

His free hand swept across her breasts in a bruising crush, then came to rest at the neckline of her bodice. His long fingers slipped inside, grasping the soft fabric and bunching it in his powerful hand. With a terrifying cry of rage he made a bold swift yank that rent the garment and the chemise beneath it to her waist. Ria gasped, too stunned to scream or struggle until she felt his hand probe her bosom in an unrestrained search for what was hidden there.

"Stop!" she cried, her breath coming in gasps as his invading hand stroked and lifted her tender flesh. "I took the map! Only the map!"

Chest bare and broad and glazed with red light reflected from the scarlet bed curtains, Chane straddled her thighs, holding her slender arms pinned in the tangled blaze of her hair. The brilliant, lustrous tresses spread around her fine oval face like the flaring rays of the rising sun. Chane's eyes dimmed as he stared, shaken and stirred, at her loveliness.

His eyes blinked as they swept to an image, alien on her fair skin, a coin-size, black-rayed sun rimmed with red, tattooed on one smooth shoulder. Disbelieving, he touched the mark, sensuously running a finger over the inked lines, expecting them to rub away. Instead the contact worked magic on him, changing his dark mood as the dawn changes night to day. Ria lay panting beneath him like a pagan princess, angry, proud, her lips white-rimmed with fury. He forgot, all at once, what he had been about. He wanted only to kiss those enticing lips, to feel them soften and yield beneath his mouth, those angry lips that spoke simple truth.

Nothing that belonged to him was concealed within the remnants of her bodice, nothing except her lush, tempting breasts and the roll of parchment that was Dagian's map, her map. He wondered as he stared hungrily down at her bared breasts, sweet soft mounds pale as the midnight moon, if that bit of parchment and ink would lead to a finer treasure.

He thought not, at least not at the moment, as a surge of lust, blinding and painful, filled his loins.

Ria moaned. His long legs, like a pair of thick twining vines, held her fast upon the bed. Immobile beneath him, trapped like a timid rabbit by a sly fox, Ria had the wild suspicion that like the beast he brought to mind, with a quick gnash of his teeth, a savage twist of his jaw, he could as easily devour her.

She could not have moved if she'd wanted to. What alarmed her was that she did not desire escape. The brutal thrust of his hand against her breast had turned hypnotically tender. His hand, hot as a firebrand, stoked a like fire within her, every gentle, exploring caress forging an aching curiosity and a desperate yearning to know how it would be to allow that forbidden fire to totally engulf her.

"You are a witch, Aurelia Kingsley, a flagrant, heartless witch," he swore as his dark hand pressed against her milky skin. She was smooth and soft and he had a reckless desire to wrap himself around her, to plunge his burning body inside her. He had a damning belief that he must, that if he did not there would be no way to cool his boiling blood.

"Only a woman," she whispered, terrified and entranced by what she saw in his fiery blue eyes. "No more, no less."

"A witch," he argued. Who but a witch would wear a mark like the one that embellished Aurelia Kingsley? "You've set me afire with a spell. Will you let me burn, Ria? Will you?"

He freed her hands that he might make better use of his. That he did by skimming his palms over her soft, bare shoulders and down her sides as if he touched the cool, fragile petals of a white, white rose. He cupped her full breasts, a hand to each, his thumbs brushing over the soft flushed nipples until they puckered and rose like sweet, ripe berries.

Ria whimpered, unable to answer, uncertain of her own mind and thoughts. A shiver of excitement ran though her shaking flesh and bone and sanity; reason left her. No man's hands had touched her before. No woman's quiet wisdom had warned her of what she should fear from a man's un-

bridled passion. Nor had any softly whispered girls' secrets
told her what ponderous joy might come of forbidden intimacy. Ria discovered all for herself as Chane bent his raven
head to her mouth, sweetly sealing her trembling lips to his.
Her body tingled and throbbed as the essence of him, heady
as wine, lingered on her lips and the velvet softness of her
tongue. She wriggled beneath him and sighed, a soft keen-
ing sound he took within him as his mouth played softly,
possessively upon hers.

Ria forgot herself and how she had come to be locked in
his embrace. Her arms, unbidden, strung about his neck,
pulling him tighter to her. She was dismayed when, in what
seemed but a moment, he broke his hold and drew his tantalizing mouth away. She was stunned when his lips, hot as
flames, sought her breast and sealed around one tightly
crested nipple. He toyed with one then the other, kissed and
licked softly where the tattoo marked her shoulder, then slid
his long legs down the length of her to lie beside her.

"Cool me, witch," he whispered, his breath a tiny flame
in her ear. "Take me in your woman's well and cool me."
His sturdy arm drew her beneath him, his titillating mouth
sought her lips again.

"Chane," she whispered. "I—" Her hands clasped his
shoulders, felt a sudden change in him, a stiffening, a
warning something was wrong. Before she could answer yes
or no, Chane, in the flash of an eye, shuddered and slumped
across her with the leaden weight of a dead man. He gave no
room to breathe, no space to move, and he was hot against
her, hot as a glowing coal. His eyes were shut, sealed as in
sleep. Ria could not rouse him, try as she might, either by
word or by touch.

Panic beset her, panic that gave her strength beyond the
ordinary. With a heave unbelievable for her tiny frame she
rolled him aside, scurried to her knees and looked, terri-

fied, upon him. A hand to his face told that he breathed, but a look beneath the tightly closed lids showed eyes rolled back with fever. And delirium. Dear God! He burned with fever. Fever had sent him to his bed and the waking-sleep she had disturbed. He had been out of his head, saying, doing things he would likely not remember when he recovered.

If he recovered. The thought set her to action. She snatched her caught skirts from beneath him and bounded from the bed, hurriedly found a clean cloth and a pitcher of fresh water. The bed curtains she flung aside that he might have fresh, cool air to breathe. She was nearly as hot as Chane as she toiled at sponging his heated skin, but her fever was a result of the shame and censure in her mind. Would she have given herself to him? She did not know, did not think she cared so much one way or the other to ever know that answer. Yet she cared deeply, painfully, that Chane Bellamy needed the madness of delirium to hold her in his arms.

Chane turned and tossed in a sea of fire, a sea of scalding, burning oil he could not escape. Moaning, thrashing, he plunged deeper, ever deeper into the consuming depths. He was drowning, drowning in the flames, dragged endlessly down by a pain that seared his left side as if he had been snagged by the barb and line of a harpoon. He fell, faster, burning hotter, until the witch came, a red-haired sea witch, bare-breasted, her shoulder scored with the mark of the Black Dawn. A witch she was, whispering tender, balmy words, a sweet witch who laid soothing hands upon him and drew the searing heat from his fevered body.

"There, you bloody fool," Ria whispered when at last the fever in him broke. Did he think himself invincible? Did he think his wound would heal if he gave it no care? She did not put such a thought above him. Nor did she doubt that when she removed his bandage she would find his injury little better than on the night it had been done. "Bloody, proud, handsome fool," she whispered softly. "I'll not let you die of pride, Chane Bellamy."

He was tranquil now, the thrashing of his arms and legs stilled. Ria tore the strips of bandage from his shoulder and discovered what she had feared, a neglected wound festered and oozing. The ragged edges of it had reddened around a pair of badly placed stitches. Heaven alone knew the source of the thread or the previous use of the needle that had made the stitches. What was certain was that they had to come out. The wound required cauterizing, for the infection had advanced beyond a stage to be cured by poultices or ointments.

She would need help, and, as if by divine decree, help arrived at the very moment she needed it.

"Ria—" Tad's young face blanched to frosty white when he saw her in the captain's quarters and on her knees beside the man's bed. When he saw the captain sprawled near naked before her, Tad's knobby knees shook until they touched. "Do—do not wake him," he whispered. "You must leave before—"

"Slackard! Dolt!" Ria snatched the edges of her torn bodice together and glared at the boy. "What excuse of a servant are you to allow your master's wound to fester until it is but a piece of rotting meat?" She leaped to her feet and dashed across the room, catching the hapless lad by the ear and dragging him to the bedside. "Answer me that!" she demanded.

"He would not let me touch it. Nor anyone," Tad whimpered. "I tried. I did. But he cuffed me for so much as lifting the bandage."

What Tad said of his master she could well believe. She let the boy go. "Then who, pray tell, put the stitches in?"

"He did it himself," Tad insisted. "He was furious mad a woman did him in," the boy explained. "He would not allow a man of his crew to see the damage."

"Bloody fool," Ria whispered. Then in a voice so loud it set poor Tad to quaking she demanded, "Get Axel Gresham! This minute!"

Tad gladly fled the cabin. While he was gone Ria picked out the badly set stitches and did her best to purge the wound. Her work was made all the more difficult by the renewed tossing and thrashing of her patient, but by the time the cabin boy returned with Axel Gresham in his wake, the wound was as ready as it could be made for the cauterizing that was called for.

"Godamercy!" Axel Gresham cried, seeing his friend and captain desperately ill. His eyes went searchingly to Ria. "Is it the injury?"

She nodded. "Badly festered," she said. "I've cleaned it as best I can, but—"

Axel bent over Chane and looked for himself. Without hesitation he barked an order at Tad. "Bring coals from the cook's fire," he said. "And be quick." Tad made a move to go but a heavy hand on the boy's shoulder turned him back before he could do as bidden. "Not a word to the men," he ordered. "Should anyone ask, one of the women has suffered a chill and the coals are for a warming pan."

Tad nodded and sped away.

Axel wore a long knife in a scabbard at his side. He pulled it free of the leather holster and doused the blade with a slosh of brandy from a bottle stashed in a cupboard. Ria toiled, too, folding a clean handkerchief to place between Chane's teeth for his protection and theirs.

"Tad and I will hold him steady," Axel told her. "You must apply the knife when it's hot enough."

Ria shuddered but agreed. Without cauterization the infection would only worsen and there was no predicting the outcome for Chane if that happened.

Tad hustled in, carrying glowing coals in an iron galley pot. At Axel's direction the boy fanned the embers while the knife lay among them, the steel blade drawing the scorching heat from the coals. Chane groaned and thrashed upon his bed, alternately shivering and drenching his bedclothes with fevered sweat. Axel strode the cabin, his anguished face twisted with worry. At length he dipped his hand in the water basin and trickled a drop on the knife's blade. The water sizzled to steam.

"It's ready," he announced.

Ria drew a deep breath to fortify herself for what she must do. Tad shook as if he were the one who would feel the knife's searing heat.

"Hold him fast," Ria warned as she bound a scrap of cloth around the knife's heated hilt. "I wish to do this only once."

Axel understood and ordered Tad to lay his weight across Chane's legs. Stronger and stouter, Axel locked Chane's arms in a secure grip, certain that between the two of them they could control the unconscious man long enough for the cauterizing. Chane was now calm and quiet. He remained still until the glowing blade, which trembled with Ria's hand, charred his flesh. A cry of rage broke from his lips, muffled but not obliterated by the pad between his teeth. He lurched, nearly throwing off the solidly built Axel. Determined to hold the hot blade in place for the seconds needed, Ria moved with Chane, though she, too, was almost knocked aside by the savageness of his jerks.

Tad fared worse than any of them. When the blade came away from his skin, Chane again lurched savagely, this time using the considerable strength in his legs. Tad, slightly built, lost his hold and consequently suffered a vicious kick that sent him sailing.

Swathed in silk curtains ripped from their anchoring rings, the boy hit the floor so hard his breath whooshed out. "Damn," he groaned and coughed.

But neither Axel nor Ria could aid Tad. Chane gave them more than they could handle. Having wrenched one arm free, he yanked the handkerchief from his mouth. His fevered eyelids burst open and his pained, furious gaze found Ria.

"Witch!" he shouted and pointed a finger at her. "I'll do you in kind."

The threat robbed him of the little energy he had. He made a feeble move toward Ria, moaned and fell flat on the bed.

"He hates me," Ria said. "And small wonder."

"Hates you?" Axel shook his head, questioning in his mind for the first time the condition of Ria's clothing. He could only conclude that Chane was responsible for the damage. Still, he knew his friend better than any other did, and he believed Chane would not have harmed the girl had he possessed all his senses. "Nay," he said. "The man is not capable of hate. Give him time to mend and get a clear head. You will like him better, and he you."

"I hope you're right," Ria said woodenly. "Or else it will be a long and disagreeable voyage."

"Give him time," Axel repeated. "As for me, I must return to the deck or the men will begin to question the absence of both captain and first officer." He paused for a swig of the brandy not used in cleaning the knife. "You will see to his care, will you not?"

"I'll stay with him," Ria promised. "Until the fever is gone for good."

"Tad will assist in any way you need," Axel said. He left the room a moment later, recalling the premonition he'd had when told of the plans to seek Dagian's trove. He wondered if Chane would be any more ready to heed a friend's doubts when he recovered.

Tad, disengaged from the curtains and rubbing his bruised behind, wondered how his captain could be more a trial to tend unconscious than alert. He was happy to leave the cabin to ask Clair for a change of clothing for her sister, even happier when the fair-haired Clair declared she must see for herself why Ria needed a fresh gown. He waited in the passageway while Clair went inside.

Frightened, hesitant, Clair crept into the quiet cabin. "God help us! Ria!" she cried when she saw her sister's disheveled hair and tattered dress. "That brute Bellamy! What has he done to you?"

Ria's face colored as she shushed Clair with a finger to her lips and quietly nodded toward the bed, a mistake. Clair nearly collapsed when she saw Chane Bellamy sprawled and sleeping there. "Nothing," Ria answered softly. "Nothing he meant to do, anyway."

She took the dress Clair had brought. Besides the one she wore, it was the only garment of hers the intruder had not destroyed, her last unless she could put together a piece or two of the rags made of her others. But that would take time and patience. While she had plenty of the first, she completely lacked the latter.

With the lamps low and her back to Chane, Ria stripped off the torn gown. Clair gasped and hurriedly positioned herself between Ria and the bed. "Are you mad?" she cried. "There is a man here."

Ria was too tired to care if she stood naked before the entire crew as she twisted her hair off her neck and splashed cool water over her skin. "Only in body," she assured the distressed Clair. "Captain Bellamy is unconscious and is likely to remain so for a long time." She splashed her face and her bare breasts and back, rinsed her arms then dried with one of the clean bath sheets Tad had provided.

"I don't know what has become of you, Ria," Clair sobbed. "This isn't proper. You shouldn't be in Captain Bellamy's cabin without a chaperon."

Ria laughed, a lilting, hysteria-tinged laugh that resonated from the walls of the cabin. "Believe me, Clair," she said dully, "my days of innocence are long past."

"Ria!" Clair paled and trembled.

Ria sighed as she patted her skin dry. "I don't mean that," she explained. "I mean my days of believing that being sweet and proper is enough to guarantee a good life, or that I am a lost Cinderella whose prince will ride to her rescue. Believe me, Clair, neither is true."

"I don't. I won't," Clair whimpered. "You are wrong. One day our luck will change and our lives will be the same as they were when Papa was alive."

Ria turned to her sister, wishing Clair were right but knowing nothing would ever be the same again, not even when they found the treasure. Nothing, not even riches, could restore those happy times.

Ria was wrong about one thing. Chane was not unconscious and, if he was not wholly awake, his eyes were slitted open enough for him to take in the hazy sight of a beautiful flame-haired girl as she stepped nimbly into a plain cotton dress. The image of her filtered into his fevered dream—the familiar creamy breasts, the strange black tattoo on a graceful shoulder, the cloud of red hair that sprang loose from the tortoise combs and floated around her shoulders.

"Witch," he whispered so softly neither girl heard the mumbled word as silently he vowed he would possess her.

Chapter Eight

For two days more Ria got no closer to the decks than a wistful gaze from the spray-washed windows of Chane's compartment. From there she watched the sun splash the vast sky with the dying colors of day, paint it pale amber and gold with a promise of morning light. Nearly devoid of sleep for the entire period, weary to the marrow of her bones, she could scarcely tell one event from the other by the time the captain's fever and delirium broke.

An hour before noon, the exhausted cabin boy was just departing for the galley to assist in the preparation of the midday meal when a last worried look at the captain showed a change for the better. "He's coming around." Tad's voice, sometimes a masculine baritone, sometimes a juvenile squeak, penetrated Ria's fatigue.

The news, long awaited, revived Ria as a reprieve from a sure sentence of death might have. She rose from her chair lively and refreshed and hastened to the bedside, a smile on her face and joy in her heart. For two days she had feared Chane's fever would prove stronger than the man himself. In all that time she had neither left his cabin nor broken her staunch vigil of caring for him. With Tad's aid, she had poured warm broth or cool water laced with the strongest medicines available down Chane's dry throat. Most, it had seemed, spilled from his lips. Ria had feared that if the fever did not kill him, hunger would. Now the tide had turned. He was waking and soon he would be well.

Chane saw Tad first, his unfocused eyes missing the glad smile on the face of the boy who stood at his bedside, his befogged mind unaware he had lost nearly three days of the past week.

"What's the damned hour?" he growled, judging that the sun was high, and thinking he was long overdue on deck. Cursing, he tossed the bedclothes aside as he made to rise.

"Captain! You cannot! Stay as you are!" the boy shouted, cognizant as Chane was not that beneath the sheets he wore not a scrap of clothes. Confounded when the captain ignored him, Tad threw himself in front of Chane to shield his nakedness from Ria's view.

Chane, a curse on his lips, swept the boy aside with a swipe of his hand. "Out of my way, you little cur," he growled, his voice hoarse as the drag of a rasp after the ravaging fever and days of disuse. "Did I not tell you to wake me at break of day?"

"Yes, captain," Tad admitted. He hastily grabbed a sheet and threw it around his master's shoulders, but not before Ria was treated to a shocking glimpse of the half of Chane Bellamy that she had so cautiously avoided seeing while she cared for him. "But that was days ago and—"

"For your neglect I'll be leaving you high and dry at the next port," Chane swore, angrily ripping the sheet away. "Damned irresponsible cur—" A host of factors—the puzzle of what Tad had said, the unwarranted presence of Ria in his cabin, the sudden loss of the strength that had brought him out of bed—seemed to converge on Chane at once. He swayed on his feet, caught Ria in a fuzzy, confused stare, then toppled backward to the bed.

He was as he had come into the world, gloriously bare, splendidly made as men went, or so she assumed until she, too, felt light-headed and close to a faint. Realizing she held her breath for minutes on end and stared as openmouthed as a dumbstruck child, Ria gulped in a breath. By then Tad, his face red as a beet, had grabbed the discarded sheet and flung it over the captain again. When Ria reached the bed, Chane had calmed but his temper had not improved. His usually sky blue eyes were as dark as his mood, his black-bristled jaw squared and hard. She dared not think what he would have done if he had not already spent his energy.

Poor Tad was made to feel the brunt of what little he did have. "Get this woman out of my cabin!" Chane ordered. "What the devil are you thinking, allowing that she-demon in while I sleep? Answer me, boy? Or would you like a turn under the lash?"

The threat was the last straw. "Look here!" Ria said, shaking a finger within inches of Chane's face. "You won't touch that boy! The lad's worked night and day—"

Chane pushed up on his elbows. "Out!" he shouted. "Put her out or must I do it myself?"

"Come along," Tad whispered and gave Ria a nudge. "The captain's himself again."

Ria sighed and started out but looked suspiciously back at the bed as Tad held the door open for her. "I suppose that was to be hoped for," she said.

Tad nodded in agreement, smiling.

She had second thoughts, however, when Tad began to close the door behind her. Her hand caught the edge before the latch closed. "Are you certain you're safe with him now that he's awake?" she asked.

Tad laughed merrily. "Yes," he said. "He's mostly bluster, my Captain Bellamy. For all his threats he's never laid a hand on me or anyone who didn't deserve it."

Ria was partially mollified and truly glad that Chane had survived his ordeal, though a bit of gratitude would have been appreciated. None, apparently, was forthcoming for her or for Tad. From behind the cabin door she heard Chane bellowing.

"Are you lame, boy? Get my dinner and quick. Or do you wish to starve me, too?"

Drained from her long vigil and the final rebuff from her patient, Ria crept into the cabin she shared with Clair and eased herself, fully clothed, upon the berth she had not used in days. She was dozing when Clair found her. She awoke to see her sister, looking fresh and pretty as a newly blooming flower, wringing her small hands in distress.

"Is he dead?" Clair ventured.

Ria sighed and swept a thick tangle of hair from her forehead. "Most definitely not," she said. "Though I am positive he will soon make the rest of us wish we were."

Her prophecy proved out within hours. Chane, revitalized by a good meal and a hearty glass of brandy, insisted on climbing to the deck. Axel had received word of Chane's recovery but was surprised to see him return to duty so quickly.

"Back among the living, I see?" Axel greeted him, as with some effort, Chane swung up the short tier of steps to the quarterdeck. "And not looking too proud of it," he observed.

"I've had enough mollycoddling from Tad," Chane warned. "Don't you start telling me how well I look."

Axel laughed. He had endured enough mornings with his friend to know he awakened with the temperament of a bear leaving hibernation. The recent long and forced sleep seemed to have rendered him doubly ill-humored. "To see you on your feet is improvement enough. I will not complain of your gaunt face and bad temper."

"My temper is well earned," Chane said, scanning the heavens and the horizon to learn the *Aurelia*'s position. "Where the devil are we?"

"A day out of Aileron."

"Sacre bleu!" Chane swore. Aileron was the small village south of Eglantine on the western side of Martinique. The *Aurelia*'s proximity to the island underscored his lost days. Even though he knew nothing would have gone wrong with the ship under Axel's command, Chane did not like, even involuntarily, having abandoned his duty. "What reason have you given the men for my staying below?" he asked in a low voice.

"I told them I had pleaded for command on the first run of the *Aurelia*," Axel said. "And that you had paperwork wanting your attention."

"They believed you?"

Axel shrugged his wide shoulders. "Some did. Others choose to believe you are wallowing with the Kingsley sisters." Axel felt a sharp stab of conscience at what he had revealed. "I trust you will not tell the ladies I made no effort to dispel the rumor."

"Wallowing?" The first semblance of a smile softened Chane's bleak expression. The men would think no less of him for that. Given the nature of the expedition once they left Martinique, he could afford no show of weakness to his crew. Glad the truth of his hiatus had been kept from the men, Chane derived a small ration of pleasure from knowing a part of the silence had been gained at Aurelia Kingsley's expense.

"As neither of the women has appeared on deck since the shooting, there is speculation you keep them locked in your quarters for your own use," Axel said.

"Wallowing."

"As most of the men would like to do."

"And you?"

"I like to think I live by a higher moral code," Axel said, his reddening skin camouflaged by the dusk. He had on a few occasions spoken with both Kingsley sisters, but Clair, unforgettably lovely, hung in his mind as the clouds hung white and pure in the sky. She possessed his dreams night following night until, in spite of his efforts to remain unmoved by the experience, she stirred even his baser nature.

But he would have died before he offended her by making his desires known. Never would he offend a sweet-spirited, angelic lady such as Clair Kingsley. Nor did he think she would ever give someone like him a second look. Not with Chane Bellamy around.

"Yes. Higher," Chane said. "That you do, my friend."

The *Aurelia* put in at Aileron under clear skies, riding in upon the calm turquoise waters of the harbor. The village, tucked on a hillside overlooking Aileron Bay, was festooned with banners and streamers in celebration of Vaval, the festival that began shortly after the new year and ran until Ash Wednesday.

The happy, pulsing sound of native drums and voices bounced across the smooth jewellike water to welcome the ship. The crew, many of whom had celebrated festival in Martinique before, worked zealously to get the craft tied up at the wharf so that they might join in the revelry by nightfall. Ria and Clair shared the excitement, at long last allowed to partake of the fresh air and enjoy the splendid view from the upper deck. However, the privilege was not given without a warning to stay clear of the forecastle, keep quiet and cause no trouble.

Clair wore a straw bonnet and her faded yellow gown. Though the gown was long-sleeved and high-necked and a bit warm for the day, she looked as lovely as a jonquil in the sunlight. Ria's checked woolen skirt was mismatched with a bodice of plaid. With no shade or shelter from the sun she steamed in her outfit, but Spruill had left her little choice in her already meager wardrobe.

Chane, she determined, knew how to dress for the heat. His buff breeches, tight as the skin on his corded thighs and hips, were of cool linen. His shirt was linen, too, a grade nearly as fine as silk and open down the front that he might feel the cooling breeze on his hair-sprinkled chest. He wore no hat and his black hair, glistening in the sun, hung in loose curls on his neck.

Her back to the rail, Ria watched him at work, haggard but determined, standing above the binnacle, barking orders to his men for a lowering of sail, a turn of the rudder that would successfully bring the *Aurelia* to mountings along the wharf. When their eyes chanced to meet, she was reminded with startling vividness of the way she had seen him last, naked and proud, spellbinding in his maleness. Only in that brief moment did it occur to her that to such a man she must look like a charwoman.

Clair missed all the activity on board, for her eyes were on the gay goings-on along the waterfront and the narrow village streets cobbled with ballast stones. Savannah had never been so festive as this. Native women in bright dresses swayed down the streets balancing enormous urns and bundles on their heads. Scantily dressed native men heaved and hauled crates and barrels from ships to waiting wagons, all the while smiling and chanting to the steady beat of drums.

Smells from a village market, unfamiliar or oddly mixed, assailed Clair's nostrils—meat basted and roasting on open spits, ripe tropical fruits piled head-high in colorful mounds, stacks of rich spices and hanging bunches of pungent herbs. Sweetest of all were the bouquets of jungle flowers set in every open window or growing wild on every archway and wall—orchids, red and golden jasmine, bougainvillea, others she could not identify.

"Have you ever smelled anything so wonderful?" Clair asked, high-spirited for the first time since they had left home.

"Never," Ria said, joining Clair at her spot on the rail and breathing in deeply the stimulating and exotic island scents.

She was bewildered by the behavior of the attractive matron who stood alone on a balcony high above the widest street in the village. The woman held a rose-colored kerchief in her hand and waved it to and fro as if signaling the *Aurelia*.

Tad joined them at that moment. It was he who made sense of the woman's actions. "That is Madame Bellamy," he said, indicating the woman. "The captain is her only son."

"He has sisters, then," Ria responded.

"But one," Tad informed her. "A child of twelve."

Ria smiled. Tad could not be much above that age himself but obviously considered the difference in years vast.

"I understood that Madame Bellamy and her family lived on a plantation beyond the city," Ria said.

"At Eglantine, the biggest and best plantation on the island," Tad boasted. "But the Bellamys own a smaller house in the village as well. During festival madame and her daughter often stay a night or two in Aileron so that they can take part in the celebration."

"I see," Ria said. The house in Aileron was no small one in her eyes. If it was but a resting place for the Bellamys, then Eglantine must be stellar indeed. And the Bellamy family far wealthier than she had imagined, which stoked her curiosity. With so much at his fingertips already, why had Chane been so eager for a share of Dagian's trove?

She was given no time to ponder her question. With the ship tied up and the sailors bustling from one end of the crowded deck to the other, Axel sauntered up to the sisters and inquired of their health.

"The air here will return a bloom to your cheeks," he said. "Enjoy it. We will be docked a week, perhaps more, and when we sail again we are not likely to be blessed with the mild weather we have known to date."

Ria heard only the part of his comment that concerned her most. "A week!" she exclaimed. "So long? Is it necessary? Surely not."

"Mademoiselles," Axel entreated, giving a small bow of his head to Ria, then a second nod to Clair, "where we sail next there may be no friendly port. A careful assessment must be made of the provisions called for. The vessel will require a more careful going-over than she got before we sailed from Savannah."

Clair was glad to hear of the delay, but Ria sighed. "I suppose all that will take a week," she acknowledged reluctantly.

"Do not be surprised if it is ten days or beyond," Axel hastened to say. He did not wish to incur Chane's wrath should the sisters grow impatient if the preparations delayed sailing beyond a week. "And may I suggest, as the captain has recommended, mademoiselles, that you acquire a garment or two lighter and looser than those in your present wardrobe." Color sped to his face as he hesitated and cleared his throat. "If I may broach a more delicate topic, no corsetry and fewer petticoats are called for in the southern latitudes. So near the equator, the heat can be overpowering if clothing is too heavy and binding."

"Thank you, Mr. Gresham," Ria said, seeing that Clair's pretty bow of a mouth was agape with shock. "We shall do our best to be properly attired."

Axel, looking almost as stricken as Clair now that the message from Chane was delivered, acknowledged her agreement.

This bit of chicanery, Ria was certain, originated with Chane Bellamy. For the time she did not stop to think that the suggestion might have been made with her comfort and survival in mind. She could accept only the misaligned reasoning that Chane, to further punish her misdeed, pointed out the shabbiness of her wardrobe. She made up her mind to do her best to accommodate him.

"The captain has another recommendation," Axel began hesitantly.

"Oh." Ria's head tilted suspiciously. Clair's golden eyes widened apprehensively.

"A pleasant one," Axel hurried on. "He suggests that you seek more comfortable quarters while we are in port."

"He wants us to leave the ship?" Ria asked incredulously. "Does he think *I* have a box full of gold left?" She huffed. "You may tell him it is quite out of the question unless he wishes to pay for our rooms."

"Better than that." He smiled. "Madame Bellamy can accommodate you in her house in the village—at no cost," he added. "She will be delighted to have guests from the Colonies."

Ria opened her mouth to refuse but Clair was ahead of her. "How very kind," she said. "We should be pleased to stay with Madame Bellamy."

"Yes," Ria said, seeing the happy look of anticipation on Clair's face. Terrified as her sister was of their undertaking, she had barely voiced a complaint against any of Ria's plans. Who could know what the future would bring—great riches or great disappointment? As much as she objected to obeying Chane Bellamy's directives, Ria could not deny Clair the pleasure of a week of luxury and comfort in Madame Bellamy's house. She could only hope they would be as well received as Axel indicated. She took consolation in knowing that from where the house perched on the rise of a hill in the village, she could keep a watchful eye on the *Aurelia*.

An hour later, Ria's fears of a cool reception from Chane's mother proved unfounded. Following Tad, who had drawn the duty of delivering them to the village, Ria and Clair entered the whitewashed structure that was Madame Bellamy's house.

"Welcome," the woman greeted them in a soft voice while a neatly clad servant trotted up the winding stairs with their valises. "So you are the young ladies my son has brought to Martinique."

"We are," Ria responded. When Madame Bellamy beckoned them into her drawing room, Ria was surprised to see the remarkable likeness of mother and son. Chane had inherited his mother's clear blue eyes and dark hair, though her tresses had gained a streak of silver at the temple.

"I am Rose Bellamy," the woman said, her English distinctly authentic. She kissed Ria warmly on each cheek, then greeted Clair with the same friendly gesture. "You cannot imagine how glad I am to have two lovely young ladies as my guests. My daughter Laure is away at a school in London for the first time this year and I miss dreadfully having someone to dote on."

Ria wondered at the choice of schools for Madame Bellamy's daughter. Then it came to her. "You are English," she burst out before she could contain herself.

The woman laughed. "Not so much as I am a Bellamy," she said, smoothing out the folds that sitting to work on her embroidery had put in her deep pink batiste and lace gown. "For twenty years I have made my home on Martinique with my beloved Renaud. I have no desire to return to the land of my birth."

"That is understandable," Clair remarked. "I've never seen a more beautiful place." On the trek to the Bellamy house she had been swept away by the richness of the verdant landscape, impressed by the copious abundance of goods in the small market and thrilled by the gaiety of the people, whether servants or merchants or common sailors.

The Bellamy house augmented Clair's good opinion of Martinique. White outside and in, it gave one a cool, restful feeling. The entire lower floor, from the foyer to drawing room with its cream-colored furnishings, was more garden than house. Potted palms, roses, hibiscus and orange trees accented every corner of the drawing room, the stairwell and the high balcony where they had first seen Rose Bellamy.

"Careful," Rose warned, "or you will become as entranced as I am and never want to leave." Laughing, she clapped her hands together twice then introduced a slimly built Creole girl as her maid, Minette. "I've had the hip tub put in your room," Rose told them as the girl led the way to an upstairs room. "Minette will bring water. Even after a score of years I have not forgotten what it is like to travel on board a ship."

Rose smiled at the look of appreciation so evident on Clair's sweet face and wondered if perhaps this lovely girl was the one who would put an end to the foolish standoff between her stubborn husband and equally stubborn son.

Ria thanked their hostess, noting a long-absent sound as she and Clair followed the servant into their room. Clair was laughing. She could not remember the last time she had heard laughter from her sister, or from herself for that matter.

"Is it not strange," Clair asked when Minette had left them, "that Captain Bellamy's mother is perfectly nice while he is—frightening?"

Ria found herself unexpectedly defending the man. "Perhaps you have misjudged him, Clair. You have, after all, seen him only at the most difficult of times for all concerned."

As she removed her bonnet, Clair shook her head. "I think Captain Bellamy is fierce and frightening and that he can be no other way."

There was too much possibility of truth in that for Ria to disagree. "Perhaps he drew his nature from his father," she commented, flopping into a most comfortably contoured lady's chair. She did not want to think about Chane Bellamy. He caused too much alarming discord in her nature, which by her own admission was becoming increasingly shrewish. She should have trusted her first judgment of the man when she had thought him arrogant and proud—and handsome—to a fault.

Somehow she had rooked herself into believing such a man could be her knight, gallant and trustworthy. Now she suspected her chosen knight had tarnished armor. Certainly his manner toward her could not fit into the realm of chivalry. Why, he was more considerate and appreciative of the scurviest man of his crew than he was of her.

Ria fidgeted in the chair as Minette and another servant returned with buckets of steaming water and filled the hip tub. Well, she considered, perhaps she had provoked him, but no knight who was true to his cause would hold that against her.

"From Madame Bellamy," Minette said, offering Clair a small bottle of aromatic oil, a cake of coconut soap and a tiny packet of silver paper.

Clair thanked Minette. When the maids were gone she whirled to face Ria, smiling softly as she opened the packet of sweet herbs to be poured into the bath with the scented oil. "Can I bathe first?" she pleaded. "I am ever so eager to sink into that water." Her happy face darkened with shame as she remembered Ria's long and strenuous ordeal of tending Captain Bellamy. "But I can wait," she said.

"Indulge yourself," Ria insisted. "I am too comfortable here to move anytime soon."

Clair disrobed in short order and climbed into the tub. Giggling and purring she soaked and scrubbed while Ria reflected on continuing her quest in the company of Chane Bellamy.

Chapter Nine

Less than twelve hours after the *Aurelia* docked at Aileron, the *Conquest* crested the horizon in sight of Martinique. One of Chane's men, aloft to check the stays and sail atop the mainmast, shouted out the vessel's name. From his post on the quarterdeck where he oversaw the securing of the ship and the preparations for the unloading of his cargo, Chane muttered a curse. He was in no mood for the Telfours.

That they were making port so soon after he sailed in did not bode well for someone. Gus had been two or more days from departure when the *Aurelia* set off. To have arrived so soon, the man had to have cut short his business and worked his crew double hours. With a disgruntled shrug, Chane returned to his work. Whatever had put a hell wind to Gus's sails could not concern him. Furthermore, he would be remaining aboard the *Aurelia* while they were in port. That at least would minimize any contact with either Gus or Lorelle.

He had put both of them out of his mind by the time Axel, drenched in sweat, came up from the hold to report on the status of the goods stowed below.

"All fared well," his friend said as he splashed water on his red face from a bucket on the deck. "We lost but a pound or two of flour where a barrel cracked. The count on all goods is the same as the manifest," he continued. "I have ordered the men to begin unloading."

Chane nodded. Requiring Axel to do the job he generally reserved for himself was galling, but he was still weak and light-headed from his battle with fever. Passing out from the heat and the exertion of climbing into the hold would stand him ill in front of his men. He was mending fast, though, and he was sure a few more days of rest topped by hearty meals sent from his mother's house would soon see him good as new. As he examined the state of his health, he could not help thinking of Ria Kingsley. He hoped he had not imposed trouble on his mother by sending the Kingsley sisters to her house.

He laughed dryly as he considered the idiocy of that thought. Rose Bellamy was well able to withstand the antics of the Kingsley sisters. Had she not for much of her lifetime put up with the bellicose Renaud Bellamy? And Chane himself?

Chane's laughter lasted only until Axel reminded him of the date. "Tomorrow night is the governor's fete in Aileron," he said. "Your mother is sure to invite Ria and Clair to attend as her guests."

Chane groaned. "If I had remembered the governor's fete I would have taken another day to make port." An annual event during festival, the governor's fete at Aileron was a costume ball that lasted the night through and included a wild and winding parade along the cobbled streets. Following the parade all owners of property customarily presented the governor with a gift.

"And likely had a mutiny on your hands," Axel said, exaggerating but pointing out that the crew would not have stood for a deliberate delay. Rum flowed free for all in

Aileron during the fete and there was a horde of village girls to be had at the same price.

"I would have welcomed a mutiny if it spared me attending the fete." Chane dreaded the ordeal but there was no getting out of it now that he was here. Every landowner was expected to attend. Not to attend or present a gift was a personal affront to the governor. Attending, on the other hand, meant spending at least part of the evening with Chane's ill-tempered father. It also meant dodging Lorelle and Gus with everyone he knew watching for a misstep.

For all that, he would be required to dance with each costumed lady and to behave as if he were enjoying himself. The way his shoulder pained him dancing was the last thing he cared for. Still, he had no choice. Unless he wished obstacles to be thrown up to his every future enterprise on Martinique he could not afford to offend the governor, especially since he was already at odds with his father.

Oddly, he welcomed the likely presence of the Kingsley sisters. Perhaps if he pretended a serious interest in one of them he could discourage Lorelle once and for all. Devoting himself to Ria or Clair would spin his father's head with wondering if his son planned to end the deadlock and acquiesce to his wishes.

Ria or Clair? It must be one or the other. The debate took only a moment. Clair Kingsley, beautiful as a fragile orchid, was the sister he would favor with his attentions, no difficult task that. All the better that her rare good looks would draw every eye at the fete. He would steer clear of Ria. Any public interaction with her would be unpredictable. She had a nettling way of inciting his temper, indeed, all his emotions. A moment or two with Ria Kingsley and he had no control over head, tongue or sentiments—a dangerous state where a woman was concerned.

Clair Kingsley it must be. Let him regain full strength before he took on Ria again.

Lorelle Telfour, having been immediately shepherded from the *Conquest* to Flores, the Telfour plantation, and placed under the watchful eye of her Aunt Sophie Telfour, longed impatiently for the governor's fete. By whatever means it took she intended to maneuver herself into the arms of Chane Bellamy. This she believed she must do before he made any public declaration of his intentions to either of the colonial women he had brought to his home. If Chane was as blind to her love for him as he pretended, and to what he must surely feel for her, then it was up to her to make him aware of both.

Lorelle weighed her choices as she rashly tossed the carefully pressed ball gowns around her sumptuous suite of rooms at Flores. She must select the perfect gown, one that showed her charms to advantage but one that was easily gotten out of with no assistance. She had made up her mind that following the governor's fete, Chane would have no choice but to marry her. There was, amid the lush garden of the governor's *maison de ville* in Aileron, a secluded gazebo. While the governor's guests danced to violins in the ballroom, she would arrange to meet Chane in the gazebo. She had a plan that was sure to bring him to her.

Lorelle smiled confidently as she found the perfect gown for the occasion, a brilliant red silk trimmed with black lace and ebony rows of jet beading. A black silk cord laced beneath the bosom secured the plunging bodice. She had a black mask of feathers and lace that would conceal her identity at the ball. Ebullient, Lorelle carried the gown to a looking glass and held the voluminous silk skirt before her. The gown was stunning, and with the laces in front, required no maid's assistance.

Perfect, as was her plan to seduce Chane. Lorelle's body tingled as she thought of the way he had linked his powerful body to hers. Her breathing quickened, a flush spread across her breasts and throat as she anticipated the ecstasy of his lovemaking. Perfect. After the fete she could have him in her bed any time she wanted. Hang Gus! Hang her Uncle Rossy and Aunt Sophie! She wanted Chane.

A gurgle of laughter spilled from her as she tumbled across her down-filled bed and closed her dark sloe eyes. Once Chane was discovered compromising the *innocent* Lorelle Telfour, he would have no choice but to marry her. Renaud Bellamy and her Uncle Rossy would see to it.

Ria and Clair spent part of the evening selecting ball gowns for the fete, choosing from the six Rose Bellamy had offered to them. Petite, curvaceous Clair soon found a gown to her liking, a pale saffron with yards of ivory lace and a scooped neckline trimmed with bunches of seed pearls. Clair and Rose were close in size, and the saffron gown was a good fit when laced tightly. Rose had furnished matching satin slippers and an elegant black-and-gold mask with streamers of matching ribbon.

Clad in the borrowed ball gown, Clair waltzed around the room while Ria made a selection from the remaining gowns. Attending the ball held little interest for Ria; her sole concern was getting under way to search for her grandfather's treasure. But Clair so looked forward to a social outing that she did not voice her objections. Taller and more slimly built than either Clair or Rose, Ria had difficulty finding a gown that did not hang above her ankles or gape scandalously away from her full but less ample bosom.

Finally she settled on the only one that was a near fit, a watered oyster silk that was completely devoid of lace or trim but hid her ankles and was only marginally too large in the bodice. A glance in the mirror made her glad for the painted satin mask that would conceal her identity and the grimace she expected to wear the entire evening. Her foot, she had discovered, was an unfortunate half size larger than her hostess's. Aching feet were sure to keep her in discomfort throughout the ball.

"Lovely," Rose declared, coming in for a look at her handiwork. Neither of the girls could complain that Rose Bellamy had made them less than welcome. She had sent up a bountiful tray of food following their baths, then insisted both of them nap before the evening meal. Rose smiled as she turned Clair before her, admiring the girl's tiny waist and display of creamy bosom. "You will be a princess at the ball, my dear. Extremely popular with the gentlemen, mark my words." And, she hoped, with her son.

"I am sure I shall enjoy it," Clair mumbled shyly.

Rose patted the girl's hand. Pretty Clair would look wonderful on Chane's arm, and with her sweet disposition would make a stunning companion for her high-spirited son. Her smile faded as she gazed at Ria. Making the other Kingsley sister presentable would require more imagination. Rose tried pinching a dart in the shoulders of the heavy gray gown but still the bosom sagged across Ria's smaller breasts. "A corsage or two pinned just so will help, and will give the gown some color, child," she said helplessly.

Ria sighed and tugged off the dowdy garment as soon as Rose left them. Except for her hair, made all the brighter by the dull gray color, she looked exactly like a mouse in the gown. She suspected she would be a wallflower at the ball, but if Clair enjoyed herself that would be satisfaction enough. Anyhow, with pinched feet she did not think she would care for dancing.

But dance Ria did, lavender orchids pinned to her bodice and in her hair, her silk skirt flowing like a sail around her.

First she took to the floor with Renaud Bellamy, a portly but handsome man a score of years older than his wife. From the time he was introduced to the girls at dinner, he had shown a surprising preference for Ria. And he had listened attentively as Ria awkwardly explained that she and her sister had hired his son for a mysterious expedition. Renaud did not pry, a trait Ria instantly admired. She was puzzled that Chane did not join his family for the meal, but like Renaud, did not pry.

She gathered, from a whispered exchange overheard as Renaud complained of the absence to his wife, that some family disharmony kept the younger Bellamy away. Knowing Chane's temper as she did, and judging Renaud to be a kindly man as he whirled her in the first waltz, she could only surmise that the fault lay with Chane.

"Is that the best gown my wife could find for you?" Renaud asked, noting that the flowers pinned to the bodice to camouflage the poor fit did not succeed. "I could have advised her on a better shade for that fine red hair."

"She did her best," Ria explained, her suspicion that she looked plain and ill-clothed confirmed. "I am not as easy to outfit as my sister."

"And not as ready to show your true colors, either," Renaud remarked, cocking a graying brow as he studied her face and came to one of the devious conclusions Chane so abhorred. "I doubt my son has seen them."

Ria felt a warmness spread over her skin at the mention of Chane. "I have no idea what you mean," she protested.

"Don't you, my dear? Do not forget you are talking to a Frenchman." Renaud laughed and gave her a vigorous spin. "You must make a point of opening his eyes. No one else is likely to do it for him."

Ria was completely puzzled. But even if she had had a mind to ask Renaud what he meant, she did not get a chance.

Rose Bellamy danced the first set with the governor, a leggy, aging bachelor whose vanity led him to wear his curled and powdered wig even though his face dripped with the sweat it raised on his scalp. As the pair whirled past, Renaud called out a good-natured warning for the governor to mind his step with Rose Bellamy.

Clair spun by a moment later, twirling across the floor in the arms of Axel Gresham. He had been at dinner and had walked with the party from the Bellamy house up the highest hill in the village to the governor's mansion, a frame structure the color of a shell's pink inner surface. The house was used solely for entertaining, the lower floor being a series of four large drawing rooms, connected one to another by accordion doors, which had been thrown open. This arrangement had the effect of dividing the guests into several small groups of couples who could, if they chose, waltz from one room to the next.

The upper floor, Ria was told, contained a dozen bedrooms, several set aside for ladies to rest and several for gentlemen, a few reserved for the use of individual guests who had come with the governor from other parts of the island.

Many of those not dancing hovered at the refreshment tables, nibbling cakes and fruit and sipping champagne or potent guava punch heavily laced with rum. Some buzzed round a table guessing the contents of tissue-wrapped gifts of assorted sizes and shapes. Others sat on padded benches that lined the pristine white walls. Still others strolled the garden, admiring a splendid view of the ocean from a high green bluff over a tumble of black rocks and foamy waves below. Like the Bellamy house the place was a veritable jungle garden inside and out. Anyone who wanted privacy might slip unnoticed behind the heavy foliage of a potted palm or banana tree or secrete themselves behind a thick hanging screen of fragrant purple bougainvillea.

Indeed, to Ria's surprise, those at the gathering were a remarkably uninhibited lot. She saw masked couples frolicking in the garden and dancing inside in a wanton manner that would have resulted in scandal had this been Savannah.

Axel Gresham was not of that persuasion. When he invited Ria to dance it was at arms' length that they swept across the floor. She was happy to see Clair safely in the arms of Renaud. She wondered what had become of Rose until she saw a couple dance by, unmistakably mother and son. A gown of green silk the color of sea mist, which Ria had admired at dinner, identified Rose.

As for Rose's partner, no mask could obscure a head inches above that of the next tallest man, or hide the thick raven hair tied in back and tucked into a silk queue bag. Nor did Ria need those features to identify Chane. The shape of his shoulders, the turn of his slim hips were as familiar to her as her own. What she had not learned of the contours and hollows of that strong masculine body in three days of bathing and tending him she had learned in the last. Face flushing, she pictured Chane as he had been at that moment.

"I see Captain Bellamy has not forgotten his family after all," she commented dryly to Axel.

Axel's sharp eyes left off searching among the rainbow of dancers for a blond girl in a yellow gown. He picked out Chane in buff coat and breeches and a simple mask of midnight velvet, dancing an animated waltz with his mother "He is fond of his family," Axel said warily.

Curiosity prompted her to pry but she justified her need to know with a belief she ought to learn all she could about Chane Bellamy. "I gather there is some quarrel between father and son," she ventured.

"A private matter," Axel said and dexterously turned the conversation in another direction when he spotted Clair and Renaud in the next room. "Your sister is most lovely tonight."

Ria had the good grace not to stomp her partner's toes, but that was only because hers were cramped within the tight, borrowed slippers and because she was accustomed to being overlooked in Clair's glow. Besides that, she had no womanly interest in Axel or any man. All men, she vowed, were but a necessary evil since she could not do what she wished on her own. With that thought in her head, she thanked Axel for the dance, declined the stranger who asked her for the next and strolled alone to the wide, vine-laden veranda to enjoy a cool breeze Renaud had told her the islanders called *alize*.

"You are enjoying the ball, mademoiselle?" A stranger's voice assailed her. Ria spun around to confront the man, young, she judged by his straight back and clear voice. His hair was fair and brushed his shoulders. His garments were of costly linen and silk, his coat tan, his breeches a dark maroon, his black shoes adorned with heavy silver buckles. His hands, bedecked with rings of silver and gold, held two glasses of champagne.

"Yes," she answered, sensing the man was merely being polite. "I find it most entertaining."

"The best is yet to come," he told her, stepping nearer and offering her one of the glasses. "At midnight when the parade ends the masks come off."

"And then?" Ria asked. She sipped cautiously from the sparkling glass.

Yves Telfour smiled. "And then everyone returns here to present gifts to the governor. The highlight of the evening, of course, is the governor's presentation of a favor to each lovely lady in attendance. After all this the ball resumes, mademoiselle." He paused a moment, moistened his thin lips with the point of his tongue. "You will, perhaps, save the first dance after midnight for me?"

"I can think of only one reason I would not," Ria said, having momentarily forgotten her recent disavowal of men. The stranger's interest intrigued her.

"If there is a reason you would not, let us dispense with it now," Yves said.

"I would not know you by name or face," Ria confessed.

"I am Yves," he told her. "I admit I have the advantage, Mademoiselle Kingsley." He smiled as her lips parted in surprise. "I would know you masked or not." His eyes went to her hair, worn long and tied back with a lavender ribbon. "There is not another on all Martinique with hair that shade. And yes," he continued, "I took it upon myself to learn your name." He saw no reason to add that he had first seen her boarding Chane Bellamy's ship in Savannah and that he had learned her name from Spruill, or that his family and Chane's were enemies of long standing.

The silken sheen of her fiery tresses made her especially attractive to Yves. He had a weakness for true redheads, but it was rare that he had a chance to indulge himself. Tonight an opportunity had presented itself. A few dances, a few glasses of champagne and maybe a kiss—he could hope for more—might be had before someone from the Bellamy family warned her to steer clear of Yves Telfour.

Ria was about to refuse the man, charming as he was, even though she assumed he must be a friend of the Bellamys. She did not know him well enough to promise mid night dances, but she chanced to look into the room behind him before she spoke. There, whirling to soft and sensuous strains of music, Chane held her sister in a shockingly close embrace. His smile was warm, his gaze devoted. She could almost see a glittering light of appreciation in his eyes. When she saw him refuse to yield his partner to another gentleman after the music ended, it was more than she could bear.

"I will reserve the dance you have requested," she told the fair-haired man. "But perhaps, before then we might practice one or two."

Chane enjoyed seeing his father strain his buttons watching as he danced two then three sets with Clair Kingsley. Albeit the girl felt like an ice floe in his arms, he held her close and gave her his rapt attention. From the corner of his eye he was pleased to see Lorelle locked in Gus's possessive arms dance after dance, and when she was not with Gus, put on a short tether near Sophie Telfour. Lorelle had deliberately looked away every time there was a chance he might catch her eye but now his partner was back to back with the black-haired vixen.

Chane bent his head close to Clair's small ear. "You have the grace of a gazelle, Mademoiselle Kingsley," he whispered, spinning closer so that neither Lorelle nor Gus could avoid seeing and hearing. Lorelle bit her lip and twisted around to gaze sharply at another part of the room. Chane grinned sardonically. If nothing else, his dances with Clair had spared him any of Lorelle's antics.

He gave a self-satisfied sigh, startling Clair, who feared she had brought the alarming response from him. Chane was barely aware of his companion's concern. He was wondering why Gus did not put himself out of his misery by wedding Lorelle? The answer was forthcoming as the couple turned and he got a look at Lorelle's insolent face. Lorelle was the reason. She devised a way to postpone the nuptials every time they were mentioned. Poor dumb Gus did not know what a favor she was doing him.

Yves, who Chane thought might have made a good friend were their families on better terms, waltzed by with a young lady snugly wrapped in his arms, his blond head inclined to gaze boldly at his partner's décolletage. Almost immediately Chane had cause to reconsider his regard for the younger Telfour brother. The woman with the curtain of red hair and the brazenly low-cut gown was Aurelia Kingsley. He did not notice that he gave Clair a spine-shattering clench as the two dancers brushed by him, but Clair felt it and decided she had had enough of the overpowering Chane Bellamy. She immediately begged off finishing the third dance she had shared with him, insisting she had a dreadful headache.

"My apologies if I have pressed you to overexert yourself, Mademoiselle Kingsley," he said, escorting her to the foyer that she might retire to the ladies' dressing room upstairs.

"No. It is the heat, I'm sure," Clair fibbed, feeling perfectly fine now that she was not so near him. Chane Bellamy was handsome, she acknowledged, but he was so tall and overwhelming with his maleness that she felt she had no breath when he held her. She much preferred Axel Gresham with his soft-spoken voice and gentle manner.

As soon as Clair was up the stairs Chane pegged himself against the wall to watch the dancers. When the music ended and the couples parted, he maneuvered a path to Ria's side.

"I believe this dance is mine, mademoiselle," he said.

"Why, no—"

Chane swept her into his arms and across the floor before either Ria or Yves could deny him. Ria allowed herself a few luxurious moments to match the rhythm of her steps to his, a few moments simply to enjoy the feel of his powerful arms, and then she rebelled at his high-handedness.

"Why did you do that?" she demanded.

"Ask you to dance?" he queried innocently from behind a quirking smile.

"You know what I mean." Her berry red lips made a pout, and she hoped desperately that Chane could not feel the fervid beat of her pulse beneath his hands.

"It seemed to suit," he answered honestly, noting with satisfaction the leap of her pulse, concluding that she was not nearly so displeased with his company as she indicated. "Do you mind?"

Ria relented. "Not if it means you will no longer roar like a beast every time you see me and not if it means that Clair and I will no longer be banished from the deck when we sail again."

His smile and the full force of those mercurial eyes, made bluer by the black mask surrounding them, devastated Ria. "You want the white flag, mademoiselle, a truce?"

"At least that," Ria said curtly, refusing to admit how much she liked being in his embrace. "Is my map safe?"

Chane touched the breast pocket of his embroidered satin waistcoat. "As safe with me as you are, mademoiselle."

"That gives me little comfort," she countered, laughing, glad the discord between them was at last mended—or at least patched.

She gave herself over to the dance, tenuously allowing her forehead to rest on his shoulder as he whirled her with the utmost fervor across the floor. The harmony lasted only briefly. He set her temper on edge when his gait slowed and, lifting her head, she noted the direction of his gaze. Skin prickling under the harsh stare, she nervously pressed the sagging neckline of her gown tight against her bosom, but, limp victim to humidity and heat it remained so only until she let go.

He was smiling at her wickedly. Ria trembled with alarm. Could he possibly remember what had happened between them the night he had been taken with fever? She did not think so. And yet . . .

Chane did not try to unravel the tangle of emotion that led him to say what came next. He admitted the knot had grown tighter when he spied Yves, standing out the dance, attempting with a wink to draw Ria's attention. Glancing away from the youngest Telfour and down at Ria he was treated to a generous display of soft white flesh, even the pinkened tips of her breasts, and in that moment his loins tightened and he imagined that Yves had enjoyed the same delectable sight. He was overcome by a sudden need to strike out at her, and followed through.

"If Yves Telfour had the same view of you as I now have," he said, "let me recommend that you stay out of the garden."

Ria lost her step and got her toe trodden on. "No gentleman would say that to a lady," she responded hotly. She tried vainly to pull away from him but found his grip too tight to break. When she did free herself a minute later she discovered that her last limping steps in his arms had led onto the veranda and behind a blind of bougainvillea vine. The music had ended and while other dancers returned to the drawing room to regroup, he blocked her way so that she was not really free at all, not with Chane edging forward to press her against the shadowed wall.

Ria bent her neck back to stare into his dark face. The blue eyes above her flared like torches. The square, chiseled jaw was clinched tight until he blew a long, hot breath that tickled across her tawny lashes as it swept over her upturned face.

"No gentleman would say it, but he would interpret your display of flesh the same as I do, Ria Kingsley," came roughly from his throat. "As an invitation." He placed his hands on her pale shoulders allowing his thumbs to inch deep beneath the gaping neckline of her gown and to burrow into the soft silken flesh of her breasts. "And if it is that," he whispered, "if you are so eager to share your charms, allow me to be the first in line."

An involuntary shudder shook Ria. Chane felt the tender vibration of it beneath his hands as his marauding thumbs flicked across the tight, aching peaks of her breasts. She moaned softly instead of voicing the defiant *no* that had been in her mind.

For Chane the sound was one of consent. His mouth crushed against hers. His hands slid rapidly down her sides to capture her wrists and pull her arms around him. Ria was completely enveloped by him, pinioned to the wall by his hard chest and thighs, absorbing his heat through the silk of her gown, feeling the rising change in his manhood. The orchids she wore, squeezed and broken between them, released a potent spice that, mingled with Chane's distinctly masculine scent, was more intoxicating than the champagne she had drunk. Ria breathed it in.

All the while his mouth continued to plunder, but he was not brutal. Ria wished he had been; then she would not have found anything to savor from his kiss, not the warmth of his lips nor the heated crush of his strong and virile body against hers, nor would a wild, weakening swirl of heat have come racing though her.

Still he had no right, not even if what he did felt good. When she came to her senses, she stiffened in his arms and at the same time aimed a sound kick at his shin.

"Yow!" he yelped and drew back, favoring the bruised leg, knowing he deserved her wrath and more. But he was totally unwilling to admit it until long after she had stalked off.

The ribbon hanging from her hair, her lips puffed and red, Ria ran to the veranda's foyer door, stopping only a second when she nearly collided with Renaud Bellamy. But that was long enough for him to see a tear in her eye and to assess her appearance. Gasping, embarrassed, Ria rushed past Renaud and beat a hasty retreat up the stairs.

Renaud, guessing what had happened, went swiftly to the veranda to see which of the governor's male guests might deserve a piece of his mind. He was incensed to see his son propped against the rail in an obvious state of arousal.

"You dishonor my name!"

Chane had been deliberating the wisdom of following Ria and making an apology. When he saw his father he straightened his shoulders and tightened his jaw. "The name is mine as well," he said. "I use it as I please."

"To take advantage of a woman?" Renaud jeered, his round cheeks puffing out. "No small wonder you have not found a wife. No good woman could abide your brutish ways."

"If I wanted a wife," Chane said coldly. "Which I do not." He ran his fingers through the mop of black curls that had fallen over his damp forehead. "You can rest assured it would not be that *diabless.*"

"Even a she-devil is too good for you," Renaud returned, though with an ache in his throat. It pained him that for the past year every encounter with his son ended with anger and shouts. He wanted only what was best for the boy but no longer seemed to have the knack of communicating his love and concern.

"Ha!" Chane said, eyes blazing defiantly as he turned to leave.

Renaud, a bitter resigned set to his face, called after him. "Where are you going?"

"To my ship."

"You can't leave," Renaud insisted, bristling again. "Not before you have made your gift to the governor."

"The governor be damned!" Chane said over his shoulder.

He left without another word to anyone, slipping through the garden to the street, leaving his mask to float with the lily pads on the surface of a fish pool. A bottle of Bellamy rum—there was one place his father had things right— would be better company than he had found at the fete.

Before Chane reached his ship, before Renaud Bellamy's red face cooled down and he returned to the fete, Lorelle Telfour, having at last eluded her chaperon, passed a sealed note to a blue-shirted serving boy. "There is a man in a buff silk coat," she told the boy. "A man with black hair, the tallest gentleman here. Give the note to him and no one else. When you have done as I've asked come back to me." She showed the boy a coin in the palm of her gloved hand. "I will reward you for your trouble."

"*Oui,* mademoiselle," the boy replied, eager for the coin.

With a tray of champagne balanced on his arm the boy hastily canvassed the four drawing rooms and made a sweep around the veranda and the garden, finding no one who fit the description the lady in the red gown had given. A quarter hour later he did find a gentleman who fit on two counts of the three, buff coat, the tallest gentleman at the governor's fete. Had he misunderstood? Had the lady said black mask rather than black hair? She must have, he decided.

Cautiously—she had insisted on secrecy—the boy slipped the note to the man's hand.

"What's this?" the astonished gentleman said.

The boy shook his head and grinned then hurried off to refill his tray one more time before the party left to parade through the village. He suspected there would be a pair who would not join the celebration. He had been a messenger to these games between lovers before. He was collecting his due from the lady in the red dress when the man in the buff coat found a secluded spot and broke the seal on the note, hastily unfolding and reading the words inside.

I await you in the gazebo at midnight.

> Impatiently,
> Mademoiselle Kingsley

Chapter Ten

With the moon vanishing behind a high drift of clouds, Ria and Clair began the parade procession at the side of Renaud and Rose Bellamy. Axel rounded out their number, taking a place between the sisters. Though the night had grown dark enough to make the winding trek to the village and through the narrow cobbled streets dangerous, each reveler had been issued a torch or long tallow candle to light the way.

At the head of the group a bevy of musicians set the pace, pounding a lively march on hollow drums, accompanying the riotous song of the company with the shrilly sweet sound of flutes. The crowd was unformed, a twisting garland of twinkling lights moving rhythmically down the hillside. Occasionally Ria would see a flame or two extinguished and a shadow or a pair of grayed shapes slide behind the dark shelter of a building or the wide trunk of a tree. As many new lights joined the parade as left but it was with those who departed that Ria's sentiments lay.

Her heels, having suffered the abuse of snug shoes all night, felt as if they must be devoid of skin. Each step became more torturous than the last until finally her sore feet could take no more. Unnoticed by her companions Ria paused to rest, watching dozens of the governor's guests pass her by, some singing and dancing, some locked in close embrace and floating past as if they walked on air. Time swept by, too, until Ria realized she had fallen far behind Clair, Axel and the Bellamys with no hope of catching up.

Deciding that she had no wish to do so anyway, not if she hoped to be able to walk the next morning, Ria sighed and withdrew from the street. Beginning the trek with the others had been a mistake, and she knew she had done it only because she believed it would take her mind off the disastrous episode with Chane. Futilely. The episode was as graphically real as the moment it happened. Even now her flesh prickled where he had touched, her lips throbbed with the imprint of his kiss.

Dejected, Ria flopped down on a wooden bench beneath a tiny shop window and tore the painted mask from her face. Evidently she was not the only one who had paraded long enough. Another young woman, one whose candle revealed an exquisite chin and alluring mouth beneath her black silk and feather mask, dropped out of the procession. Like Ria she watched others pass for a few moments then withdrew from the street.

There the similarity ended. The dark-haired woman in the stunning red dress snuffed her candle and moved stealthily into the shadow of a canvas awning, waiting until the tail of the parade waved by. When the last of the procession had passed and the voices were but an echo in the deserted street she turned and scurried up the hill down which they had all come.

"Ria! There you are. I was frantic when I realized you were not beside me." Clair, with Axel at her elbow, dashed across the street to join her sister. "Is anything wrong?" she asked nervously.

"Yes," Ria said woodenly, slipping the confining shoes off her burning feet. "I am lame for life." With no concern for modesty she stuck both her bare feet from beneath her drooping silk skirt.

Thinking she might have fallen and injured an ankle, Axel knelt before her and held his torch so that it shone a light on her aching feet. "Blisters," he said. "Bad ones."

"Oh, Ria," Clair cried, her lovely mouth marred by distress. "You won't be able to return to the ball."

"No," Ria admitted without regret. She had forgotten, for the moment, the stranger to whom she had promised a special dance. "But that is no reason for you to stay away."

"I couldn't leave you alone," Clair insisted.

"Nonsense," Ria protested. "Surely some of the servants are awake at the Bellamy house." Shoes and mask in hand, she stood. "I believe it is only a few doors away. If Mr. Gresham will escort me there, the two of you may have time to rejoin the parade and the ball."

"But..."

"I will not spoil your fun, Clair. Go with Mr. Gresham."

Beneath the torchlight Ria thought she saw a deepening of color on Axel's face. And why not? Like all men, like Chane, he found her sister enchanting. Clair was the sort of woman men wanted to cosset and protect. She wondered, as she limped barefoot down the street, what quality there was about her that brought the opposite response.

Lorelle, out of breath and dizzy with excitement, fell upon one of the velvet-cushioned wicker settees within the octagonal walls of the governor's gazebo. In the farthest reach of the garden, all but obscured by a thick stand of bamboo and a heavy cluster of head-high, red-leafed poinsettias, the small structure was a perfect meeting place for lovers. Lorelle considered herself lucky that she had not come upon any trysting couples who might have arranged an assigna-

tion in the gazebo. Once she had caught her breath, she
scrambled to her knees and peeped out of the latticed walls.
From her vantage point she could see the chain of flickering golden lights beginning to ascend the hill.

"Soon," she whispered, a restive spirit dogging her as she
frantically plucked loose the laces that cinched the clinging
bodice of her red silk gown. Hurriedly, she shimmied out of
the garment, gave it a purposeful jerk that ripped one of the
cap sleeves almost off and tossed it capriciously to the floor.
She drew a long, exhilarating breath into her compressed
lungs the moment her corset joined the gown on the floor.
She had to be ready. Soon Chane would appear winding
along the path through the bamboo canes expecting his
prissy Mademoiselle Kingsley.

How a man could desire a woman with no more color
than a bucket of cow's milk puzzled Lorelle as she stepped
out of her red satin slippers and sat down to roll her sheer
black stockings and garters off her slim legs. His *graceful-
as-a-gazelle* Mademoiselle Kingsley looked as if she would
bruise at a touch and faint from a kiss. That bloodless bitch
was not the woman for Chane Bellamy. Lorelle knew that
even if he did not. Mademoiselle Kingsley would be bland
as milk too. Chane needed a woman of spirit and blood, a
woman with all the endowments of good Caribbean rum, a
woman who would risk everything to have him. He needed
Lorelle Telfour.

"Soon," Lorelle mumbled as she placed her hands just so
and gave her skimpy chemise a powerful pull that rent it
from neckline to waist.

"Mademoiselle?" The hoarse whisper came with the
breeze from the edge of the bamboo stand.

"Here," Lorelle returned, quivering as she felt her skin
turning to gooseflesh. He was here. Her heart beating a
hundred times too fast, she crouched low in the gazebo. She

did not want to give away her identity too soon. Not so soon that Aunt Sophie would not have found her reticule and the carefully placed note left in the ladies' resting room. Lorelle smiled as she imagined Aunt Sophie reading the words her niece had written with extreme care so that the penmanship appeared to be that of a man.

The note would bring her aunt in a run and she did not doubt that her Uncle Rossy would be in tow. And—all this she could picture in her mind as she waited for Chane to break from the bamboo stand—she would tearfully exclaim that her honor was besmirched, that Chane, beset by lust, had seduced her and must, by right, wed her with all expediency.

"Mademoiselle—"

She heard his footsteps, eager, rushed. He must be as anxious as she was, a thought that both thrilled Lorelle and raised her ire. His eagerness was for the insipid Mademoiselle Kingsley. But that was not whom he would find. Lorelle's red lips curled like a bit of hot wire as she whispered silkily, "I await you, my love."

Head tossed back, she stood and pushed the torn shift from her shoulders, allowing it to float sensuously to her feet.

Yves Telfour never saw the woman's face. The full naked breasts, the slim bare legs, the dusky shadow where they met brought a painful jolt to his groin. He had hoped for a kiss. This was to be a sumptuous feast. With no fanfare other than an impassioned moan, Yves leaped into the gazebo and rushed at what awaited him.

Just then the moon broke from behind the clouds and a silvery streak of light shone into the gazebo.

When he saw her face, his fervor and his ready manhood died at the speed they had been born. Sputtering a curse, fumbling at his clothes, he shoved her away.

"Lorelle! What the devil?"

Lorelle, equally appalled, flung her arms across her body to shield herself. Grimacing, spitting, she spun away from Yves. "Get away from me, you snake!"

Yves clambered to his feet, badly shaken, brooding over how much trouble this encounter was going to cause. Cursing, he shifted out of his coat and tossed it over Lorelle's torso. "Cover yourself!" he ordered.

Stomach queasy, he reeled away from his brother's fiancée, sweat pouring from his brow and armpits as he damned Lorelle to perdition. His stomach eased when he arrived at the conclusion that this predicament was no fault of his. Gus didn't have to know about it at all. Lorelle was responsible. She had been waiting for someone, and it surely wasn't him, or Gus. She would be no more anxious than he was for anyone to know what had happened. He hoped. Feeling leaden, racked with worry, Yves shuffled toward the opening of the gazebo and into the swinging fist of Gus Telfour.

He awoke some minutes later to see Gus shaking Lorelle so hard her teeth rattled. "I've had enough of playing second to every stud who catches your eye," he told her. "Do you think I don't know what you are? Do you think I don't know you wait here ready to play the doxy for Chane Bellamy while you deny me even a kiss?"

With Lorelle shielding her face, he tossed to her the reticule given him by an efficient maid.

Gus bent over her. Lorelle spit in his eye and laughed, but only until Gus slapped her hard enough to crack her neck. Scared, but defiant still, she rubbed her stinging cheek. "Do you think you can beat Chane Bellamy out of my mind?" she taunted. "Or out of my heart?"

"If that is what it takes," he warned. "It is my curse to love you, Lorelle. But even I have limits." Angrily he wrenched her arm behind her to make certain she listened as he bent his angry face over hers. "You will wed me, Lorelle. You will wed me when I say or you will find yourself on the streets using your talents to buy your bread."

Something about the gleam in his eyes warned Lorelle this was a time when a lie would do better than the truth. "*Oui, Gus,*" she said softly, pretending defeat. "I will wed you when you wish." Loosely wrapped in Yves's frock coat, Lorelle stretched out a hand and laid it on Gus's heaving chest, slowly drawing her fingers downward. "I will need a little time to have my gown made," she said sweetly. "And for Aunt Sophie to plan the festivities."

Gus shuddered and weakened beneath her sensuous touch. "I have a trip at hand," he said, his voice losing the harsh edge. Grimly smiling, he caught her wrist and held it tightly as he slipped a gold-and-emerald ring from his hand and onto the middle finger of hers. "We marry when I return," he said. "And, *bonne amie—*" Gus touched his lips to her forehead "—I will cover you with jewels on our wedding day."

"Truly?" Lorelle smiled then looked slyly away. She knew the journey he spoke of would be the one in pursuit of Chane and the treasure he believed Chane sought. Long before either man set sail she would have gained the treasure she sought.

"Truly," he assured her. Then seeing that Yves stirred said gruffly, "Clothe yourself."

Yves pulled himself to his feet. "I did nothing," he said weakly.

Gus roughly shoved his brother against the fragile lattices, breaking them. "If I thought you had I would have killed you," he growled. As for Chane Bellamy, that coward who had most assuredly slunk away from his rendezvous when he saw Gustave Telfour in the gazebo, Gus's intentions were far less generous.

* * *

The days dragged by at a snail's pace for Ria, partly because her blisters pained her, partly because sitting and waiting left her too much time to think. She ran the gamut of all her troubles beginning with her father's untimely death, her persecution, as she had come to view it, at the hands of Hyatt Landis and now the hostile impasse with Chane Bellamy.

What had developed between Chane and herself had never been part of the bargain. Her feet swathed in compresses made with juice from the aloe plant, she fell back on the softness of a pile of pillows on the comfortable bed she shared with Clair. She had seen a pair of felines mating once, claws and teeth bared, yowling and clawing as if they would leave nothing but hide and bone of each other. They had come together raging still, a vicious mating forced upon them by the primitive instinct that united male and female. With Chane she felt herself dancing the same primitive dance, fighting the intuitive pull of nature, losing the battle.

Ria groaned as the image thrust its way into her fertile imagination. She would not lose. She was no hapless animal driven by nature's fires. She was a woman with a good head on her shoulders, a woman who would choose her destiny rather than be led to it by the impulses of a randy male. She would dress as she pleased and go where she chose. She would not suffer the arrogant captain's rule again.

While Chane offered her much fodder for complaint, she could not fault his family on any count. Their hospitality was excellent. Even while Ria was indisposed, Rose had included Clair in every social function during the busy week of festival. Renaud Bellamy had sent fresh fruits and jelly nuts to aid Ria's recovery, once even stopping by her room to assure himself that she was on the mend.

"If there is time once you recover, I should like to show you Eglantine," he said after presenting her with a tin of nutmeats. He smiled but Ria detected a troubled look in his eyes. "I should like there to be something about your visit to Martinique that is pleasant."

"All of it has been pleasant," Ria lied politely. "And when I recover from the aftereffects of vanity, I should be delighted to see Eglantine." She laughed and wriggled her bare toes. "I have heard it is the grandest of plantations."

Renaud snorted. "My son did not tell you that."

"No," Ria admitted. "But I heard it described. . . ." Her voice trailed off when she saw that Renaud had more to say.

"I have spawned a son who is blind to his heritage and his destiny." He paced to the open window, turned and came back to the foot of her bed, where he stood for a long time looking at her in a curious searching way. Ria feared he had noted the flush that had come to her face or that she was listening too eagerly to what he said of his son. "But perhaps I have no patience." His mood had changed abruptly. Ria suspected he was harboring a smile behind a stoic face and she wondered why. "Perhaps destiny takes care of itself."

The smile broke through as he patted her head and bade her goodbye. He was quite sweet, Ria thought, as was his wife, who had been especially attentive to Clair.

During the few days under Rose's care, Clair had blossomed like one of the sunny hibiscus blossoms so abundant in the garden. Still timid, but now only as became a lady rather than in the cringing, shrinking manner that had made her such a trial that last year in Savannah, Clair outshone every girl in the village. Or so Rose Bellamy proclaimed. Ria did not doubt that in the absence of her young daughter,

Laure, Rose had developed a fondness for her sister. Ria could only be grateful for the change in Clair.

She was especially grateful that Clair had developed enough confidence to do the shopping necessary before the *Aurelia* sailed again. Ria made her list and trusted Clair's judgment of the purchases.

"All will be up to you," Ria told her. "We dare not wait until the last day to shop."

"It will be a change for me to look after you this once," Clair said.

She smiled as Ria counted out a few of the coins she had left. There were not many, but she trusted Clair to make the best possible use of them. Her sister had always had a better eye for fashion, and Rose had directed her to shops where she could find the cool linen blouses and soft cotton skirts they would need when they sailed south.

Clair was ebullient as she set out with Minette carrying a grass basket to hold her purchases. Clair could not remember the last time she had felt money in her pocket and shopped with the freedom to buy. Her enthusiasm for the task heightened as she browsed the crowded shops. In one she chose leather sandals that, because of the way they laced, were sure to fit both her feet and Ria's. In another shop she spent an hour plying among skirts in a palette of colors. She chose some of the boldest colors for Ria, who could carry them off, and for herself muted tones to suit her more subtle coloring.

The blouses, loose garments that could be drawn up high on the throat or worn loose about the shoulders, were delightfully sheer and available in dozens of patterns and colors. Clair chose plain ivory and white since those would blend with any of the skirts. To complete the outfits she selected a girdle and vest that laced about the midriff over blouse and skirt and would fit the loose garments to the figure. Ria's were black, hers a royal blue.

Clair could not resist buying for herself a strand of beads made of creamy white shell and pink coral, and for Ria a set of combs carved of mother-of-pearl, which she rationalized would be useful in controlling her sister's unruly hair. With those luxuries tucked in Minette's basket, most of the shopping was done. All that was left were the last two baffling items on Ria's list: a boy's garments.

Clair could not imagine what use Ria would have for them or where in the shops Rose had recommended she was likely to find any. Deciding Ria intended to make a present of the items to Tad, who had become a friend, she consulted Minette about a shop that would carry them.

"Oui, Mademoiselle Clair," the maid said. "I know a shop that will have exactly what you want. It is a street away, nearer the docks," she explained. "Not far to walk."

Pleased that she would not have to disappoint Ria, Clair willingly followed Minette into what she quickly realized was likely the poorest section of the village. She had begun to worry for her safety when the maid turned a corner and led her into a broad bustling square, which proved to be a market and a favorite gathering spot for both sailors and merchants. Small tables and chairs hugged the narrow walkways between stalls of vegetables and fruits, stacks of coconuts, tables of fresh fish and buckets filled with fist-size oysters.

The "shop" Minette went to turned out to be a stall looked after by her uncle. True to the girl's words the items Ria wanted were there and the price was agreeable. Clair quickly made the final purchases and, smiling proudly, turned to tell Minette she was done.

"You are perhaps hungry, mademoiselle?"

The smell of baking bread from an open-air oven reminded Clair that it was long past lunch. She guessed that

Minette must feel the same. "If you know a place here," Clair said, "we might have tea and a bun."

"*Oui,* mademoiselle!" Minette eagerly took her to an open café where an ebony-skinned woman, a cousin of Minette's, served tea and sweet biscuits. A pot of tea steaming at her table, Clair relaxed in a chair and nibbled a thick biscuit while Minette, nearby, conversed with her relative.

The heat of the sun tempered by the gentle breeze felt delightful on Clair's skin. For once disavowing her need to protect a delicate complexion, she removed her bonnet and looped the ribbons over the back of her chair. The activity in the market reminded her of that of a swarm of bees in search of nectar, a lot of to and fro, a lot of testing and trying as people moved from one colorful stall to another. She tried to take in all that she saw but was soon overcome by a pleasant drowsiness. Indulging herself by closing her eyes and lifting her face to the balmy breeze, she missed a familiar face among those perusing the market.

William Pollack did not miss Clair. Wondering how the girl came to be alone in the market, he edged close to her table, taking care not to give away his presence.

The abrupt but whispered call of a familiar name shook Clair out of her repose and gave Pollack a start. Not wanting to be discovered near the girl, he hid himself behind some bundles of hemp and coils of rope.

"Chane." The call came from amidst the clatter in the market, this time louder and nearer. Clair, immediately alert, gave a quick nervous glance around and observed Captain Bellamy threading through the rows of stalls with the speed and ease of an eel in water. Pursuing him, though hindered by long skirts, was an attractive dark-haired girl.

Clair hoped the captain would not spy her among the throng in the square, but it seemed, to her dismay, she drew his eyes as a magnet draws a scrap of metal. Smiling broadly, he changed his course and steered her way.

"Mademoiselle, I require a favor of you," he said, sliding uninvited into the empty chair at her small table.

"Oh no, I couldn't," Clair said, shaking her head, wanting nothing to do with him.

"You need not do anything," he said, insisting she hear him out. "Except sit quietly and smile."

Lorelle, her professed interest in acquiring a trousseau having gained her liberties, had easily managed to give her maid the slip when she spotted Chane in the market. But now she had lost him as well. Annoyed that he had not heeded her call, she whispered a vicious curse as she bypassed the sweltering heat cast from the market's brick oven. She could scarcely blame Chane for avoiding her after the scene Gus had caused in Savannah. Nevertheless she had to see Chane now. She had to tell him of the danger he was in from Gus the minute he sailed. Stopping to scan the crowd, Lorelle lifted the heavy dark hair from her neck. Chane would be grateful, of course, grateful enough to challenge Gus. And then—

She uttered a cry of delight as she spotted the black curls and the wide shoulders that could only belong to the object of her affection. Hasty steps brought her past the last stall separating them.

"Chane!" she cried. An elated smile showed Lorelle's perfect teeth, dazzling white beneath her red lips. "I was afraid— Oh!" Her black eyes darted across the table to the fair-haired woman who sat timidly sipping tea.

"Lorelle." Chane slapped his knee. "How nice to see you." He nodded to the girl. "I have been looking forward to introducing you to my fiancée, Mademoiselle Clair Kingsley."

"Fiancée!" Lorelle hissed.

Chane feigned a crestfallen look. "I am disappointed," he insisted. "You have already heard the news of my betrothal." Smiling devilishly, he reached across the table to pat Clair's hand.

Clair, more undone than Lorelle, nearly choked on the swallow of tea that had just passed her lips.

"So it is to be like this," Lorelle said icily.

Chane gave her a wide-eyed look of innocence, which changed her mood from chill to hot rage. Putting all her might into the swing, Lorelle stung him with a slap that left the full print of her palm and fingers on his cheek. Then, skirts flying, she ran through the market.

Thinking that he had seen the last of Lorelle and that now she might cease in her pursuit of him and play fair with Gus, Chane turned his branded face to offer an apology to Clair. Clair, however, was already on her feet, having spilled her tea with the abruptness of her move but not caring in the least about the waste. All that mattered to her at the moment was getting away from the contemptible man she could neither appreciate nor understand.

"You must be mad!" she cried. "Minette!" With a quick spin Clair was gone, dashing through the market in the direction opposite to that Lorelle had taken, wondering how such a wretched boor could possibly be the son of Renaud and Rose Bellamy.

Lorelle, blind with rage, ran for the docks, thinking she would throw herself into the warm blue waters and drown. Chane would be sorry then, sorry to have lost Lorelle Telfour. She never reached her destination. Chance sent her on a collision course with a wiry seaman who thought for an instant, as the lovely young woman fell against him in a tangle of limbs, that luck shone on him that day.

When Spruill saw whom he held and considered that she might relay to her cousin and his captain that he had not kept his word and stayed hidden while the *Conquest* was in port, he changed his mind.

"Beggin' yer pardon, Mademoiselle Telfour," he said, pulling his cap low on his brow, hoping she would not know him.

"Spruill, isn't it?" Lorelle said, eyes narrowing as she considered that she was not the one who should suffer for the horrid injustice done her. That reward belonged to Chane Bellamy and his colonial bitch.

"Spruill, aye," the seaman said hesitantly, rocking his weight from one foot to the other.

"Would you like to earn yourself a few pieces of gold, Spruill?" Lorelle offered.

"I am not opposed to that," the seaman replied, his tense shoulders easing. "If 'tis no risk to old Spruill."

"You are not afraid of a woman are you?"

Spruill cackled. "Only if she 'as the pox."

Lorelle drummed her slender fingers together. "I hear there are men who will pay handsomely for a woman," she offered.

"That be true," Spruill responded, thinking he was beginning to catch her meaning. "If she be not much used."

"This one is virgin, I believe." The Kingsley bitch had that untouched look about her.

"Then she be worth 'er weight in gold." His steely gaze met Lorelle's coal black eyes and an understanding was born between them. "In the right place."

"That is the place I want her," Lorelle said coldly. She slipped a handful of coins meant for her trousseau from the lace reticule on her wrist. "But it must not be on this island."

Spruill nodded. "There's a ship 'ere that deals in cargo o' the sort ye mean, the *Madrid*. I can see the girl be in the 'old when she sails."

"It must be soon," Lorelle said. "Tomorrow at the latest. I will make it worth your while," she added. "And what you get for her elsewhere is but gravy on meat."

"I need only know where to find the piece." Spruill cackled.

Lorelle's wary eyes swept the dock but saw only seamen going about their business, none among them who gave a whit that she parleyed with a member of her cousin's crew. William Pollack, who had fled the market rather than have his captain stumble upon him, eased himself against a piling near the pair, pretending to pass the time tying knots in a length of cord. The black-haired girl he did not know, nor she him. Spruill he recognized as the man who had fled the *Aurelia* the night before she sailed. He kept his back to Spruill and his ears open to him and the girl, though he heard but a word or two and learned little other than that the dark-haired beauty was furious with Captain Bellamy and up to no good.

Lorelle leaned in closer to the shifty-eyed sailor who was so eager to accommodate her. "She is no stranger to you, Spruill." Lorelle smiled cruelly. This was far better than drowning herself over a man undeserving of her. Let him suffer. Let him know how it felt to lose someone who mattered. "She is Mademoiselle Clair Kingsley and she is here in Aileron. At the Bellamy house. Monsieur Chane Bellamy's fiancée."

Chapter Eleven

Chane was of the opinion there was but one sensible woman in the world and that was his mother. Clair Kingsley was as flighty as her sister was feisty. He could not imagine why the girl took such issue at doing him a niggling favor. As he saw it he had done a sizable favor for the Kingsley sisters by agreeing to help them in their quest. Mademoiselle Clair had a memory as short as her pretty little nose if she had forgotten what he had suffered at the hands of her sister.

Which brought him to another troubling point. Axel had reported that Ria was indisposed, though he had not been clear on the cause of her malady. Chane wondered if what had passed between them at the ball could have perturbed her so much that she had taken to her bed. He had thought her made of stronger stuff. His father's accusations stung his ears yet. Tonight, though, his mother was dining aboard his ship and he would have the opportunity to learn if he was in any way responsible for Ria's distress.

Unlike the two women who had fled the market, Chane lingered an hour or more tending to the business that had brought him in contact with Lorelle and Clair. He preferred to choose the stores for the *Aurelia* himself, in particular the rum and brandy for his cabin and the barrels of beer for the men. Now that he was not supplying his ship from Eglantine's warehouses, he must select all wares carefully. Some distillers on Martinique did not take the care with their brew that Renaud Bellamy demanded.

He was not anxious to dwell long on remembrances of his father, and he did not. A dozen dipperfuls of beer, a few sample swallows of rum and his troubles were of no more concern than the gadfly that had taken a liking to the scarlet plume attached to his tricorne. That buzzing nuisance he caught and crushed beneath his boot heel.

"Fiancée? You are certain he said fiancée?"

"He told the girl he was betrothed to me." Clair looked up from the sopping lace-edged handkerchief she used to stem her tears. "And when the girl was gone he laughed. At both of us, you can be sure."

Ria was sure of nothing except that she was the greatest of fools to have chosen Chane Bellamy to lead their expedition. She could hardly have fared worse if she had asked Hyatt Landis to captain the *Aurelia*. This, however, was the final straw. The man was deranged. First he mauled her, then he declared himself betrothed to her sister. What was she to make of it? What was she to do about it? The certain answer almost brought tears to her eyes. *Nothing*.

Chane had the map and he was assuredly not about to yield it to her simply because she changed her mind about the choice of a captain. If she welshed on their bargain, he would undoubtedly refuse to relinquish the *Aurelia*. The best she could hope for was that Axel could shed some light on the strange circumstances when he dined with them later in the evening while Rose was out. Axel was loyal to his captain and friend, of course. But he, of the two, she judged honest and sensible. He would help.

"Wash your face, Clair," Ria gently ordered her sister. "Mr. Gresham will arrive within the hour and if you do not stop that crying your face will look like a poached shrimp."

The table was set in the garden, where the bushels of fragrant flowers appeared almost as delectable as the dinner Rose's cook had prepared for the girls and their guest. The fish, so abundant in the waters off Martinique, were prepared in the Creole style as were the spiced fruits and curried rice dishes. Ria's appetite could not do the cook's efforts justice. Clair's was paltrier yet. Axel, however, saved them from insulting the servants by consuming enough of each dish to make it appear they had all partaken.

By the time they were at dessert, a custard floating in a rich sherry sauce, Ria had overcome the case of nerves that suppressed her appetite.

"A peculiar thing happened to Clair in the market today," Ria began. "Captain Bellamy introduced Clair as his fiancée."

Axel's cheeks bulged as he hastily swallowed, sputtered and coughed. His face from brow to throat was bright scarlet by the time he found his voice. "Did he? To whom?"

Though he attempted to sound as if what she had told him was the most normal of statements, Ria noticed that his large fists were tightly clenched around the napkin in his lap.

"To a young woman," she continued, repeating the story as Clair had told it, since her sister would not speak for herself.

"Hmm," was his reply to all she said, but Ria could see that he was deep in thought.

"This young woman was evidently quite disturbed by the news." She pushed the uneaten custard away from her. "As was Clair."

He looked apologetically at Clair. "I regret the experi
ence was distressing to you, mademoiselle. And while
cannot undo what happened—though I wish I could—per
haps if you understood the provocation," he continued
"you would be less upset."

Clair's cheeks flushed. "Perhaps," she said softly.

"This young woman," he inquired, pushing his half-eaten
dessert away and throwing his napkin to the tabletop, "she
was dark-haired?"

"Dark-haired. Dark-eyed," Clair confirmed.

"Did you hear her name?"

"Lorelle."

"Lorelle Telfour," he said as if that explained the whole
of it. "Lorelle was Chane's—Captain Bellamy's— She
was . . ." Bright color suffused his face again. "The girl ha
become a pest."

Ria's face was immediately as bright. "I think we under
stand what she was to Captain Bellamy," she said sharply
"What we do not understand is why Captain Bellamy hu
miliated my sister."

"Chane—Captain Bellamy—he can be impulsive." He
made a penitent nod to Clair. "I assume he hoped to dis
courage Lorelle's unwanted attention by presenting himsel
as an affianced man. I assure you he did not assign the sam
seriousness to the issue as you did, Mademoiselle Clair."

"I suppose it is too much to hope that *he* would apolo
gize to Clair," Ria said. Her displeasure with Chane had no
been lessened by anything Axel had said and, in fact, sh
was more chagrined than before. She wondered if Chane'
association with Lorelle Telfour had begun as had her own

Had the man no feelings for anyone but himself? Wha
of that poor girl Lorelle? How must she feel, disdained b
a man she had trusted? Publicly rebuffed. Stricken with
shame and dread that these things were only the beginning

of what she and Clair might endure from Chane, Ria felt her stomach begin to lurch and churn. Excusing herself before she became ill, Ria hurried inside, leaving Axel and Clair alone in the garden.

Happy for the chance to speak to Clair privately, Axel waited for the door to close behind Ria then riveted his gentle eyes on the blond girl beside him. "Mademoiselle," he stammered. "I cannot actually apologize for the transgressions of another man, but I can assure you will not undergo any further mistreatment from Chane Bellamy. He is brusque. He is cavalier. But he is a good man beneath it all."

"If you say so I believe it," Clair said, feeling the first faint, shy stirrings she had ever felt for a man, and believing that for the first time since the loss of her father she might trust someone other than Ria.

"I will speak to the captain about this. You have my word that he will not humiliate you again," Axel said emphatically, his eyes, all his senses so intent on the lovely girl that he was oblivious to all else.

Axel's and Clair's rapt attention to each other afforded Spruill and the burly mate, Luis, from the *Madrid* a chance to slip through the briar hedge that protected the garden. Scratched but easily concealed in the thick foliage, Spruill and his cohort crept toward the couple. When they sprang the attack both were taken by surprise. Axel leaped to his feet to defend Clair, but Luis, prepared for his move, swung a leather sleeve filled with metal shot at his head. The blow caught Axel squarely in the temple, hewing him down before he could voice an alarm.

Spruill looked at the downed man and cackled. "Tell yer captain 'e'll be needin' a new fiancée."

Clair, stunned speechless, fought but was no match for Spruill. Overpowering her, he clamped a drug-soaked cloth over her mouth and nose. Her final struggles were feeble against Spruill's iron grip and the drug's numbing effect. Terror-ridden to the last, she went slack in the seaman's arms. He eased her to the chair. While Luis hauled Axel out of sight behind a bush, Spruill slipped a dark cape and hood over Clair's shoulders and face.

"Easy as dyin'," Spruill said as they carried her through the garden, out the back gate and into the street, holding her between them as a pair of seamen might a drunken strumpet. Luis, adding to the picture, carried a half-empty bottle of rum and sang at the top of his lungs to allay any suspicion that they were not what they appeared.

Ria heard the off-key song as she emerged from the house to rejoin Axel and her sister. Thinking they were strolling the garden she took her time returning to the table, not concerned until the sight of an overturned chair and a napkin flung on the ground alerted her that something was amiss. Still it was not until she spied one of Clair's kid slippers caught in the gate that she felt as if a hand squeezed her heart.

By then Axel was moaning and struggling to stand. Ria raced to him. "Clair!" she cried. "Where is Clair?"

Trying to get his head clear enough to understand what had happened, Axel first stared blankly at Ria, then at the table where Clair had been. *"Mon Dieu!"* he cried. "They have taken her."

A search of the village failed to turn up a trace of Clair. No one had seen a beautiful blonde with or without a couple of men. Or if they had, they were tight-lipped as was often the case among seagoing men. By nightfall no progress had been made. Neither Renaud's offer of a reward nor Chane's threat of death jarred a memory in the village. Ria was frantic, and Axel almost mad with the knowledge that the girl had been taken forcibly at a moment when he assured her she had his protection.

His injury had prevented his taking part in the search, but once the doctor pronounced him fit he was ready to initiate another hunt on his own. "I would forfeit my life for hers if I could," he solemnly assured Ria. "I will turn the sea out of its shores to find her."

"I cast no blame on you, Axel."

"I cast it at myself," he said bitterly. "I will never forget the way the man laughed as I took the blow. *Mon Dieu!*" he shouted. "I remember the other's words." He looked pointedly at Chane. "The man said tell your captain he will need a new fiancée."

Ria turned on Chane abruptly. "How could he have known—of that? How could anyone?"

Chane's face clouded. He smelled a cunning she-fox in this. "Was there anything familiar about the men?" he begged of Axel.

"The voice was one I've heard before." Axel leaned his pounding head into his hand. Thinking hurt but he had to remember. He forgot the pain when the recollection became clear. "Spruill," he said. "The one who invaded your cabin on the *Aurelia,* Mademoiselle Ria."

"What is this about?" Renaud demanded, having listened to all he could without speaking.

"We had a man make trouble on the *Aurelia* before we sailed from Savannah," Chane explained briefly. "If Axel is right, he is the man who has taken Clair." He rose and, looking like a bull set for a charge, started for the door. "There is but one vessel out of Savannah that has docked here since the *Aurelia.*"

"The Telfour vessel," Renaud said.

He started after his son, but Chane refused his father's help. "I had best see to this alone," he warned.

That he knew a private and unwatched entrance to Lorelle's suite of rooms did not weigh well on his heart as

Chane climbed the English ivy trained to the wall of the
Telfour mansion. In the tropics the ivy grew vines nearly as
stout as a tree trunk and if a man moved fast upon them,
they were as good as a rope. Veiled in darkness, Chane
climbed up and over the wrought-iron balcony. As he expected, the door between Lorelle's bedroom and the balcony was open to the breeze.

Chane crept into the spacious room, needing no light to
guide him to the tester bed where Lorelle Telfour slumbered. She slept nude. He knew that of her just as he knew
which side of the four-posted bed she preferred. Silently he
pulled back the sheer curtain and slipped his hand across her
mouth.

Her dark eyes, like small black pools in the night, opened
wide with fear, then, as she recognized Chane, they registered glee. When he kept his hand across her mouth and she
got a good look at the grim threat in his expression, the
emotion in her eyes reflected the outrage she saw in Chane's.

Easing down beside her, he moved his hand from her lush
mouth to the slender white cord of her throat, daring her to
scream. "Where is the girl?" he whispered hoarsely.

Lorelle curled her fingers into claws but did not strike out.
"How should I know?" she hissed.

He bared his teeth and squeezed her neck lightly. Her
pulse, already rapid as a raging river, leaped faster still. "Do
not tempt me, Lorelle."

"I'm not afraid of you," she countered, gasping a breath.
"You are no murderer."

"No," he said. "I thank the gods I have not joined you
in heaping that sin on my head."

Lorelle blanched. Murder. She had not thought of that.
Her plan to dispose of the girl, her revenge, had sprung
from frenzied rage. She had never considered what the girl's
fate might eventually be. Even so, she did not repent and

confess. The girl might easily come to enjoy her new life. Her heavy-lashed eyes were darkly insolent. Chane was not so saintly himself, a fact she pointed out to him. "You joined me in plenty of other sins," she reminded. "And you liked it."

"I do not deny it, Lorelle," he said icily. "I enjoyed our lovemaking. But I remind you I did not initiate what was between us. And it is over now. Leave me be. Marry Gus while he will still have you."

"Ha! Gus will always wait," she boasted, though she was not as sure as she sounded.

Chane shook his head. "I think not," he warned. "Because tomorrow I will tell Gus and Rossy and all Martinique how you spent every hour of the time you stole away to be with me."

The prospect shook Lorelle more than the possibility that she was a party to murder. She shivered with dread at what might become of her should her uncle and aunt learn of her liaisons with Chane. "I'll tell you where your fancy fiancée is," she said bitterly. "But it will avail you nothing. Not now." The black eyes gleamed with wicked satisfaction. "She is aboard the *Madrid* and the *Madrid* is at sea."

"Bound for what port?" he demanded.

"That I don't know," she replied. "And it would do you no good if I did. She sailed at dusk. You'll not overtake her in time to save your Mademoiselle Kingsley from being sold to a man with a taste for unsullied girls."

"God forgive you, Lorelle," he said, unhanding her as if he held a writhing serpent. And me, he said silently, for getting Clair Kingsley into this. "If I do not find her I will be back, you witless chit," he warned. "Know it."

"Chane." Black hair flowing over her naked shoulders, Lorelle ran after him as he walked to the balcony. "Do you love her so much?"

"Love her?" Chane's laugh was dry. "Not a whit. The girl means nothing to me."

He was over the rail, only a shadow among the vines when Gus Telfour, who had found sleep elusive, chanced to stroll to his window. At first he did not want to believe his eyes. Since the governor's fete, Lorelle had been compliant and pleasantly responsive to him, had led him to believe she had gotten over the folly of desiring Chane Bellamy. Had she not spent the past several days completing her trousseau for their wedding? And now this. Bellamy slinking out of her rooms like a weasel from the coops.

In the first flare of temper Gus threw on his clothes and started out after Chane, prepared to issue a challenge that would end this rivalry once and for all. Before Gus got far, he recalled Chane's sureness with a pistol and skill with a sword. He turned back on the stair. There were better, surer ways to even a score. Biting down angrily on his thin lower lip, Gus headed for Lorelle's room. He would begin with her.

With Axel aboard the *Aurelia,* Chane laid out his plan for finding the *Madrid* and Clair. "We won't find Spruill," he said. "He is wise enough to have gotten himself off Martinique with the *Madrid.* He will have them drop him off at the next port, wherever that is." He muttered a curse. "Someone in Aileron will know where the vessel is bound. I've sent the crew out to scour the village for any word of her destination, and I've offered a reward tempting enough to make them cut the information out of anyone disinclined to tell."

Chane's faith in his crew proved out before two hours had passed. William Pollack dragged aboard the *Aurelia* a sailor lately of the *Madrid*'s crew. "Tell Captain Bellamy what you have told me, mate," Pollack cajoled.

The man, who had taken sick aboard the *Madrid* before she made port in Aileron, fidgeted as he found himself surrounded by the *Aurelia*'s crew.

"'E's a blimey bastard, is Galvez," he stammered. "'E pitched me off the *Madrid* when 'e saw I was poorly."

Chane approached the cowering man. "Galvez is captain of the *Madrid?*" The seaman nodded affirmatively. "I'll see you're compensated for your trouble here if what you tell me is worthwhile," Chane promised. "Where was the *Madrid* bound?"

"Santa Marta," the man said. "An' the girl ye want was rowed out to 'er after she was under way. She ain't the first 'sack o' sugar' Galvez 'as carried to Santa Marta."

"Maybe the last," Chane said harshly. "What will Galvez do with the girl?"

"Sell 'er. There's a man o' wealth in Santa Marta who's got a taste for pale-haired virgins. An' that one Galvez took—I seen 'er in the market—will bring a top price."

Chane knew the man he spoke of, a Spaniard called Juan Santander. He owned a stretch of land running from the coastal Spanish Main to high in the mountains. And he ruled it like a king. Once Clair was within the boundaries of Santander's ranchero no one would bring her out. Immediately Chane knew his choices had narrowed to one. The rescue of Clair Kingsley had to be made before the *Madrid* reached Santa Marta.

A pulse pounding in his forehead, he shouted at his crew. "We sail in an hour!" He ordered a trio of his men to recall those who still searched the village. When they were gone and Pollack and the seaman paid their due, he turned to Axel. "Go for Aurelia Kingsley," he said. "And make certain she wastes no time packing her trunks."

Axel's big jaw fell. "You can't mean to take her along," he protested. "There might be bloodshed. She—"

"Get her," Chane growled. "If we succeed in saving the other girl we will have them together again and we will proceed to the Guiana coast for that blasted treasure of hers." Face grim, he barked more orders to his crew as Axel left the ship in a run.

Axel could not argue with Chane's logic. Clair would need her sister's comfort when they found her. Apart from that, if he knew Ria as he believed he did, she would not want to be left behind.

With Ria on board, her clothes and Clair's stuffed into a single valise, the *Aurelia* hoisted her sail and caught the wind at the appointed time.

Late that night, when the wind carried them and the men had a moment to slacken the pace at which they had worked, William Pollack made himself popular with the whole crew. When it was his turn to sleep he milled around the deck and below sharing the fistful of francs given him by the captain. Distributed man by man the reward was but enough to stand a sailor a short night of drinking in a tavern, but the goodwill it bought was worth more than ten times the amount to Pollack.

Sore-muscled and weary he rued not having come to the captain earlier to report what he had overheard between Spruill and the Telfour woman. He cursed his shortsightedness, but he had not known there was a kidnapping afoot. His regret was not for the fate of Clair Kingsley. He would have nabbed her himself had the opportunity arisen. Pollack did have to admire Spruill's nerve, snatching the girl right out of the Bellamys' garden, but now that Clair was gone, the search for the treasure would be delayed until she was found or determined dead.

For that reason and because of a long-standing desire for a go at Clair Kingsley, William Pollack wished godspeed for her rescue. Satisfied he had made a start at winning the loyalty of the crew, Pollack pitched his hammock on the forecastle. He liked to sleep in the open when he could. A man was safer there than in the hold and got his own air to breathe. Sometimes, if he was fortunate, something more.

Pollack raised his grizzled head from the hammock's rough netting and watched as a lad, too well dressed to be a common seaman, strolled past him on the forecastle. It was not Tad, the cabin boy. Something about the lad did not ring true—the turn of his hips was too round, the shape of his shoulders too slight. Not until the lad pulled the knit cap from his head did Pollack realize whom he watched. Long loose hair streamed out with the wind, red as blood in the moonlight. Aurelia Kingsley, at the rail above one of the gun ports, lifted her face to the midnight sky.

The moon vanished and the girl seemed to go with it, all with a suddenness that sent a chill around William Pollack's heart. He thought of her heritage, recalled a tale of the gory end of a man who had crossed the Black Dawn. Gooseflesh rose on his tough hide, staying until the moon reappeared and the girl was where she had been. Pollack hastily put the lapse of courage out of his mind.

"You there!" The challenge came from the captain. Pollack heard the clack of his boots on the deck and feigned sleep.

Ria heard his approach, too, the step double time as it closed the distance between them. Turning her back on him, she tried unsuccessfully to stuff her windswept hair beneath her cap but missed a few wisping strands.

"Seaman! Identify yourself!" Chane bore down on the man who had been loitering on the forecastle longer than reason allowed. No man of his crew was as small as the fellow he'd observed, not even Tad. He did not like to think he had gotten under way with a stowaway on board. He caught the fellow by the shoulder and bore him around so hard he heard the man groan.

Chane did not believe his eyes when he saw the face, not until he pushed the black stocking cap from the small skull and saw the wild red hair spill out. "Ria!"

Ria pushed his hand from her shoulder. "Yes," she said. "Taking the air if you do not mind. And dressed for it so that even you cannot complain."

"Complain?" Chane allowed his eyes to lock with hers, holding her prisoner beneath his gaze, making her squirm with unease. As if that was not enough he tantalized her by gently grasping an errant strand of her hair and, surprising her further, slowly coiling it around one of his fingers. She found the touch oddly satisfying until he gave the strand a sharp tug and he was once again the Chane Bellamy she knew so well. "I have no complaint, mademoiselle," came his whispered taunt. "Not if you wish to entertain my men."

Ria wondered at his moderated voice and implication until she saw men blatantly staring at the two of them. All who were above deck—some who had been curled up to sleep, others who stood at watch—had turned their eyes to the captain and his oddly garbed passenger. She could feel their stares nearly as tactile as hands upon her, running the length of her and back with a curious yearning gaze.

Chane was no different from the men. His eyes moved like the stroke of unseen fingers from her face to her throat. Though from throat to waist to wrists she was concealed within a man's loose shirt of plain white linen, she felt unnaturally bare. When his probing eyes dropped to the breeches buttoned across her belly and hips the protest waiting on her lips was forgotten.

She freed her hair from his grip, gave her head a shake and said, "I—I think I've had enough air. I'm going below."

Eyes gleaming like a pair of distant stars, teeth shining from within the curve of a savage smile, he approved her decision. "A good idea, mademoiselle. I will escort you."

Ria regained a little of the defiance that had prompted her to dress in shirt and breeches and take herself to the deck. She shrugged away. "Don't trouble yourself," she said.

He laughed softly, making her quiver. "I assure you my only intent is to save myself more misfortune." With that he gripped her upper arm so tight she believed the bone would break if she offered any resistance as he moved her from the forecastle to the companionway's low door.

She felt his harsh grip increasing as he thrust her inside and down the stairwell toward the cabins. Her heart sunk when he dragged her toward his compartment instead of releasing her to enter the one she occupied.

"Whatever you have to say I do not want to hear it," Ria told him.

"But you will," he said roughly and shoved her inside. Chane closed the door with a kick that shook the latch into place. He planted himself so close to Ria that she began to tremble with dread of what might come, and with anticipation if she was honest in her emotions. One brow, a dark stroke on his shadowed face, arched sharply. "Let us understand each other, Ria. I will do my utmost to save your sister. I blame myself for her plight."

"As well you should," Ria said sullenly.

"But," he cautioned, his face like a devil's as he held back his rage, "I will not be mocked or played the fool on my ship, not to salve my guilt, not to satisfy your desire for revenge."

"I will not be locked below," Ria warned, her body betraying her will with a disturbing curl of longing to reach out and touch the contours of the powerful chest so near her. He smelled of salt spray and faintly of bay soap. He had shed his coat while on the quarterdeck. His shirt was damp and clung to his skin, revealing the pattern of black curling hairs on his chest. She remembered how the black pelt tapered and made a dark tempting trail that ran across his belly and farther below. Her eyes followed her thoughts until she realized their transgressing descent and snapped her head up.

"No," he relented. "I grant you that is unkind in this heat. But you come above only when I am above and you stay always within my sight on the quarterdeck." Again he laughed softly, mirthlessly, his mouth afterward forming a diabolical smile. "What you do not know of men is that a week out of port and they will all wish to put themselves between your legs." His eyes were upon her so harshly, his face set in such a spirit of invasion that she wanted to press her stockingd knees together. "And in that outfit," he said bluntly, cruelly, because he wanted to rip the scandalously tight breeches from her hips and sink himself into the carmine center of her soft white flesh, "you only point them the way."

Ria cringed but her heart beat fast and hard inside her chest. "And does that include you, Captain?"

His derisive gaze assailed her, his eyes dark and gleaming. Her taunt had struck open the rage in him, unleashed it with a single slash as if she had taken the sharply honed point of a knife and slit the gossamer hold he had on his longing for her.

"If that is what you like, Mademoiselle Ria," His husky voice raked her, his arms swept around her, his hands hauled her to him like the violent force of a storm-whipped sea. One hand cupped her bottom and dragged her up the length of his thighs, pinioning her pelvis against the engorged flesh that ached to claim her. "Is that why you display your woman's secrets?" he jeered. "Is that why you make the way to them swift and sure?" The other plundering hand found and cupped the curve of her breast beneath the mist-dampened shirt she wore. To her horror Ria saw that the wet garment, pasted to her skin, displayed faint mauve shadows and outlined all too vividly the taut buds of her breasts.

"No," she whispered.

He was beyond absorbing what she said. His eyes, glinting with desire, sought that which filled his hand so softly. "Do you offer them to me, Ria? Again?"

The provocative hands gripped her roughly, triggering a treacherous moan of desire from her lips, drawing his assault there as well. The onslaught of his kiss was reckless, a tidal wave against a tender shore, his mouth the churning sea beating at her lips, his tongue the crest of the swell breaking past a seawall, invading, filling the cavern of her mouth.

The rapturous taste of her, the heady scent of flowers and the sea drove him with the relentless force of the tides. He could not stop himself any more than he could have stemmed a rampant ocean current. He laid her back against the wall, coiled his hands around the soft flesh of her thighs, plunged his hands between them ebbing his fingers to and fro until the weight of her hips came cascading against him, wending the same primitive motion.

His breath was a hot sea wind at her temple. Her body melted, twisted, turned in a whirlpool of desire with him at the core of it, propelling the swirling, maddening rush that welled and washed across the tender reef that guarded her maidenhood. A cry of need tumbled from her lips. "Chane..." she pleaded as a wave of pleasure swept within her, a tiny ripple that swelled and rose and promised.

A rapacious knock and Tad's uneven voice dashed the silvery wave upon the rocks of reality. "Captain, you are needed!" the boy shouted through the timbers of the door.

Chane shoved away from her, his breath a rasp that heaved his chest. His eyed were hooded, still glittering with the dying storm of passion. "Damn you!" he swore.

Ria, trembling, scandalized by her response to him, did not know if he meant her or the cabin boy, who yet rapped and called at the door. But it was her his scathing gaze assaulted. Appalled, feeling as stricken as if she stood stark naked on a street, Ria dropped her head. "I never intended—you complained of my gown before—I only wanted—" she stammered, revealing pitifully, humiliatingly her agony over the first incident, the fateful kiss at the governor's fete.

And now this. Her passion-drugged face, her labored breath told as clear as any voice how she had responded to the foray of his hands, the pleasure it had given her. She shook, like something cast from the sea, unwanted, unworthy. From her eyes tiny salt tears welled and fell.

"Captain!" the boy called.

"I hear!" Chane roared at the door, ending the disturbance. With his heated eyes on Ria his face grew hard, his features sharp and sanguine as a war of emotions took a toll on him. Half of him wanted to finish what he had begun, half of him condemned it. The look of confusion and betrayal on Ria's face, the threatening tears haunted him. She reminded him too plainly of his baser side. She had a gift for bringing it to play and now the added talent of prickling his conscience for his foolhardiness. He could not name what there was about her that drove him beyond reason. She was not the fairest girl who had fired his lust, not the sweetest maid who had set him ablaze. Yet something about her made him as mad and frenzied as a whale beached upon a bar of sand.

"It seems, mademoiselle," he said thickly as his hands worked at tucking in the hem of his rumpled shirt, "that since I met you I am destined always to be apologizing to one Kingsley sister or the other." He walked to the basin and paused to splash cool water on his heated face, used his wet hands to comb down the black curls she had tangled with her fingers. "Had I known where it would lead," he said, drying his hands then tossing the towel carelessly on the floor, "I believe even the lure of Dagian's trove would not have been enough to tempt me to this fate."

"What do I care about treasure?" Ria declared, ashamed of what she had done, chagrined that passion had so easily swept the most important of missions from her mind. "I want to save Clair. If she is lost to me nothing else matters."

He stared at her long and hard, wondering if she meant what she said. In Savannah nothing had mattered more to her than the treasure. At times, he had suspected her to be as treacherous a female as Lorelle Telfour. Even now, believing she would forgo the treasure to save her sister was difficult. He smiled harshly, but of no consequence, since he had every intent of doing both.

Breathing hard, trying to purge the last vestige of ache and need of her from his body, he strolled to the door. "My men will require a good reason to risk their lives," he told her.

"What better reason that saving an innocent girl?" Ria asked incredulously.

His hand to the latch, Chane laughed harshly. "Honor is not so great a commodity among seamen. Any woman's honor is suspect to such men. They work for gain. They will have to know there is some reward to be had for their efforts. They will have to be told of Dagian's trove before we overtake the *Madrid.*"

"You think that wise?" Ria had a vivid image of the crew refusing to save her sister and instead demanding an immediate alteration of course to search for the treasure, that they might sooner have their share.

Eyes glinting, nostrils flared, Chane assessed her, defiant even in desperation. Would she ever heed his warning and stop questioning his judgment? He paused to consider that he had, on several occasions, given her cause to question. Not on this, though, and now he desired her assistance, not her enmity. "I know my men and how to bring them to my will," he said flatly. "They must know they will profit from finding your sister, otherwise they can refuse to stand against the *Madrid* when we overtake her."

"Then do whatever you must," she conceded, at the moment ready to offer all the riches her grandfather had stolen and hidden, anything to assure Clair's rescue.

He nodded. "Tomorrow at first light I will assemble the crew. I want you there, looking like a woman," he added mockingly, looking up and down her much as he had done on deck. "A modest one. Take that garb and cast it in the sea," he sneered. "You must appeal to the decency in the men, while there is some of it left. The rest," he said, his hand lifting the latch, his back to her, "is up to me."

Chapter Twelve

Blue for loyalty, red for courage. Ria chose a striped skirt with the colors needed, colors she hoped would touch a soft spot in the heart of each man of the *Aurelia*'s crew. A blouse of white for purity, Clair's. She was not as sure of her own purity now as she had been at the outset of the journey. No one who remembered and longed for the touch of a man as she did was entirely pure, not even if she tied the blouse's neckline drawstring snugly up to her collarbone.

The black peplumed weskit she chose for sorrow, hers that she might have lost her sister to a fate so dreadful she could not bear to think what it might entail. Her flaming hair she parted and combed into smooth waves held fast with the combs Clair had selected for her. The length of her tresses she smoothed back and twisted into a tight bun she secured with a few scattered hairpins.

Chaste was the look she wanted. A small shaving mirror tacked to the wall hinted she had achieved her goal.

Tad tapped on her door. "The captain is ready," he said. "And the men assembled."

Tremulously, Ria followed the lad up the stairs and through the companionway, past the seamen who stood in wait. The murmur of their voices followed her like the portending fin of a hungry shark, cutting behind her, nipping the hem of her skirt until she had gained the quarterdeck and stood beside the captain.

"Hear this!" he shouted. "Mademoiselle Kingsley wishes to make an appeal."

Ria stepped forward. Having been banished from the deck until they reached Martinique, she recognized none of the crew other than those she had seen while boarding and departing the ship. Save one man. That was Pollack, but she did not expect sympathy from him. She felt the legion of their eyes upon her. All knew of Clair Kingsley's disappearance and that the *Aurelia* was in pursuit of the ship believed to have taken her.

A few knew the blond girl had been taken against her will. Of those, few cared that an injustice had been done. Fewer still would voluntarily lift a finger to save Clair Kingsley. Most of them, as the captain had said, weighed risk against gain. On Ria lay the task of shifting the balance to her favor.

"My sister," she offered, her voice quivering as she looked into the hard faces, the implacable eyes of the crew, "is held captive on a ship called the *Madrid*. We have learned from those who instigated this crime against her," she continued, "that she, an innocent, is to be sold to a man who will use her as a whore and a slave."

"Pity," came a voice and a belying laugh from deep in the throng.

"A pity, yes," Ria said haughtily. "For if it happens, you lose a share of the reward I offer to those who aid in her rescue."

"Gold?" One man stepped forward, a burly fellow big as an oak, his face as pockmarked and rough-skinned as tree bark.

"Gold," Ria repeated. "Enough to take a man from this life to one of ease."

"Does she speak true, Captain?" The man turned his odious face to Chane.

"She does, Gosse," he answered. "She is granddaughter to the Black Dawn and it is his treasure she offers for her sister."

The voices rumbled like thunder as memories strained for an accounting of the loot attributed to the Black Dawn's cursed coffers. Gosse, out of that din, was the first to lend his might to the cause. The best of the lot, he would have been tempted out of sympathy for the girl, but sympathy coupled with a reward hooked him through.

"You have me with you, Captain, mademoiselle!" Gosse shouted.

"We are all or none in this," Chane said, balancing at the edge of the quarterdeck, his men below him except for those aloft who could not leave their posts even for business as important as a girl's life. "If a man of you is not for risking his skin to save the girl, then we turn back now."

William Pollack, lost in the rear of the gathering where Ria had not seen him, stepped forward and lent his assent to the cause, surprising Ria by cajoling the last of the men who resisted joining.

If he'd known he'd be faced with this sorry situation, he'd never have spoken against the sisters. But, if he could sway the crew to his purpose now, he knew he would have them when he needed them later.

"I knew the kidnapped girl in Savannah," Pollack said. "A gentle, sweet thing no man should ill-use." He turned his head to meet the eyes of all who stood around him, nodding to any who had a look of uncertainty, then turned back to make his simple pledge. "I am with you, Captain, and ready to cut the throat of any man who will not aid you."

Pollack got a spirited chorus of agreement from the crew. They liked him already. He had played fair and generous when he had no obligation to one of them.

A cheer rang out across the deck, a cry of affirmation that the *Madrid* and her crew were done for. Pollack congratulated himself. He had saved most likely the treasure. Ria Kingsley, he knew, had the temper her hair hinted at. If she thought her sister doomed because his fellow crewmen refused to aid her, no man on the *Aurelia* would profit from Dagian's rich trove. The treasure map would surely be reduced to ash or sacrificed to Neptune's waiting hand.

Smiling to himself Pollack returned to his post as did the rest of the crew. One slapped his back. Another made a jest of what Pollack had gotten them into with his laudable ideals. Pollack jawed good-naturedly with those who approached him. He had their trust now; he had confirmed it. When the time came they would follow his lead again as they had minutes before, with not much questioning. By then there would be fewer of them to get a share of the waiting treasure. His treasure.

"Well done," Chane told Ria when he came down briefly to join her at a light supper in his compartment, a supper she had agreed to share only because she believed, erroneously, that Axel would join them. "The right mix of gentility and daring. A lady with pirate blood," he said. "What man of the sea could resist following that?"

"Quite a few," she confessed, glancing around nervously to be sure Tad had not left them. "I was not sure of them until the last, when—"

"When Pollack gave you his support?" He drank deeply from a glass of sparkling wine. "You were wrong about Pollack," he said, reminding her of the first quarrel between them, the one that had set the tone for every exchange to follow. "Are you ready to admit it?"

Ria looked guiltily into her glass, but found on the shimmering surface of the red wine a reflection of Chane's handsome visage. She took a long swallow. Had she been wrong about Pollack? Savannah and Hyatt Landis seemed a distant world away, little more than a faded, forgotten care when weighed against her present plight. And yet suspicion nagged and pricked her conscience, robbing her of any gratitude to the man from her past. She would leave William Pollack to his foibles among the shadows of doubt until her heart and head could agree on the true nature of the seaman.

"Pollack was loyal to my father's enemy," she said bluntly. "I find it impossible to believe such a bird could change his feathers."

"He's been a good man," Chane contradicted. "Faithful to his duty, quick to go beyond what is required." He paused as Tad refilled his glass. "I cannot fault him."

"Hyatt Landis felt the same about him," Ria said. "Which is why I find it strange he left that employ to work as a carpenter's mate under your command."

"He is a good man, a better mate than the man before him," Chane responded.

"Even so, you cannot compensate him half what Landis did."

Chane sighed indulgently. "A man does not always take to the sea for the sake of a fortune," he said. Even so she had raised a question in his mind. The work of a ship's carpenter was hard and ofttimes dangerous. "I know you despise Landis," he remarked, "and it was clear he held some animosity for you. I do not know or understand the cause of the discord between you."

Tongue loosened by the wine, Ria, after a moment of hesitation, poured out her story to Chane Bellamy, telling of the privilege and prosperity that marked her life while her father was alive. Palmira had been one of the richest plantations in the Georgia colony, her father among the most astute planters and merchants. A charitable man, he had not turned his back on those who had less. He had sponsored many young men of integrity toward a like prosperity, among them Hyatt Landis.

She told of her father's mounting dissatisfaction with the British crown and of his eventual devotion to the cause of revolution; how, when under siege, he had bound the people of Savannah in a spirit of resistance to the British forces descending on them.

"He was betrayed," she said sadly. "Blamed for leading the British through the swamps and to a slaughter upon his unsuspecting men. Before my father could prove his innocence he was murdered by men under his own command, men who had known him all their lives, men who knew him incapable of treason, men like Hyatt Landis."

"You think Landis was the one who betrayed him?"

"I do," Ria said. "Landis, a penniless solicitor, was my father's most recent protégé in business. After his death we discovered Landis had power over my father's holdings. He told Clair and me there was little left, that my father had mismanaged his business and that was the chief reason Marcus Kingsley had betrayed his cause. He said that my father feared independence from Britain would cost him the business associations he needed to replenish his fortune."

"Was there not an investigation? Evidence offered to support the charge of treason?"

Ria nodded. "One that took all of an hour. A man, not one of my father's, himself accused, testified that my father had ordered him to lead the British upon the sleeping encampment. The wretch was pardoned but disappeared shortly afterward. My father's death was termed accidental by the military court. Clair and I found ourselves virtual paupers afterward. What property of my father's that remained had been willed to his widow, including Palmira. Hyatt Landis, my father's former solicitor, was suddenly a man of wealth.''

Chane lapsed silent. He could understand Ria's distrust of Landis. Had he not also been suspicious of the man? Incensed by the injustice the girls had suffered, he could understand Ria's determination to seize upon the opportunity her grandfather's map offered.

''Will you return to Savannah when you have the treasure?'' he asked. ''Will you avenge your father?''

''I have thought of nothing else since his death.'' Ria dropped her lids to conceal the hurt in her eyes. ''And when I learned of the treasure, I believed that if I had the money to further my cause I could prove Landis's duplicity and clear my father's name.''

''And you no longer think that possible?''

She pushed her empty glass aside. ''With Clair's life in jeopardy it hardly seems the most important endeavor.'' Her voice broke, her open pain touching a tender chord in Chane's heart, making him regret briefly that he had added to her misery. ''Have we truly a chance to save her?'' She looked pleadingly at him. ''Or is this attempt to overtake the *Madrid* only a desperate ploy?''

''No ploy,'' he assured her, hoping he told the truth. He was on his feet and at the map table a moment later and beckoning Ria to his side. ''If the *Madrid* puts in first at St. Lucia, as I believe, then swung south to these lanes, we should overtake her here.'' He had learned of Spruill's family connection to a fiend of a man who once worked for his father. Both had come to Martinique from St. Lucia. His guess was that Spruill would hide out where he had family and friends until he was sure the *Aurelia* had left Martinique.

With a steady finger Chane traced the lines he had charted and where they met, forming an imaginary mark above the intercept point. "She is a cumbersome vessel lacking the *Aurelia*'s speed. And she will not expect us to look for her this far south," he said. "If I am right we will overtake her late in the day. Before sundown if we are lucky. The crew is armed, the guns ready. And you, mademoiselle," he ordered, though his usually brusque voice was tempered by a gentler tone, "will remain here in my cabin until the fighting is done."

"I will," she promised. For once Ria was willing to agree to his command, though if she had possessed the skill to fight like a man nothing would have barred her from being in the thick of the battle to save her sister.

Chane did not go below again before the sun fell. He had not been lucky enough to overtake the *Madrid* before nightfall. Because he had not, the *Aurelia* cruised with her lanterns out, even the cook's stove cold in the galley lest a spark or drifting plume of smoke give them away before she spotted the *Madrid*. Two hours after midnight, the man on watch from the foretop spied a league and a half away the lights of a ship that was surely the *Madrid*.

Giving his men orders to hold the distance between the *Aurelia* and their quarry, Chane went to his cabin for a short rest before the dawn. He had forgotten about Ria. He found her curled on the cushion of a window bench in a soft wash of moonlight, lost in sleep, looking innocent with her hands folded beneath a smooth cheek, her hair in a long braid that coiled like a shining satin ribbon over one shoulder.

There was nothing innocent in the quickening of his loins, nothing pure about the dry ache in his throat as he recalled the fiery sweetness of her parted lips. Tempted, he crossed the compartment and with the quietest of movement touched the bow of her mouth gently with a single finger, touched rose red lips soft as petals, lips that had never succeeded in slaking his thirst for more of their delectable nectar.

Breathing out a long solemn sigh, he left her when he saw that he had caused her limbs to stir. He would get no sleep at all if he wakened her, not if he wanted the girl this badly, not if a look from her soft green eyes drove reason from his mind so easily. With eyes closed, Chane turned away from her. He needed his wits about him when the *Madrid* saw, at first light, that they were discovered.

Ria awoke to the sound of shouts and, confused at first by her strange surroundings, tumbled from the narrow bench where she had slept. Startled wide-awake by the fall, she rose quickly and flew to the bank of stern windows in the great cabin. Fumbling at the latches, she cried out her despair. Finally, after a minute of effort, her unwieldy fingers obeyed and she flung open one sash. She saw that the *Aurelia* pulled abreast of another vessel.

Her rapidly pounding heart skittered and her knees shook when she saw the identifying letters painted in black and gold on the vessel's stern—*Madrid*.

"Clair!" Ria cried frantically when she saw pressed at a porthole glass the desperate, terrified face of her sister. Ria marked the window in her mind, glad she had done so an instant later when Clair's image behind the glass disappeared. A brittle ball of anguish formed in her stomach. Was Clair gone because of fear or force? Should she break her word and hurry to the quarterdeck to tell Chane where Clair was held?

Distraught, anxious for Clair's safety, Ria wondered and worried on both matters. Then she found a third to disturb her, considering for the first time the possibility that the *Aurelia*'s forces might be overcome. If so, Ria would be alone and defenseless below deck. Even Tad had gone above for the encounter.

She began to scramble through the cupboards and chests in search of a weapon, hoping to find the one the captain had taken from her the night she shot him. That flintlock pistol, which had once belonged to Marcus Kingsley, fit comfortably in her hand. She knew its workings well enough to use it, even if her aim was less than true. Unless Chane had given the pistol to one of his men it was among his things.

There! Ria snatched the flat leather case that held the flintlock from the tray of a chest. Breathless, she sat down to load the weapon.

From the quarterdeck Chane ordered the three-pounders and the swivel guns on the port side of the *Aurelia* to be made ready to fire as, from the forecastle, Axel signaled the *Madrid* to bring her to. The confusion on the *Madrid*'s deck showed her lack of preparation for an attack. The men, acknowledging by their behavior that they were a slovenly crew, ran from their quarters, several jumping upon the quarterdeck in an attempt to strike the flag and surrender before the *Aurelia* fired a broadside.

Galvez, the *Madrid*'s captain, and Luis, his lieutenant, cut down two of their own crew and tossed the bodies to the lower deck as a warning to any others who might attempt a mutiny under fire. But Galvez's desperation was his undoing. Half his guns were without powder at their ports, half his crew, men he had forcibly impressed and with no wish to die for him, dived down the main hatch when the *Aurelia* fired a warning volley across her stem.

"Return fire!" the Spaniard shouted at the top of his formidable lungs.

The gunner at the *Madrid*'s forward gun did as ordered but the ball struck the water short of its target. The *Aurelia*'s second salvo clipped the *Madrid*'s bowsprit; a third cut her mizzenmast and brought the heavy yard and sail smashing onto the quarterdeck. Galvez leaped clear before the crash but Luis went down beneath the splintered mast and heavy rigging. With him six of the *Madrid*'s crew were lost as well.

"Fire!" shouted Galvez. Another gun opened up and fired. This one struck, boring a hole the size of a man's head through the *Aurelia*'s rudder, splitting it off and shearing the head. The jolt from immediately beneath her almost toppled Ria out the open window of the captain's quarters. Stunned, she drew back and out of sight until she felt and heard the *Aurelia* fire a fourth volley.

The victorious shout from the *Aurelia*'s crew brought Ria forth for a timorous look at the damage done. The fourth volley had hit the *Madrid*'s hull at the waterline. Another as well placed would sink her and Galvez knew it.

"Bring up the girl!" the Spaniard yelled.

The *Aurelia* was close enough for her crew to throw grappling lines and swing across for hand-to-hand fighting if it was called for. Galvez had not yet struck his flag, but Chane held back his men when he saw the Spanish captain clutch a handful of blond hair and, leading Clair by the head, bring her into clear view.

"Stay!" Chane shouted to the first wave of sailors ready to rappel to the *Madrid*.

Galvez hoisted Clair to the near rail and, with her arm twisted painfully behind her back, held her teetering over the water. "Eez theez what you seek, Bellamy?"

Flintlock in hand, Ria watched from the window. She choked back a scream when she saw her sister manhandled by Galvez. She feared, as she had never feared anything, what Galvez would do. The water below Clair teemed with debris from the *Madrid*'s shattered hull and deck, sharp splinters of wood, coils of rope and rigging, any of which could kill Clair should she fall. Even if her sister survived a fall, Ria knew as no one else did that Clair Kingsley could not swim. If Galvez let Clair fall into the sea, her heavy skirts would carry her under as surely as an anchor tied to her limbs.

"Harm the girl and you forfeit your ship and your life, Galvez!" Chane warned. "Give her up unhurt and we will leave you to patch your ship and sail again."

"She eez worth a hundred pieces of gold to me!" the Spaniard retorted. "Pay or lose her!"

Chane raised his arm and signaled his men to fire when he lowered it. The *Madrid*'s crew rushed to the rail and, defying their captain, begged Chane to hold back. None, however, dared challenge Galvez who brandished a pair of deadly pistols in his chest bands and was known for his cruel accuracy with the sword. The deadlock lasted five minutes, ten. All the while Chane's hand remained aloft. Across from him Clair had gone limp, hanging on the rail only because Galvez cruelly held her arm.

"Yield, Galvez!" Chane shouted, fearing that if he ordered the guns fired Clair Kingsley would not survive her plunge to the water.

The deadlock broke when a man of Galvez's crew cracked from the strain before his captain and yielded. Drawing his sword, he blindsided the Spaniard, or so he thought. Galvez, alert to all sides, heard the man's approach, turned and fired, lodging a pistol ball in his attacker's leg. Wounded, the man reeled off balance and, unexpectedly, into Galvez before the captain drew his other pistol.

The hold Galvez had on Clair Kingsley slipped as he fought with the wounded crewman. When another man came on the heels of that one to seize the pistol from Galvez's band, the captain lost his grip on Clair completely.

Ria screamed. Clair, in a faint, slumped, tottered on the rail and in an instant pitched headfirst over the edge, miraculously missing the debris below. She plunged deep into the water and was gone. Ria, thinking herself as near as any to where her sister had fallen, threw down her pistol, ripped away her red-and-blue skirt and flung herself from one of the stern windows. She did not clear the surface before Chane likewise threw off the weightiest of his garments and flung himself into the dangerous blue waters.

On board the *Madrid,* the crew ended Galvez's tenure as captain of the vessel, killing him with his own pistol before the fate of the tyrant's last victim was known.

Eyes open to the stinging salt water, nose burning from the bite of the brine, Ria saw the treacherous barnacled ribs of the *Madrid*'s hull. A few feet away and in danger of being swept beneath and against the razor-sharp barnacles was Clair, her full skirt floating like a bell in the water as Clair hung suspended a foot or two below the surface. Her long loose hair had snagged on a piece of flotsam at the surface. That alone had saved her from sinking into the dark water beneath the ship.

Ria kicked and swam furiously to put herself between the *Madrid* and Clair, that she might give her sister a boost to the surface. Before she reached her sister, the *Madrid,* taking on water, listed to the larboard side. A portion of her hull struck Ria's shoulder before she could swim clear. Pain sharp and cold, tore down her back.

Lungs bursting, one side of her feeling as if it had been torn asunder, Ria swam desperately for the surface and the portion of masthead around which Clair's hair had tangled. Before she reached it, she saw the shorn wood dip under the water and stream away from her. Giving an anguished sputtering cry and defying the dizzying sweep of pain that gripped her back, Ria dove beneath the surface for her sister. Though nearly blind from the salt water in her eyes and the agony of its sting in her wound, she thought that she saw Clair swept upward by a twisting black-limbed creature that had caught and folded the drowning girl over its back.

Three bodies broke into light and air at the same moment, Ria with an agonized cry, Chane with a curse on his lips and Clair, blue-faced, no sign of breath in her lungs.

"Throw a line," Chane shouted, treading furiously with his strong legs to hold both Clair and himself above water. He was obeyed before the echo of the words died.

"She's not dead," Ria vowed as she worked furiously mindless of the racking pain, to free her sister's hair from the flotsam.

"*Mon Dieu!*" Chane swore, feeling his heart squeeze off beating as he saw the widening halo of blood around Ria's neck and shoulders. "Another line!" he shouted, working against time and the inevitability of unwelcome company in the shark-infested waters off Santa Marta. With Clair secured he turned to Ria, saw that her strength was fading and that, as he feared, the scent of her blood and his thrashing had drawn sharks. Gray-black bodies circled beneath them one, the largest of three, bumped his thigh with a fin. "Hold still," he called to Ria, who had seen them too.

Easing his legs upward in the water, Chane floated on his back, conserving all movement as he reached for Ria's outstretched hand. Slowly he brought her toward the dangling safety line. "I have it," she gasped, her fingers anxiously clutching the wet hemp. "But I don't think I can hold on." Her right arm felt numb, her head light, the weight of her body like a sinking rock as she tried to hoist herself from the water.

Seeing that Axel was towing the unconscious Clair to the *Aurelia*'s deck and safety, Chane eased alongside Ria in the water, getting one hand on the rope and the other around her rib cage. Molding his body against hers, feeling a quick reaction in his loins even in this moment of duress, Chane muttered a curse for that part of him that wanted her even when his life and hers were at stake. The curse did not hold back his arousal, as he slid the rope around Ria and tied it off in a sturdy knot beneath her soft, unbound breasts.

Dazed by shock and the loss of blood, Ria felt Chane pressed against her, his hard body, his maleness as threatening to her well-being as the frenzied sharks who had smelled her blood. But she was too weak to fight him or her fluttering reaction to him. Strength declining, Ria felt her head loll back against Chane's shoulder and she surrendered to his arms and the loop of rope he'd secured around her. She trembled uncontrollably when his corded legs wrapped around hers and the heavy thrust of his manhood lay against her soft buttocks.

"Damn you, Ria," Chane swore softly in her ear as the whole of her body melted against his and he was set afire with wondering how much sweeter the feel of her would be were he deep in her lush flesh. "Why could you not stay put in the cabin?" he chastised.

"I saw Clair fall," she mumbled. "She doesn't swim." Drawing warm, restorative heat from him, wondering dimly

why the accusing tone of his voice did not match the ten
derness of his embrace, Ria slackened still more against him

Chane groaned. Her legs were bare, her skin like fine sil
beneath his hand as he supported her limp frame, scarcel
able to refrain from exploring the gentle curves and tempt
ing places beneath the short garment she wore.

Except for the danger of the sharks, still circling, he coul
take her where they were, his need of her so great he coul
make love to her in the water, mindless of the crews of th
Madrid and the *Aurelia,* who watched from the decks.

"Heave!" he called out to those who manned the rope
The sharks were getting bolder, bumping his legs and Ria's
perhaps sensing they might lose their prey. A pair of th
scavengers skimmed the surface, searching for the lost mea
their tail fins like pirate sails, as the men hoisted Chane an
Ria clear of the water.

He wrapped her in his arms as they tumbled onto th
deck, covering as much of her near-nakedness as he coul
until Tad threw his captain's discarded coat around her.

"Clair!" Ria cried, the sight of her sister reviving he
strength.

With Clair stretched out on her stomach, Axel straddle
her back, applying pressure to her bloated chest, squeez
ing, lifting, pressing the water from her lungs.

Ria, drenched, her naked legs in a crouch, joined in th
effort. She cradled her sister's head in her hands and waite
what seemed an eternity for a sign of life. It came after the
seemed no hope—a gush of water from Clair's open mouth
a twitch, a cough and then a cry as her hand curled feeb
around Ria's.

"You're safe, Clair. Safe now," Ria assured her siste
"Get her below," she said to Axel. "Tad, bring blankets a
the brandy from the captain's cabin."

Axel Gresham nodded and smiled, but a tear he did not bother to wipe away tumbled down his bristled cheek. Effortlessly, he lifted Clair into his arms, paused as he got a hurrah from the crew, then carried her to the companionway. From behind her Ria heard Chane breathe a great ragged sigh of relief, then he was bounding across the deck, hair and clothes dripping, commending his men for their steadfastness as Ria and Tad departed the deck.

"Send the skiff over and bring on board the wounded crewman," he ordered. "Tell the others we will take to port any one of them who wishes to quit the *Madrid*. Those who want to stay with her have my accord to do as they wish. We'll do no looting," he shouted, reading the mood of a segment of his crew as he strapped his pistol and sword to his lean hips. "We are not a pirate band. Move now! Make haste!" he shouted. "The rotten sight of her sickens me."

The men moved off, doing as their captain had ordered, though not without a grumble or two once out of earshot of their leader. "Maybe 'is pockets be full but mine are not," said the seaman Norbie to the hefty Gosse.

"Cap'n Bellamy 'as been fair with us," Gosse countered. "'E backed Galvez down an' not a man o' us got a scratch from the ruckus."

"Aye, that be true," said Norbie. "But the captain got what 'e wanted from it, another fair lass for 'is bed."

A third man joined in the lowering of the skiff and climbed down with Gosse and the others. "Did ye see 'em on the red-haired wench in the water?"

"Aye," said Norbie and laughed. "I'd 'ave 'umped her too, 'er with nothin' but the sea between me and 'er 'arbor."

Laughing, even Gosse joining in, the three cast off for the *Madrid*.

An hour after the fray ended the *Aurelia* made sail, not toward the harbor at Santa Marta, which was nearest. Chane was uncertain of his welcome in the *Madrid*'s home port. He set his course for the isle of Aruba, where he could make repairs to the damaged rudder and replenish the supplies for the voyage to the Guiana coast. The *Aurelia* had suffered no other loss, but she was unwieldy with her rudder split. For where they were going next, Chane wanted his vessel at her fittest and fastest.

Three of the *Madrid*'s crew elected to join with him. The others, seeing an opportunity in remaining with their captainless ship and making her seaworthy again, chose to stay.

In their cabin Ria, ignoring her injury until she was sure of Clair's recovery, comforted her sister and offered a prayer of thanks for her safe return. But she grieved a little, too. Gone was the vivacious Clair who had emerged in Martinique. Now her sister was more subdued than ever, fearful of the slightest sound, afraid to allow Ria out of her sight. Of her ordeal aboard the *Madrid* she would not utter a word. That, above all, tore at Ria's heart.

Chapter Thirteen

Clair fell asleep clutching Ria's hand, and Ria, more bogged in guilt than pain, sat wet and shivering at her bedside.

"If you do not allow me to tend that cut, tomorrow you will need your sister to care for you," Tad threatened. The welfare of both Kingsley sisters had been heaped on his head by a captain Tad thought remarkably contrary for a man who had proved himself victorious over a foe.

Ria glanced at the boy nervously shuffling his weight from one skinny leg to the other, while he eyed the box of medical supplies he had brought to the cabin. He was right. She remembered well enough how Chane's neglected wound had quickly festered in the tropic heat. She had swallowed a sizable amount of water, too, and if that did not make her ill, staying wet after suffering shock surely would.

The possibility of finding herself unable to care for Clair prompted Ria to action. Tad would have to clean her wound. There was no one else to do it since she could not possibly reach the affected area, not even when the feeling in her arm had returned. Groaning as she carefully slipped her hand free of Clair's, Ria stood and stretched her knotted and complaining muscles. She almost wished her arm had remained numb. One entire side of her ached as if it had an arrow embedded in it.

"Give me a minute to slip out of these clothes," Ria told the cabin boy. "Then you may do whatever is necessary."

Tad fled the cabin and Ria peeled the captain's coat and her ripped blouse from her shoulders, wincing as she lifted her arms over her head. Taking a minute to tie up her tangled wet hair out of the way, Ria then snatched a sheet from the bed, draped it around her and called the boy. Before he started the tending of her wound, which she dreaded, she asked him for a glass of brandy, hoping it would warm her shivering flesh and undo whatever ill a belly full of seawater might cause.

Tad plainly found his stint as surgeon's mate distasteful, a tribute to his youth rather than his lack of concern for Ria Kingsley. He liked her plenty, but the idea of washing and applying ointment to a woman's naked back had him scarlet-skinned and shaking. Gangly to begin with, Tad stumbled over his long feet coming across the cabin, and at her bedside, dropped the pot of ointment before he got control of his trembling knees and hands.

Modesty was practically a stranger to Ria's mind under the circumstances. Urging him to proceed, she loosened the veiling sheet to expose her back and sat tiredly on the corner of her berth, the white folds of cloth held firmly to her breast while on the back side the edges of it floated open down to the dimples above her buttocks.

"That must hurt," Tad mumbled, his eyes lingering on the deep and jagged gash which ran a good six inches across her upper back.

"It does, so take heed that you do not add to the pain," Ria warned. Staying him a moment more, Ria drank deeply of the brandy, choking and coughing as it scorched her blistered throat.

Tad waited and, when she had drunk her fill, set the glass aside. He was more nervous than she as he gently sponged the blood-caked skin with a cloth dipped into a basin of warm water.

"How does it look?" Ria questioned, glancing over her shoulder at the boy.

"Goo— Bad!" he said, nudging her head to the front. "Like you lost a foot of hide at least. Must have smarted like the devil when you did it. I know I couldn't have stood it, then or afterward. All that blood and the sharks about." He dropped the soiled cloth in the basin and picked up a towel to blot her skin dry, never pausing in his nervous prattle. "The cut is not so deep as I thought before I cleaned it," he said. "No stitch is needed but you will be sore as the dickens a long while and there may be a small scar."

"Oh," Ria said, rolling her aching shoulder back so that the sheet clutched to her breast inadvertently fell lower on her bosom.

It was not the dazzling cleavage that held Tad spellbound. He had found an equally amazing sight, one that had him swallowing a surprised gasp. Slightly above the crest of Ria's left breast was an odd mark shaped like a flaring sun, black and red, inked into the pale skin.

Rough sailors wore such marks, but he had never imagined that a beautiful woman would submit to such torture as a tattoo required.

Tad stopped dabbing Ria's skin with the towel, stopped everything except staring mutely at the mark on Ria's creamy shoulder. Entranced by the tattoo, he did not notice that the cabin door swung fro nor did he hear the long stride of Chane Bellamy until the captain caught him by the collar and hauled him out of the compartment.

"See to my dinner!" Chane shouted brusquely to the boy when he had set him upright in the hallway.

Tensed, Ria twisted around to give Chane a piece of her mind. "He was not done with me," she said, haughtily tossing the sheet over her shoulder so that it hung around her like a toga.

"About as done as a boy should be at his age," Chane returned, a sneer in his tone. He gave the door a kick that slammed it shut. "Does it give you pleasure to tempt a lad who cannot possibly deliver what he might promise?"

It was too much, his idiotic temper, his impossible logic, both directed at a hapless lad. She had felt the brunt of it too often herself, and this, when both she and Clair had been but a step from death, was too much. "You, sir, are the offspring of an ass!" With that jabbing remark on her lips Ria spun off the bed, and seeing a black mist of rage before her eyes, swung fiercely at his face.

Chane, undaunted, broke her swing by swiftly capturing her wrist. "And you are a ship's cat," he retorted. "Chasing anything and everything."

"I have had enough of your insinuations," she said. "I am neither cat nor tart! Least of all your tart!" She jerked her arm from his, wincing as a spasm gripped a sore, misused muscle.

Seeing that he had pained her, Chane frowned, ruefully admitting to himself that he had come to the cabin with the honorable purpose of assuring himself that she and her sister would recover quickly and completely. Seeing Tad ogle her had set him off before he took the time to consider how ridiculous his response was. Contrite, angry at himself, he bowed slightly to her. "Once again I must apologize, mademoiselle," he said. "The first and foremost line of conversation between us."

"I do not need apologies," Ria spit back, eyes lit with anger and glittering like shards of green glass. "I do need

Tad to apply that ointment to my back," she admonished. "If you will kindly call him to the cabin so—"

Chane, wishing to make amends, gently put his hand on her injured shoulder and turned her around. "I am sorry," he said softly. "You did not see the state you put the boy in."

"He is but a boy," Ria reminded, imagining, ridiculously, that she felt a genuine tenderness in Chane's touch. Responding to it she allowed him to guide her to the connecting room and to sit her down upon the berth.

"I will dress the wound," he said. "I owe you the favor."

Ria submitted to his handling of her injury. He was sure to be more skilled than Tad and, she basely admitted, she liked the idea of his waiting upon her. Sitting cross-legged on the berth, Ria moaned softly as he rubbed on medication and folded, with exceeding care, strips of clean bandage over the cut.

The sting of it had diminished by the time he finished, either from the power of the brandy in her system or from the strength of the ointment he applied. He did not, however, stop at applying the soothing concoction and a covering to her wound. His hands, when done at that task, tarried on her tight shoulders, kneading, rubbing, working out the soreness in the stretched and abused muscles.

Ria yielded completely, his gentle ministrations leaving her drowsy, his warm, skilled fingers easing the lingering tension from her body and mind. "Feels good," she mumbled, rolling her head with the rhythm of his kneading. "I could...umm..."

"Ria?" Chane had intended only to aid Ria in relaxing enough that she might rest after her ordeal. As was usually the way of things when he was with her, nothing went as planned. His hands moved over her shoulders, seemingly of

their own volition, coveting more of her. He yielded to their
misguided descent, sweeping his palms recklessly over the
sweet rounded mounds of delight the loosely draped sheet
revealed to his hungering eyes.

And when she did not resist him, did not ward him off
with word or move, he slid to the narrow berth beside her,
his hands around her waist, lips at her throat like a flame.
Pangs of guilt, as misguided within him now as his unbridled temper had been minutes before, rose to condemn what
he had begun. He had not come to her for this. He had not
come to make love to her, not when she was weak and
frightened, exhausted from the events of the day. But that
was surely what he would do if in another moment she did
not tell him nay.

"Ria," he whispered hoarsely, crushing down his mind's
valiant effort to resist what his body desired and demanded. "I have wanted you, my sweet *diablesse*," he
whispered. "I have wanted you since the first fiery lash of
your temper struck me as I stood unsuspecting on that sorry
wharf in Savannah. How you flew at us, Landis and me,
lashing at the both of us, leaving welts on innocent and
guilty. I felt myself stung to the quick by a vicious she-devil
who had materialized out of the wind." He laughed, his
breath rasping and hot against her throat. "I could have
hauled you aboard the *Aurelia* that very day and torn that
prudish dress off your delectable little body. I could have
made love to you then, claimed you, tried to tame you. I
knew I must, someday," he whispered. "Inevitably." His
mouth swooped to hers, seizing the softness and pillaging
for the treasure locked within. "Witch," he whispered,
pulling away to pluck the ribbon from her hair so that it fell
like a rippling skein of red silk over both of them.

Sea-scented, damp, exhausted, the shielding wrap of the
sheet gone from her shoulders and spread on the berth

where it might best serve, Ria yielded to the weakness made greater by the brandy and the sensuously hypnotic stroke of his hands.

Enthralled, she languished in his arms, head thrown back and her white throat bared to him, a storm rising in her body, wind and rain and lightning. An incredible thrill, roaring like thunder through her, came as he eased her across his thighs, turned her so that she faced him. Against him he felt the charge of the storm in his taut body, electric, wild, a fury ready to spring forth.

Ria's head spun. Sensations new and wanton roiled within, burning her like a fever, chilling her like a north wind. Chane's arms folded her, his eyes dark with passion fiercely electrifying, his mouth consuming, dizzying her with kisses.

Deep in her churning, overwrought mind Ria knew there was more to be said and understood between them before the intimacy that was inevitable became complete, exacting and irrevocable. Yielding to the sweep of the storm was easier than fumbling with the burden of reason. She could fly with the storm, ride on the wind, touch the turbulent clouds of passion, unquestioning, if she dared.

Low in her throat she moaned, her head, heavy, reeling, bobbling on a neck suddenly unable to hold it upright. At her thighs Chane tugged possessively, lifting her astride him, knowing that to lay her down would be unbearably painful and that this first time for her must be all pleasure. He demanded that of himself even as his need grew, surging like a gale in his loins, raging like a tempest in his veins.

"How I want you, Ria." His mouth moved on her breast, his tongue lashing out to curl and tease the tight rosy bud. "How I need you, sweet *diablesse!*" Hands wrapping her waist, he lifted her, his mouth a hot biting wind traversing her flat belly, tormenting as he made his plea. "I must have you, Ria."

A hot, searing bolt of lighting struck the core of her as she strained and involuntarily rolled her hips against him. "Yes, oh yes," she whispered into a burgeoning wind, a spiraling current that drained her of sensibility and reason. Her heart pounded as if it would split at the walls, her lungs convulsed and ached as if they would burst. "Chane..." she gasped, clutching him, as the last wind-tossed leaves of reason swept from her, leaving her lost in a choking, dizzying fog. The compartment turned, the ship spun end over end. And Ria, brandied, battered and beguiled, tumbled from Chane's arms into a dead faint.

"Mon Dieu!" Chane swore. "Ria!" He held her tenderly in his arms, castigating himself with shame as he remembered the extent of her injury, the amount of blood that had flowed from the wound before he pulled her from the sea. By all of hell! He was the grandest of fools. The greatest of knaves. He would have forced himself on her, filled her with his raging passion when what she needed most was rest and sleep.

Laughing harshly at his folly, unable to stifle the echo of his conscience, Chane gently eased Ria beneath the sheet, plumped a pillow beneath her head and called Tad to sit the night in her cabin. He had no patience for the boy's diffidence to his orders. He could read what was in Tad's mind and, as it was not so far from the truth, he did not bother to deny that he had made love to Ria Kingsley.

The time would soon come when he would.

A pair of chains rigged to what remained of her rudder, the *Aurelia* made slow headway toward Aruba. Adding to the difficulty was a near calm that made the sails almost as useless as the rudder.

Ria awoke to the strange sensation of a motionless ship, her back feeling as if it had taken a brutal flogging. She felt too weak to open her eyes until she recalled that while she slept Clair had been alone. Stricken that she had been negligent in her duty, Ria pushed up on her elbows and attempted to sit up.

"Lord of mercy!" she cried weakly, aware in that moment of another presence in the room and that beneath the sheets she was as naked as— "Chane?" she whispered, her last waking moment in his arms coming vividly to mind. Flushed, feeling fevered with dread, she glanced at the pillow beside her, the sheets upon which she lay, but got no clue from them.

Had she— Had he— Her body told her nothing except that it had been much abused. Fitful with doubt, she could not discern whether any of that abuse had occurred after Chane came to her cabin. Or after she swooned as she must have. Surely she had not— He had not—

"Mademoiselle?" Tad bent anxiously over Ria. She looked dreadfully worse following a night of sleep.

"Clair?" she sputtered, grateful Tad understood from the single word her need to know of her sister's health.

"Fitter than you," he assured her. "Still abed, but she has had tea and is asking for you."

"My robe is in that cupboard." Ria pointed to a small compartment directly behind the boy. "If you will give it to me and turn your back, I want to see Clair."

"Better not," Tad warned. "The captain said you were to stay abed today, said you would be in no fit shape to take to your feet."

"Did he?" Ria challenged, swathing herself in the top sheet and swinging her legs over the edge of the berth. "And pray tell why not?"

Tad's face glowed red. "Because of your injury, I'm sure," the boy said, turning his flushed face from her. "Best do as he says."

Scowling, still wondering what had happened before Chane left her bed the night before, Ria hustled to her feet, unsteadily making her way to the inner compartment where Clair reclined on a stack of pillows.

"Are you well, Clair?" Ria demanded, flopping down beside her sister, taking the small limp hand that lay at Clair's side and squeezing it fondly.

The pretty face had a scratch and several bruises along the cheek but they did not compare in severity to the ones ringing her small wrists.

"Now that I know you are mending, too," Clair said, having, to Ria's delight, found her voice again. "Tad told me you jumped in the sea to save me. Ria—" the soft brown eyes welled with tears "—Ria, you should not have risked—"

"Nonsense," Ria said. "We are sisters, are we not?" Clair nodded, sniffling. "And I have no doubt you would have done the same for me." Ria laughed. "Even though you cannot swim."

"I would have, Ria." Clair smiled weakly and pressed her sister's hand. "I have been frantic since Tad told me how badly you were cut."

Ria looked up to be certain the door was closed between the compartments. "I have been sick worrying that Galvez used you badly, Clair. You must tell me. I know there are other bruises. I helped you into your nightgown."

Clair's eyes were downcast and it seemed for a time that she would lapse into silence again. Finally she stammered out a reply. "He did not use me in *that* way," she said feebly. "But he 'displayed my wares' as he called them to see if I was worth the price he planned to ask for me. And he put his hands wherever he would." She sniffled. "I think I will never feel clean again."

"Galvez's men cut him down when he pushed you into the sea." She sighed heavily. "They at least did not sanction his actions."

Clair shuddered. "I could not trust a one of them," she said, having learned from Tad that three of the *Madrid*'s crew had come aboard. "Promise me they will never come near me again."

"I'll ask the captain to make sure of it," Ria promised before a knock interrupted. "Yes?" she responded.

"It's Mr. Gresham," Tad said. "Come to see for himself that the two of you are alive."

Ria opened the door without getting Clair's consent, afraid her sister would refuse and wanting to restore Clair to normal interaction with others as soon as possible.

"We are alive," Ria said. "If somewhat worse for the ordeal." Noticing that Clair cringed at the intrusion, Ria made a point of saying, "Credit Mr. Gresham with the actual saving of your life, Clair. If he had not pumped the water from your lungs, I think none of us would be here looking so ill at ease with one another."

Axel smiled awkwardly. "You are looking enormously better, mademoiselle."

"I am grateful to you, Mr. Gresham," came Clair's demure reply. "I confess I do not know adequate words to tell you how very much."

"No words are n-necessary," Axel stammered. "That you have not been too badly hurt by what befell you is adequate thanks." His shoulders hunched forward, seeming to weigh on him. "I cannot forgive myself for not defending you in the Bellamys' garden, mademoiselle. I—"

"Please," Clair entreated. "You did all that could be done." She smiled at him. "I trust you are recovered from the injury done you."

"I am," he said. "And now, reassured of your well-being, I'll leave you to rest undisturbed."

"He cares for you," Ria declared when Axel had left them.

Clair blushed. She was not quite ready to deal with such a possibility, but when she was, she thought there might not be a kinder, more affable man than Axel Gresham. "Do you think he could?" she asked tentatively.

Chapter Fourteen

The calm sea lasted three incessant days, the heat rising and the still air thickening with each passing hour. The mood of the men, many superstitiously believing that a calm presaged more ill to follow, worsened with the weather. Some of them clamored for the reward promised for saving Clair Kingsley. With bravado alone Chane put them off on that count, determining it was neither the time nor the place to reveal that Dagian's treasure was yet to be found.

To placate them he promised a part of the reward would be distributed when the *Aurelia* reached the port at Aruba. While they were at their worst he did not want them thinking a hoard of gold was hidden on the ship. Gold had been the catalyst for many a mutiny, and he did not care to add his name to the bloody list of those overthrown for a pirate's fortune.

He had not visited Ria again, thinking it best if the girls remained segregated from him and his crew. There was another point of contention among the men. Idle sailors think of mischief, and there were only so many hours of the day they would submit to replacing rigging and repairing sail. Even he, who would surely be the last to know of such, had overheard a mumbled comment that a man might, if he dared, find something better than a mast to wrap his legs around.

It did not help that they suspected Clair was no longer lily-white after having been with Galvez and that they had seen Ria pulled from the water nearly naked. Recalling the untoward eruption of lust he had felt for Ria afterward, he could hardly expect coarse seamen to welcome a forced celibacy. To keep them from draining the beer barrels that they had turned to for combating the heat and boredom he had had to place a man on constant watch in the hold.

So when at last the wind whipped in, filling the sails and cooling the dangerous disposition of the crew, it was Chane Bellamy who silently celebrated the timely change of luck.

Luck, however, proved fickle as she was wont to do. Two of the Dutch crewmen Galvez had snared and forced to join his band and who had come aboard from the *Madrid* brought sickness with them. Within four days of leaving the defeated vessel adrift, half the *Aurelia*'s crew had caught the ague. The others feared contracting it as much as they feared death.

And with good cause. By the fifth day two men, one from the *Madrid,* one from the *Aurelia,* succumbed to the sickness and had a speedy burial at sea.

"We are low on medicines," Ria told Axel, who had been put in charge of the surgery. Ria had done her best to aid him, finding there was nothing so good for curing an ailment as having the responsibility of others with worse illness. She learned, in short order, to work despite the pain from the gash on her back, at times completely forgetting the wound, at others finding her body so weary it was oblivious to the pain. "We have enough for another day," she reported, having examined the dwindling supplies. "None after that."

"By the day after tomorrow we make Aruba," Axel said wearily, his white shirt sweat-soaked and plastered to his skin. "If this fair wind holds."

Ria nodded and left Axel to make a last check of the ailing men, whose number had overflowed the surgeon's ward and now filled every unused space in the hold. She intended to help in the galley now, where Clair had taken the place of the ship's cook, who had come down with the fever early in the morning. But first, tired and dirty and wondering if there was enough gold in Dagian's trove to make this ill-fated journey worthwhile, Ria climbed to the upper deck. She needed a lung-cleansing breath of air before she went to the stifling galley.

Chane saw her come above and with a wave motioned her to the quarterdeck, the first time he had sought her out since the night he had come to tend her wound. Since then all communication between them had been but a nod or a hasty word or a request sent by way of the cabin boy.

"How do the men fare?" he inquired, noting that she looked as spent as he felt. Her shoulders sagged slightly and she seemed to heave out a wearied sigh. Her face, like her clothes, was smudged with grime. Yet there was a quality about her that superseded her look of exhaustion. Her shadowed eyes and pinched face, her weary step as she climbed to the quarterdeck, did not eclipse her beauty.

Beauty? Yes, he admitted. She was beautiful. Though he recalled with precision that had not been his first impression. He had thought her passably pretty that first day and her sister the one endowed with exceptional looks. Oddly, either the girls or his opinion of them had changed since. Her reply to his question interrupted any further examination of how his perception had altered.

"Most of them show improvement," Ria said, wondering why he looked at her as if he were seeing her for the first time. "One or two, I fear, will not last the night."

Clumsily, she wiped away the lank tendrils of hair that stuck to her damp brow. She was aware the long hours and the heat in the hold played havoc with her appearance. But, Chane, too, showed signs of strain. He had the haggard look that comes of too little sleep and too much worry, his blue eyes circled, his face drawn. Short of able men, he had been at the wheel for a day at least without rest, sparing Axel so that the second officer might be able to supervise the care of the sick.

So while she knew she must look a fright, she doubted she looked much worse than the captain, even with her clothing soiled and rumpled from carrying bowls of broth and tea to the hold, her hair, for economy of time and energy, merely bound into a straggling braid.

She was, of course, aware too that the captain had a peculiarly magnetic appeal that neither lack of sleep nor worry could dim. The deep blue eyes, so like the sky that framed his face, while circled had not lost the ever-burning fire in their intriguing depths. His voice, even as he talked of matters as gravely disturbing as the life and death of his men, sent a shuddering thrill snaking along her spine. He was in need of a shave, his cheeks dark with a day's shadow beard. She wondered, at the most improper of times, how the dark bristles would feel against her fingertips, beneath her lips.

Called out of her musing by the pleasant sound of his voice, she willed herself a reluctant return to the present.

"More would be lost except for your care," he said, wondering at the direction of her thoughts, which evidently were not with him. Did she find his nearness distasteful now? Did she regret what she had done, almost done, in that frenetic state following her injury? Did she remember how very close he had come to making love to her? Did she despise him for taking advantage of her moment of weakness? He cleared his throat and spoke. "Axel has reported your perseverance in making the weakest eat and drink when they would have refused."

Ria breathed a weary and winsome sigh. "I could do no less for men who willingly risked death to save my sister," she said. "I regret it was that encounter that brought sickness to the *Aurelia*."

He took a hand from the wheel and laid it briefly, consolingly on her arm, a tender, gentle touch that awakened the half-remembered passion she had last felt in his arms.

"We have no guarantee the fever would not have struck without that," Chane assured her. He wanted to spare her the ache of remorse, realizing in that moment that he cared for this untidy, spirited woman as he had never before cared for anyone. Chane longed to take her below and tell her his thoughts, but this was not the time to speak of love, if that alien emotion was what he felt. When his ship and his crew were mended, when she was rested and he at his best, then he would broach the topic, but not now, not with death and despair after them like a pair of demons.

"Perhaps," Ria said dispiritedly. "I wish I could be sure."

"What we can be sure of is that for every man who credits you with saving his life, another will offer blame at your feet—and mine. A man would rather die in battle than turn out his gut over a ship's rail. When he fears death—and the ague is a shameful death for a man of the sea—he is quick to fault another. Beware," he said, voice lowered and hoarse with concern, "that you do not go to the hold without Axel or Tad at your side."

"No," she said. "I won't." But as she left him she could not help wondering if she was in any greater danger from the crew than she was from him—or herself. She did not know yet what had passed between them, but she knew, with certainty, what would have if she had not fainted. She would have yielded to him, begged and pleaded with him to show her the golden mysteries only a man and woman who desire each other could know. Another thought leaped to her mind, one nebulous in impact. Suppose they had made love and he had found her sorely lacking?

Would that not explain why he had conveniently kept his distance since? She might have been a mere convenience to him, only a woman who, when she was weak and defenseless, might be persuaded—or forced—to satisfy his lust. Would Chane scoff at her tender, budding feelings of love? Would he take and trample them underfoot like a discarded bouquet? Stricken, sensing that she was too plain, too bold to ever hold the heart of a man like Chane, Ria turned away, tears brimming in her green eyes.

Had he not given ample indication that she was no more than a diversion for him, that to desire his love was far too lofty a wish? What had been his words that night at the governor's fete? With no pretense of flattery, or tenderness, he had said, "If you are so eager to share your charms, allow me to be the first in line."

In spite of the sweltering heat, Ria shuddered as she hurriedly went to the galley. She could not bear the thought that for Chane, making love to her might have been nothing more than payment for all the trouble she had been to him.

Ashen-faced, Ria slipped into the galley. She looked so unwell that Clair called out in alarm, thinking her sister had contracted the pestilence that had settled over the ship like a dark vengeful cloud.

The day passed and evening came with no more men coming down with fever, a good sign that the plague had run its course and that the others would be spared. Late in the night, however, those two most seriously ill died. While their bodies were carried from the hold another man worsened as well, his fever so high the only hope for him was to be stripped and bathed with cool water until his fever broke.

With Axel above, saying words over the two recently departed seamen, and Tad collapsed across a barrel sleeping off his fatigue, Ria discovered that the cask of water Tad had last brought from the hold's lower level was empty. She had not the heart to wake the boy, not when the water casks were only a few yards away. Too tired to think clearly, Ria did not realize she was breaking her promise to Chane by going below for water. A bucket in one hand, a candle in the other, she started down the ladder that led to the lowest section of the hold.

She had reached the last spindly rung when a hot gust of air, which should not have been stirring in the closed compartment, blew out her candle. "What luck," she mumbled, the blackness surrounding her like a wall as the tiny flame sputtered and died. She though of going back for another light but decided there was no need. Tad had shown her the location of the water kegs and she believed she could find them and fill a bucket without benefit of light.

"I been waitin' my chance," came a voice low and rough as the menacing growl of mad dog. "Why should the cap'n 'ave all the fun an' me none when I may be dead o' the fever a day from now?"

Before Ria could react a hand yanked her from the ladder, sending the empty bucket she had carried rolling across the floor. The stump of the candle she had held tumbled at her feet as another hand, gritty and foul-tasting, slapped over her nose and mouth, stifling the start of a shout for help. Thrust roughly backward and to the floor, Ria fell hard, the hefty man's weight coming down with her and knocking the startled breath from her.

Stunned, trying futilely to get her teeth into his hand, Ria fought him, kicking and clawing, but she could not tell if her nails drew blood. Her kicks did not deter him, and if it could be possible, her desperate resistance drove him on. Laughing, assaulting her face and throat with his wet mouth, he shoved her skirts high and, grunting at his easy success, painfully pinned her legs with his knees. "This puddin' ye will like better'n the cap'n's," he jeered. Crushing her to the floor, he ripped open his breeches.

She was suffocating, feeling the blackness of the hold swirl and sweep into her head. She choked on the stale air in her lungs, felt cold sweat bubbling on her skin. He had not allowed her a breath since he had grabbed her, and now, deprived of air, she was slipping away so easily. Clair. What would become of Clair? she wondered as a black, smothering fog settled in around her.

With a last agonized gasp beneath the heavy hand Ria stopped struggling; her flailing arms fell limp at her sides though her frenzied mind raced on. Who could have imagined death could come so easily? she thought dimly. So quickly? So unexpectedly? So horribly?

"No, ye don't," her attacker growled and snatched his hand from her mouth. "I'll 'ave a live piece under me, I will," he roared.

Ria gasped a breath into her starved lungs, and another, unable to scream until the life-giving air filled her and the blood flowed strong and fast in her veins again. Coughing, chest heaving, she recovered sooner than her attacker expected. When she did she cried out, once, weakly, only to be silenced by the suffocating hand thrust over her mouth again.

"That's it." He laughed venomously and then his hand was on her thigh, crudely seeking to shove her tightly pressed legs apart. Grunting, groaning, he fell across her. Desperately, Ria bucked against him, trying to dislodge him, failing. "That's it! Fight!"

Ria had not thrown him off but in her struggle had felt some object within arm's reach. Wildly searching the darkness for it, she dragged her hand over the pitch-black of the floor hoping whatever she had touched might serve as a weapon. What she found was a length of rope, the rolled handle of the heavy wooden bucket, her chance to get away alive if not intact.

"Ria? Are you there?" The voice drifted down from above, bringing hope to one and striking quick fear in the other. Ria's attacker cursed but continued to hold her fast, even as he eased off her and into a crouch. But that gave Ria the stretch of freedom she needed to heave the bucket, like a discus, at his head.

The wooden staves struck hard on the back of his skull, knocking him clear of her and in a groaning heap on the floor of the hold. Giddy, gulping air, Ria sprang for the ladder, luckily finding it before the man came to. By the time she scrambled to the top a friendly circle of light had appeared, and she saw the worried, kindly face of Axel Gresham.

Axel snatched her out of the well. "A man is there!" she cried, pointing to the lower hold. "He tried to force himself on me."

"Tad!" Axel yelled, rousing the boy, who was on his feet before the sound of his name died. "Stay with Ria!" he ordered, then with a great leap disappeared down the well.

Tad saw the deep red marks on Ria's throat and face. He guessed what the trouble had been and that he was likely to get a thrashing, or wish for one when he heard what the captain had to say to him. The boy's pulse pounded in his ears at the thought of it. He had promised faithfully to stay at Ria's side at all times and now, sure as he had fallen asleep, disaster had struck.

The two of them, Ria and Tad, eyed the well and ladder, listening nervously to the bumps and booms in the inky blackness of the hold, and then to a lengthy, frightening quietness. Hovering together, they waited with great trepidation as the thump of footsteps started on the ladder rungs, both wondering if they should stay or run until a familiar towhead emerged with the lantern light.

"The bastard climbed out through the hatch," Axel explained, grievously disappointed at being a minute too late getting below. "Do you know him, Ria?"

She shook her head, grimacing as she painfully learned that her neck was wrenched and sore. "I had no light. I heard his voice but I do not think I could pick it out from others."

"He will know as much," Axel said rapidly. "And there is nothing to be done about it now. But you," he insisted, "look peaked as the worst of them here. I am taking you above for a draft of fresh air and then you retire to your cabin for the night."

"No," Ria protested, and led him to the sailor whose fever soared. "That man needs sponging. He's burning hot."

Axel turned her away. The man she had left only minutes before was still, his fever-reddened eyes rolled back in death. "He's past help," Axel said. "Tad will watch over the others. And you will rest."

She did as directed, too tired and tested to resist. True to his word Axel took her into the fresh cool air, led her to the rail and, with his arm stoutly around her lest she crumple with fatigue, insisted she drink from his brandy flask.

"If I do," Ria said, resting against him as she breathed deeply, "I'll fall asleep before I turn around."

Axel laughed lightly and put the flask to her swollen lips. "If you fall asleep before you turn around I'll see that Clair gets you into your bed. Now drink."

Ria drank deeply then handed him the flask. Axel turned it up and drank a long swallow. Good, she thought, he needs it as much as I do.

"More," he said, handing her the flask again.

Ria sighed, then put a hand to her throat at the agony even that caused. "I'll be a sot," she offered, putting up her other hand to refuse.

Axel insisted. "I'll take the blame for your downfall," he said. "Drink."

Ria drank again, thinking never had anything been as agreeable as the warm burn of the brandy, never had anything been so fresh as the cool breath of the night air. Never, ever, had she been as tired. "I warned you," she said as her knees gave way and she slumped and nodded against his big body.

Axel caught her in his arms, scooped her up and headed for the companionway. "Sleep," he said. "You deserve it."

From the quarterdeck behind the binnacle where he had stood since the departing pair came above, Chane watched their leaving with feral eyes. Axel and Ria going below to bed. Together? His best friend. And his... What? What was Ria to him? He refused to think on it. Denied silently that the girl meant anything at all to him. True, in a moment of weakness he had thought he cared for her, but now, clear-headed, he saw the emotion for what it was. Lust, misguided lust. Was not Axel entitled to the same? Did not Axel have as much right to Ria Kingsley as he had?

But if so, why did he feel an irrepressible urge to do violence to his best friend? A man who was a brother to him.

* * *

Ria went above early the next morning, finding the wind brisk, the sea a glistening sapphire blue that rivaled the sky for the deepest and richest color. The sails whipped above her, full and white against the wind. Refreshed from the first sound sleep she had enjoyed in days, she could offer a smile to each of the men heaving and towing lines on the deck. The attack in the hold, while only hours old, seemed but a bad dream if she did not dwell on it too long. She preferred not to dwell on it at all. She would be more cautious, that was called for.

Chane had warned her about being alone, and he was sure to chasten her for disobeying. She might as well get that over early and not have it waiting for her all day. Seeing that he, too, was above she made for the quarterdeck where he stood, head thrown back, shoulders squared, motionless, but as compelling as a ship's grand figurehead. She assumed, as she approached, that Axel had told him of the attack.

"The men are better this morning," she said, a friendly, hopeful smile upon her lips. "Several are on their feet and will be back to their duty once they have had a day of rest and a few good meals put in them."

"I am glad of that," he said dryly. "And it is good to see you on your feet as well. Your adventure must have been stressing."

Adventure? A delicate way of putting it. She would hardly refer to a near rape as an adventure. Ria's cheeks colored beyond the flush the brisk wind had given them. "It was not pleasant," she said. "But Axel took good care of me."

"I have no doubt of it," he retorted, staring at her with cold blue eyes. Having had his direst suspicion confirmed, he felt rage surge within him, a teeming, boiling brew of anger that had him ready to tear his best friend limb from limb. The ferocity of his wrath nearly blinded him. The thought of Axel's big hands on Ria's lush, ripe breasts, Axel's hungry mouth kissing her sweet red lips, Axel spilling his seed inside her when he, the rogue of the two, had held back his passion rather than press his advantage. Now here she was before him, rosy cheeked, gay, still glowing in the aftermath of Axel's lovemaking. He could have throttled her there on the deck. With difficulty Chane forced himself to refrain from any display of his outrage. He would not give the satisfaction of letting her know he was bothered in the least. "Axel is a capable man," he said, one black brow lifted sardonically.

"He is kind. I don't know what I would have done without him."

For a moment he was dumbfounded that she continued the provocation. If her purpose was to make him feel the fool she had done that. He had thought her an innocent temptress, drawn to him, only him, by the lure of a passion she did not completely comprehend. Now he knew her for what she was, wanton, a woman ready to welcome any man to her bed, a woman no different from Lorelle Telfour.

His gaze swept her, crudely reassessing. Did she think Axel would wed her now that he had taken her? Did she want a husband and the gold, a strong but malleable man to share her wealth, a man who would do as she bade him? Had she learned from Axel that he, Chane Bellamy, had no desire for a wife and then turned her wiles on the more persuadable Axel?

Ria, refusing to allow the seaman's vicious attack to prey on her mind, held her face to the warming sun, allowing her long russet hair, left unbound, to float like a fan in the breeze. A wayward strand of it rippled and fell against Chane's cheek and besieged him with her enticing floral scent. A quiver of desire tightened his loins, but a picture of Axel's big clumsy body pressing down on Ria's milk white skin assailed his mind.

Another diabolic notion beset Chane. Axel, with his "high moral code" would wed Aurelia Kingsley if he had taken her virginity. The thought stoked his rage. "Never," Chane vowed under his breath. Never would he allow that to happen. He would have another chance to make love to Ria Kingsley, and when that occasion came he would not hold back. Axel, he knew, would never abide such a betrayal from the woman he intended to wed.

Chane had been silent so long Ria was startled when he spoke, and cut to the quick when she heard his hurtful words. "You are no doubt needed in the hold," he told her, his mouth twisted derisively. "Surely that silly little adventure of last night had not made you forget those who are ill."

Ria's face colored as if he had struck her. He blamed her! He believed she had invited the attack when she had only gone to the lower hold alone because of her concern for a dying man. "No, of course not," she said, her voice tinny and weak as she recalled the way she had ardently thrown herself at Chane, the fervid liberties she had allowed, welcomed, in his arms. Only she had hoped—believed— What? That he cared for her? Clearly he did not, nor did he think it unlikely that she would invite any rutting seaman to do what he had done.

"By the scourge of hell!" He pounded one fist into the other and swore. His face was hideously contorted, his eyes so venomously dark Ria inhaled sharply and fell back, thinking herself the object of his sudden ire. Then she saw the outline of a sail in the distance and realized it was the approach of a ship that had set him off.

By then the lookout had spotted the sail, too, and gave a shrill warning shout.

"Conquest!" the man aloft yelled.

"Neptune take her!" Chane spit out. "And the damned brothers Telfour!"

Chapter Fifteen

With the windswept divi-divi trees visible in the distance on Aruba's barren hills and the *Conquest* hying a league off the *Aurelia*'s stern, Chane ordered her sail lowered so that he might ease her into the port at Oranjestad. Water and wood were scarce on the Dutch island, but Chane knew a man who ran a gold mill above the port city and knew the fellow would have timbers on hand, albeit at a steep price, if they were unavailable in Oranjestad.

He rued the time the refitting of a rudder would take. Nothing would suit him better than being done with this travesty of a treasure hunt, and most particularly with Aurelia Kingsley. Damn her traitorous heart! He had actually believed she was special, a woman who knew her mind and would not be diverted from having what she wanted, nor driven to accept any substitute for her ideal. Until last night he had thought so, he had even thought it was he and none other she would yield to—until she proved she was nothing but another devious Eve with a basketful of apples for any and all.

Damn Aurelia Kingsley! With his hands behind his back he paced the quarterdeck, scowling at any who looked his way, sending any hapless man of his crew packing if he so much as crossed his path. The red-haired witch made him feel more of a buffoon than any cuckolded husband. How had he allowed himself to be hoodwinked by a girl who was more pirate than her infamous black-hearted grandfather? He despised the chit, even despised her name.

Axel, with no forewarning of the captain's wrath, chose the time when there was a lull in activity below deck to come above and make his first report of the day to Chane. He'd had no opportunity to inform Chane of the attack on Ria, having been called to aid a convulsing patient immediately after he had turned the exhausted girl over to her sister. All through the long night he had been in constant demand, the recovering seamen more a trial than those who were too weak to complain.

Overjoyed by the proximity of land and the thought of a new supply of medicines, Axel did not notice the sneer on his friend's face or guess that the hard glaring light in Chane's eyes could be meant for him.

"I must speak to you about Ria," Axel intoned, standing close so that no one else would hear the words he had not wanted to trust to a messenger, even Tad. With virtual bedlam on the ship already, Axel did not want to create more divisiveness by having hostile men guess at the identity of the culprit. There was no way to tell who carried the guilt unless one of the sailors admitted having a sore head, which was not likely to happen.

"I have no time to waste talking about a woman," Chane retorted and stiffly turned his back on his friend.

Axel was not deterred. He was accustomed to Chane's crabbed temper and, because of recent events, thought Chane had a right to show his raw side. Mostly Chane's bark was worse than his bite, though the reverse would probably be true when he heard what had happened to the girl.

"Ria was attacked last night," Axel continued. "Set upon while she was drawing water in the lower hold. Had I not come along when I did—"

Chane knew an instant of remorse for his hasty word, a savage fury for the swine who had dared harm Ria. "Raped?" he demanded.

"No," Axel said, his voice brittle with ire as he remembered the shock and terror on Ria's face when she had come out of the hold. "She fought the man off but—"

Chane read the concern in Axel's eyes and resentfully mistook it for more than it was. He skeptically raised a dark brow. "You believe her story?" he queried, jealousy surging up out of his dark side to overwhelm his first, more noble, reaction.

Axel was taken aback by his friend's scornful response. Chane was not the most sensitive of men where women were concerned, but even he did not sanction rape and assault on a female, particularly one under his protection. "I saw the marks on her throat. I saw the fear in her eyes," Axel replied firmly, though a shadow of annoyance crossed his face.

Shoulders hunched, Chane leaned toward his friend. "And is that why you found it necessary to 'comfort' her afterward?"

"She needed comfort, yes," Axel said, his body tightening with disgust at Chane's disregard for Ria's welfare. "What would you expect? She was understandably distraught. I brought her above for fresh air and got some brandy down her before I took her to bed."

Chane laughed, loudly, bitterly. "And what did you get down her . . . in bed?" he asked.

Dumbfounded, body rigid with anger, Axel stood and stared at the man who had been his closest friend for most of his life, a man dearer to him than a brother, a man he had, in most ways, always held in high regard. Chane met his militant stare, facing him off so that to an observer they looked like a pair of snarling, bristled dogs spoiling for a fight.

"If you think that of me, you endow me with your own vile attributes, Chane Bellamy," Axel said at length. "I, for one, would not abuse a woman, especially not one who has just suffered a brutal attack, especially not one I have come to admire." Giving Chane his back, he left the deck.

Torn between following the lead of his uncurbed rancor or standing fast with the trust of a longtime friend, Chane quivered as an ugly battle raged inside him. In the end suspicion held him back, kept him from following Axel and clearing the dissension between them. After all, he would not call it abuse if Ria was willing, if she invited Axel to bed her, as, Chane believed, she had more than once invited him.

With the gulf between the friends widening, the *Aurelia* put in at Oranjestad. Chane, true to his word, distributed the promised gold coin to each of the men, in return exacting a pledge of silence concerning the *Aurelia*'s mission, trusting those who broke it would not garner any believers. Those seamen who were able rumbled down the gangplank and, like ants to a hill, burrowed into the doorways of taverns and bordellos ready to buy as much rum and trouble as the gold in their pockets would pay for. Pollack had been chosen to remain on board with a small handful who had drawn first duty.

Chane, when he saw the *Conquest* dock a distance down the wharf, retired to his cabin, seething. He regretted his falling out with Axel and his denial of compassion for Ria, but was unable to stem the briny flow of resentment of them both in his heart. With an oath that blasted Tad's ears,

Chane ordered the boy not to disturb him with anything short of a fire engulfing the vessel. Tad, skirting the captain's ominous wrath by surreptitiously anticipating every need, poured a glass of Madeira, searched the cupboards for the drafts of the *Aurelia*'s hull and keel and spread them upon the map table. Then he stood waiting, knees locked to halt their knocking, for whatever was required of him next.

Scowling, Chane scanned the drafts, then looking up, remembered the boy. "Have Mr. Gresham take the Kingsley sisters ashore," he growled. "There is an inn called the Dove that is respectable enough for women. Take a room for them there and make certain they understand they are not to be underfoot aboard the *Aurelia* before the repairs are done."

"Yes, captain," the boy said, grateful he would have an hour of reprieve and hoping that by the time of his return the captain's mood would have lightened to bearable.

Ria would not stand for it! Not that she minded a few days at an inn. She longed for a luxurious bath such as she had enjoyed at the Bellamys' village house. She desired a place to launder and peg out her clothes that they might be free of the stench of sickness. She yearned for the feel of solid ground beneath her feet, the glorious sight of sky meeting land, but she did not take to being ordered off the ship by a diffident boy.

If Chane thought the worst of her, believed she had led on one of his men then changed her mind about what she had begun, let him tell her himself. If he could not abide the sight of her let him make his feelings clear. But this she would not stand for, not being shunned and shunted off the ship again like unwanted cargo.

Incensed, she stalked across the hallway to his door and thundered against it with her balled fist. "Captain! Chane! I'd like a word with you!"

Having set the Madeira aside, and well into a bottle of rum, Chane reacted physically to the sound of Ria's voice before his mind identified it. A wave of need coursed over him, a hot, jangling wash of desire to throw open the door and pull her inside and fling her upon his bed, red hair spread beneath her like a silken shawl, to thrust inside her and make her forget—

Beading sweat poured off his brow, down his muscular chest. "*Mon Dieu!* Cannot a man have the privacy of his cabin!" he roared.

"Chane?" This time her voice quavered. She pictured his face, blunt, harsh as his words. "I want to tell you what happened," she pleaded, leaning her forehead against the planks, needing the support of something more solid and strong.

"Damn you!" Standing, he gave a splintering kick to the chair he'd vacated. "I've no time for it, I tell you! Get to the Dove, the two of you!" He snapped off the words. "Give me the peace of a few days without females on my ship."

"My ship," Ria whispered as she hung against the door a moment, eyes closed, pulse racing, feeling completely desolate and miserable. She should have known better, she determined, than to unlock her heart for any man. It was bound to get broken and tossed at her feet, unmendable, unwanted.

Defeated, Ria pushed away and like a bedraggled wet lamb returned to the fold. In her cabin, as she collected her belongings, she remembered that she had begun this quest with a mission at heart. There was the place to keep her sentiments, within herself. Then they might all be focused on finding the treasure and using it to clear her father's name. She would forget the man who had made her lose sight of her goal, and she would not lose her way again.

* * *

Two days later, sitting with her sister enjoying a choice meal in a small private room of the inn, Ria avowed she no longer cared a whit what Chane Bellamy thought of her. She was ready to wager no mishap to come could be as devastating as those she had lived through since leaving Savannah. But she did not anticipate another brooding soul who believed himself greatly wronged by Chane Bellamy.

Gus Telfour, with too much idle time on his hands as he waited out Chane's refitting of the *Aurelia,* chanced upon the lively tavern room of the Dove. As he sat, morose, amid the robust, laughing men who filled the tavern, drinking one ale after another, rehearsing his revenge over and over in his furtive mind, a new means of reprisal occurred to Gus. Chane had seduced his fiancée, sullied, spoiled his beautiful Lorelle. Why not return the favor?

The fair-haired American fiancée of his enemy was but a wall away. He had seen her enter the private dining room with her red-haired sister. Having wrested the story of her abduction from Lorelle and having come upon the defeated *Madrid* sitting dead in the sea while her crew ran a patch to her hull, Gus presumed any further calamity befalling the girl would doubly aggrieve Chane. Bellamy's fiancée did not appeal to him, her pale loveliness that of a crystalline snowflake when he preferred dark, torrid beauties. But he would not suffer to kiss the girl, to leave his brand upon her as Chane had left his on Lorelle. Let Bellamy live with Gus Telfour's taint on his beloved, let the bastard reap what he had sown. Why not?

The idea grew in appeal with each frothy mug of ale, until, emboldened by an advanced state of drunkenness, Gus, eyes hooded, strolled into the private room the girls occupied. Because he was well dressed, a gentleman on first impression, Ria was not overalarmed when he sauntered up to the table and deposited himself in a vacant chair.

"Mademoiselles Kingsley." The man nodded and almost immediately turned his wobbling blond head to Clair. "I am a friend of your fiancée, mademoiselle, aware of his devotion to you and most anxious to make your acquaintance."

Clair's pert little chin quivered. Distrusting all strangers since her kidnapping, she paled.

Ria took it upon herself to answer the obtrusive man, her tone civil but not without a sting. "My sister is not engaged to Captain Bellamy."

"He says differently," Gus replied thickly, his bleary gaze resting for a time on the red-haired girl. His brother had sworn she was the wench he had expected to find in the gazebo that damnable night of the governor's fete. The bitter thought of that debacle made the taste of revenge all the sweeter. "And so do I," he jeered.

Quaking with indignation, Ria slowly stood, hands clenched at her sides. "You are unbearably rude, sir!" she spat, eyes blazing. "And you are intruding where you are not wanted! Please leave!"

"Not before I leave a gift for the betrothed." Gus laughed and, ignoring Ria's heated demand, scooted his chair close to Clair. Before either girl guessed what he was up to, he grabbed Clair's tiny wrists and snatched her into his lap, immediately bending her back, thrusting his hand roughly beneath her tangled skirts, all the while crudely forcing her rosebud mouth to open beneath his deep invasive kiss.

"Let her go!" Ria shouted. Outraged, she set on Gus like an attacking wildcat, clawing and hissing, grabbing him by the hair of his head and violently snatching out tufts.

With a threatening yell, Gus abruptly broke off the kiss. He swung wildly at Ria, his big hand cuffing her shoulder, his long fingers catching hold of the cotton blouse she wore.

Enraged when he saw a handful of his golden curls stream
from her fingertips to the floor, he gripped Ria's garment
fast, jerked her brutally forward then savagely slung her out.
Ria, cast completely off her feet, landed painfully twisted on
the splintered floor, haphazardly somersaulted across the
small room, tangled like a burr in the heavy curtain covering the doorway and rolled on to an ungainly stop in the
middle of the tavern room.

Gus, unsteady but alert to the urgent need to depart the
Dove, had one last assault in mind. With Clair on the verge
of apoplexy, he forced his mouth to her swan white throat
and while she sobbed and shouted hysterically, drew a dark
red blood mark on her fair skin. "Tell Bellamy it is a gift
from Gustave Telfour," he boasted.

A sailor came to Ria's aid and helped her from the entan-
glement of the curtain. Another, but a blur to Ria's eyes,
streaked past and caught Gus Telfour before he bolted from
the Dove's rear door. A minute later the blond reprobate lay
in the garbage heap beyond the door, bloodied, bruised, his
nose a new shape, and unable to rise under his own power.

Inside, getting her battered wits about her and with some
assistance from the attentive sailor who had aided her from
the curtain, Ria dizzily rose. Unaware her melee with Gus
had left her blouse in tatters, the back of it but a scrap dangling against her skirt, one sleeve torn away.

"Gawd! Look at this!" her rescuer cried as, disbelieving, he caught sight of the vivid tattoo on Ria's bared
shoulder.

Ria, aghast, tried to cover the mark, but one of the crowd
of the curious she had drawn snatched her hand away that
all might see. "It's the bloody Black Dawn's mark," one of
them announced, his ale-clouded eyes gaining a sudden in-
quisitive gleam. "Who be ye, girlie, to wear that mark?"

"Turn loose!" Ria shouted as the men circled her like a pack of marauding wolves around a helpless prey. "Stop!" Caught in a dozen hands, she was turned and twisted by one man after another wanting to see the unbelievable tattoo, her umbrage and her fear ignored. Nothing she said, no defense she made dissuaded the men from having a look. When one, her rescuer turned tormentor, stretched his callused hand to touch the mark, Ria felt a panicky scream rising in her throat.

A guttural sound, like an ominous death toll in the dark of night, stayed the seaman's violating touch. "Unhand the girl!" that malevolent voice growled.

Ria shuddered with the others, her dazed brain racked to place the terrible and familiar voice. She saw and knew a moment later, recognizing the sardonic scarred face, the coal black eyes, the broad, death-wielding knife in his belt.

"Dom!" she cried. "You! But how—" And then a gasp, an agonizing realization that if Dom had left Savannah her grandfather was surely dead.

The demonic head nodded, knowing the girl had assumed correctly. "'E sent me" were his only words before he gathered up Clair and took the girls safely to their rooms.

Chapter Sixteen

Eight sultry days of unremitting work, beginning with the formidable task of unloading the *Aurelia*'s cargo, ended with the fitting of the newly built rudder. Another day saw the vessel restored with supplies and an empty-pocketed crew.

Only Gustave Telfour's midnight departure on the *Conquest* had saved him from the further vengeance from Ria and Clair's new protector, Dom, and the growing wrath of Axel Gresham. Both men put aside that reckoning for a later date. Clair was devastated by the assault, losing what little ground she had made toward recovery of any trust of men since her kidnapping. The best that could be said of her was that she was no longer as eminently afraid of Dom. She would not leave the security that lay behind a locked door and the knowledge that somewhere near, from a secret place, the barbarous Dom kept a sentry watch.

Ria waited out the long days watching the progress on the *Aurelia* from the window of her room at the inn. She had observed the refitting and testing of the rudder, and fervently anticipated the day of their departure. When Tad came, his timid rap sounding like a sparrow's peck on the thick door, she was ready to leave Oranjestad and begin the last stage of the quest to recover the Black Dawn's trove.

Clair, however, dug in her heels and refused to leave the inn. "I will not go!" she declared, stubbornly planting her tiny, trembling frame in a chair, crossing her arms and rejecting all pleas to board the *Aurelia*.

Ria had expected resistance, but also expected that she could easily persuade her sister to follow her course. This time, though, she could not.

"No!" came Clair's tearful response. "I refuse to go again where there are bawdy, hateful men and no woman is safe. I will not leave this room!"

"Clair, you must," Ria beseeched, giving patient entreaty a last try. "Finding Grandfather's trove is our only chance for rising above men like Hyatt or Galvez or Gustave Telfour, men who would use us ill for a song. If we are to be beyond their reach we must have wealth. What else is armor to a woman? Answer me that. A pretty face is not enough. And wit will not do it. Be brave, Clair! Only for a few weeks and then you need not worry over anything, any man, again."

"I can't," Clair said, sobbing and shaking her red blond curls.

"Very well," Ria replied, despairing of what she was about to do but seeing no other way. She knew that in a contest of patience, Chane Bellamy's fell short of hers. She did not want to begin this last leg with his black temper at a fever pitch because she and Clair had caused another delay. Tad had said the captain was ready to sail but for their boarding. Swishing her skirts, Ria left off begging and crossed the room to gather up her belongings. "Stay here if you please," she said. "But I think you will soon find that you have no choice but to come out of this room." Ria traipsed to the door, turning back for only a brief moment. "And, as you may recall, the men in Oranjestad are as bawdy as any on the *Aurelia*."

Giving Tad a shove, Ria started briskly for the darkened stairwell.

"Ria! Come back! You cannot leave me here alone! Ria!"

With Clair's shouts ringing in her ears Ria descended the uneven stairs, pausing momentarily at the landing when the shouting stopped. By the time she reached the tavern room she heard Clair's hurried, frantic steps behind her. Before Tad could push open the weathered door of the Dove, Clair had a clinging, leechlike hold on her sister's arm. She sobbed uncontrollably but matched Ria step by step until they were aboard the *Aurelia*.

Ria was not to have as easy a time with Chane. His temper, while not hot, was sour, his face as he greeted her hard as that of a stone statue, his eyes cold as blue bottle glass, giving no hint of his thoughts.

He ordered more than invited Ria and Dom below as Axel took watch at the wheel.

"We'll put in a day at sea before we tell the men where we are bound," Chane announced, having closed his cabin door to any eager ears. He flipped open a small chest in which nestled a dozen bottles of rum. He removed one and handed it to the pirate, guessing accurately that a show of hospitality would take the edge off Dom's suspicion of the need to parley.

"You, Dom, will be more help than the map in keeping us to the right heading," he said, his voice giving a grudging respect to the pirate.

"Nay." Dom held his voice low as he used his blade to hoist the cork from the bottle. "I can tell ye naught of that trove except that it was the richest Dagian ever took."

"You saw it?" came from Ria and Chane in near unison.

"That I did," Dom admitted. With the neck of the bottle between his lips he guzzled a long drink of the rum, then wiped his mouth on the back of his arm. "Trunks full 'o gold, bullion an' coin. Jewels fer a queen, pearls, rubies, an emerald big as a man's fist. 'E took it in the grandest battle o' all, pirate against pirate in the Spanish Lagoon on Aruba's leeward shore. Dagian an' 's crew—a fiercer band never lived—defeated Robby Scorpion and Red Jon Lane." With a glistening black light that would have brought a shiver to the most fearless of men, Dom's eyes glowed as he recounted the battle. "'E sunk 'em both in the lagoon but not before 'e robbed 'em blind."

Ria shuddered as she heard Dom's tale, more words than she had believed the man had in him, and all a testimony of the foul deeds of her grandfather. "Then it was a pirate's treasure he took," Ria stated, finding some solace in knowing that her grandfather had shed no innocent blood on the treasure.

"Aye," Dom said. "'An 'e was entitled. Robby an' Red Jon 'ad banded together against 'im, thinking they could outwit the Black Dawn. I was wounded bad," Dom continued. "Only a green lad then and no good with me knife. Got run through an' would 'ave died 'ad not the cap'n's surgeon sewed me up afore the others." He drank deeply of the rum again and it seemed to loosen his tongue even more. "I never forgot that kindness or that the cap'n kep' me in 'is own cabin till I mended. By all accounts I rolled and pitched with the fever fer a week or better. An' when I come to, the treasure was 'id."

"No man of that crew could have gone back for the treasure since?" Chane inquired. He did not like to think he might have wasted his effort to find an empty hole. "Maybe one of those who buried it has lived well on Dagian's trove."

"Ha!" Dom shook his head. "No man knew the spot but the cap'n. 'E took but four men ashore to dig the 'ole, prisoners from Robby Scorpion's crew. Ye'll find their bones with the spoils," Dom explained.

"And the men of Dagian's crew? Wouldn't some of them have looked for the treasure in later years?" Chane persisted.

Dom drank and, with the bottle at his lips, turned his head slowly from side to side. "Lost in a storm with the *Black Dawn,*" he said. "But for five o' us who rode it out in the longboat. An' of us only the cap'n an' me lasted out the year. Robby's brother murdered the others before ol' Dag fed 'im to the sharks." Dom laughed as he remembered the spectacle. "Denny Scorpion was like a scarecrow dancin' out the plank." He plugged the half-empty bottle and stashed it under his arm. "The cap'n let 'is spoils sit after that. 'E 'ad aplenty without it."

"Did Grandfather never tell you the location, Dom?" Ria asked, recalling Chane's complaint that the precise location was deviously coded.

"'E said ye knew it," the pirate replied. "On 'is deathbed 'e said it." The light in the black eyes went out and the heavy lids dropped low over the dark, cold orbs. "An' 'e made me promise to see ye got the trove. Like 'e wanted."

The hooded gaze rested on Chane and said more than any words could in warning there must be no treachery where Dagian's granddaughters were concerned.

"She will get it," came Chane's gruff reply as he slid the map from within his shirt and rolled it flat on the table. "Minus my share," he added emphatically. "And all the sooner if she is forthcoming with what she knows of the code. I've deciphered most of it," he revealed, unfolding a small square of parchment with figures inked in neat rows across it. "I can get us ashore at the right point." On the map he arced his hand from Dagian's drawing of the ship to the line of the coast. "Now if you, mademoiselle, will tell me the rest, I can get an exact fix before we go ashore."

"But I don't know," Ria protested, urgently bending over the table and poring over the map for any clue Chane might have missed. "Grandfather Dag didn't tell me. He said nothing of coordinates. I don't know."

Scowling, Chane braced his arms on the table and bent his head perilously close to Ria's, believing that out of spite or suspicion she withheld the information he needed. "Tell them to me now," he demanded. "What is the use of waiting until we are in the middle of a jungle? Which is what we will find here." His finger stabbed a spot on the map.

"I'm telling you the map is all my grandfather gave me," Ria returned determinedly. "All there is to know is on the map, everything we need. He said so." Ria snatched up the parchment for a closer look.

Chane snatched it from her hands, knowing in his heart that were Dom not with them he would find a way of making her tell. "Be mule-headed," he snapped. "Why should I expect your stubborn character to change now? But I warn you, Ria, you will regret your folly when you are attacked by mosquitoes and up to your neck in snakes and leeches while I sit and decipher coordinates you are too stubborn to tell me." His eyes flashed at her. "And make no mistake," he said as an afternote, "you will tramp every yard through that jungle with me."

"I wouldn't dream of allowing you to go alone," Ria retorted, through her anger sensing the futility of continuing to deny she knew more than she had told him of the codes.

Little changed but the days. Chane did not risk pressing Ria more, not with Dom and his treacherous blade always handy. Axel had few words for Chane either, as had been the way of it between them since the docking in Oranjestad. No less stubborn than he had accused Ria of being, Chane did not take it upon himself to mend fences with his friend. But neither did he expect a continuation of Axel and Ria's affair. While she had Dom to watch over her, Axel was no more likely than he himself to get close to Ria again.

The weather was much fairer than the atmosphere on the ship. The *Aurelia* made good time, her crew amenable to shortening the voyage by finding the swiftest current and keeping to it.

Ria had the good fortune to be above deck when the *Aurelia* first cruised along the Guiana coast where her grandfather had marked the anchor spot on his chart. She would not have known the ship passed over that exact point had she not noted a look of recognition in Dom's eyes as he gazed toward the shore.

"This is the place," Ria whispered.

"Aye," Dom answered, his vociferous ways having been of a day's duration.

Ria had an impulse to climb the rigging for a bird's-eye look at the land, but restrained it. She wanted to shout out her joy, but a wild outburst might deter the men from their work, and she guessed from the careful way they hung at their posts that while the *Aurelia* was cruising so near the reefs nothing should distract them. Instead she stood, excitement mounting, looking out over the crystal water and wondering how soon—a day, two?—she would have her treasure.

"Anchor here!" Chane shouted, having made a pass of the shore and brought the ship around. He waved Ria below as a flurry began on deck, men running and yelling, rigging loosed, sail coming down, the anchor cast to drag the bottom and hold them through the change of tide.

Ria had hoped to go ashore before dusk, but soon saw that was not to be. Tad confirmed that the landing would be delayed until morning when he came to ask that she dine with the captain and Mr. Gresham. That Clair preferred to dine alone came as no surprise to Ria. Her sister had been above but once since leaving Aruba, and that at Ria's insistence that she get some air.

The four of them, Dom included, sat around the table in Chane's compartment partaking of the celebratory fare Tad served. Midway through the second course, and past the perfunctory courtesies a group of people on the outs exchange, Chane announced his plan for retrieving the treasure.

"The men understand what is at stake here and that they profit only if we profit," he said. "They are ready to do their part."

"When do we start?" Ria asked impatiently.

Chane lifted a wineglass to her in a solitary toast. "At dawn, mademoiselle. It seems the appropriate time to begin this venture."

Ria agreed.

"My plan is that you, mademoiselle, Dom and myself take two seamen ashore with us. We carry five days of rations, mattocks and spades, a weapon for each man—"

"And for me," Ria insisted. "I'll not be the only one unarmed."

"A weapon for you, too," he conceded reluctantly. "Axel stays with the ship and, of more concern, the men. They are a good crew but many are new to my service and their loyalties uncertain. I do not want to find out at the point of a sword precisely what those loyalties are. Axel—" he began.

"I know my charge," Axel cut him off. "No man will move against another or against the ship while your party is ashore." His glance at Chane was hard, but when his eyes went to Ria the look was soft. "The *Aurelia* and your sister will be safe in my care, mademoiselle."

"Thank you, Axel," Ria returned, relieved to know Clair could be safely left behind while Dom accompanied her ashore.

"As we are all assured of our duties, I suggest we finish our dinner," Chane said. "For us—" he nodded to Ria and Dom "—this may be the last good one for a time."

When the meal was cleared and brandy poured, Chane and Axel put aside their grievances long enough to establish a signal should trouble befall either the shore party or the ship.

"What have we to fear on shore?" Ria asked, certain the men knew more of the nature of this land than she did.

Chane finished his brandy ahead of the others, propped his elbows on the table and proceeded to tell her what to expect. "Besides the jungle," he said, "which is formidable enough, there are natives in this region, wanderers, not a hospitable tribe. Let us hope they are not in the area while we are ashore."

"They be a murderous lot," Dom said, making his first contribution of the evening. "The cap'n 'ad a run-in with 'em when 'e 'id 'is spoils and 'e 'ad to shoot a dozen or better. It was them what cost 'im 'is leg," he said. "They 'ad a kind of poison on their darts what made a wound that would not 'eal."

Ria shuddered and the men, too, seemed visibly shaken by Dom's announcement.

"That was..." Chane broke off and drummed his fingers on the table. "Two score years ago or better," he said. "That the same natives would remain is unlikely. The French are not so far up the coast that they would not have ventured here and eliminated any tribe that is a threat to their settlements. Still, we'll carry extra powder and shot.

Even without savages, there will be enough hardship in the jungle.''

His words brought an end to the evening. Axel rose, and with a perfunctory thanks bade the lot of them a good-night and godspeed. Dom downed the last of his brandy and stood. Ria left her brandy unfinished but offered her thanks to all for their efforts to date.

"There is something about this place that makes me believe success is at hand,'' she said, relaying a feeling that had come to her the moment the anchor stayed the ship and she saw the verdant shores beyond where gentle waves broke upon the sand.

"Much of that hinges on you, mademoiselle,'' Chane responded, a look of resolve in his eyes. "If you please, I would like a word in private.''

Ria's heart leaped, racing like a doe before a hunter. Even so it took all she could do to persuade Dom that Chane Bellamy would do her no harm if he stepped without the door while they talked.

"Say what you could not say before the others,'' Ria demanded, hoping the handsome captain would apologize for his unjust accusation and that, as the search neared an end, she and Chane might share more than a common goal.

Her hopes were dashed like a ship tossed upon a rocky shoal when she saw the twitch in his firmly set jaw and heard the contemptuous undertone in his voice. "That I will, Mademoiselle Stonehead,'' he said. "Or will you relent and give me the next coordinates now that it is the eve of our going ashore?''

Ria sighed and returned as scornful a look as she had received. "I can only repeat what I have told you before,'' she snapped. "I do not know anything more.''

"Why should I believe you?" He stood near the windows, his chin high, his arms belligerently crossed over his chest.

"Why should you not?" she parried. "What have I to gain by withholding anything? I am more anxious than you to know the exact location of the trove." Eyes gleaming, she sashayed across the chamber to within an arm's reach of him. "May I suggest, Captain Contrary, that rather than argue a moot point we put our heads together and determine whether what we need is contained within the map."

Chane's squared jaw went slack as he considered the biting logic of what she said. He had allowed his temper to do his thinking, and now he reluctantly admitted to himself Ria had nothing to gain by withholding the keys to the codes. He further admitted, though it pained him, that she had given him far more trust than he had given her. What galled him, what pricked him like a thorny rose vine, was that he did wish to put his head together with hers, head and arms, lips and legs, all that a man and woman could put together—and she had chosen Axel instead.

Still he was not ready to concede on every point. "I am willing to give that a try," he allowed. "Though if there is another clue on the map, it is beyond my talent to find."

"My grandfather said it was all there. I cannot believe that after he was so careful with the making of the map, my grandfather forgot to include everything we need to know."

"No, that isn't likely," Chane acknowledged.

"Where did you find the first clue?" Ria asked, bending to the map table where the parchment still lay spread beneath the lamp.

Chane stood beside her. "A man often uses his name to hide a code," he explained. "Your grandfather signed with the mark of the Black Dawn." He touched the familiar sun symbol in an upper corner. "Count the points," he said.

"Nine. One for each letter," Ria said.

"Using nine in the computation took me from the ship to here," Chane explained. "The landing point. The smaller sun symbol on the ship, I determined, has seven points. Using seven in the calculation took me here." He showed a point ashore.

She spent a long while examining the map, eventually realizing she'd found no more than Chane had. "He must have been certain the marker he left would endure," she said softly. "And it *will* be there, waiting where we are sure to see it.

"And that is where we will find another symbol," came Ria's excited pronouncement. "Carved on a stone or a tree, waiting somewhere we are sure to see it!" In the wake of her enthusiasm she forgot herself and laid a hand on his arm.

"Of course," Chane returned, automatically clasping the feminine hand that lay on his forearm and drawing it gently between both of his hands. "If—"

"Yes," she said, wanting the words he had broken off, wanting them to be conciliatory, wanting them to say what she saw in his eyes.

He had drawn Ria close and brought her fingertips to rest upon his chest, forgetting for a moment his disdain of her, her evident preference for his friend. He felt a trembling in her hand, knew that she must feel the thunder of his heart, the rush of blood that her touch had triggered. When she lifted her face to him, speared him with a look from eyes that held the tender green promise of spring, he weakened more.

"Ria," he whispered, his breath catching in his throat. Differences be damned, he thought. Axel be damned. The way she looked at him had him ready to forget there had ever been discord between them. "Ria, I—"

A thump beyond the cabin brought his mind crashing back to blunt reality. He recalled that Dom stood with his broad back against the cabin door, ready to break it down if he suspected a misdeed.

"Yes," she prodded, her voice breathlessly low.

Chane thrust her away. Another time, he promised himself. Another time would come for this, a time when he was not bewitched and would not be tempted to tell her he did not care that Axel had loved her first. "I want you on deck before dawn," he barked. "Do not be late!" He cut her in two with the harshness of his stare. "Or you will regret it!"

Chapter Seventeen

The smooth water was dark as India ink when the skiff cast off from the *Aurelia*, manned by the burly Gosse and another seaman called Jeune. On the stern bench sat Chane Bellamy, clad in black from his knee-high flanged boots to the braid-trimmed tricorne atop his head. A band of black leather crossed his chest and a pistol was tucked beneath it. Another belt at his waist held a second pistol and a broadsword of gleaming silver.

Dom, in the bow, was just as somber in a shirt of black jersey and breeches of a charcoal-and-black stripe. Twin bands of leather made an X on his chest, and pistols hung from each. In the dim light of morning Dom's craggy face was that of a fearsome gargoyle, only the glistening gold rings in his ears giving a hint he was human.

Ria sat beside Dom, forced to face both Chane and the straining seamen as the skiff skimmed the glassy water, which was as smooth as a gliding gull until they neared the shore.

"Hold fast!" Chane shouted as a wave leaped up and tossed the light skiff's bow high. The stern bounced on a second whitecap when the bow went down, but settled in a band of milky foam before the next crest caught it and repeated the maneuver. Gosse and Jeune never missed a stroke of the oars and seemed oblivious to the copious spray of foam that coated their arms and chests, as it had already had Ria's back and Dom's.

Only Chane arrived on the shell-strewn sand without getting drenched. Ria looked and felt as if she had been in rain, her homespun skirt speckled with salty droplets, her black vest and white blouse soaked through, her braided and pinned-up hair damp and briny. Dom boosted her from the skiff to the sand so that her feet at least were dry. Shaking out her skirt, she took a few steps up the gentle slope of beach while the men got their weapons and tools from the skiff.

A hand shielding her eyes from the rising sun, Ria looked in every direction for a path, but found no sign there was or ever had been one. Beyond her the jungle was like a blanket of green leaves spread on the land, so thick where it met the beach that it might as well have been a wall of stone. Snaking green tendrils of vine spilled out of it and lay upon the sand, waving in the breeze, making it appear as if the thick jungle crept out surreptitiously to greet her.

Silently Ria cursed Chane for making her toss out her breeches. Those were the only sensible clothes for the terrain. Her skirts would not last ten minutes in the bramble and thorn before her. She was thankful she'd had the foresight to don her riding boots. Old and worn as they were, they would save her legs from being slashed to ribbons.

A glance back at the men showed them hauling the skiff above the tide line. While they were occupied Ria bent down and caught the hem of her skirt at the back, bringing it between her legs to tuck into the wide leather belt she wore at her waist. When she was done she had the look of one clad in a Dutchman's full breeches. Comical perhaps, but Ria was satisfied that with her skirt out of the way she could move through the jungle with as much ease as the men.

Seeing that they were yet occupied with the skiff, Ria moved farther up the beach, one hand on the hilt of the knife she'd been issued, the other on the handle of the pistol that hung at her side. Curious about what was ahead, she started into the jungle at a spot where the vines were slightly parted and a small stream trickled out.

"Hold up! Are you touched?" Chane roared.

Ria spun to see him in a wide-legged stance, his hands planted angrily on his hips. "I wanted to have a look around," she countered. "I wouldn't have gone far."

He stomped through the sand toward her, a look on his face that made her feel both a shiver of dread and a purely female reaction to a man as handsome and imposing as Chane Bellamy. With the sun in his face, his eyes glittered with reflected light like the sapphire waters behind him. Even the frown he wore could not minimize the attractiveness of that face. Ria, aghast, could not tear her eyes from him even though she knew he was bearing down on her with malice in his heart.

"A few steps and you would have been lost." He swore as he caught her by the shoulder and gave her a shake. "You stay in my sight every minute. Understand?" Ria nodded as he pulled her to the beach to where the men waited. "We all stay together," he charged the lot of them. "Each of us within arm's reach of the one in front. This jungle will swallow a man—or a woman—in the time it takes to draw a breath. I do not want to spend my time here searching for one of you," he growled.

Glaring again at Ria, he lined up with the ship and got his position on the beach. When he had his point he marked it with a conch shell set atop an oar staked in the sand. Behind Dom, who would chop a path with his sword, Chane placed first Ria, then himself, followed by Gosse and Jeune. With everyone in position he gave the order for the expedition to begin. The party headed due west, moving like a train of slugs through the living wall of green.

"How far?" Ria asked when a quarter hour had passed but their progress into the jungle was no more than thirty feet.

"Less than a league," Chane told her, his gruff voice revealing none of the pity he felt that she was the least properly garbed for the rough going. Her ridiculously wrapped-and-tucked skirt did not give much protection from the whipping vines and sharp thorns near the jungle floor. Early into the foray her bare forearms were scratched and red, and like everyone else, she constantly batted her neck and shoulders to scatter the swarms of biting insects and hungry mosquitoes that constantly assaulted them.

Pity did move him to pull a kerchief from his coat pocket and to drape it around her exposed neck as a line of defense against the insects. "Thank you," she mumbled with a quick look of surprise and gratitude cast over her shoulder.

She tied the white square high beneath her chin and twisted the trailing ends beneath the neckline of her blouse, narrowing by some inches the amount of skin that was exposed. Ahead of her, the swish and chop of a broadsword measured time. Behind her the slow steps of the men crunched the sword's fodder. More than once she heard Jeune grumble to Gosse that he would rather be adrift at sea than in the devil's wooded playground.

"Yer worse'n an ol' woman, Jeune," Gosse pitched back. "Yer asked to come."

"Clot-head that I am," complained Jeune. "I could be aboard the *Aurelia* fillin' a mug o' beer."

The whole of the day passed as the first quarter hour had, with the five of them buried by vine and branch, moving often in a darkness as black as that of any cave. They took the midday meal standing in single file. The only change came as Dom and Chane alternated in the lead, each taking an hour at the front to chop and clear for the others.

Ria gave up wondering when this part of the search would end, devoting her strength to keeping up with the men. Step after step sweat poured down her brow and between her breasts like a river of steam. Bites peppered her aching arms, which were sore from swinging at the perpetual black cloud of gnats before her face or deflecting limbs and leaves from her path. Not a word had been spoken in hours. Had there not been an occasional grunt from Gosse and Jeune, she would have wondered if they still paced behind her. She did not have the energy to waste looking back. Weary enough to be knocked flat by a feather, Ria was nodding off as she walked when a shout jostled her to life.

"Halt!" Chane called unexpectedly from the lead.

Ria obeyed when she had drawn abreast of him. "Oh," she whispered. "How amazing!"

A clearing was a strange sight after what they had come through. This one was as wide as a ship was long, a crescent of grassy ground leading to a massive stone that must have burst from the earth's core in some bygone age. A layer of gray green lichen covered the craggy surface. High as two men the monstrous stone sat in the first sunlight they had seen since morning. It had the formidable look of a huge reptilian ogre stretched out to warm his blood.

"The sign should be here." Chane spoke low, his voice reaching her ears only as they slowly approached the stone. Their steps were measured as they cautiously searched the waist-high grass for whatever creatures might lurk unseen within it.

Dom and the seamen paused at the edge of the clearing, Gosse and Jeune dropping to the ground for a rest, the wary Dom keeping watch on both jungle and clearing.

"He made it hard to miss," Ria said when she stood close enough to touch a rendering of the sun symbol so large she could have curled within the circle at its nucleus.

"Praise him for that," Chane remarked as, using the tip of his sword, he counted the points in the sign. "Ten," he mumbled.

"Eight," Ria contradicted.

Chane swore softly. He was devoid of patience after the long trek through the jungle, much of that time spent in the act of hacking a trail for the others, another part of it spent in self-reproach for spitefully insisting that Ria come along when plainly the jungle was no place for a woman. But even he had not expected a tangle as thick as a nest of snakes in hell, or that it would take a full day to cut through to the first mark. Still, even when regretful, he could not find it in him to magnanimously offer an apology for exposing Ria to so much hardship, particularly when she insisted on correcting his count.

"I am tired but not blind," he said, his brows lowering significantly. "Look again. There are ten points."

"Yes," Ria admitted without looking up from the spot where she used the blade of her knife to scrape a patch of silvery lichen off the stone. "Ten on the large sign, eight on the smaller."

She stepped back to reveal the fruit of her work, another sun symbol the size of her hand beneath and to the right of the larger one.

"Damn Dagian for that!" Chane swore. "He could not make it simple."

"No," Ria intoned. "Grandfather Dag was never a simple man. But if his safeguards have kept the treasure intact all these many years, I will not complain overmuch," she said. "Not at all if we camp here for the night."

"That was my plan," Chane admitted. He needed time and light to calculate the next set of coordinates. "We'll think ourselves dropped in a pitch barrel as soon as the sun dies and that is no more than an hour away." With a shout he sent Gosse and Jeune to gather wood for a fire while he and Dom beat out a pad in the grass for their camp.

Ria took the moment to slip off a few yards to attend her personal needs, imagining while she was in that vulnerable state that she heard the scurrying of nearby feet. She was glad to return to the camp and the company of the men, gladder still to have come upon the sign that proved her grandfather's map was genuine. Tired as she was, she felt restored by the discovery. It was with some elation that she set to the task of preparing the evening meal, not kingly fare but good strong coffee and beans, boiled over the fire and eaten with what was left of the bread and cheese they had lunched on at noon. Gosse had found mangoes while he gathered wood, and had made a pouch of his shirt to bring one for each of the party.

None of the party needed an invitation to sleep after the meal was done. Even Ria's exuberance was dying down as they bedded down around the fire like spokes from a wheel, each hoping the drifting smoke would offer a little relief from the pesky mosquitoes. "I'll stand the first watch," Chane announced, reminding them all there might be perils worse than insects. "Two hours to a man," he said. "Dom after me, Gosse next and you the last, Jeune."

"Aye, Cap'n," said Jeune, smiling wearily, grateful he was to get nearly a full night's sleep before his turn came.

Ria fell asleep wondering what could befall them. Panthers, she imagined, were the largest predators in the jungle, but not even the thought of one of the black creatures

slipping into camp could keep her eyes open. She slept as if
drugged, never moving, hearing neither the night sounds
from the jungle nor the rasping snores of the men before a
hand rudely thumped her shoulder.

"Jeune is gone," Chane whispered. "Get up."

Ria sat up, not sure of the time until she saw crimson
streaks in the band of sky above the clearing. Dom, to her
left, squatted beside the fire, fanning it with his hat until the
glowing coals lit a flame to the twigs and leaves he had laid
upon it. The flare of the fire and the glow of the sun from
over the treetops came at the same moment, flooding the
clearing with a blaze of red light.

Dom and Chane had rolled their blankets; Gosse sat
cross-legged on his looking at the abandoned blanket next
to him. "He might have gone back to the ship," Ria offered, remembering the man's complaint about having
joined the land expedition.

"'E's a bloody fool if 'e forgot 'is musket," Gosse returned, picking up the weapon the other seaman had left at
his watch post. "But I would not put it past 'im."

Ria shuddered. She was glad Chane stayed close to their
camp while she made breakfast for the men. The food was
cold by the time Dom and Gosse returned from a two-hour
search, having found no sign of the missing man. Either
Jeune had voluntarily headed down the path at the first sign
of light, or the jungle had come in and taken him. The last
possibility gave Ria a chill of foreboding, but she cast her
vote with the others to continue the hunt for the treasure.
They could not hope to catch Jeune before he reached the
ship, and even if they did, there was no point in backtrack-
ing to retrieve a man who did not want to be on the expedition.

After the meal was eaten and supplies left for Jeune on
the outside chance that he returned to the stone, the re-

maining four plunged on, southwest by the new coordinates, and through a part of the jungle thicker than what they had traversed the day before. With only three men to take turns cutting the trail, the going was slower—and, if it was possible, the day hotter. Chane was on his second tiring round in taking the lead, Ria on his heels just beyond the swing of his sharp blade, when a muffled shout and a rustle of leaves sounded over Dom's shoulder.

"What—" The pirate whirled, his sword drawn, his pistol raised in the other hand. He found nothing to meet his attack. The jungle had closed behind him, obscuring the path over which they had come. Like a morning mist beneath the sun, Gosse had vanished.

Linked together so that they would not lose another of the party, the three searched for the missing man and shouted until their throats were raw. But Gosse, stout as an oak, strong as an ox, had disappeared as easily as a sparrow on the wing.

"*He* did not turn back," Chane said as the three huddled on the path, passing round a skin of water to soothe their parched throats. "We can if we choose," he offered. "A day of hard going might get us to the ship before night. More likely not. An hour as we are going should see us to the next point on the map."

His eyes rested on Ria and shone in a way she had never seen them, with a flicker of pity, a flicker of wrath, another of resolve. She could not put it all together before he glanced away and at Dom's dark, unreadable visage. Her face, she imagined, told exactly what she felt, an equal measure of both fear and confusion.

"I say we go on," Ria offered, her voice small as she realized he was leaving the choice to her, a deed so remarkably out of character that it was frightening. *The direction*

*did not matter if they were no more likely to make another
hour one way over the other.*

Chane caught her hand and squeezed it tight, staring at
her a moment silently. The fingers strongly gripping hers
were scarred with scratches, but his hand was reassuringly
warm. Ria felt her courage grow as he held her, knowing in
that moment that if in an hour she, like Gosse and Jeune,
mysteriously disappeared into the jungle, she would not be
alone. Chane had said as much with his eyes.

"Hold my shirt." His face was somber, his voice choked.
"Let go for nothing. Dom will hold to you until we stop
again."

Ria gripped his garment tight, stalking him close as a
shadow. Dom looped the long fingers of one hand in the
neckline of her vest and carried a cocked pistol in the other.
Only the jungle spoke, its language a primitive blend of
faraway bird calls and whispering wind, a hum of myriad
buzzing wings, a trilling call of hidden tree frogs, an eerie
warning song none could understand.

A pistol shot ended the song. Ria, feeling that the blast of
it had split her eardrums, was lurched back and to the
ground as her vest ripped down the back seam. She toppled
at Dom's boot-clad feet, saw them kick, and above them a
flutter of bright feathers, a flurry of brown-skinned arms.
And Dom was gone. Like Gosse. Like Jeune.

"God help us!" she cried as, snatched to her feet, she was
thrust ahead into a torturous jungle thicket that shredded
clothes and skin alike.

"Run!" Chane shouted. "Run, damn you!" He had a
viselike hold on her arm and would not let her stop, not
when tears streamed from her punished face, not when her
heart pumped hard enough to burst, not until they realized
they had run clear of the jungle and toward a rise of rock—

and a score of brown-skinned men, each armed with a feather-adorned spear.

"*Mon Dieu,*" Chane whispered, gauging the distance between the natives and a slit in the rock as he ground to halt. "We might make that cave."

Ria gasped for breath but nodded that she was for trying. She clung to Chane, moving as he did in a slow walk toward the opening. After running the last gauntlet of the jungle, Chane was almost as bare as the natives, his shirt ripped off, his breeches black tatters on his muscular legs. He still carried his pistols and sword but he had thrown off his pack when they started to run.

Ria was as bad off, her blouse a bit of rag and thread, her skirt tasseled and torn from the knees down. Her hair had tumbled loose and worked free of the tight braid that had held it. Tangled, laced with bits of leaf, it flowed down her back like a blaze of wildfire.

She did not know her fiery tresses were her momentary salvation, a color legend among the natives who moved toward her. She would not have believed anything could save her from the fate that had befallen Dom and the seamen, not when she saw that she and Chane had no chance of gaining the opening of the cave ahead of the natives and their spears.

Ria began to shake when the band surrounded them, herding them along with frequent nudges from the sharp points of the spears. She panted in horror when one, overtly curious about her hair, lifted the mane from her shoulders with his spear, holding the length of it aloft so that the sun seemed to set it afire.

"Yaaah!" One of the native men leaped back, lowered his head, raised his spear, then buried the dagger point of it in the ground. Others followed his lead, dropping back with the first man until half the band was grouped with him.

One of those who had not fallen back stabbed his spear tip at Ria's shoulder, cutting away what remained of her blouse. Being naked was the least of Ria's worries, but she instinctively covered her bared breasts and voiced her indignation at the man who had stripped her to the waist.

The fellow, black eyes round with fear, fell back with the others and jabbed his spear into the ground. Another, silver-haired, decades older than any of the lot, was undaunted by what he saw and boldly reached out a hand to touch the cloud white skin. Ria fiercely slapped his hand away but got a spear tip thrust against her throat for her audacity. With Chane held at a standstill by two spears pricking his back and another scoring his chest, Ria submitted to the savage's examination. Grinning broadly, the elderly brown-skinned savage caught a length of her hair and rubbed the lustrous tress between his thumb and fingers. But it was what he unexpectedly saw underneath the hair that stupefied him. The old man stood and stared like one paralyzed, stared until his hand began to shake.

Ria felt the trembling fingers brush over the mark, rubbing back and forth over the sun tattoo as if to rub it off. When the mark did not smudge, the old man dabbed spittle on his fingers and tried again to wipe it away.

"Yaaah!" he shouted.

Without warning the trio holding Chane lowered their weapons to the ground and, along with the rest of the band, buried the spear tips in the soil.

"Do—do you think this is a ritual?" Ria whispered. "A taunting game of cat and mouse before they k-kill us?"

"I hope it's an opportunity," Chane answered, making a halting move toward the cave, stopping after one step to see if it would be his last, disbelieving when it was not. He moved again and, getting no response from the host of savages, dragged Ria the two yards to the cave mouth and then hastily inside.

Chapter Eighteen

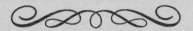

The narrow aperture led to a chamber behind the wall of rock. Enough light spilled in through the long, high slit that Chane could easily see the savages when they entered. He had enough powder and shot for half the number. After that it would be sword against spear for as long as his arm and his luck held out.

Ria, face blanched, clung to his side, trembling so hard he kept a protective arm wrapped around her waist to steady her. Chane was all too aware of her damp, silky skin beneath his fingers, the tangled skeins of her hair brushing his ribs, the undercurve of her full breasts resting against his arm.

"Will they follow?" she whispered. "Play with us more before..." Before they run us through with spears and do whatever they did with Gosse and Jeune and Dom. She could not give voice to the horror, could not quite form a picture of the unknown torture those savages had surely performed on the missing men, not allow herself to think of poor dear Clair, waiting for her sister's return from the jungle—forever.

"Maybe not," Chane answered gently. What need of feeding her fear? They would die soon enough. Why die in their minds a dozen times before the actual moment came?

Glancing down, he saw that the hazy light bathed her lush curves in rippling shadow so that with her weapons strapped at her sides and her long loose hair whipping around her naked shoulders she appeared wild as a pagan goddess, an ephemeral Diana risen out of the wild forest. He learned in that instant that a man had emotions greater than fear. In that daunting flash of consciousness he thought not of death but of life, of long years spent with a fine woman at his side, of dark-haired children laughing and playing at his knee, of rich fertile land that was his to till and to pass down to his sons and his daughters. He thought of loving the woman he held in the curve of his arm.

"Ria," he whispered, his voice ragged as the wind on a jagged mountain peak. "Ria, my sweet, if you do not find a way to fashion more of a cover from that skirt you wear, you will meet death with a man making love to you."

Her laugh had a bittersweet sound. "Should I be appalled?" she asked, wrapping her arms about his waist, unabashedly burying her face in the silken mat of black curls on his wide chest. A hiccuping sob became muffled against his flesh as she sagged against him. Inside her a light went out, a light of vengeance under the banner of justice. She thought sadly of her last years since her father's death, Clair's past years, all spent dreaming of revenge.

Looking at them now, as if they all passed before her eyes at once, she rued the waste of sentiment and time. Her father would not have wanted his daughters' lives so used. Now that it was too late to undo a minute of those bartered years she saw that she should have sought happiness over revenge.

"Are you not—appalled?" Chane asked. His powerful muscles, tensed in readiness for an attack, quivered when the assault came from an unguarded front. Ria's bare breasts, a pair of sensuous crescent moons, hot white fire, quivered against him and sent the blood roaring in his veins.

Tears streamed from Ria's eyes. Now that she was to die, perhaps within a stone's throw of the riches that might have exacted the revenge she had wanted so long, the treasure seemed to matter little. A moment of happiness before the end came seemed a greater treasure than any gold.

"No," she choked out between sobs. "I—I would very much like for you to make love to me, Chane."

"Shush," he said, thinking it the cruelest of fates that he was offered a prize he wanted above all just when the savages mounted their attack. "I hear them moving."

Holding her at his side, Chane edged cautiously to the opening and peered out into the clearing where the band had accosted them. Beyond the open area the sun burned low in the evening sky, a flaming crimson ball that lit the clouds and treetops like a flame to tinder. "Gone. Out of sight, at least," he said, turning away from the opening and turning Ria in his arms. "And if you are sure of what you say..."

"I am," she whispered, her open palms upon his chest, her face uplifted to his. Her voice shook but she said what was in her heart. "I want to know everything there is to know of life before mine is over." Every fiber in her body echoed her words as her arms rose to circle his neck. "And most especially, I want you."

"And I, my sweet," he said, passion rising in him like a storm surge as he heard her tender words, "would not deny a woman her last request."

There had been a time for gentleness but it belonged to another lifetime. He bowed her back with his kiss, the onslaught of his mouth wild as the teeming jungle beyond their sheltering cave. His hands, like the quick sure claws of a beast, pared the heavy leather belt from her waist. Another swipe loosened the drawstring of her skirt and the ragged garment and underlying petticoat floated swiftly to the sandy floor. He was careful disposing of the weapons she had worn, laying them aside cautiously so that he did not hasten the demise both feared awaited them.

Ria, trembling, seeking passion over fear, drank in his kiss as if she would fill herself with potent wine, opening to him, welcoming his ravaging, savage lips, the cleaving thrust of his tongue into the dark silky sanctum of her mouth, a foretaste, a promise of what was to come. She whimpered when he broke the sensuous bond to wrest off the gun strap across his chest. She felt closer to life than to death when he held her, as if he carried her to the wellspring of existence and plunged her into the everlasting waters, a place where time never ended.

Sighing softly, Chane touched his lips to the tousled mass of red hair at the crown of her head. "Help me, sweetling," he whispered, dragging her hands to his waistband.

Ria fumbled with his belt buckle. Clumsily, hurriedly, she drew the ends free and into his anxious, waiting grasp. Chane eased to a crouch to put aside his weapons. He rose slowly, his hands at her sides, sliding from the curves of her thighs to the dip of her waist as his mouth blazed a fiery comet trail of kisses from her soft belly to her creamy breasts to her slender, pulsating throat.

His hands wove into the silky tassels of her hair, his fingers slipping through the luscious length of it, red as the sky at the first shimmer of dawn. "I should have done this the first moment I saw you," he said softly, huskily, drawing back her head, savoring the sparks of passion her eyes held. A whimpering cry, a sweet birdsong of anticipation, rose from her throat. Beyond the cave a crack of thunder boomed in the burgeoning night, a brilliant sliver of lightning that hissed and lit the hot still air, a torrid parallel of what Chane felt in his flesh, a storm, a tumultuous deluge of rising want and need.

His mouth swept down on hers like rain to a drought-stricken land. Her soft lips tasted of flowers, fresh and sweet from newly fallen droplets. Her hair flowed around her like the rich red loam of the earth. His eyes clouded with a vision of what was to come. To earth they would soon surrender their bodies, but not, he swore upon the heavens, without a last defiant act of life and love. Whispering her name, tenderly lifting her, he carried Ria to the ground, laid her upon the skirts she had discarded, helped her out of the boots she wore.

Ria wished for time as she lay upon her makeshift bed, a crimson fan of hair for her pillow. She loved Chane—that she knew and accepted even as she accepted the inevitable death. Her heart swelled with love as he stood above her, peeling off his boots and breeches, proud and tall in the white glow of a sky-searing lightning flash, man, lover—boldly aroused lover—the first and last lover her virgin body would ever know. Pulse quickening, eyes afire, she welcomed him to her rough pallet with wide arms and a throaty cry of his name, the cry of a worshiper to a high priest, Chane, who would teach her the secrets of creation and of life and love.

She was pale against the dark earth, her hair like a flaming torch against the darkness when the lightning slashed and flared in the heavens. He knelt beside her, grazed her gilded breasts with his fingertips, followed the tender touch with his questing lips tasting salt and sweet on her skin, feeling her arch and lift to the pressure of his mouth. Like Ria, he wished for time, for eternity, but feared there might be only an hour or a handful of minutes before—

Tormented, tortured in heart and soul, he rose purposefully above her. He stroked her pale luminous skin, quicksilver beneath his trembling hands, knew, and ached with knowing, that it was as painful to die of regret and want as from the thrust of a spear. A cry of love tore huskily from his throat, as he willed himself to think only of the moment, only of Ria glistening like a silver sea beneath him. His hungry mouth dove down to hers, soft and lush beneath his urgent, questing kiss, her breath warm and fragrant as ripe summer fruit as it mingled with his.

A rasping cry, a chaotic shudder of desire came as his pulsing shaft, hot as a brand, hard as horn, fell against her belly. Timorously, curiously, she brought her hand between them, and brought a hoarse cry of need from his lips.

"Ahh, Ria! I wish—" His breath caught.

"Love me, Chane," she whispered, "while there is time."

"Ria . . ." he groaned, abruptly plunging into her, feeling her stiffen and moan as the tender, untouched veil of her maidenhood tore beneath his erotic onslaught. He had been wrong, he thought, about Ria, about so many things. And then he did not think, could not as a shimmering, dizzying wash of pleasure, hot as sparks, began when she arched to meet him.

Ria cried out, lifted her hips, rose to receive the stabbing thrusts, enveloping, taking him deeper, forgetting the brief splintering pain of his entrance. Her arms tangled around his neck, her fingers knotted in his thick hair, her lissome legs twined around his long, powerful limbs, moving, rocking, sailing the air with him as if she were a scarlet bird in stolen flight on the broad soaring wings of another. Where he took her she had never been, might never go again, high above the turquoise sea and amber plain, beyond the lilting alabaster clouds and starry blue-black skies to where the world was a rippling glow of silver and gold, the sun a shimmering ruby hung in the distant heavens.

In that otherworld Chane moved his hands beneath her rounded hips, sweeping her infinitely higher. His mouth lay ravenous against her silken throat, his breath uneven, vaporous and hot against her tingling skin as he carried her ever nearer the burning ruby sun, chanting her name, whispering of love and loss. Outside their lair, rain pattered the ground, raising a soft mist that wafted through the dark cave and over the couple entwined on its ancient floor, raising the sweet, musky scent of their mating to the damp jungle air.

Together they climbed, winged, doomed lovers flying into the fiery sun, knowing first a slow melting heat and then a full shattering magnificent blaze of ecstasy, rapturous flames leaping, licking, rhythmically igniting a sweet burning fire storm in them. An explosion shook Ria, a roiling, seething heat, molten, brilliant, beautiful. Chane shuddered into the flames with her, his body racked and spent as, with a gasp, he spilled his seed inside her.

They slept afterward, the hard ground a soft billowy cloud, drugged by their lovemaking and the aftermath of a day filled with death and danger. Chane and Ria slept unworried, unhurried. Until morning light spilled in like a flood of cold water.

When sunlight struck his face, Chane lumbered to his feet, a harsh cry of surprise emanating from him. He had not expected to see another sunrise, nor to spend what he had believed his last night on earth sleeping.

"Mon Dieu!" Barefoot he padded to the cave mouth and, not without trepidation, peered out into the hazy morn. "Ria!" came like a trumpet call. "Up! Have a look!"

She rose quickly, giving her snarled tresses a toss over her shoulder. Daylight and modesty seemed to go hand in hand so that in spite of her haste she grabbed her skirt, gave it a shake to remove the grit and held it against her as she rushed to the cave door.

"This is unbelievable," she whispered, seeing outside a bounty of fruit heaped before the aperture—mangoes, bananas, coconuts, other varieties unknown to her. Coconut shells split in half held clear fresh water. Her thirst grew keen in her dry throat, hunger gnawed and knotted in her belly as she looked upon the jungle feast, wanting to partake but fearing it was part of a trap, a tempting bait to draw them into a deadly snare. Her eyes went imploringly to Chane. "Could it be safe to go out? To eat?"

"I think it might be as safe as staying inside and doing without," Chane told her. "In which case we will die of thirst in a few unpleasant days. Either that or we take a chance making a run through the jungle."

"It might be poisoned," Ria offered, a hand rising tremulously to his arm when it appeared he would go beyond the cave walls.

"I think it is the best they have to offer," Chane said, his voice lowering with his eyes. Boldly he stepped outside, dragging her with him, though she let out a gasping protest. He had his sword in hand and he pointed it at the dust, at a series of lines roughly drawn. A sun symbol was outlined in flame. Above them, chiseled into the rock was a second symbol, like the one in the sand. A replica of the one on the great stone where they had spent their first night in the jungle, a replica of the one on Ria's shoulder.

He turned to her and gently caught the hands that held a scrap of soiled and shredded cloth to her bosom. "I think, my sweetling, that the sun sign on the stone is significant to them." He bent his head to her shoulder and kissed the black and red tattoo that marred her pale skin. "When they saw the same mark on you, a lovely white-skinned witch with hair like the sun, we were saved."

"Saved," she mumbled, stunned and reeling from his words and the tantalizing feel of his mouth, soft and moist, on her skin.

"Saved," he repeated, drawing her close, cupping his hands under round, firm buttocks, lifting her against him. "Which I might have realized yesterday had I not been scared out of my wits that they would stake and skin you and dine on your liver."

Ria shuddered. "What about your liver?"

"Too tough," he said. "Too hard. Hard as..." He crushed her against his manhood, rising hotly between them.

Ria gasped. "Let me eat or I will be no good for that or anything," she said, though she expended none of her fading energy to break his embrace. She did, in fact, prefer his lovemaking to the most palatable food, but she did not see a reason to tell him anything that would encourage the self-satisfied smirk on his enticing lips.

"Already a shrew-wife," he mumbled, letting her go so quickly that she staggered to keep her balance. Kneeling before her he scooped up a coconut half and offered her the first drink. Ria swallowed down the water greedily, as if she filled a well gone dry. Cool, invigorating droplets ran from the corners of her mouth. Chane lobbed them away with his fingertips, catching the surprised gasp that came as her slow-witted mind caught and considered his last words.

"Wife?"

"I have need of one," he told her earnestly. "Provided she has the mettle to get back to the ship." Then, growing serious, his eyes darkening, he gently caught her hands and squeezed them tight. "What say you, Ria? I know there have been quarrels between us and words spoken that ought to be called back. I know we have not spoken of love. But that is because I would not admit that I loved you until I thought I would lose you forever. I do love you, Ria. I have loved you since I saw you spitting fire at Hyatt Landis that first day I laid eyes on you. And," he said, his voice low and sorrowful, "I have fought loving you ever since."

Ria laughed, then cried, tears flooding her face, trickling unchecked to drip and fall from her chin. She had come all this way for a treasure and she had found it in the heat of a relentless jungle, a glorious, naked, exasperating man who mattered more to her than all the gold and jewels from the earth's bowers.

Chane mistook her hesitancy. "Think on it at least, Ria," he said, his crestfallen look touching her heart. "I am not the most even-tempered of men and you may think you could never love me as I do you, but for the sake of all we have been through together, think on it at least."

"Dolt!" Ria cried, throwing her arms around him, and gazing lovingly into his eyes. "Wonderful, naked dolt! My only fear is that you will never love me as much as I love you."

"Ria," he whispered, the sweet sound of her name saying so much that she closed her eyes and waited in breathless anticipation for his kiss. When it did not come after what seemed the longest stretch of time, she opened one eye a crack to find him gazing oddly at the tattoo gracing her shoulder. "*Sacre bleu!* I am a fool," he said softly. "That is it. Six! The last of the codes."

Concluding that she was not to get her kiss, Ria opened her eyes fully. "What are you saying?" Her fingers splaying curiously over the mark she had regretted all the time she had worn it. "That this tattoo is the key to the treasure? But what does it matter now? I care only about getting back to the ship alive," she insisted. "I do not care a whit if we are rich or poor as long as we're together."

"Sweetling, we will not be poor by any count, since I will no doubt please my father to the point of overflowing by taking a bride." He put a finger to her lips when she started to question him about what he had said. "In good time you can know all about the rift between my father and me," he said. "Preferably after we are wed and you cannot change your mind about having me. But right now," he insisted, "we are close to Dagian's trove, and I for one would like a look at what has nearly cost both our lives."

They ate, gorging themselves on the sweet, nourishing fruit, quenching their thirst with the cool water, using the last of it to rinse their bodies, unabashedly cuddling and kissing in the open air of day, occasionally suspecting that watchful eyes followed every move, but neither fearing nor caring. Afterward Ria shook out her skirt and tied it beneath her arms, making a short loose smock of the garment, while Chane donned his boots and breeches. While he plotted the last coordinates from the map, figures he had fortunately committed to memory, Ria knotted the ends of her discarded petticoat and made a sack for what remained of the fruit, their sustenance on the long trek back to the shore.

Chane found the suspected treasure den a few yards from the cave where they had made love, in a smaller cleft of the same wall of rock. A pile of stones within the tiny cave looked suspiciously as if it had been stacked by human hands. When, as Chane moved the stones, he uncovered bones and bits of brass and leather that had survived the years, they guessed they had found the graves of Robby Scorpion's unlucky men. The chests were beneath the bones, two rotting caskets of wood and brass, smallish, such as a lady might use for traveling, each stamped with the sunburst of the Black Dawn.

What was within had not suffered over time—gold coins bright as newly forged stars, twinkling jewels like shards of a rainbow fashioned in fittings of gold and silver. Chane selected and hooked a necklace of emerald and gilt around Ria's neck. "A wedding present," he whispered, "for my pirate bride."

Ria selected a sword hilt for her groom, chased gold set with glittering rubies and sapphires. She hung it on his belt. "For my knight," she proclaimed, and dubbed him so with a kiss.

They did not linger long with their riches. They bagged only what they could safely carry, mostly to satisfy the men who waited on the *Aurelia,* and a generous portion of coin and jewels for Clair, who would need a dowry someday. Whether they would ever return for the bulk of the treasure was of no concern at the moment. The aging day mattered. Chane wanted to be at the rock that bore the sun sign before nightfall. So with no remorse he stacked the stone as he had found them, hiding the decaying chests, replacing the bones that had guarded the treasure since Dagian's time.

Just before noon, laden with pockets full of coins and jewels, and what Ria's makeshift bag would hold, the pair struck out along the trail, retracing the steps that had brought them to the trove. Not a sign remained of the articles dropped in their flight. Packs and tools, food and water skins, even the map were gone. The path itself had almost disappeared, almost reclaimed by the jungle in the space of a day. Had not Chane's sword hacked branches along the way, neither could have sworn they followed the same steps.

Luckily nightfall brought them to the huge stone, grateful and weary, too spent to do more than make a nest in the grass and eat the last of the fruit before they curled together and slept.

Morning brought a surprise—a water skin filled with
sweet, fresh water, a mound of fruit, as on the day before,
no more than a foot from where they slumbered. Ria shivered when she saw it, thinking of the brown-skinned men
who moved like the invisible wind through the jungle, everywhere and nowhere, following, watching. Would they
change their minds about sparing them? Did they bait and
toy with them to heighten the pleasure of a last kill? Ria
poured out her fears to Chane even as she feasted on the
savages' gift of food.

"I think they worship you, sweetling. As I do." He kissed
her soundly, tasting the juice of potent jungle fruit on her
lips. "If it were not a full day's march to the sea, I would
show you how much," he threatened.

Ria sighed. "If I didn't believe there were a hundred pair
of eyes watching us I would demand you make good your
boast," she countered.

He laughed, a lusty regretful sound, as he pulled her to
her feet, bound up the remaining fruit and hooked the water skin over his shoulder. Before the last gray streaks in the
sky faded before the sun, he ushered Ria out of the clearing
and, ordering her to hold to his belt, began the arduous last
leg of the trek through the jungle.

Sometime near sundown, when they had stopped to rest
and eat, a sound of distant thunder seemed to roll across the
treetops.

Ria, tugging Chane to a halt, looked up at the sky to see
if the rumbling forecast of imminent storm and rain was
upon them, but what she saw through the thickly laced
boughs was bright, shining sun. "Do you think the storm
will hit before we reach the shore?" she queried, wondering if she had the reserves to last through any burden added
to that of their jungle march. Her legs and arms ached al-

ready from exertion and the constant bombardment of hostile leaves, limbs and insects.

Chane shifted his heavy sack to the ground and moved Ria into the circle of his arms, finding the sweet taste of her lips, the warm softness of her body more strengthening than a hearty meal. "Sweetling," he said, reluctantly tearing his mouth from hers, "that thunder is cannon fire, and I fear it bodes more bother for us than any storm."

"You think the *Aurelia* is under attack," she said, understanding at once that their vessel sitting off the coast might have been seen by a passing ship. She could not understand why that should lead to hostilities. "Who would fire on her?"

"That I don't know," he answered. "But I am certain we did not make this shore without some man of our crew tattling of our mission." He shrugged. "Galvez might have had friends who would avenge him. And," he added, grinning in a way that started Ria's heart hammering, her pulse fluttering with desire in spite of her fatigue, "it does not defy belief that I might have gained an enemy or two who would put a blade in my back should the opportunity arise."

"I'll be sure to keep a watchful eye on your backside," she said, giving him a swat to the posterior as he hoisted the sack of loot and food and started again along the difficult trail.

Chane's prediction proved true when at last they stumbled out of the thick green snarl of jungle to the sandy beach, beyond which the *Aurelia* and another ship lay offshore.

The last of the cannon fire had died out half an hour before, but the battle on the decks must have ended only shortly before they emerged from the jungle. Dusk had fallen, but the sky and the darkening waters were lit by a ravenous leaping flame consuming the mainsail atop the

Aurelia's tallest mast. To save the ship, the crew swarmed around the stout wooden mast and hacked it off. As it fell they used the rigging to guide the flaming canvas and wood into the sea.

"The *Aurelia* is defeated," Chane said, a quiet rage in his voice as he led Ria to the shelter of a formation of tumbled boulders on the shore. "Damn Gus Telfour," he ground out as he got Ria hidden behind the stones. "That is the *Conquest* bringing the attack. Damn him to hell! I'll cut out his eyes for this!"

Ria sank down to the sand, thinking herself the most cursed of women. Having been granted a man so handsome and bold that all others paled in his shadow, having been granted love that filled her empty heart and soul with a bounty so precious she ached to think about it, she must face losing both. She knew, as she knew another sunrise would come on the morrow, a black dawn if ever there was one, that Chane would not rest until he regained his ship—or lost his life in the trying.

Shoulders slumped, head bent, Ria thought of Clair and Axel and shamed herself for the selfish thought of her pending loss. Clair, perhaps this moment being raped by the *Conquest*'s crew or her captain. She shuddered with dread as she remembered what Gustave Telfour had done to her sister. "We have to help them," she said, noting that Chane eyed the place in the jungle's edge where the skiff had been hidden. "The two of us with weapons might be able to—"

"You'll stay here!" Chane ordered, the thought of subjecting her to whatever he might find on the *Aurelia* bringing an unbearable image to his mind.

"I'll go with you or I'll swim after you," Ria said, broaching no argument. "I am a strong swimmer."

Chane shook his head in defeat, knowing she would do what she threatened. "You are a stubborn, pigheaded, beautiful fool!'' he told her, signaling his defeat with arms that swept out and enclosed her in a violent hug. ''I love you, Ria!''

''I love you, my darling imperial knight, too much to be separated from you—in life or death.''

''Then we go together,'' he said, softly, tenderly, nudging her down when she started toward the skiff. ''After we have eaten and rested and given the *Conquest*'s crew time to get crocked on my good rum and the men's ration of beer.'' Determined he would take back his ship, Chane buried the sack of loot in the sand beside the rocks for safekeeping, then spread the last of their food before them. They ate the fruit, drank and washed with the water. Ria dozed, resting her head on Chane's shoulder, her cheek against his heart, until an hour passed, and two, and he stirred her awake with a bevy of kisses strung across her face. ''Time to go,'' he told her. ''Time for your pirate blood to rise, sweet Ria.''

Ria stretched and sat up. ''If Clair has been harmed I'll be no better than Grandfather Dag at showing mercy.'' She strapped on the knife and pistol.

Preparing for battle, she looked more pirate than not, her long red hair like flowing blood in the moonlight, her bare limbs gleaming like ivory lances, her face proud and fierce as she looked toward the ships. Chane, girding on his courage and resolve, was no genteel planter's son, no gentleman sea captain as he loaded his weapons and tested the blade of his sword. Shirtless, his corded chest strapped by a leather band and pistol, his black, ruffled hair hanging wild around his savage face, his chilling eyes gleaming with a barbaric and menacing light, his jaw jutting ruthlessly, he swore that Gus Telfour would pay endlessly for his treachery.

Chapter Nineteen

As the moon dipped behind a drifting cloud, Chane and Ria shoved off in the skiff, Chane manning the oars with slow, deliberate strokes. He expected the watch would be lax, the victorious men too sure of themselves to believe the shore party would attempt an attack under any terms, certainly not at night. Tomorrow Gus doubtless planned to send men ashore to waylay the five he must have learned had gone in search of the trove.

"Are you up to a long swim?" Chane whispered as the small craft slid through the water. "We'll have to scuttle the skiff a few yards out. Even a man tumbling drunk could hear a boat bumping the *Aurelia*'s side."

"I can do it," Ria said, gripping the bench tightly as she thought of plunging into the dark water beneath an even darker sky.

"Can you swim and hold your pistol clear of the water?" he asked next. "If the weapon is to fire you must keep it dry."

"I'll keep it dry and I'll use it," she swore.

Moments later they trod water, both wishing for a bit of the sun's heat and light as the skiff slid beneath the lapping black waters of the sea. With an awkward crawling stroke and a pistol held above her head, Ria swam behind Chane to the ship, where they found footing in the fallen rigging the conquering crew had been negligent in clearing away. Before climbing aboard they paused long enough to catch their breath, then, like an agile pair of squirrels, they surged up the sagging lines to peer cautiously beneath the railing. The three men assigned the watch lolled about on deck, and they were not hard at their duty—not with a couple of rum kegs to keep them company.

The only sound of activity came from below and from the captain's cabin, where a blaze of lights shone from the stern windows. The *Conquest,* sitting a short distance off, was quieter still, her lanterns out and her decks like a ghost ship's.

"Mon Dieu!" Chane swore softly as his eyes swept from stern to forecastle and surveyed the damage done to his ship. They came unexpectedly to a sight that made his blood boil. Only by the greatest constraint did he not bound to the deck and challenge all.

"Axel." Ria whispered the name that had been on his lips. "And others. Do you see them? Lashed to the foremast. He's wounded, I think." She clawed for a hold that would hoist her to the deck, but Chane stayed her with a well-placed hand. He tipped his head in the direction of the three on watch. Two of them had pitched over and lay on the deck scratching and snoring like a pair of hounds before a hearth fire. The third tipped back a mug and chugged enough to ensure he would soon join the others.

He was not long about it, clumsily stretching out beside the sleeping men, his stocking cap pulled over his face. Shortly his loud snores harmonized with those of the other two. Chane waited a few tension-charged minutes longer to be sure the trio slept soundly, then made his move. Voicing an order for Ria to stay put, he swung to the deck and, heart drumming his dread, hurried to Axel's side. Until he reached him he was not sure if his second officer was dead or alive. Axel's torn shirt was blood-soaked and his head hung limp as a gourd on a rope. But he breathed. Chane saw the steady rise and fall of his friend's chest and could have given a rousing cheer.

Recognition of the two prisoners who shared Axel's punishment nearly took Chane to his knees with surprise. Both were conscious, but barely, gagged as Axel had been. The pain-filled eyes of both faces showed they were no surer of their fate at the hands of Chane Bellamy than at the hands of the men who had trussed and tortured them. Chane put his back to them as he sliced the ropes that held Axel to the mast. "Where is Clair?"

"Below," Axel answered in a crackling, dry-throated voice. "I think they've a mind to sell her where Galvez intended. If so, she's not been harmed."

Chane motioned to Ria that her sister was all right, then went to work cutting the tight bonds on Axel's wrists and ankles. "Why are the Telfours bound?" he asked, his whisper hoarse as his eyes rested hotly on Gus's bloodied, shaking head. "Did they not bring the attack on the *Aurelia?*"

"Gus started it," Axel answered, sinking from exhaustion to his haunches once the ropes fell away. "Whoreson that he is." Grimacing, he rubbed his wrists and gingerly touched a crusted wound on his side. A low groan came as he probed the depth of the cut. "I could have sent Gus packing, but that bloody bastard Pollack mutinied with half the crew and would not fight."

"Pollack! Damn him!" Chane's lips twisted with anger, anger directed at himself as he remembered Ria's unheeded warning of the man's character.

"And Gus had a man to equal him. Our old friend Spruill and his cutthroat pals put those two in bonds and made a truce with Pollack. The devils are in your chamber even now, planning the way they will divvy up the spoils of this raid."

"They will be disappointed," Chane growled, his heated pulse throbbing in his throat. "Are any of the loyal men of our crew alive?"

"Some few they needed to man the ship when we sail," Axel told him. "They are bound in the hold."

Ria, unable to wait any longer, lithely swung under the railing and eased close to the men. "And Clair?"

"In her cabin or with Pollack," Axel said sorrowfully. "I cannot be sure. But the men have not— They have complained of being kept from her," he explained, heartsick, hoping what he told her was right.

Chane quickly outlined a plan for getting to his men and arming them with weapons Pollack was not likely to have found. "What of those two?" he asked of Axel, staring remorselessly at the Telfour brothers, still bound to the mast. Gus Telfour's eyes strained nearly out of their sockets pleading for release. Yves was more pitiful than his brother, tears streaming from his eyes and mixing with a trickle of blood from a nasty head wound.

"Gus would never have gone as far as this," Axel admitted reluctantly. "I say we give them the chance to join us. When we are back on Martinique the governor can deal with their penchant to turn pirate."

Chane agreed, but not before he advised the Telfours their only choice was to keep quiet and follow his orders. He got a quick compliance to his request, even to that of leaving them at the mast, and Axel, too, so that their disappearance, if noticed, would not raise an alarm before Chane could release his crewmen.

For a man of Chane's size, squeezing into a gun port meant leaving a portion of hide on the frame. For Ria the going was easier. What was difficult for her was not barrel-

ing in to face Pollack and Spruill and demanding her sister
be handed over. She realized the recklessness of that when
they came upon one renegade crewman who was not so
drunk that he did not attempt to prevent their descending
the companionway ladder to the hold.

"Blood—" the man started before Chane wrapped an
arm around his long neck and pulled him to the floor. A
quick punch rendered the staggering man unconscious, but
his bellow had raised an alarm to the man on watch in the
hold. Alerted, he waited with a heavy fist when Chane
leaped below. The crack of the blow was loud enough to
bring a horrified gasp from Ria and to make her break her
word that she would stay hidden above. Pistol in hand, she
made the risky descent.

A pool of light from a single lantern gave a dim glow to
the hold. A pair of shadows convulsed within the murky
light. Ria's eyes sought them out. She found them weaving
amid the barrels and the trussed bodies of the *Aurelia's*
men, Chane and another man struggling, blows flying so
fast and hard that she could not tell who had the advantage. Chane, locked limb to limb with his opponent, sported
a line of blood from his lip, his adversary a split over an eye,
but neither man ceased pummeling the other. Grunting,
groaning like a pair of battling bears, they continued until
Chane caught his foot in a tie line and fell. The seaman
lunged at him for a blood kill, hastily drawing a knife from
the scabbard on his hip. He went down swearing he would
slit Chane's throat.

Chane parried the death-wielding slash with an uppercut
that sent the seaman's aim off the mark. But the sharp descending blade sliced his side along the rib cage and rendered his next swing at the assassin a forceless swipe.
Momentarily dazed by the scathing pain, Chane found
himself pinned and vulnerable when his head cleared.

A knife hung poised above him. "Now ye die, ye high scum!" came in a growl from between a set of yellowed teeth.

Death came, but not at the quarter expected. A shot from Ria's pistol bored a passage through the seaman's throat. In an instant the man's hand jerked and quivered in midair, his mouth fell open and his eyes stared knowingly into the world he was about to enter. He fell to the floor like a boneless thing, blood gurgling from his mouth and wound, the gleaming knife locked in his lifeless hand.

"Dear God! I've killed a man!" Ria gasped, the smoking pistol held loosely at her side. Her lids, abruptly heavy, slid low. Her body shook.

Groaning, a hand pressed to his bleeding side, Chane pushed up from the floor. "Do not feel guilty for saving my life," he warned. "That one was vermin and likely murdered a good many of my crew this very day."

Unable to stanch the flow of blood from his side, Chane ripped the knife from the dead man's hand and slid it to Ria. "Cut the men loose," he ordered. "That shot you fired may bring others if they deem it more than one of their number celebrating his good luck."

Ria hurriedly sawed through the bonds of a seaman, demanding the wide sash he wore the minute the man kicked free of the ropes. "I need a bandage for the captain," she explained.

"It's 'is, an' me bloomin' britches, too, if 'e wants 'em," the man swore, taking the knife from Ria's quivering hands and hastily going to the aid of his companions. "There's two score of 'em, Cap'n," he said to Chane, "countin' that blighter Pollack an' 'is 'brother' Spruill. We're a dozen an' there's near as many tied up aboard the *Conquest* who'll stand with us. I 'eard this one say there were but two guards on the *Conquest* tonight."

"You are Sam Webber, are you not?" Chane stopped and submitted to Ria's efforts to bind his wound, wincing when she pulled Webber's sash tight around the open cut.

"Aye, Cap'n," the man said, never ceasing in his work of cutting the others free.

"Take another man who can swim and release the men on the *Conquest*," he said. "Bring them back with all the weapons you can find."

"Aye, Cap'n." Webber tapped another man and together they started up the ladder.

"Webber," Ria called before the man was out of sight. "What's become of Tad?" All the men in the hold were free and she did not see the lad anywhere among them.

Webber hung his head, but remembering Ria's remorse over killing the pirate, deemed truth a necessity. "Bloody rogues were madder than 'ell when Pollack an' Spruill would not give 'em the girl. They slit the lad's throat."

"Webber!" Chane said harshly as Ria slumped atop a cask. "Godspeed, man. A quarter hour and we take our ship."

The man responded with a nod, then with his companion behind him, scurried through the hatch.

Ria, face covered with her hands, sat and thought of Tad as Chane armed and instructed his men. Poor, sweet Tad had been her first real friend on this perilous voyage. She did not want to believe she would never see him again. More than that, she did not want to see those responsible for Tad's death go free. Fury building in her, she wished them all the fate of the one she had put a bullet through.

Chane looked around and found Ria reloading her pistol when he and his band were ready to advance on the pirates. His men, he noted, stood back in awe of her. He could easily see why. Her abbreviated garment clung damply to her curves, held snug at her waist by a gun belt and scabbard.

Her pale, lovely arms and legs bore a maze of scratches. She had the look of one fresh from battle and the ire of the Black Dawn in her glowing green eyes.

But no matter how fierce she looked, Chane was not willing to make the risk to her life any greater than necessary. "The safest place for you is here hidden among the casks," he said, fearing even before he spoke that his words would fall on deaf ears.

"I am going to Clair," she retorted. "If, as Axel said, she is in her old cabin, I can scale down the side and reach her window."

One of the crewmen confirmed that Clair was held in the cabin she had occupied since they sailed.

"Let one of the men—" Chane began.

Ria savagely shook her head, a blazing torch of red hair in the lantern light. "I plan to coax her out," she explained. "She would not yield to one of the men, so it must be me." When Chane's lips moved to voice a last protest, she stopped him before he began. "It must be done. If I know Pollack, he will think of putting a hostage before him once the fight begins. I prefer you get a clear bead on him." She rose, a savage Amazon princess ready to battle any man who stood in her way, even the one she loved. "Do not miss."

"Pollack will get no better than he deserves. Nor will Spruill," he said hoarsely, his voice racked with pride for the woman he had chosen, a woman who had in the course of a few weeks changed from a naive determined girl into the equal of any historic heroine. No Deborah or Joan of Arc could have been braver or more beautiful or more certain that what she undertook was right and essential. Nor could he have loved any woman more than he did Aurelia Kingsley. She was fire in his blood, sweet, heavenly wine on his lips, the very life-giving beat of his heart.

He could not part from her without a last savage, carnal coming together. With a snarl on his lips he swept her into his arms, tilting her head back with the onslaught of a ferocious kiss that was a vehement claiming, a zealous pledge, an unbreakable promise that what had begun between them would not end, would not yield to any foe, not even death.

Her release from his embrace was a bittersweet agony. For one poignant moment in his arms she had been able to forget she stood in the heart of treachery, to forget the rough men who watched and envied their leader.

"Wait for me ashore," he entreated. "Should we not prevail—"

Ria would have none of that and silenced him with a quick parting kiss.

Chane held her close a moment longer, feeling her heart beat in time with his, and then, as delay became risk, he boosted her up the ladder ahead of the men. He saw her safely out a gun port, trusting he would next see her triumphant at his side.

Only a fraction as brave as her beloved believed, Ria rappeled along the side of the ship, having shed her heavy boots for the silence of her bare feet against the rough, splintery boards. For once in her life she was glad of the wicked power of rum, which rendered men blithering, worthless dullards, too far gone to believe their eyes when a woman swung past beneath them.

Had she not known that Chane's brave men waited at strategic points below the railing, she could not have gone on. It was, in fact, because her fear was so great that she was able to risk her life to save Clair. Thinking what would surely be Clair's fate once Pollack knew he was lost, was vital to staying sane. She could not abide living should Clair, sweet and innocent, be used and butchered.

Her heart seemed suddenly buoyant when she reached Clair's window and saw her sister crouched in a corner, the cabin's only movable furnishing, a straight-backed chair, jammed against the door. Clair's clothes were torn and there were bruises on her arms and cheeks, but other than that and the evident trembling of her slender body, she looked fit.

Trembling nearly as violently herself, Ria tapped the window glass. Clair jolted, then shrank even farther into her corner, both hands across her mouth. But Ria would not give up until she forced her sister's frightened eyes to search out the source of the sound. Eventually Clair came round, and once assured the tapping was not from one seeking entrance through her door, spotted Ria's face pressed to the glass. She rose and flung the window open at once.

"Heavens! Ria! How did you get here? I feared you were dead. They would tell me nothing. I—"

Ria reached in and put a finger to Clair's quivering lips. "Hush, and shed your petticoats. Leave off your shoes, too, and get out of that tight vest. You are coming out and we are swimming to shore. There will be more fighting in a few minutes."

"Swim?" Clair's mind flashed to the horror of her last dip in the sea. "I can't, Ria. I will drown. You know I will."

Beneath her Ria was aware of men swimming alongside the ship, men from the *Conquest* come to aid Chane's band. The fighting would begin soon. Already she heard a shout raised from the great room only yards away. "Do you trust me, Clair?"

"Of c-course," her sister stammered.

"Then shed those clothes and climb out. Any minute you will have Pollack breaking down that door, and he, I promise, will be worse than a dunking."

Sobbing, Clair tore off her garments down to her shift and heaving off the cabin's bunk, slid through the window only seconds before a din of voices rose from within the ship. Ria heard thundering footsteps from the alleyway and stair and then a vicious pounding as Clair's door was flung open.

"Jump clear, love." Chane's voice rang from a shadow hung at the lower end of a shroud. To his men he bellowed a lusty call to attack.

"Aye, my captain," Ria whispered as she saw him ease over the rail. Pulling Clair with her, Ria pitched off into the waiting sea.

Clair was no easy company, as afraid of the dark as she was of water. She fought and wept until Ria cajoled her into floating on her back so that she could be towed ashore. Still it was with bone-aching exhaustion that Ria found the sandy bottom near shore and tugged Clair to the shelter of rock where she and Chane had hidden earlier.

The tilt of the battle on the *Aurelia* was impossible to determine, though Ria kept a watchful vigil through the whole of the night, waiting, wondering, fretting, cursing.

"Damn the bastards!" she charged the higher power when, at the threat of dawn, no rescue had come from the ship.

Clair awoke on those profane words from her sister's lips. "Ria," she mumbled, rubbing her eyes. "No lady—"

"I suspect no one will ever again accuse me of being a lady," Ria said flatly, cutting Clair off as the sun challenged the fading night with a brilliant marbled sky, a sky of blood and light that shone with equal vengeance on good and bad. Ria held her breath until she could see what had become of the *Aurelia*. Her decks had been quiet for hours and Ria did not know if that boded ill or fair for her.

Finally, when the sun's rays swept the glistening silver-blue water, setting both vessels afire with a crimson glow, Ria could see men upon the decks already at work righting the mast, and restoring the downed sails and rigging. She had hoped to see the Bellamy flag flying, the wild rose of Eglantine on a field of blue, but none was aloft as yet.

Beside her Clair yawned, not yet clearheaded enough to contemplate her uncertain fate. Ria preferred to allow her a period of blissful indifference. The terror might come soon enough.

A first sign of it felt like a blade piercing her heart when a foursome lowered one of the small craft over the side. Too distant for her to make out the faces and forms of the men, she could not ascertain if friend or foe made ready to come ashore. While she knew she could doubtless lose an enemy party in the jungle, she knew as well she would never flee not knowing what had become of Chane, not at any cost.

Regretfully, she put an arm around Clair, in anguish over her sharp words moments before. She wanted desperately the last words to her sister to be kind. "They are coming for us, Clair," Ria said softly, looking into her sister's troubled face. Gently she laid her brow against Clair's. "You are dear to me, sister. Know that always. I love you."

Clair excitedly shoved her away. "They are running up a flag!" she cried.

Ria whirled to see the banner, felt the wound anew in her heart when she saw a scrap of black waving from the pole. "Black," she said weakly and turned away. "A Jolly Roger. A pirate flag."

"No!" Clair grabbed her sister's shoulders and spun her around.

The billowing flag Ria saw caught in a morning breeze proved to be a woman's black skirt—hers. Someone nimble with a needle had sewn on rays of red and made a replica of the symbol she wore on her shoulder. "The Black Dawn!"

Laughter bubbling from her throat, Ria ran down the beach and into the water to meet Chane. "You took your bloody time!" she shouted to him.

Giving her a look of mock indignation he threw up his hand. "I'll have you know these are gentlemen whose ears you blister, Mademoiselle Pirate," he said. "Keep a civil tongue in your pretty head."

Ria recognized Webber among the three who roared with delight at Chane's jest.

"I thought you dead, you bloody rogue!" Ria told him, throwing her arms around his neck when he had leaped from the boat to join her in the shallows near shore.

"We lost but two men," he told her solemnly. "But those cowards of Pollack's hid like rats on the ship, and I would not send for you until we hunted down the last man of them." He held her tightly. "You are no worse for your adventure, I hope."

"No better, either," Ria said, thrilling at the feel of him warm and wonderful beneath his wet clothes, his body reacting to her nearness.

"I will make it up to you, sweetling. I promise," he said softly, deeming it wise to wait until later to tell her that Pollack, faced with hanging, was ready to testify to her father's innocence of the charges that had led to his court martial and death. Pollack was more than willing, too, to implicate Hyatt Landis in the deed.

A wave curled toward them, a watery mount that threatened to knock them both off their feet unless they moved swiftly toward shore, which they did. The spent wave lapped their ankles. Forgetting there were other people about, Chane allowed his hands to drift low and cup Ria's rounded buttocks, holding her snugly against him.

"You are scandalizing Clair," Ria told him, though she did not in the least pull away. Instead, she tilted her head back for the kiss she felt she deserved after being scared senseless all the night. "And setting a poor example for your men."

"If perdition is this sweet, let me always be a sinner," he whispered, dipping his head to hers and obliging her with a kiss.

His hands ascended to her hair, a glorious silky tangle much in need of a comb. His tongue delved between her lips, finding her mouth honey-sweet, a drugging nectarous taste he knew he would never tire of. Reluctantly he wrested his mouth away. Pleasure, however intoxicating, would have to wait.

"I have men aboard in need of a doctor," he began.

"We can come back for the treasure another time," Ria offered.

"Should the need arise," he said. "I believe what we buried beyond those rocks will keep the lot of us in luxury all our days." He stretched out a hand to Clair, who, after a moment's hesitation, joined them on the beach.

"Y-you are—" Clair stammered.

"Deeply in love," Ria told her.

"Soon to be wed," Chane added, throwing an arm round each of them and ushering them to the boat while his men dug up the bags of Dagian's loot he had buried in the sand. He laughed as he thought of the joke fate had played on him. What had started out as defiance of his father's will had brought him round to Renaud Bellamy's wishes. "Much to my father's surprise," he added, his blue eyes twinkling.

"Somehow I think not," Ria said, mostly to herself. Renaud Bellamy, she thought, might be a slyer fox than his son.

"What say you, sweetling?" Chane asked.

"I say I love you, Chane Bellamy. Forever and a day."

Beside her in the skiff, Chane cradled her in his arms, h
eyes darkening to a smoldering blue as his mind leaped
the night and Ria beside him in his bed.

"And on that day, my love, we start anew."

* * * * *

Harlequin® Historical

WESTERN SKIES

This September, celebrate the coming of fall with four exciting Westerns from Harlequin Historicals!

BLESSING by Debbi Bedford—A rollicking tale set in the madcap mining town of Tin Cup, Colorado.

WINTER FIRE by Pat Tracy—The steamy story of a marshal determined to reclaim his father's land.

FLY AWAY HOME by Mary McBride—A half-Apache rancher rescues an Eastern woman fleeing from her past.

WAIT FOR THE SUNRISE by Cassandra Austin—Blinded by an accident, a cowboy learns the meaning of courage—and love.

Four terrific romances full of the excitement and promise of America's last frontier.

Look for them, wherever Harlequin Historicals are sold.

Relive the romance...
Harlequin and Silhouette
are proud to present

by Request

A program of collections of three complete novels by the most requested authors with the most requested themes. Be sure to look for one volume each month with three complete novels by top name authors.

In June: **NINE MONTHS** Penny Jordan
                                    Stella Cameron
                                    Janice Kaiser

Three women pregnant and alone. But a lot can happen in nine months!

In July: **DADDY'S**   Kristin James
             HOME   Naomi Horton
                                 Mary Lynn Baxter

Daddy's Home... and his presence is long overdue!

In August: **FORGOTTEN**   Barbara Kaye
              PAST   Pamela Browning
                                  Nancy Martin

Do you dare to create a future if you've forgotten the past?

Available at your favorite retail outlet.

Harlequin® Historical

HARLEQUIN HISTORICALS ARE GETTING BIGGER!

This fall, Harlequin Historicals will bring you bigger books. Along with our traditional high-quality historicals, we will be including selected reissues of favorite titles, as well as longer originals.

Reissues from popular authors like Elizabeth Lowell, Veronica Sattler and Marianne Willman.

Originals like ACROSS TIME—an historical time-travel by Nina Beaumont, UNICORN BRIDE—a medieval tale by Claire Delacroix, and SUSPICION—a title by Judith McWilliams set during Regency times.

Leave it to Harlequin Historicals to deliver enduring love stories, larger-than-life characters, and history as you've never before experienced it.

And now, leave it to Harlequin Historicals, to deliver even more!

Look for *The Bargain* by Veronica Sattler in October, *Pieces of Sky* by Marianne Willman in November, and *Reckless Love* by Elizabeth Lowell in December.

Harlequin® Historical

THREE UNFORGETTABLE KNIGHTS . . .

First there was Ruarke, born leader and renowned warrior, who faced an altogether different field of battle when he took a willful wife, in KNIGHT DREAMS (HH#141, a September 1992 release). Then, brooding widower and heir Gareth was forced to choose between family duty and the only true love he's ever known, in KNIGHT'S LADY (HH#162, a February 1993 release). Now, Alexander, bold adventurer and breaker of many a maiden's heart, meets the one woman he can't lay claim to, in KNIGHT'S HONOR (HH#184, an August 1993 release), the dramatic conclusion of Suzanne Barclay's Sommerville Brothers trilogy.

If you're in need of a champion, let Harlequin Historicals take you back to the days when a knight in shining armor wasn't just a fantasy. Sir Ruarke, Sir Gareth and Sir Alex won't disappoint you!

If you'd like to oreder the Harlequin Historicals mentioned above—*Knight Dreams* (HH#141); *Knight's Lady* (HH#162)—please send your name, address, zip or postal code, along with a check or money order (please do not send cash) for $3.99 for each book ordered, plus 75¢ ($1.00 in Canada) postage and handling, payable to Harlequin Reader Service, to:

In the U.S.	In Canada
3010 Walden Avenue	P.O. Box 609
P.O. Box 1325	Fort Erie, Ontario
Buffalo, NY 14269-1325	L2A 5X3

Canadian residents add applicable federal and provincial taxes.

Coming in October!

From

Harlequin® Historical

It was a misunderstanding that could cost a young woman her virtue, and a notorious rake his heart.

Award-winning author of JESSIE'S LADY and SABELLE

Available wherever Harlequin books are sold.

Harlequin® Historical

BELLE HAVEN

A colony in New England. A farming village divided by war.
A retreat for New York's elite.

Four books. Four generations. Four indomitable females....

You've met Belle Haven founder Amelia Daniels in THE TAMING OF
AMELIA, Harlequin Historical #159 (February 1993).

Now meet the revolutionary Deanna Marlowe in THE SEDUCTION
OF DEANNA, Harlequin Historical #183 (August 1993).

In early 1994, watch Julia Nash turn New York society upside down
in THE TEMPTING OF JULIA.

And in late 1994, Belle Haven comes of age in a contemporary story
for Silhouette Intimate Moments.

Available wherever Harlequin books are sold.

Harlequin is proud to present our
best authors and their best books.
Always the best for your
reading pleasure!

Throughout 1993, Harlequin will bring you
exciting books by some of the top names in
contemporary romance!

In August,
look for
Heat Wave by

BARBARA DELINSKY

A heat wave hangs over the city....

Caroline Cooper is hot. And after dealing with crises all
day, she is frustrated. But throwing open her windows to
catch the night breeze does little to solve her problems.
Directly across the courtyard she catches sight of a man
who inspires steamy and unsettling thoughts....

Driven onto his fire
escape by the sweltering heat, lawyer Brendan Carr
is weaving fantasies, too—around gorgeous Caroline.
Fantasies that build as the days and nights go by.

Will Caroline and Brendan dare cross the dangerous
line between fantasy and reality?

Find out in HEAT WAVE by Barbara Delinsky...
wherever Harlequin books are sold.